GAIL Z. MARTIN

THE SWORN

THE FALLEN KINGS CYCLE: BOOK ONE

---

orbit

www.orbitbooks.net

ORBIT

First published in Great Britain in 2011 by Orbit
Reprinted 2011

Copyright © 2011 by Gail Z. Martin

Excerpt from *The Dread* by Gail Z. Martin
Copyright © 2011 by Gail Z. Martin

A CIP catalogue record for this book
is available from the British Library.

ISBN 978-1-84149-913-0

Typeset in Times by Palimpsest Book Production Limited,
Falkirk, Stirlingshire
Printed in the UK by CPI Mackays, Chatham ME5 8TD

Orbit
An imprint of
Little, Brown Book Group
100 Victoria Embankment
London EC4Y 0DY

An Hachette UK Company
www.hachette.co.uk

www.orbitbooks.net

For my family and friends, who believe

Prologue

Nearly a year and a half has passed since King Martris Drayke of Margolan won back the throne from Jared the Usurper, and still Margolan is not at peace. Jared's brief reign was long enough to drive the kingdom to famine and revolt, beggaring its farmers and stirring tensions between its mortal and undead residents, the vayash moru.

Jared seized the throne by killing his father, King Bricen, and the rest of the royal family, save for his half-brother, Martris, the only legitimate challenger. Martris (known as Tris) escaped with the help of three loyal friends: Ban Soterius, the captain of the guards; Harrtuck, one of the king's guardsmen; and Master Bard Riordan Carroway. Tris and his friends fled to Principality to plan their counterstrike. Along the way, they gained a number of unlikely allies: Jonmarc Vahanian, an outlaw turned smuggler; Carina, a gifted healer; Carina's brother Cam, a former mercenary; Gabriel, one of the lords of the vayash moru; *and Kiara of Isencroft, who was fleeing an arranged marriage with Jared. When the group rescued a young girl, Berry, from the slavers who had captured her, they unexpectedly found King Staden of Principality in their debt.*

During the journey, Tris discovered his ability as a powerful summoner, a mage able to intercede among the living, dead, and undead. Summoning magic is rare and dangerous, as its great power easily corrupts many who wield it, including Tris's grandfather, a mage named Lemuel. Lemuel became possessed by the spirit of the Obsidian King, and Lemuel's misuse of his summoning magic plunged the Winter Kingdoms into a cataclysmic war in a generation past. That long-ago war splintered the Flow, one of the great currents of magical energy. Learning to control the Flow and his own wild magic before they could destroy him pushed Tris to the brink of sanity and survival.

The battle for the throne took a harsh toll on all of Margolan, and Tris Drayke paid the price in blood as he honed his skills as fighter and mage in order to go up against Jared and Jared's dark mage, Foor Arontala. Ban Soterius played a vital role in the rebellion, assembling deserters and refugees into a strike-and-hide force to harry Jared's troops and stop the massacre of civilians. Tris's victory nearly cost him his life, and it won him a tattered kingdom with a bankrupt treasury. Although he gained the crown, it became painfully clear that the peace and prosperity of Bricen's reign would be dangerously elusive.

Tris's marriage to Princess Kiara of Isencroft is a love match, and Kiara is pregnant with their first child, a son they hope will inherit his father's magic. Isencroft is a neighboring kingdom to Margolan, and the two kingdoms share a stormy history. The attempt to forestall war a generation ago unwittingly sowed the seeds for strife in a new generation. When Donelan of Isencroft eloped with Princess Viata of Eastmark more than twenty years earlier, Eastmark threatened war. Bricen of Margolan forced peace by creating a betrothal contract between his heir and Donelan's heir. When Jared murdered Bricen, Kiara scandalized both courts by throwing her allegiance to Tris and helping him unseat Jared the Usurper.

Isencroft's fortunes have suffered in recent years due to poor harvests and drought, and Kiara's marriage means that Isencroft and Margolan share a joint crown until a suitable heir for each throne is born. The idea of a shared crown with a kingdom that in times past was an invader has fueled dissension in Isencroft, leading to riots and the rise of the Divisionists, a group that seeks to keep Isencroft free of foreign entanglements.

A Divisionist sympathizer infiltrated the Margolan palace staff and nearly succeeded in killing Kiara and her unborn child. The attack was stopped by Bard Riordan Carroway, a trusted friend and Margolan's master musician. The wounds Carroway sustained protecting Kiara could cost him his livelihood. Kiara recovered from the attack, but the poisoned blade may have damaged the child she carries.

Jonmarc Vahanian, who was rewarded for his courage with the title of Lord of Dark Haven, returned from war to claim lands that were the traditional sanctuary of the undead vayash moru and shapeshifting vyrkin, immortals who were not pleased to see a mortal lord claim his due.

When rogue vayash moru led by Malesh of Tremont broke the Truce and slaughtered mortals, Jonmarc retaliated, and he bargained his soul for vengeance. Carina, newly betrothed to Jonmarc, became a pawn in the war. The magical energy of the Flow, damaged in the Mage War of a generation past, became too dangerously unstable for mages to use, and Carina risked her life to "heal" the energy. Jonmarc and Gabriel defeated Malesh's forces, but the Truce remained damaged, and retaliatory killings between mortals and the vayash moru still threaten the fragile peace.

Carina's brother Cam returned to the service as Champion of King Donelan of Isencroft. Cam was captured by the Divisionists, and while a prisoner, he uncovered a plot to kill the king and put the Divisionists' man on the throne. Alvior of Brunnfen, the traitors' challenger, is Cam's elder brother. When

Cam managed to blow up the Divisionists' stronghold to warn the king, he nearly lost a leg in the explosion, but he gained the unlikely assistance of Rhistiart, a silversmith-turned-squire. After the king's personal healer did all he could for Cam, Donelan sent Cam to Carina in Dark Haven, hoping that she could complete the healing.

In the first year of his reign, Tris went to war to put down a rebellion by the traitorous Lord Curane and his blood mages. Tris waged a bitterly fought siege that unleashed a virulent plague. His triumph over the traitor lord took a great toll on Margolan's army and came at a high personal cost. When Tris returned to his palace, he found his queen badly injured by an assassin's blade and his best friend wrongfully accused of high treason. Summoning the spirits of the dead to find the traitor and clear his friend's name, Tris was sorely tempted to use his powerful magic for vengeance, but the memory of the penalty Lemuel paid for his twisted magic stayed Tris's hand.

Six months have passed since the Margolan army returned from battle and since Jonmarc Vahanian put down the vayash moru *uprising. Jonmarc and Carina wed, and Carina is pregnant with twins. Tris and Kiara nervously await the birth of their son, uncertain how the poison has affected this child on whom the future of two kingdoms depends. In Isencroft, the Divisionists have scattered, but Cam fears that the threat has merely gone into hiding and that Alvior may have found foreign allies to challenge Donelan for the throne.*

Peace in the Winter Kingdoms has always been elusive. With the kingdoms weakened by war, insurrection, and poor harvest, the threat of invasion and revolution looms large and all the magic in the world may not be enough to hold back the bloodshed.

1

"Every time you go, I can't believe six months have passed already."

Prince Jair Rothlandorn of Dhasson looked up as his father, King Harrol, stood in the doorway. Jair smiled and sighed as he closed his saddlebag and secured the cinch. "And every time I get ready to leave, I can't believe I've survived six months away from the Ride." Carefully, Jair folded his palace clothing into neat piles and placed them in a drawer to await his return. For the Ride, the only clue that would mark him as the heir to the throne of Dhasson was the gold signet ring on his right hand.

Jair walked to his window and looked out over the city. Valiquet was the name of both the Dhassonian palace and its capital city. The sun gleamed from the white marble and crystalline sculptures that had earned Valiquet its reputation as "The Glittering Place." Long a crossroads for commerce and ideas, Dhasson was perhaps the most cosmopolitan of the Winter Kingdoms. Its long tradition of tolerance for all but the Cult of the Crone had spared it the conflicts that often tore at the other kingdoms and had made it a magnet for scholars and artists. Beautiful as it was, for the six months Jair was home, the city felt like a glittering prison. Jair sighed and returned to packing.

Harrol watched as Jair gathered the last of his things. For the last eleven years, ever since Jair's fourteenth birthday, he had made the Ride. Although this trip would take Jair away from the palace, Valiquet, and Dhasson for six months, Jair's belongings fit neatly into two large saddlebags. "You miss her still."

Jair turned back to look at his father. "I miss her always." He was dressed for the road, in the dark tunic and trews that were the custom in the group with which he would ride sentry for the rest of the year. Jair slid up the long sleeve of his shirt, revealing a black tattoo around his left wrist, an intricate and complicated design that had only one match: around the wrist of his life-partner, Talwyn. On his left palm was an intricate tattoo that marked him as one of the *trinnen*, a warrior proven in battle. He stared at the design on his wrist for a moment in silence. "I wish—"

"—that the Court would accept her," Harrol finished gently. "And you know it's not to be. Even if it did, Talwyn is the daughter of the Sworn's chieftain and she's their shaman. She can no more leave her people than you can renounce your claim to the throne."

"I know." They'd had this conversation before. Although every heir to the Dhasson throne made the six-month Ride, only two before Jair had married into the secretive group of warrior-shamans. Eljen, Jair's great-great-granduncle, had renounced the throne, throwing Dhasson into chaos. Anginon, two generations removed, had worked out an "accommodation," accepting an arranged political marriage in Dhasson to sire an heir while honoring his bond to his partner among the Sworn by making it clear the Dhasson marriage was in name only. Neither option was to Jair's liking, and it was at times like these that the crown seemed to fit most tightly.

"You may find that this year's Ride leaves little time for home and hearth," Harrol said. "Bad enough that plague's begun to spread into Dhasson. What I've heard from Margolan sounds bad. I know the Sworn stay to the barren places, where the barrows lie. Please, avoid the cities and villages. And be careful. Nothing is as it should be this year. I fear the Ride will be more dangerous than it's been in quite some time. I have no desire to lose my son, to plague or to battle." Harrol embraced Jair, slapping him hard on the back. But there was a moment's hesitation and the embrace was just a bit tighter than usual, letting Jair know that his father was sincerely worried.

"Don't worry. I'll be home before Candles Night. And perhaps this time, I'll bring Kenver with me. The Court can't argue that he's my son, whether or not they recognize my marriage. Whether he can take the crown one day or not, they can get used to the fact that I won't deny him."

Harrol chuckled. "If the boy can be spared from his training, by all means, bring him. If he's half the handful you were as a lad, it should keep you busy fetching him out of the shrubbery!"

Neither Jair nor his father said more as they descended the stairs to Valiquet's large marble entranceway. There was no mistaking the two Sworn guardsmen who awaited Jair. They were dressed as he was, in the dark clothing and studded leather armor of the Sworn, wearing the lightweight, summer great cloaks that would help to keep down the dust and discourage the flies. Jair shouldered into his own cloak.

"Good to see you once more, Commander."

Jair recognized the speaker as Emil, one of the guardsmen he had known since he'd first begun making the Ride. Emil's greeting was in Dhassonian, but his heavy accent made it clear that that language was not his native tongue. His companion, Mihei, a warrior land mage, echoed the greeting. No one would mistake either of the men as residents of Dhasson. Both wore their dark, black hair straight and long, accentuating the tawny golden cast of their skin. Their eyes, amber like the Sacred

Lady's, marked their bloodline as servants of the goddess. A variety of amulets in silver and carved stone hung from leather straps around their necks. The leather baldrics that each wore held a variety of lethal and beautiful *damashqi* daggers, and the weapon that hung by each man's side was neither broadsword nor scimitar but a *stelian*, a deadly, jagged, flat blade that was as dangerous as it looked, the traditional weapon of the Sworn.

Jair was dressed in the same manner, but it was obvious to any who looked that he did not share the same blood. Tan from a season outdoors, he was still much lighter than his Sworn companions, and his dark, wavy, brown hair and blue eyes made his resemblance to Harrol obvious.

"It's been too long," Jair responded in the clipped, consonant-heavy language of the nomads. "I've been ready to leave again since I returned."

Jair knew his father watched them descend the sweeping front steps to the horses that waited for them. Even the horses looked out of place. They bore little resemblance to the high-strung, overbred carriage horses of the nobility. These were horses from the Margolan steppe, bred for thousands of years by the Sworn for their steadiness in battle, their intelligence, and their stamina. Jair fastened his saddlebags, shaking his head to dissuade the groomsman who ran to help him. Then the three men swung up to their saddles and rode out of the palace gates.

They did not speak until the walled city was behind them and they were on the open road. Mihei was the first to break the silence. "When we stop for the night, I have gifts for you in my bag."

"Oh?" Jair asked, curious. "From whom?"

Mihei smiled. "Kenver—and his mother. Kenver chased me down the road to make sure I'd packed the gifts he made for you. *Cheira* Talwyn didn't chase us, but I wouldn't care to face her displeasure if I were remiss in making sure you received your welcoming gift."

Jair smiled broadly, knowing that he had packed several such gifts for his wife and son in his bags as well. "Are they well?"

Emil laughed. "Kenver is a hand's breadth taller than when you left, and begging for a pony to ride with the guards. Talwyn's driven us all mad these past few weeks with her wishing for time to pass more quickly."

"Tell me, where do we join the tribe?"

Mihei's smile faded. "The Ride's taken longer this year than in any season for many years."

"Why?"

"Many times, we've found the barrows desecrated. *Cheira* Talwyn says the spirits are unhappy. We'll join the others just across the river, below the Ruune Vidaya forest," Mihei replied.

Jair didn't say anything as he thought about Mihei's news. The Sworn were a nomadic people, consecrated thousands of years ago to the service of the Lady. They were the guardians of the barrows, the large mounds that dotted the landscape from the Northern Sea down through Margolan into Dhasson and to the border of Nargi. Legend said that long ago, the barrows had continued, down into Nargi and beyond, to the Southern Plains. But when the Nargi took up the worship of the Crone Aspect of the Lady, they destroyed the barrows and fought any of the Sworn who dared cross into their lands. The Sworn had left them to their folly, and the legends said that the Nargi had paid dearly for destroying the barrows.

Within the barrows were the Dread. What, exactly, the Dread were, Jair did not know. No one had seen the Dread in over a thousand years. Only the shamans of the Sworn, the *cheira*, ever communicated with their spirits, and then only through ritual and visions. But it was said that as the Sworn were the guardians of the barrows of the Dread, so the Dread were guardians of the deep places, and it was their burden to make sure that a powerful evil remained buried.

The three men rode single file, and Jair noted that both Emil and Mihei seemed unusually alert for danger on this leg of the trip. Normally, the two-day journey from Valiquet to meet up with the Sworn was uneventful. Now, Jair realized that the others' heightened vigilance had affected him, and he found himself scanning the horizon.

"Look there," Jair said as a small hamlet came into view late in the afternoon. Any other year, the fields would have been full of men, women, and children working. Instead, even from a distance, Jair could see that the fields lay untended, although it was only weeks until harvest. As they drew nearer, an over-powering stench filled the air, and Jair saw shifting gray clouds hovering over the village and the pastures.

"Dark Lady take my soul, what's happened?" Jair breathed as they drew nearer. The air stank of decay, and it was clear that the gray clouds were swarms of flies. The sunken, half-rotted corpses of cows, sheep, and horses lay in the pasture. There was no noise, except for the buzzing of flies, so many that it sounded like the hum of a distant waterfall.

"It's the plague," Mihei said, as they passed the turn to the lane that led into the village. The smell was overpowering in the late-summer heat. He began to chant quietly to himself, and Jair recognized it as the passing-over ritual the Sworn said for the bodies of the dead. Jair made the sign of the Lady, adding his own fervent prayer for safe travel.

"What have you seen of plague?"

Emil shook his head. "Rarely have I been so glad to avoid cities as this season. Most of what we hear comes from the news of the travelers and tinkers we pass on the road. But it's bad enough in some of the larger towns that the dead lie stacked like cordwood because there isn't time to bury them, and the living have abandoned their sick and fled."

"Sweet Chenne," Jair murmured. "What of the other kingdoms? Have you heard?"

"There's a rumor that Principality has closed its border to Margolan refugees. It's said that Nargi is patrolling the river more frequently, as if anyone would think about sneaking into that rats' nest. Has your father closed Dhasson's borders?"

"Not yet. But it may come to that."

"Watch out!" Mihei's shouted warning came as figures crashed through the underbrush toward the road. Jair's eyes widened as he drew his *stelian*. Four creatures burst from the forest, dressed in rags, moving in a frenzy of rage. They had been men once, but there was no reasoning in their eyes, nor sanity. They stank of waste and sweat and were covered in filth and dried blood. Three of the madmen swung tree limbs that looked to have been ripped from their trunks. One of the men wielded a large branch with finger-length thorns, heedless of the blood that flowed from his hands as the thorns tore at his discolored flesh. Their faces and arms were covered with large, red pustules and bleeding open sores. The sight of three well-armed men on horseback should have deterred even the most determined thieves. Instead, the four howled with rage and ran at them, swinging their makeshift weapons.

"What are they?" Jair shouted as his horse reared.

"*Ashtenerath*," Mihei replied, slashing down with his *stelian* as one of the madmen tried to lame his mount with the branch it swung. Mihei's weapon cleaved the man from shoulder to hip, but the remaining attackers pressed forward, paying no attention to their companion's fate.

Two of the madmen circled Jair, yammering and howling in their rage. The third launched himself toward Emil, and his thorny club scored a gash across the flank of Emil's horse before Emil sank his blade deep into the man's chest. The *ashtenerath* collapsed to his knees with a gurgle as blood began to pour from his mouth. Still, he swung at Emil's horse with his club until Emil's *stelian* connected once more, severing his head from his shoulders.

Jair struck at the *ashtenerath* that ventured the closest, slicing through the madman's shoulder and severing the arm that swung the club. The thing pressed on, paying no attention to the pain or to the rush of blood that soaked his tattered rags. Aghast, Jair brought his *stelian* down, slicing from the bloody stump of his attacker's shoulder through his ribs until the body lay severed in two.

With a cry, Mihei engaged the fourth man, who had advanced on Jair's horse from the left. Mihei's horse reared, and a well-placed kick tore the *ashtenerath*'s club from its hands. Blind with rage, the berserker hurled himself toward Mihei. The horse reared again, knocking the attacker to the ground and crushing him beneath its hooves as its full weight landed on the berserker's chest, spattering gore and soaking the horse's front legs to the knees in blood.

Silence filled the clearing as Jair and the others watched the tree line for another attack.

"By the Crone! What spawns those things?" Jair asked as he wiped his *stelian* clean and resheathed his weapons.

Emil and Mihei looked around the bloodied roadway. "Usually, *ashtenerath* are created by potions and blood magic, men pushed past sanity by torture and drugged into a bloodlust," Mihei replied. "They're expendable fighters, just a breath removed from walking corpses, and it's a kindness to put them out of their misery."

"A blood mage did this?" Jair asked.

Emil shook his head. "In a way. The plague began in Margolan, and it was the traitor Curane's blood mages who created it, as a way to stop King Martris's army. Only it got away from them, and it spread beyond the battlefield. Maybe it's the nature of the sickness, or maybe it's because it was magicked up, but a handful of the ones who catch the plague don't die right away. The madness takes them and they become *ashtenerath*. We've heard of attacks before, but this is the first time we've been set upon ourselves."

Jair looked down at the mangled bodies on the roadway and repressed a shiver. He'd fought skirmishes against raiders and seen men die in battle. In the eyes of his opponents, he'd seen determination and unwillingness to yield, but never complete madness.

"Come now. We've got to purify ourselves and the horses to make sure we don't spread the sickness," Emil urged.

They rode another candlemark before they found a clearing near the road with a well. Emil signaled for them to stop. They dismounted, warily watching the underbrush for signs of danger. Mihei stood silently, staring into the forest, but his hands were moving in a complicated series of gestures that Jair knew worked the warding magic of the Sworn. As Mihei set the wardings, Emil built a fire and began to take a variety of items from his saddlebags. Jair drew a bucket of cold water from the depths of the well, and Mihei gestured for him to set the bucket near the fire.

Mihei took pinches of dried plants from pouches on his belt and ground them together in his fist, then released them into the fire. Smoke rose from the fire, heavily scented with camphor, thyme, and sage. Mihei bade them enter into the thick smoke that billowed from the fire and to draw the horses near as well. "Breathe deeply," he instructed, and Jair closed his eyes, taking in a deep breath of the fragrant smoke. "The smoke wards off fever and strengthens the body's humours."

Next, Mihei took a flask from his bags and uncorked it. Jair immediately recognized the smell of *vass*, the strong drink favored by the Sworn, made from fermented honey, hawthorn, and juniper. Mihei poured a liberal draught into the bucket of water, then added crushed handfuls of fetherfew and elder leaves, finally dropping in two gemstone disks, one of emerald and one of bright blue lapis. Mihei began to chant, his fingers tracing complex runes in the air over the mixture. He gestured for each man to unfasten the cups that hung at their belts and fill their tankards with the brew. Jair tossed the noxious-tasting concoction back, stifling the urge to choke on the strong bite of the *vass*. He was gratified to note that Emil also seemed to be catching his breath.

Mihei finished his drink in a coughing fit, but held up a hand to wave off help. When he had recovered, he took three dried apples and a handful of dried fruit from his bags and soaked them for a few moments in the liquid, then offered a handful of the fruit to each of the horses, which they took greedily. Then he moved from Jair to Emil, using a rag to wipe away any blood from the *ashtenerath* that had spattered their cloaks or clothing, tending at the last to his own cloak. Next, he bathed the horses' legs and underbellies to ensure that any splattered gore was wiped away, and made a paste of the liquid and some herbs from his pouches to tend the gash on Emil's horse. Finally, he walked around the others, chanting as he went, spilling out the liquid to make a wide circle in which both men and horses could spend the night.

"And you know this works, how?" Jair asked as the wind caught the scented smoke and carried it away.

Mihei shook the last of the liquid from his hands and sat down beside the fire. "Talwyn said our great-grandfathers used these mixtures the last time a plague swept across the Winter Kingdoms. Few among the Sworn died, even though many others perished."

They settled down around the fire and Emil took lengths of hard sausage, goat's cheese, and crusty bread from his saddle-bags, enough for all of them. Jair rinsed the bucket well and drew up another bucket full of icy water. When they had eaten, Emil took two pouches bound in cloth and leather strips from his bag and handed them to Jair. "I promised I'd give these to you just as soon as I could," he said with a grin.

Jair smiled and took the packages, carefully unwrapping them. On the inside of the piece of bleached linen was a berry-stained handprint, just the size that might belong to a three-year-old boy. Beside it was a charcoal drawing of a horse and a man standing next to the stick figure of a smaller person, and Jair had no doubt it was Kenver's image of his homecoming. Wrapped in the middle of the linen was a disk of finely polished hematite, wound with four strings of colored leather plaited with strands of Talwyn's long, dark hair. Though Jair possessed no magic of his own, he knew it to be a powerful amulet, imbued with Talwyn's shamanic magic.

"Talwyn said it would heighten your awareness of the unseen, and guide your dreams," Emil said with a smile as Jair raised both the linen and the charm to his lips and held them tightly in his hand.

"Thank you," Jair replied, tucking the linen safely into his pack and tying the charm around his neck. It lay against another amulet, this one forged of silver and bronze set with amethyst, a token Talwyn had given him at their wedding. She had told him then that the charm would allow her to enter his dreams, and although Jair spoke of it to no one at the palace, it was only that contact, at the border between wakefulness and sleep, that made it possible for him to endure their separation.

"We'd best get some sleep," Emil said. "We've got another day's ride to meet up with the others." He spread out his cloak beneath him, using his saddlebag as a pillow, and took his blanket from the roll behind his saddle. Jair and Mihei did the same, and Mihei shook his head when Jair moved to sit by the fire to take the first watch.

"Get some rest. I'll take this watch. Don't worry—I'll be happy to rouse you when your turn comes."

Despite the amulet, Jair's dreams were dark. The afternoon's battle replayed itself, but in his dream, throngs of *ashtenerath* pursued them, undeterred until hacked to bits. He woke with a start, relieved to find the campsite peaceful. Mihei had put another log on the fire, and from the smell of the smoke, more warding leaves. Jair settled himself back into his blanket and tried to sleep once more.

As he balanced between waking and slumber, Jair saw Talwyn's image in the distance. She smiled and beckoned for him to come closer. She was singing, and the sound of her voice cheered his heart. Finally, he stood next to her, and Talwyn welcomed him with a kiss. Then she placed a hand over the pendants at his throat. "Watch carefully, my love. The roads are filled with danger." Her eyes widened. "Wake now. Take your sword. The shadows are moving."

Jair jolted awake an instant before Mihei cried out in alarm. Jair and Emil were on their feet in an instant, swords in hand.

"What do you see?" Emil said, scanning the night.

Jair could just make out a trace of movement in the shadows.

"Spirits. *Dimonns*. Don't know which, but whatever's out there isn't friendly," Mihei replied. "I strengthened the wardings."

Jair looked down, and where Mihei had traced a large circle around them and their horses with the cleansing elixir, a ring of stones now marked the area.

"There! Can you see?" Emil pointed into the darkness where darker shapes moved swiftly across the tall grass of the clearing.

Mihei nodded, raising his hands as he began to chant. As Jair watched, a phosphorescent mist rose in the clearing, first just ankle-high, then suffusing the night with an eerie green glow. In the glowing mist, the shapes became clearer. Disembodied shadows slipped back and forth in the mist, but their outlines looked nothing like men. Some were misshapen hulks with wide, empty maws. Others were wraiths with thin, grasping arms and impossibly long, taloned fingers that stretched toward the living men and horses within the wardings.

The horses shied and Jair feared they might bolt. Mihei spared the animals a moment of his attention, looking each of the horses in the eyes and murmuring words Jair did not catch. Immediately, the horses quieted.

The black shapes rushed toward the stone circle, and a curtain of light flared between the three men and the advancing shadows. The shadows howled and shrieked, spreading themselves across the glowing barrier until they blotted out the moonlight. Jair glanced at Mihei. The land mage's forehead was beaded with sweat and he was biting his lip with the effort to reinforce the strained wardings.

"Tell us what you need and we'll do it," Jair urged.

"Keep me awake," Mihei said. "My guess is that someone used this forest as a killing field, and the spirits have never left. Their anger could have drawn the *dimonns*. The deaths in the village could also make the *dimonns* stronger."

"What do they want?" Jair asked.

"Blood."

"If they're drawn by the wronged dead, can you appease their spirits, reduce the *dimonns*' power?" Jair had drawn his *stelian*, even though it was clear that it would be little protection against the shadows that wailed and tore at the gossamer-thin veil of the warding.

"I'm no summoner," Mihei replied. "I can't help the spirits pass over to the Lady. But if we survive the night, I can find where their bodies were dumped and consecrate the ground.

That should satisfy the spirits, and without them and the *ashtenerath*, the *dimonns* should leave."

"Should," Emil repeated doubtfully.

Mihei looked to Jair. "I need some things from my bag." Jair listened as Mihei recited a list of powders and dried plants, and he went to gather them from the vials in Mihei's bag as Emil stood guard, weapon at the ready.

"Mix them with my mortar and pestle," Mihei instructed. "Then make a paste of it with some water." Jair did as Mihei requested, dripping water into the mortar's rough bowl until a gray, gumlike paste stuck to the pestle.

"Bring me a small wad—save the rest, we'll need it."

Jair rolled a coin-sized wad of the gum between thumb and forefinger and brought it to Mihei, who placed it under his tongue. "That should help. When I trained with the mages, there were all-night workings where we didn't dare fall asleep. The muttar gum will keep me wide awake, although I'll pay for it tomorrow."

"Anything else we can do?" Emil asked.

Mihei nodded. "The *dimonns* will try to reach my mind. They'll send visions and nightmares. If I begin to lose my focus, you have to bring me back. All our lives depend on it."

"How should we wake you?"

Mihei shrugged. "Douse me with water. Pinch my arms. If you have to, slap me across the face. Better a few bruises than to be sucked dry by the *dimonns*."

Grimly, Jair and Emil took seats next to Mihei. Jair fingered his amulets, but his connection to Talwyn was gone. Just on the other side of the coruscating light, the *dimonns* stretched their shadows over the domed warding, mouths full of dark teeth snapping against the barrier. Talons scratched against the ground and cries like tortured birds of prey broke the silence of the night.

A motion caught Jair's eye. Something solid moved through the tall grass, and to his horror, the face of a young girl, no more than six or seven seasons old, pale and wide-eyed, rose above the mist. The image wavered, and as Jair ran his fingers over the amulets at his throat, the girl seemed to flicker and shift.

Emil started toward her, and Jair blocked his way. "She's not real."

Emil struggled against Jair, his eyes on the child. "They'll kill her."

"She's not really here."

"Let me go!" Emil broke away from Jair and stepped through the warding. Immediately, the shadows massed and the image of the girl winked out. Emil's scream echoed in the night. With a curse, Jair dove after him, making sure to keep one foot within the warding as Mihei began to chant loudly. Jair caught the back of Emil's great cloak and pulled with all his might. Claws tore at him, slicing into his forearm and shoulder. He twisted out of the way of snapping jaws and he pulled again. This time, he succeeded, landing hard on his back as Emil tumbled through the warding.

Emil's skin was pale, as if in the few seconds beyond the warding he'd been nearly drained of blood. Long, deep gashes had sliced through his vambraces, down his right arm. Razor-sharp teeth had left their imprint on his left thigh. Emil was trembling and jerking, groaning in pain.

Jair glanced up at Mihei, but the land mage's full concentration was fixed on the battle beyond the warding. The ghostly child was gone. Jair had seen enough of battle to have a rudimentary idea of how to lessen Emil's pain, and he rifled through Mihei's bag until he found the flask of *vass*, mixing a few fingers' depth of *vass* in his tankard with cohash and poppy. Jair pinned Emil with the weight of his body and forced his jaws apart until he could drip the mixture between Emil's teeth. Emil's eyes were dilated with pain, and his blood stained the dry grass red. Little by little, Emil's breathing slowed and the thrashing ceased. Jair slid his fingers along Emil's wrist.

"He's got a pulse, thank the Lady."

"Cleanse the wounds," Mihei said in a distracted tone. "Use the *vass*. It'll sting but it's the best we have. *Dimonns* don't carry plague like the *ashtenerath*, but their wounds fester."

Jair did as Mihei said, gritting his teeth as he drizzled Emil's wounds with alcohol and Emil flinched, gasping with the pain. Jair tore strips from Emil's ruined shirt to make bandages and bound up the wounds as best he could. When he had done all he could for Emil, Jair applied the *vass* to his own torn arm and shoulder, then returned to Mihei's side.

Outside the warding, the *dimonns* struck with increased fury.

"They've tasted blood," Mihei murmured. "They're hungry."

"Wonderful," Jair said dryly. "Now what?"

"Just keep me awake. It's taking a lot out of me to keep the wardings up. You could sing."

Jair looked sideways at him. "I can't sing, even for Talwyn. You know that."

Mihei managed a tired half smile. "Pain is an effective way to stay awake. It's that or step on my foot. "

In reply, Jair trod on Mihei's toes. "Ouch!"

"Awake now?"

"Yes, thanks. You can save the other foot for later."

As the candlemarks wore on, Jair paced the warded circle. For a time, he drummed on the empty water bucket with the pestle, playing a rhythm that kept both of them awake. When Mihei began to waver, Jair brought him more of the muttar gum and fanned his face. But as the stars overhead reached their zenith, Mihei was tiring. The golden glow of the warding dimmed, and the *dimonns*, sensing victory, massed against the shielding.

Alarmed, Jair started to his feet, one hand on his *stelian* and one hand touching his amulet in a gesture of protection. Beyond the warded circle, the phosphorescent glow had gone dark. Mihei's eyes were bleary and his lips were dry and cracked as he struggled to reinforce the magical barrier. And although Jair had treated his own wounds, the gashes where the *dimonn*s had cut him burned. He was sweating, although the night was cool, and his heart was racing from more than mortal fear. Emil lay still and pale on the grass. Whatever poison was rapidly coursing through Jair's blood, Emil had received a larger dose.

I'm going to die, Talwyn, Jair thought, fingering the metal charm. *Forgive me.*

The metal tingled under his touch and Talwyn's image formed clear in his mind for the first time since the *dimonn* attack had begun. *Hang on. Rescue . . .* The voice faded, but hope was enough to shake off Jair's fatigue. He ran to Mihei and shook him by the shoulders, rousing him as the glow of the warded dome dimmed nearly to darkness. The shrieks of the *dimonn*s were louder now, and just beyond the thin golden glow, Jair could hear the snap of teeth.

"They're coming for us," Jair whispered, afraid that the *dimonn*s might hear. "Try, Mihei. Try to hold the barrier until help comes."

Mihei nodded. His eyes widened, and he slammed them shut, squeezing them tightly as his head jerked back and forth. Alarmed, Jair reached toward him.

"No. Visions. I see . . . our deaths. All dead."

Acting on instinct, Jair gripped Mihei's shoulder with his right hand and tightened the fingers of his left hand around the amulets that hung at his throat. He willed his breathing to slow, picturing a river of golden light flowing between his amulets and Mihei, warm and powerful energy to reinforce the mage's failing magic. Mihei drew a long, shuddering breath and seemed to relax.

21

In the distance, Jair heard hoofbeats.

A crack like thunder split the night, and a wall of flame burst into light at the edges of Mihei's wardings. A streak of light burned through the darkness, and the *dimonns* scattered, howling in anger as strong magic crackled through the cool night air. Mihei collapsed to his knees, and the last glow of his warding faded.

The fire flared, and in its light, Jair could see five shapes approaching. By their outlines, all had swords at hand. As they stepped closer, Jair could see that the five were Sworn, and leading the group was Talwyn, clad in leather armor, dressed for battle. As Talwyn and the others reached the stone circle, the ring of flames disappeared as quickly as it had come, leaving only blackened grass behind.

"Open the circle," Talwyn said, and Jair rushed to move stones out of the way to welcome the others into the warded space.

"How did you know?" Jair asked, as Talwyn knelt beside Emil.

"When I touched your dream, I sensed evil near you. Something was strong enough to keep me from reaching your dreams again to warn you. Janeth knew the route Emil and Mihei were going to take. We'd had to backtrack from where they left us because flooding had taken out the bridge on the river, so we weren't as far away as Emil and Mihei would have expected. Even so, we had to ride hard to get here in time."

Jair glanced at their sweat-soaked horses, then looked back to Emil. "The *dimonns* tricked him. They showed us a child beyond the wardings. She looked like Emil's daughter."

Talwyn nodded. "That's hard to resist, even if you know better." Jair looked away, not at all certain he could have resisted the bait had it been Kenver's image the *dimonns* had projected.

"Can you heal them?"

Talwyn checked over both Emil and Mihei carefully before

she nodded. "Yes, but not here. I'd like to be somewhere less exposed." She looked up at Jair and cast a worried glance at his wounds. "I'll need to look at that arm, as well."

"Gladly," Jair replied. The warmth of the wound had grown to a low fever, and he didn't want to imagine how Emil was feeling.

At Talwyn's command, the Sworn warriors lifted Emil and Mihei and carried them to their horses, draping each man over his saddle and securing them in place. Jair waved off assistance and swung up to his saddle, favoring his damaged arm but able to ride. They rode in silence, on high alert, for a candlemark until they came to an inn.

"We stop here," Talwyn said, and the others slowed beside her.

"Is it safe?" Jair asked warily.

Talwyn smiled and raised a hand. On the upper doorpost, a rune suddenly began to glow, fading again into invisibility. "One of our people marked this place. It's safe."

The inn was quiet, empty of the usual travelers. Jair had no doubt that plague had dampened business, and if the locals suspected that the road ahead held horrors, then it was no surprise that few ventured this way in the dark. The innkeeper's eyes widened as he saw the company of Sworn enter, but he gestured them upstairs at the sight of the injured men, and he promised to send up food and ale. Jair took a deep breath to steady himself as he climbed the stairs. His fever had worsened during the ride, and his head had grown light. He stumbled near the top, and one of the warriors caught him by the shoulder. Talwyn glanced sharply toward him, but Jair shook his head.

"Emil's worse, and Mihei's completely spent. I'll be all right." As he spoke, his voice seemed distant, and the upstairs corridor of the inn tilted as he fell, and blackness took him.

2

"Don't let go of the life threads. I've nearly got him." King's Healer Esme shifted her position at the bottom of the birthing bed, while Queen's Healer Cerise took her place beside Queen Kiara, holding one hand on the queen's forehead to ease her pain. Martris Drayke, the Summoner King of Margolan, sat on a high stool beside the bed, focusing all of his spirit magic to anchor Kiara's life force and to strengthen the wildly fluctuating blue thread that was the life of his son.

Blood drenched the sheets. Kiara was pale from the loss of it, alternating between fever and chills. Nearly everything that could go wrong with a birth had gone wrong, and as candlemarks of labor slowly passed, the pain had worn through Kiara's warrior resolve until her cries echoed from the stone walls.

Sister Fallon had come to attend the birth, aiding the healers and sustaining Tris's magic through the long night. Rune-seer Beyral waited in the shadows to read the portents for the new prince. Tris knew the other reason the mages had come. Birth, like death, was a time when the veil between the world of the living and the world of the dead was at its thinnest. Drawn by the light, ghosts were the least dangerous of the beings that clustered at the threshold. And though the child had been ensouled since the time of quickening, neither Tris nor the mages

24

were taking any chances. Now, Tris was glad for the mages' presence, and they helped to maintain a warding around the room. It was taking all of his power to keep two fragile life threads glowing brightly. Behind the bed, Tris could see the shimmering outline of a ghost. Viata, Kiara's mother, had also come to watch over the birth.

"Hang on," Tris murmured as Kiara groaned with another contraction. Tris had already bound her life force to his own, magic made easier by the ritual wedding bond they'd made. But the baby's thread was slippery, evasive. Whether or not the boy would become his mage heir remained to be seen: Magic was almost never unlocked so early. Most mages became aware of their abilities as they approached puberty. And yet, as Tris struggled to keep a grip on the pulsing blue life thread, there was something very different about this energy. To his mage sight, it was almost translucent, instead of burning with a clear blue light. And it was damn difficult to anchor.

Cerise pushed a wad of leaves between Kiara's lips and murmured a litany against pain as Kiara cried out with the strength of another contraction. To ease her labor, every knot in the room had been loosened and every closed drawer opened. Around the room candles burned to light the child's way. Still, nothing helped. Tris winced, sharing her pain through the bond. Kiara's strength, while formidable, was fading quickly. And despite precautions—including placing his sword Nexus beneath her bed to cut the pain—nothing had eased this birth.

"He's crowning. One more strong push should do it. Please, Kiara, push him out to me," Esme urged. Tris could hear exhaustion and determination in Esme's voice.

With a final push and Kiara's anguished cry, the baby eased into Esme's waiting hands. Kiara fell back, utterly spent. Tris reinforced Esme's healing magic to ease Kiara's pain, but his attention was riveted on the child. The baby's skin was tinged blue and he did not cry out. Gently, Esme loosened the cord from around him as Tris laid a hand on the small form still slick with blood. He sent a desperate surge of magic to strengthen the baby's life force. The baby jerked in Esme's arms and began to cry, drawing a ragged breath. Tris reinforced his hold on the babe's life thread as Esme took a knife with an obsidian blade and cut the cord, knotting off both ends securely.

"Sweet Chenne, look!"

Esme pointed beneath the bed. Nexus's runes had burst into flame. Tris watched as the runes realigned themselves, magically shifting to form a new message. He read the runes apprehensively. "Light sustains," he murmured, and looked to Beyral and Fallon, whose expressions revealed them to be as baffled as he was.

"What is his name?" Esme's question drew Tris back to the moment, to the child Esme gently placed in his arms. Thin strands of white-blond hair covered the top of the baby's head in a fine fuzz. The child stretched and opened his eyes. They were a brilliant green.

"Cwynn. His name is Cwynn." Tris could only hope that the spirit of the ancient warrior whose tales of magic and bravery were legend would smile on this fragile infant who shared his name. Carefully, Esme gathered up the bloody remains of the birth and brought them in a wooden bowl for Beyral to read the omens.

Tris moved to show the baby to Kiara, gently setting him against her chest so that Cwynn could nurse. Although Kiara was exhausted, Tris could see the pride and affection in her eyes as she watched the baby suckle. "He's beautiful," Tris said, bending down to kiss Kiara's forehead. "Like his mother."

"Will he be all right?" Tris met Kiara's eyes, and he could guess what she was really asking. For months, they had worried over the possible effects that the wormroot on the assassin's blade might have had on the baby.

"His thread is strong," Tris replied. "That's a good beginning."

But even now, as he stretched out his mage sense toward the baby Kiara cradled in her arms, the strange translucency made that thread shift in his sight.

Beyral's chanting drew his attention. The bone and ivory runes were smeared with birth blood, a powerful and ancient magic. Beyral lifted the runes in her hands, and then let them fall. Her eyes grew wide. Every rune and bone had landed with the blank side up.

"What do you read?" Tris asked, hesitant to hear the answer.

Beyral stared at the runes in surprise. "The afterbirth portends great power. But the runes are silent. There is no omen, no reading at all. I've never seen this."

Tris looked to Esme. "What of the wormroot? Did it affect him?"

The healer shrugged. "There's something different about the child. I can feel it in my magic, but I don't know what it is. Everything appears as it should be. We won't know about other effects, or whether or not he inherited your power, for quite a while." She lowered her voice and turned so that her back was to Kiara. "He might be fine. But if not...if there is real damage...he may not be able to take the throne."

Tris felt a wave of cold fear sweep through him, and he struggled to keep his composure. "I won't give up on him without a fight. You know that."

Esme nodded, and laid a hand on his arm. "Protect him. I don't know what the difference means, but whatever it is, he'll need you. Both of you."

Tris swallowed. "The birth was so difficult. Could Kiara bear another child?"

Esme met his eyes. "She needs to heal. But it may be wise, given the circumstances."

An heir and a spare, Tris thought. He glanced back to where Kiara lay with Cwynn in her arms, and the tangle of emotions he felt made him want to laugh and cry all at once. Tris moved back to stand beside the bed and Kiara looked up at him.

"He eats like a warrior. That's a good thing."

Tris reached out to touch her cheek. "Goddess! I never realized what a battle it is to bring a child to the world. Both of you need to rest." One of the midwives took Cwynn from Kiara's arms to sponge him off in a bath of warm herbed wine. She swaddled him and returned him to Kiara, who let him rest against her skin as he slept.

"You need to rest, too."

Kiara reached out to take his hand in hers. "I will. Thank you for holding on." She looked down at the sleeping infant. "He's a fighter, Tris. I know it. He wouldn't have made it through everything if he weren't."

Tris squeezed her hand tightly. "I know. And whatever comes, we'll fight for him. Someday, the runes will speak."

Kiara smiled tiredly. "Or maybe he'll make his own destiny."

"Don't we all."

Later that night, when Tris was assured that both Kiara and the baby were sleeping soundly, he sat down at the large war room table with Fallon and Beyral. Both of the Sisterhood mages looked as exhausted as he felt after the long, grueling candlemarks they had all spent making certain that the new prince and the queen survived the birth. Two others joined them: Mikhail, Tris's *vayash moru* seneschal, and General Ban Soterius, one of Tris's closest friends.

"Is there anyone at the Citadel of the Sisterhood who might be able to figure out what's happened to Cwynn?" Tris asked. He cradled a hot cup of *kerif* in his hands, hoping the inky black drink might help him stay awake.

Fallon shook her head. "No one I would trust with the prince's life." She met Tris's eyes. "Sister Landis still hasn't forgiven the mages who went rogue to help you fight Curane's traitors, or those of us who used our magic to help you win back the throne. She wants the Sisterhood to focus on magic for its own sake, not on kings and wars. I understand why she thinks that way. Foor Arontala showed just how much damage a mage can do in support of a bloodthirsty king. And you saw for yourself the carnage Lord Curane's blood mages created—along with this damned plague." She sighed. "Landis has managed to reduce a complicated question to a simple yes or no. From her perspective, since mages can do damage when they become involved in the outside world, then they cannot be allowed to interfere at all."

"Which means that the non-Sisterhood mages like Arontala can do what they please unopposed, while the strongest and best-trained mages spend their days chronicling elaborate spells to boil water," Beyral muttered.

"Surely at some time in the history of the Sisterhood, a pregnant mage was exposed to wormroot," Tris persisted.

Fallon grimaced. "I've already asked Landis for access to her Citadel's healing histories, and she's refused. It will take some time to acquire any books from the Library at Westmarch, but I've sent a messenger with a request."

"Can Royster use the resources at Westmarch to help us? Isn't the library run by the Sisterhood?"

A smile touched Fallon's lips. "Many things work differently in the north. Yes, Royster's still in charge at Westmarch. But the Keepers of the Library at Westmarch have never listened to the leader of the Sisterhood. They share their secrets as they please. Landis knows that she can't stop Royster from helping us, no matter how she fumes and argues. But it will take weeks for the messenger to arrive, and more time before he returns."

Tris leaned back in his chair. He was nearly a head taller than many men, and lean. The hard-fought war for the throne had put muscle on his rangy frame and brought a weariness to his features that seemed incongruous to his twenty-two summers. White-blond hair, shoulder length, fell in disarray around his face, and stray wisps fell into his green eyes. "Margolan needs a reason to hope for something better," he said quietly, setting his empty cup aside. "Sweet Chenne! Look what the kingdom's suffered in the last two years."

He glanced up at the portrait of his father, King Bricen, that hung over the mantel. "It took Jared less than a full year to empty the treasury, beggar the kingdom, and leave the army in shambles. The farmers still haven't all returned to their lands, and the plague's killed off so many people, I don't know how they'll get the crops in. It's going to be another hungry winter."

"It's not just Margolan at stake," Soterius said quietly. "Isencroft has a civil war on its hands. Donelan won the first round against the Divisionists, but any weakness in your heir is likely to make the opposition bold."

Soterius shook his head. "Think about it. Every time someone's tried to fix one problem, they created a new one. By the Whore! Carroway couldn't concoct a tale as wild as the truth. The whole betrothal contract between Isencroft and Margolan was supposed to stop a war with Eastmark a generation ago. Instead, it made the whole mess with Jared even worse. Now that you and Kiara are married, Donelan's got a civil war on his hands because the Divisionists think it's all a Margolan plot to take over Isencroft. And here we sit, with a brand-new heir to two thrones who might not be able to rule." He ran a hand across his forehead as if his temples ached. "Goddess true! I've lived through it, but when I put it into words, it sounds like something out of the ballads!"

Tris grimaced. "Thanks to Carroway, it *is* something out of the ballads, or did you forget he wrote us into his songs and stories?"

Soterius rolled his eyes. "Don't remind me. It was bad enough surviving everything it took to get you on the throne. I don't need to hear it sung about and embellished every time I go to an alehouse for a drink!"

Tris leaned forward and rested his elbows on his knees. "When will we know how badly the wormroot has affected Cwynn— or whether it's damaged him at all?" Tris looked to Fallon hopefully, only to see the mage shrug.

"There's no way to tell," Fallon replied, choosing her words carefully. "If he learns to walk and talk like other babes, it's a sign the wormroot hasn't damaged him. What concerns me more is how it might have affected any magical talent he might possess. You're one of the most powerful mages in the Winter Kingdoms, and heir to the magic of Bava K'aa, one of the strongest sorceresses of her time. Kiara has the regent magic, and while it hasn't manifested strongly in her, the stories tell of powerful battle magic by the kings and queens of Isencroft in dire times. Magic can skip a generation. Your mother had none of her mother's power. But often, the magic breeds true. We don't know what the wormroot might have done to Cwynn's ability to wield magic."

"That's not entirely true." Everyone turned to look at Beyral. A necklace of charms and runes rattled as Beyral leaned forward. "During the last great Mage War, the Obsidian King experimented on the weaker mages he captured. He wanted to understand the source of power in order to drain magic from his opponents to strengthen himself. When his spirit was bound and his fortress breached, we saw just how far his experiments had gone." A haunted look came into Beyral's eyes. "I heard one of the old Sisters speak of it. In his dungeon, he had a score of captured mages, many of them Sisterhood. He'd sired children on them, and then used magic and potions to alter the babes before birth. None of the women or their children survived, although the Sisterhood did its best to save them."

"How did they die?" Tris asked quietly, suddenly cold all over.

Beyral met his eyes. "Some were consumed alive by magic gone wild. Others died birthing babies that were monsters. We found bodies in the Obsidian King's dungeon of more women and of babies too grossly deformed to survive. It's best for all of us that he left no heir."

But he did. Tris felt Fallon's gaze even as he averted his eyes. Only a few people knew the truth. The Obsidian King had taken the sorceress Bava K'aa prisoner. Her rescue had been one of the only bright spots in the cataclysmic battle. That Bava K'aa had been pregnant with the child of the Obsidian King was a secret that her rescuers took to their graves. That secret was kept for over fifty years, until Tris defeated the new incarnation of the Obsidian King and learned the truth. The child of that forced union had been Serae, Tris's mother. *There was nothing wrong with mother. She didn't have any magic at all. Maybe the Obsidian King didn't try his experiments on Bava K'aa. I know Lemuel's spirit fought him as best he could.* Tris struggled with the fear that welled inside him.

"Tris?" The sound of Soterius's voice roused Tris from his thoughts and he looked up, hoping his expression masked his feelings.

"I didn't know about the experiments," Tris replied. "But do we know whether wormroot was one of the drugs the Obsidian King used? Cwynn looks perfectly normal, even though he had a difficult birth."

"The journals of the Obsidian King were recovered after the war," Beyral said. "Two of them were entrusted to the Library at Westmarch for safekeeping. The third journal was lost. It's believed to have been destroyed."

Tris kept his face impassive. Thanks to a gift from a powerful *vayash moru*, the "missing" journal lay safe inside a locked trunk upstairs in Tris's rooms.

"We may have more to deal with than the heir," Fallon said. "For centuries, a loose alliance of mages has kept sentry along Margolan's borders. They aren't Sisterhood, but they do represent all of the elemental magics: land, water, air, and fire. Their job has been to be aware of the currents of magic, with the hope that they might spot hostile magic before it reaches Margolan."

"Then why didn't they do something to stop Arontala?" Soterius demanded.

Fallon turned toward him. "Their role is to watch beyond Margolan's borders for an invader with strong magic. But to your point, the Sentries did make the Sisterhood aware that two mages of increasing power were in Margolan. One of them was Foor Arontala."

"And the other?"

Fallon inclined her head toward Tris. "Martris Drayke."

"What do your Sentries tell you now?" Tris asked, leaning forward.

"Two currents in the Flow run beneath Margolan. The Eastern current was healed from the damage that made it unstable. The Western current is troubled."

"Is it damaged?" Tris asked. Rivers of magical energy crisscrossed the Winter Kingdoms. Known as the Flow, the rivers enhanced magic.

Fallon shook her head. "The Sentries believe that someone is working strong blood magic beyond the Northern Sea." She met Tris's eyes. "They're certain it's a spirit mage. A very strong summoner, and a dark one."

"What happens beyond the Northern Sea is none of our concern," Soterius muttered. "We have our hands full with our own problems."

"Things like a dark summoner have a way of becoming everyone's problem."

3

"Go!"

Lord Jonmarc Vahanian gave the signal and a dozen black-clad fighters made their way from the cover of the forest toward the shadow of a massive barrow. An unnatural fog clung to the grassland, giving them cover. The brown-robed mage responsible for the fog was right behind the fighters, and Jonmarc could hear the land mage Sakwi chanting under his breath.

He felt a shiver run down his back. For a few steps, the air around him grew as cold as winter, and he knew it was the invisible warding Sakwi had warned them about, a warding set for *vyrkin* shapeshifters or the undead *vayash moru*. Behind Jonmarc, a dozen *vyrkin* and *vayash moru* fighters awaited a signal that it was clear to advance.

Jonmarc rose from the cover of the waist-deep fog behind one of the guards who watched the doorway cut into the barrow's side. Rounding into a perfect Eastmark kick, Jonmarc's boot caught the guard in the chest and slammed him to the ground. Before the man had a chance to cry out, Jonmarc drew a blade across the man's throat. Three guards fell with muffled groans as the other fighters found their marks. Jonmarc gave a curt nod to Sakwi, and the land mage raised his hands and closed his eyes, reaching for the magic that spelled the barrow's entrance.

A sudden gust of wind swept across the long summer grass. Sakwi opened his eyes and nodded, then gestured with his hands toward the forest. An owl hooted in response, taking flight, followed by the swift advance of the *vayash moru* fighters.

"We're already dead and the *vyrkin* heal faster than mortals," Laisren, the lead *vayash moru* fighter, said tersely. "I don't like you going in first."

Jonmarc glared at him. "You wouldn't have made it through the warding. Otherwise, I'd be happy to let you go first."

Sakwi walked toward the torch-lit entrance to the barrow. Runes were carved into the wooden doorposts and the lintel. The land mage's hands moved slowly across the runes, which glowed in response, shifting from fiery red to cool silver. Sakwi nodded and gestured for the others to move forward. They slipped silently down the stone stairs that descended into the depths of the barrow.

The *vyrkin* shimmered and their forms blurred, changing them from men into large gray wolves. As they'd agreed beforehand, the group swiftly sorted themselves: mortal, *vayash moru*, and *vyrkin*. Jonmarc and the other mortals wielded close-range weapons in the tight space, and the torchlight glinted on their daggers and short swords. At the front, Jonmarc held his crossbow at the ready. Behind him padded one of the *vyrkin*, and Laisren, who would need no weapon beyond his strength, speed, and fangs. The others followed them, with Sakwi close behind.

The passageway opened to a large room. Three black-robed men startled as the fighters burst into the chamber.

"You have no right to desecrate—" The man's protest died in a bloody gurgle as Jonmarc's quarrel tore through his throat. The *vyrkin* launched himself at the second robed man, taking him to the ground and silencing his spells with a snap and a snarl that nearly tore the man's head from his neck. Laisren moved faster than sight could follow to pursue the third man, who had turned to flee. Laisren caught him by the shoulder, wheeling him so that he could see the terrified man's face.

"You desecrate this place," Laisren growled, closing one pale hand around the man's neck. "You foul it with the blood of innocents to wake a power you don't comprehend. You can't possibly atone for what you've done."

The man struggled and gasped for breath, then spat in Laisren's face. "I have no need to atone," he gasped, jerking in Laisren's grasp before his spine snapped and he fell to the floor.

"Sweet Chenne," Jonmarc whispered as he and the others looked around the chamber. The body of a *vyrkin* hung chained by its hind feet above a basin filled with blood. Two other wolf corpses lay where they had been thrown into a gutter carved into the rock along one wall. Both had been skinned. Around the room, cages lined the rock walls. The bars shimmered with magic.

Jonmarc moved toward the cages, careful not to touch the glowing bars. He heard Laisren swearing under his breath beside him. In each of the cages lay *vayash moru*, injured too severely to rise, although it was night. Several had been eviscerated; others bore the deep gashes of axes or lay carefully because of multiple crossbow quarrels through their bodies, wounds that would have easily killed a mortal. One lay completely still, with the hilt of a *damashqi* knife protruding from his heart, his panicked eyes the only clue that he remained aware. *Vyrkin* lay in other cages, some in human form, others still shifted, all showing the gashes of an ax or multiple wounds where they had been run through by swords.

"How could they have captured so many *vayash moru*?" Jonmarc asked, stunned.

Sakwi began to move from cage to cage, muttering words

that sounded like water flowing over rock. As his hands traced the outline of the cage, the bars lost their glow and the cage doors swung open.

"Most of these are young in the Dark Gift," Laisren replied, moving with Jonmarc to gather up the bodies of the maimed prisoners. "They're vulnerable in their day crypts. The fanatics know to injure them without striking the heart or cutting off the head. It takes the young ones so long to heal that they're helpless from the pain."

"What about him?" Jonmarc said with a jerk of his head toward the body impaled by the knife as he hefted one of the prisoners into his arms.

"He was old enough to be more cautious," Laisren said, walking toward the *vayash moru*. With one swift motion, he removed the knife from the man's heart. The man's body convulsed and he gave a deep groan.

"Get on your feet," Laisren said, helping the injured *vayash moru* up. "We've got to go."

Jonmarc glanced around the chamber. A small corridor branched off, sloping down into darkness. "What do you suppose is down there?"

"If it's what's been feeding on the blood, you don't want to know," Laisren said as they headed for the stairs, carrying the bodies of those too badly injured to walk.

This time, Sakwi and the *vayash moru* led the group, armed and ready for a fight. Two mortals remained behind.

"Burn what's left." Jonmarc did not turn as he climbed up the stairs. When they had reached the top, running footsteps sounded behind them, followed by the roar of fire. They hurried toward the shelter of the forest, and Sakwi raised the fog around them once more. Dark shapes darted through the fog, huge gray wolves called by the land mage to protect their *vyrkin* brothers.

"I hope you've told them we're off the menu," Jonmarc said with a warning glance toward Sakwi.

The land mage gave a grim smile. "Of course."

Just before they reached the tree line, the *vayash moru* took to flight, carrying bodies of their fallen comrades. Inside the forest, horses awaited the mortals. A few of the *vyrkin* were well enough to ride in human form; the rest, Jonmarc and the others strapped carefully behind their saddles, wrapped in blankets.

"I hate to think what Carina's going to say when she sees this," Jonmarc said to Sakwi as they swung up into their saddles.

Sakwi smiled. "Since she's been married to you, I must say that her vocabulary has grown. She'll do what she always does. First, she'll curse like a merc, and then, she'll send the rest of us running to fetch her healing supplies."

"I wish I didn't bring her so much business. At least, not this kind."

"How many more like this do you think there are?"

Jonmarc shook his head. "They're like rats. Every time you think you've found all the nests, another one shows up. We won't know until we find more of the day crypts violated. The Blood Council's issued a warning to their families, but Dark Haven's been getting so many refugees—living and undead— because of the plague, we don't know where the newcomers are going to ground. Same with the *vyrkin*. They move here to keep from being hunted in Nargi or Dhasson, and before they can find a safe place for their pack, the Shanthadurists are on them."

"Can King Staden help?"

Jonmarc shrugged. "He's sent some troops, but I get the feeling he's stretched thin, keeping peace as the refugees pour in. There've been some outbreaks of plague near the Dhasson border. Plague's gotten so bad in Margolan, Staden's closed that border."

"Didn't Cam just leave for Isencroft? He's got to cross Margolan to do it."

Jonmarc nodded. "Carina wasn't too happy. Said she didn't fix her brother up just to have him catch the plague, but Cam's as hardheaded as Carina."

"They are twins, after all."

"Cam's a soldier first. He's fixed up well enough to return to service, and Lady knows, King Donelan needs him. Anyone who can escape Isencroft's Divisionists and live to tell about it can get across Margolan in one piece."

"He was barely in one piece when he got to Dark Haven."

Jonmarc grimaced. "Yeah. Only Cam would blow up the place where he was being held prisoner to warn the king."

They rode the rest of the way in silence. Finally, they reached the forest's edge and saw Dark Haven looming in the distance. The manor house was large, austere, and forbidding. Jonmarc reached up to brush a strand of long brown hair from his face as the wind swept across the flatland that separated the forest from the manor. *Vyrkin* in their wolf form went first, intent on flushing out any surprises lurking in the high grass. They howled an all clear for the others to follow.

When they reached the manor gates, Jonmarc was not surprised to find Carina waiting for them. He swung down from his saddle and went to her. Short, dark hair framed her face, and even the full cut of her healer's robes could not hide that she was well along in her pregnancy. Jonmarc knew she was appraising him as he approached, looking with a practiced eye for injuries.

"How bad?" she asked as he reached her.

Jonmarc laid a hand on her shoulder. "Our side got lucky this time—no injuries. Laisren's informants had good information. Sakwi took down their magical protection, and we were on them before they knew what was happening."

Carina's green eyes searched his, and he knew that she could tell he was evading a full answer. "And the prisoners?"

"It's bad. Real bad." She started to move past him and he grabbed her arm. "Carina, please, let the other healers help, at least with the *vyrkin*. If you collapse again..." He didn't finish the sentence, but he glanced down toward her belly, growing large with twins. "Please," he repeated quietly, "be careful."

Carina nodded, but her gaze was already going to where Laisren and the others had begun carrying the limp bodies into the manor house. "I know. There's just so much to do." She reached over to squeeze his hand. "I'll be careful. I promise."

He watched her go, forced to smile as she took charge of the rescue operation, summoning guards to help transport the wounded, and sending servants to gather supplies.

"You were successful?"

Jonmarc turned. Gabriel, his sometime seneschal, sometime business partner, had approached with the annoying preternatural silence of the *vayash moru*. "Yeah," Jonmarc replied. "Got in, got out, killed the Durim we could find, and burned the hole. But there's nothing to say there aren't a dozen more holes like that one, and I don't know if we can keep the peace if this goes on much longer."

Gabriel's expression was troubled. "It's not the first time plague has brought oppression on my people. Ironic, isn't it? We can't die of the plague because we're already dead, and yet so many mortals want to destroy us rather than letting us help."

Jonmarc glanced at him. No one would mistake Gabriel for anything other than an aristocrat. Even dressed as he was this night, in a simple black tunic and pants, everything about his manner spoke of power and breeding. Long, flaxen hair fell shoulder length, framing an angular but not unpleasant face. But while Gabriel had the face and form of a man in his early thirties, Jonmarc knew the other had existed for over four hundred years, to become one of the most powerful lords on the Blood Council that ruled the *vayash moru* in Principality and beyond. "You've seen this happen before?"

Gabriel nodded. "Once a century or so. Fashions change. Monarchies change. People don't."

Jonmarc pushed back a strand of long, brown hair and wiped the sweat from his forehead. He'd risen from smuggler to Lord of Dark Haven when he'd helped Tris Drayke win back the Margolan throne. When he'd gone to war against an uprising of renegade *vayash moru* to avert a bloodbath, Jonmarc had become the protector of the mortals, *vyrkin*, and undead within his lands. He tugged at the collar of his shirt against the summer heat that made the air sticky, even in Dark Haven's northern climate.

His fingers brushed the long scar that ran from his left ear down beneath his collarbone, and the two pink puncture marks at the base of his throat. The scar was old, a "souvenir" of a long-ago battle with magicked beasts. The punctures were new, evidence that he had survived the rogue *vayash moru*'s attempts to kill him. Around his neck, two faint scars were a permanent reminder of the years he'd been a prisoner of the Nargi, forced to fight for his life in their betting games. There were more scars beneath the shirt, and they were proof, if anyone still doubted, that he deserved his reputation as the most fearsome warrior in the Winter Kingdoms.

"Between the Durim and the Ghost Carriage, I don't know how many more refugees Dark Haven can hold," Jonmarc said as he walked next to Gabriel into Dark Haven's massive entry hall. The lower floors had been repurposed as a hospital for as many of the *vyrkin* and *vayash moru* as possible. Upper floors where daylight might intrude had rooms for the worst injured of the mortal refugees. Carina presided over it all, directing the cadre of mortal and *vayash moru* helpers, as well as the handful of mages who came to lend their magic to the effort.

"Have you heard more from Kolin? Does he expect to have another Carriage run soon?"

"Last I heard, he said to expect him in about a month," Jonmarc replied. "Said he'd be going back into southern Dhasson, near the Nargi border, for a dozen or so *vyrkin* and *vayash moru* they smuggled out of Nargi. Depending on how often he has to hide out from the patrols, that should mean a new load soon."

"We can take them at Wolvenskorn, if there's no more room here," Gabriel offered.

Jonmarc gave him a sideways glance. "You're helping fund it, aren't you? The Ghost Carriage? You and Riqua."

Gabriel smiled, making his long eyeteeth plain. "Of course. Riqua and I have been among the hunted too many times ourselves to stand by when we could be of help. We're fortunate to have a brave network of mortals and a few *vayash moru* who refuse to leave the others behind. I know too well what it's like, hiding in cellars and caves, waiting to be betrayed and burned. So we help others 'disappear' and take them to safety."

"That's why they call it the Ghost Carriage." Jonmarc grimaced. "I just hope Kolin doesn't push his luck too far. Nargi border patrols are nothing to fool around with. I've gotten in and out of Nargi myself a few times, if you recall."

"Usually in about the same shape as the ones you brought in tonight, as I remember."

"True enough."

"Another long night."

Carina looked up at Carroway and nodded. "Seem to be a lot of them lately." She laid a hand on her swollen belly and Carroway gave her a look of concern. "I'm all right. Honestly. Just tired."

42

"Do I need to tell you what I think?"

Carina smiled and patted Carroway's arm. "I can guess. But there's work to do."

"You know, when Tris sent me to Dark Haven, I don't think he expected you to put me to work!"

"Think of it as part of your healing. It gets you out of bed and moving around, plus it keeps you from feeling sorry for yourself."

Carroway grinned as he got to his feet. He stretched out his hand to her and winced as she pulled herself up. After six months, he wasn't good as new, but his left hand had regained nearly enough strength and mobility for him to begin trying to play the lute again. A knife had impaled his hand as he struggled with the assassin who had tried to kill Kiara. That injury left him worse than crippled. For Margolan's Master Bard, it was a devastating blow. He sighed.

"Maybe I should just go back and focus on arranging music and events," Carroway said. "Macaria's been trying to tell me that it's not the end of the world if I can't play."

Carina shook her head. "You've made progress. You're getting flexibility back in your fingers. And the hand pains you less than it did before. Don't give up. Laisren and Jonmarc both think that you'll be fine with a little more time. And both of them have been banged up badly enough to know."

"You're just saying that because I'm good, free help," Carroway joked.

Carina gave him a tired smile. "Well, there is that, too. I don't know what I'd have done these last few months without you and Macaria—and Cam before he went home to Brunnfen."

"Think he'll have any problem crossing Margolan? I heard they closed the border, with the plague and all." Carroway gave a tired grin. "Which also means you can't get rid of Macaria and me now, even if you wanted to."

Carina shook her head. "As I heard it, you can leave Principality to go to Margolan, but you can't enter Principality from Margolan. And no, I don't think Cam will have problems getting to Isencroft. As for Brunnfen, well, we haven't been home in twelve years. Now that Father and Alvior are dead, it's nice to be welcomed back, but it takes more than a letter to make it home again."

"You're worried."

She shrugged. "Of course. I'd have gone with him if I could." Her hand fell to her belly, and she looked out across the windowless room at the badly wounded *vyrkin* and *vayash moru* Jonmarc and Laisren had brought in from tonight's attack.

Carroway laid a hand on her shoulder and she looked up at him. "Cam will be fine. You'll see. And as for this mess," he said with a look at the crowds of injured refugees that huddled in the room, "we'll figure something out." He grinned. "After all, they've heard the stories about how you and Royster and Taru fixed the Flow of magic when no one had been able to in over fifty years. And if that didn't make you a legend in and of itself, then when word got out that you could take away the pain from *vayash moru* and ghosts, and that you were willing to use your talents on *vyrkin*, well," he said with a chuckle as Carina blushed, "you can't blame them for hoping that if they reached the protection of Dark Haven and its brigand lord, the legendary healer Lady Carina Vahanian could take care of them."

Carina sighed and gave him a black look. "And whose fault is it that the stories have grown with the telling, hmm?"

Carroway grinned. "Once a bard, always a bard, even with a busted hand."

The servants arrived with the supplies Carina had requested, and she signaled for Carroway to help. At the far end of the room, Macaria began to play a calming song on her flute, and after a few moments, Carina could see her patients begin to relax despite their pain. Macaria was an excellent musician, and her music had a bit of magic that could sway the moods of listeners.

Carina maneuvered to kneel next to her first patient, one of the most severely injured *vayash moru*. He had been gutted, slit from ribs to waist, and his organs protruded from the wound. Other gashes were evidence that his captors had not been satisfied to cripple him, inflicting a dozen more deep cuts to increase his pain. Sakwi knelt next to her. "The magic in the cages didn't just keep them prisoner; it also hampered their natural self-healing. All the Durim had to do was injure them too badly to fight when they captured them during daylight, and the cages kept them from healing enough to break free or fight back."

Carina muttered curses under her breath as her hands glided over the gaping wound in the man's belly, pushing his entrails back into place. The dark ichor that replaced blood for *vayash moru* covered her hands.

"Use this," Sakwi said, creating an elixir from herbs he took from pouches on his belt, mixed with a sharp-smelling liquid from a flask he pulled from one of the pockets of his robe. "If they've poisoned the wounds, it should clean them, and it may lessen the pain."

The *vayash moru* groaned as Carina gently touched the wound. He looked to be in his early twenties, and Carina guessed that he had been undead less than fifty years to be captured so easily. A faint blue glow formed beneath her hands as Carina's healing magic began to work, cleansing the wound and supporting the *vayash moru*'s own regenerative powers, helping him heal more quickly. After a few moments, the gut wound had closed, and Carina could see that the other gashes that had marred the man's arms and torso had begun to heal.

The *vayash moru* grasped her hand feebly. "Thank you," he managed. Carina nodded, and signaled to a servant who brought a flask of goat's blood and a goblet, pouring a drink and holding it for the weakened *vayash moru*.

"What's your name?"

"Deinol."

"How were you captured, Deinol?" Carina asked as she and Sakwi gathered their supplies.

Deinol took a long sip of the blood and closed his eyes. "I was betrayed by family. My wife and children kept my secret, and I remained with them until they died. But my granddaughter's husband saw a chance to advance himself by courting the favor of the magistrate. He must have alerted the Durim."

"When you're ready to travel, Lord Gabriel's people will help you find a safe day crypt."

Deinol met her eyes. "I want to fight. I want to join Lord Vahanian's militia, if he'll have me. There are more out there, like the ones who captured me. I want to stop them."

Carina nodded. "I'm sure Jonmarc will be glad for the help. Now, rest."

Sakwi was already treating the next patient, a *vyrkin* whose front leg had nearly been severed by a vicious ax blow. But before Carina could kneel beside him, she heard a shout.

"Carina, I need help!"

An auburn-haired girl in her middle teens knelt next to an injured *vyrkin* in human form. The man had begun to convulse, his body rigid and shaking, eyes wide and staring. Carina and Sakwi hurried to help as the girl skillfully maneuvered a rag between the man's teeth.

"Berry, I need some herbs from my storeroom—valerian and withania, along with red wine. Will you—"

But before Carina could finish the request, Berry was already gone. Sakwi placed a jade disk in one of the man's hands and a disk of emerald in the other, and began chanting to ground the convulsion. Berry returned within a few minutes with the needed ingredients, and as Berry and Sakwi held the man in place, Carina mixed an elixir and removed the cloth from between the man's teeth so she could drip the mixture into his mouth. Then, Carina placed her right hand on the top of the man's head and her left hand over his heart, focusing her healing magic until a faint, blue glow created a nimbus beneath her hands. She willed the humours to sort themselves, separating water, fire, land, and air into their proper courses. As she worked, the man's tremors gradually lessened until he lay still and sweating.

Carina managed a tired smile as the man groaned and opened his eyes. "You had a nasty blow to the head," she said as she moved her hands carefully down the injured *vyrkin*'s body, watchful for strained and torn muscles from his seizure. "I know *vyrkin* heal quickly, but you need to make sure you rest or it will cause another fit. You can sleep here without worrying. We'll watch over you. You're safe now."

The *vyrkin* looked up at her with the clear violet eyes that marked him as a shifter. "Is anywhere safe, m'lady?"

Carina took his hand. "I wish I could answer that," she said quietly, glancing to Sakwi, who took a carefully wrapped wad of herbs from his belt. Carina showed it to the *vyrkin* before carefully inserting it into his mouth, behind his back teeth. "Chew on this. It will ease the pain and help you sleep. Berry will stay with you for a few moments to make sure it takes hold."

Berry looked up at Carina. She was almost fifteen summers old. Her auburn hair was caught back in a simple braid, and she wore a plain linen shift. *I wonder how many of the wounded would believe that Princess Berwyn is fetching them water and binding their wounds?* Carina thought. Berry's eyes sparkled with excitement, and Carina knew Berry was thrilled to be part of the action, showing the same reckless courage she had displayed two years before, when Jonmarc had rescued her from slavers. Her father, King Staden of Principality, had sent her to Dark Haven to avoid the plague. Carina doubted he had envisioned that Berry would take such a lively role as Carina's assistant, but she was glad for Berry's help and her enthusiasm.

"M'lady, you asked me to give you an update." Carina turned to find Lisette behind her. Tall and red-haired, Lisette was Laisren's partner, and though she appeared to be in her early twenties, Carina knew that Lisette was over two hundred years old. Originally assigned to be Carina's lady-in-waiting, Lisette and Carina had become fast friends and Lisette was one of several *vayash moru* Carina had trained to help her with healing both mortals and the undead.

Carina took a deep breath and stretched, hoping to ease the stiff muscles in her back. "I hope it's good news."

Lisette smiled. *Vayash moru* didn't tire as quickly as mortals, and with the constant influx of new patients to be cared for, Carina was thankful for the stamina of her undead helpers. "As good as this day gets, I suppose. Sister Taru and her assistant made one pass through the upper floors, and they've put to rights those with minor ailments. Those who've been healed well enough to leave have gone home, to make room for the ones waiting in the bailey to be seen. Taru's assigned three mortals—a hedge witch, Sister Glenice, and one of the village women—to watch over the patients on the upper floors during the day so we can take our rest."

"Has Neirin started the shelters yet?" Neirin, Jonmarc's grounds manager, had promised to build large canvas structures in the bailey to house those who had yet to find a safe place to stay once their healing was complete.

Lisette nodded. "He's got crews working day and night— mortal and *vayash moru*. It should be ready by tomorrow night."

"Sweet Chenne, how did the world come apart at the seams like this?" Carina murmured tiredly, looking out over the room full of injured *vayash moru* and *vyrkin*.

"As it always does, one crazy person at a time."

Carina jumped at the voice behind her and turned. A man she didn't recognize smiled and extended his hand. "I'm Sior." Sior looked to be in his thirties, with a close-trimmed beard and rich brown hair flecked with gray. His violet eyes revealed him as *vyrkin*, but there was something familiar in his face that made Carina pause. "I was a packmate of Yestin's."

Carina caught her breath. "That accounts for the resemblance. I'm sorry for your loss."

Sior inclined his head. "He died bravely, in battle, defending his friends. There are worse ways to go." He looked out across the rows of patients and his eyes darkened. "Lord Jonmarc sent me to let you know that I've rallied the packs and brought as many as can be spared from guarding our dens. We've pledged our service to fight or assist in any way necessary. I was told that we could be of most help here."

Carina smiled tiredly. "Thank the Lady! We can use help here with the *vyrkin* and *vayash moru*. I'd be especially grateful for a translator—we've got a few who were too badly injured to shift and I want them to know they're safe before I start working on them, so I don't lose a hand. If your people can help here, I can send the mortal workers upstairs to help the day shift."

Sior bowed. "At your service, m'lady. We are in Lord Jonmarc's debt."

It was nearly dawn when Carina and Sakwi tended the last of the wounded *vyrkin* and *vayash moru*. Carina could see the fatigue in Sakwi's face. The land mage began to cough hard enough that it racked his thin frame, but he held up a hand to fend off Carina's help.

"Nothing you can do, m'lady, great as your power has grown. My cough is my burden, I fear," he said, and shook a powder into his hand that smelled of hot pepper and garlic, which he put under his tongue. His dark, luminous eyes widened for a moment, and his face flushed with sudden heat.

"I wish you'd let me try."

Sakwi found his voice again and laid a hand on Carina's shoulder. "Perhaps when things are quieter—if such a time ever comes. These folk need your help more than I do." His eyes narrowed. "You're not the only one with a sense for how others fare. Time for you to rest, Carina."

With a sigh, Carina nodded. "Mother and Childe! It's taking all we have to care for the injured, and we haven't begun to deal with the refugees yet. Berry just received a letter from her father. The plague's grown worse in the city. Taru says that once the weather turns cold, it could spread faster with everyone packed inside." She shook her head. "I feel guilty about resting when there's so much to do."

Sakwi smiled and glanced at Carina's belly. "If you won't rest for yourself, then rest for the two little ones. You can't push yourself the way I know you're used to doing."

"You're right." She was quiet for a moment, looking out over the now mostly silent room. The *vayash moru* patients had fallen into their deathlike slumber at sunrise, even though the windowless room gave no hint of the dawn outside. The *vyrkin*, too, were quiet. Able to go abroad by daylight, the *vyrkin* preferred the night, and many had fallen asleep from sheer exhaustion.

Carina met Sakwi's eyes. "I thought that when we put Tris back on Margolan's throne things would get back to normal. But it's never going to be the way it was again, will it?"

Sakwi shook his head. "It doesn't work like that. I'm afraid we're doomed to live in 'interesting times.' Your friend Royster might love chronicling times like these, but the dull periods of history are much nicer—for the living and the undead."

"I just hope that when the plague has run its course, there's still someone around to tell the story."

4

"You're sure this is the right road?" Rhistiart fidgeted in his saddle.

Cam glanced over his shoulder. "I'm sure. I used to live in Brunnfen, you know."

Rhistiart shrugged. "You said yourself that that was a long time ago."

"It's not the kind of thing you forget."

"You're reasonably sure they aren't going to try to kill us again, aren't you?" This time, Cam detected a hint of true nervousness in the voice of his silversmith-turned-squire. He couldn't really blame Rhistiart. The two had met as prisoners of the Divisionists. Cam had enabled Rhistiart to escape with a message for King Donelan, and then had managed to make his prison explode, warning the king of the traitors' position and nearly getting himself killed in the bargain.

"Reasonably." The truth was, Cam wasn't entirely certain. He and his twin sister, Carina, had been forced from their home twelve years ago by their father, a man who despised magic in any form.

"I thought your brother was one of Leather John's friends," Rhistiart added.

"Alvior was." His eldest brother, Alvior, had supported the

Divisionists against King Donelan, then managed to escape, barely eluding the king's guards. "But it's Renn who's been in charge since Alvior sailed off across the sea, and Renn was always partial to Carina and me. He was just little when we were sent away."

"Think it's a trick?" Rhistiart fingered the hilt of the sword that hung at his belt, but Cam guessed that in a fight, Rhistiart would do better throwing crockery than trying to score with a blade.

"Maybe. I hope not. We'll be careful."

"So if Renn's letter is true, you're the new Lord of Brunnfen?"

Cam gave a harsh laugh. "Wait until you see the place before you get too impressed. Brunnfen is one of the oldest manor houses in Isencroft. It's cold and damp both summer and winter. Brunnfen was built for defense, not as a home, so it's got precious few windows and it's dark. Has its share of ghosts, too, and more than a few have bad tempers. I didn't have the chance to ask Renn, but if Mother died pining away for Carina and me, and Alvior murdered Father, the place might have two new ghosts—just what I need."

"Do you think Lady Carina will ever come home?"

Cam sighed. Rhistiart was loyal and had proven to be unexpectedly brave, but the former silversmith had a penchant for talking day and night. Cam, who was used to the company of soldiers or to traveling with his twin sister, doubted he'd spoken as much to anyone in the last ten years as he had to Rhistiart, mainly because the man refused to accept silence as an answer. "Her home is in Dark Haven, with Jonmarc. If anything brings her for a visit, it's Renn. She practically raised him when he was little. They were very close."

Cam paused, then turned to look at Rhistiart. "So what made you decide to leave Dark Haven? You had a good offer to apprentice with a *vayash moru* silversmith. I saw his work—

each one was a masterpiece. He sells his creations to every palace in the Winter Kingdoms—and to the nobles who can afford him. You could be home in a warm bed and safe." He grinned. "And don't try to tell me it's my winning personality. Carina set me right on that long ago."

Rhistiart smiled wistfully. "I expect I'll go back to Dark Haven in a year or two and take him up on the offer. He's immortal; he's not going anywhere. But this," he said with a sweep of his arm to take in the road ahead of them. "This kind of adventure comes once in a lifetime. How could I pass it up?"

Cam grimaced. "If you recall, 'this kind of adventure' nearly got the two of us killed a few months ago." Cam's injuries from the fight with the Divisionists had almost cost him a leg and had sent him to Carina for healing. Even now, he walked with a limp that would probably never go away, and he would be minus one finger on his left hand forever.

Rhistiart's eyes got a joking gleam. "Besides, Dark Haven isn't exactly a great place to meet women. But at the palace..."

Cam chuckled. "I don't know. I saw some mighty fine *vayash moru* ladies who seemed to think you were interesting."

Rhistiart shivered. "No thanks. Nothing against the *vayash moru*, but I prefer my women warm, and I'd rather take them out for dinner than *be* the dinner."

Cam laughed. "Don't expect a lot of choices at Brunnfen. The moors are a cold place, and it's thinly settled. Most of the women are hardworking farm girls, although they'll likely warm your bones."

Rhistiart drew his cloak more closely around him. He and Cam were an unlikely pair; Cam was of medium height and stocky, with a broad chest and thick, strong arms. A cloud of dark, curly hair framed his face and could make him seem as forbidding as storm clouds. Rhistiart was slim and spare, with lank, yellow hair and finely boned hands suited to the work of an artist. He was short enough that they'd had to search for a horse that was a comfortable height for Rhistiart to climb into the saddle unassisted, and had settled on a roan mare that seemed petite compared to Cam's large warhorse.

"You're going to wed once you get back to the palace!" Rhistiart protested. He grinned. "Now, I figure if you can snag a girl with your obvious charm and breeding, there might be someone who'd favor me."

Cam chortled. "Rhosyn has no illusions about my 'charm' and 'breeding.' Her father's the brewer for the palace, so she's seen me well into my cups, and bless her, she seems to love me anyhow."

He grew pensive at the thought. Although messengers between Isencroft and Dark Haven were few—and with the plague in Margolan, becoming more rare—Rhosyn had bargained and badgered seemingly every trader headed to Principality to carry a letter or a keg of ale to Cam in the six months he'd been recovering. Thanks to Jonmarc, *vayash moru* headed to Isencroft were willing to carry Cam's messages back to Rhosyn. Rhistiart was quite right; when Cam returned to Aberponte, there'd be a handfasting within a fortnight.

"That's well and good for you, but I'm a free man and I plan to enjoy it!"

Cam gave Rhistiart a sideways glance. "Last I knew, you were a 'wanted' man thanks to your late employer's wife."

Rhistiart screwed up his face and spat. "Crone take her soul. Although, in a perverse way, perhaps I owe her some gratitude. After all, if she hadn't cheated me out of my share of the partnership when her cuckolded husband died, I wouldn't have been hiding in that old fuller's mill. And if I hadn't been hiding there, freezing my balls off, I wouldn't have met you and nearly been murdered by the Divisionists. But then, I wouldn't have saved you or met the king, and while you were drugged and recuperating, King Donelan formally pardoned me for 'service to the crown.' So," he said with a grin, "I've been a fugitive, an outlaw, and a hero, all in less than a year." He stretched. "Life is good."

After that, they rode in silence for a while. Cam glanced back, surprised at the lull in conversation, to find Rhistiart dozing in the saddle. He chuckled. Annoying as the silversmith could be at times, Cam had to admit he was good company, and Rhistiart kept him from brooding overmuch on the challenges that awaited him when he returned to King Donelan's service.

It had taken more than three weeks to ride from Dark Haven to Isencroft. Along the way, Cam had gotten a good look at what a combination of war, famine, and plague had done to Margolan in the wake of Jared the Usurper's brief, violent reign. It would probably take a generation to restore Margolan to its former prosperity, even under King Martris's fair and judicious hand. The thought that civil war and poor harvests could wreak the same havoc in Isencroft chilled Cam and made him restless to return to Aberponte. But first, there was Brunnfen to deal with.

By midday, they crested a small hill. In the distance, Cam saw Brunnfen, and beyond it, the Northern Sea. Brunnfen was just as he had described it to Rhistiart: a fortresslike box of gray stone looking out over a high cliff across the cold sea, as unwelcoming in appearance as he remembered.

"You weren't kidding," Rhistiart said, bringing his horse up alongside Cam's. "Looks more like a prison than a manor."

Too many memories crowded in on Cam at once. "It often felt like a prison, even before things went badly with Father," Cam said quietly. "Ah well, no use putting it off. Let's get this over with." Cam jerked the reins and his horse started down the road toward Brunnfen.

Before they had closed half of the distance, Cam saw a figure running toward them, waving its arms. Cam's hand fell to the pommel of his sword out of habit, although he wasn't quite close enough to hear what the man was shouting. His eyes widened as the runner grew closer.

"Cam! Cam! You came! I didn't think you'd really come, but you did! Welcome home! Welcome home!"

The runner was breathless, stopping just a few paces before Cam's horse. He was a young man, a few years more than twenty seasons old, with straight, long brown hair caught back in a messy queue. Most of the strands fell into his eyes, eyes that were unmistakable in their resemblance to Carina's. The man stood a little taller than Cam but was of an entirely different build, almost painfully thin, with an angular face and intelligent green eyes.

"Renn?" Cam breathed.

Out of breath, the runner could only nod. Cam slipped down from his horse and approached Renn slowly, and then clasped him tightly in an embrace. "You were barely waist high when we left," Cam said, his throat tight. "Just a kid."

Renn managed a grin. "Yeah, and now I'm a skinny, over-worked stand-in for the real lord of the manor."

Cam took another look at Renn. Alvior had imprisoned Renn in the dungeon when Renn had discovered his older brother's disloyalty. Although a summer outdoors had restored some color to Renn's skin, the young man's eyes had a hauntedness Cam knew too well was a lasting reminder of captivity. It was also clear from the sinewy muscles in the young man's arms that he had been truthful about taking an active role in keeping the manor afloat in the absence of an "official" lord.

Renn glanced at Rhistiart and seemed to look down the road behind them. Cam could guess what he sought. "I warned you Carina wouldn't be coming," he said gently. "Just Rhistiart—he's kind of my squire—and me. Carina's due to have twins late this fall."

Renn met Cam's eyes with a sad smile. "Twins. That's what got you two into the mess with Father in the first place."

Cam nodded. "Aye. Father might have suffered the ill omen of twins for Mother's sake, but it was Carina's magic that he couldn't abide. And if you're wondering, Carina believes that it's likely that at least one of the babies will have her healing talent."

"Is she really married to Jonmarc Vahanian? The outlaw?"

Cam clapped Renn on the shoulder. "Jonmarc's still the most fearsome fighter the Winter Kingdoms have seen in a long while, but he's a legitimate businessman these days, amazingly enough." He chuckled. "Well, as legitimate as any business is in Principality, if you know what I mean."

Renn laughed. "I haven't traveled the kingdoms like you and Carina, but if the tales I've heard at the pub have been true in half, my sister's descended into a shadowy place filled with rogues, *vayash moru*, and scoundrels."

"Yeah, and that's just the manor house," Cam said and chuckled. "You ought to see the rest of the place!"

Cam got back on his horse, and Renn walked between Rhistiart and Cam as they headed toward Brunnfen. To Cam's amusement, Renn chattered enough to silence even Rhistiart. Cam was unprepared for the rush of emotions that swept over him. Returning to Brunnfen after nearly twelve years in exile, he was surprised by the intensity of his feelings, as he rode across the threshold of a place he never expected would be his home again.

"Unfortunately, you won't know most of the servants," Renn said. "Some of the older ones, like the nurse who would have looked after you and Carina, died. Others were driven away when Alvior became lord." Renn grimaced. "As you can imagine, he wasn't easy to get along with—even before he took up with the Divisionists. It got bad enough, just before he threw me in the dungeon, that we barely had enough staff to run the kitchens and look after the stables.

"Then, when King Donelan's men set me free, I had a manor with no staff, since they'd all fled for their lives, thinking the king was going to arrest them for helping Alvior. I had a terrible time convincing them to come back in time to get any planting done."

Renn sighed, suddenly seeming much older than his years. "I've managed to get the manor back up almost to full staffing, although we're practically penniless." He grimaced. "Alvior apparently gave quite a bit of Father's money to the Divisionists. Whatever he did with it, it's gone. But with crops in the fields and the herds gathered, we won't starve, and that alone was good enough for most of the servants, plus the guarantee of a roof for the winter. They're scared that Isencroft might get the plague, and Brunnfen is out of the way enough that I guess they thought it was better to come here than to try their luck in the city."

"You've done a great job, Renn," Cam said as a stable boy ran out to take their horses. Cam looked around at the familiar courtyard. The buildings were the same, but when he inspected them more closely, he could see the toll that neglect had taken. Despite Renn's efforts, Brunnfen looked shabby and down on its luck, and while it had always been a forbidding place, it had never before looked impoverished.

Renn smiled weakly. "I mostly made it up as I went along, but I wanted to keep it from falling apart before you could get here." He paused. "You're going to stay, aren't you?"

Cam met Renn's eyes. "I can't, not right now. Donelan needs me. The Divisionists dispersed, but they're not broken. If plague does come, along with a lean harvest, there could be riots.

There's nothing like hunger and fear to bring out challengers to the throne."

"So it's true," Renn murmured. "You really are the King's Champion."

Cam nodded. "Aye, although I'm a rather busted up old warhorse these days, I'm afraid. But Carina fixed me well enough to soldier, and as long as I have breath, I'm sworn to Donelan's service."

"Did he tell you he's getting married?" Rhistiart blurted. It was so unexpected Cam suspected Rhistiart was about to burst from his long silence.

Renn raised an eyebrow. "A potential lady of the manor?"

Cam laughed. "The daughter of the Brewers Guild master in the palace city." He pursed his lips as he thought. "Although... that gives me an idea. Someday my bones won't bounce back from battle, and then I imagine I'll need a place to retire. It would be nice to have good ale. Tell me, how is the grain harvest looking?"

Renn grinned. "If you want something to ferment, you've come to the right place. We've got a good crop of grain in the field, and a bumper crop of apples and plums. Not to mention fields of potatoes."

Cam's smile widened. "And in my experience, no matter how bleak it gets, men will always find coin for something to drink. Perhaps I can borrow someone from Rhosyn's father's guild to set up shop in Brunnfen. With a percentage coming to the lord, it might work out well all ways around."

"See, thinking like the lord already," Renn said, clapping Cam on the shoulder. "Come on inside, both of you. I won't promise you the kind of dinner you get at the palace, but the cook's been working up a welcome home meal and I don't want it to get cold!"

Two servants appeared in order to carry the travelers'

saddlebags upstairs and take their cloaks. Cam and Rhistiart followed Renn into the great room. After the long ride, Cam's limp was pronounced and his injured leg ached. Renn seemed not to notice the limp. The room was much as Cam remembered it, a long, cold hall with a huge fireplace at one end. It was too warm to have the fire lit, though come winter, a bonfire would scarcely heat Brunnfen's cold stone. A layer of candle smoke hung near the ceiling from the tallow candles. The unmistakable smell of roasting goose filled the air, along with the scent of leeks, onions, and fresh bread. Cam's stomach growled, and even Rhistiart looked hungry.

Three places were set on the long, empty table. A pitcher of ale and tankards sat next to pewter dishes that were dented and dinged from hard use. Cam looked at the bare walls and frowned.

"I remember there being tapestries," he murmured.

Renn sighed. "There were. Alvior had them burned after Father's death, Crone take his soul. Not that I was necessarily fond of the pictures on the tapestries, but they did help keep down the chill. Quite a few things disappeared like that—either destroyed when Alvior was in one of his moods or, more likely, sold off to raise money for his pet rebels."

They sat down at the table and a plump woman in her middle years brought out a roast goose on a platter. Cam could tell the woman was trying to get a good look at him without staring.

"I hope this is to your liking, Lord Cam," she said with an awkward curtsey. "Master Renn told us you're used to the fancy food they serve at the palace."

Cam eyed the goose and the baking dishes full of vegetables that two serving girls placed on the table. He met the woman's gaze. "Believe me when I tell you that after three weeks on the road, no meal has ever smelled or looked as good."

The plump woman blushed. "Thank you, m'lord. I'm sure you don't remember me, but I was a kitchen girl when you and m'lady

Carina were just little. You used to nip dried fruit from the pocket of my apron and I pretended not to notice."

Cam laughed. "I do remember!"

The woman chuckled. "Now that you're home, I'll bake up some fresh cakes for you by evening."

There was silence as the three men ate. Even Rhistiart paid more attention to his plate than to conversation. When they were finished, the servants brought out a warm plum pudding and a pitcher of mulled wine, then left them alone once more.

Cam leaned back and sipped at his drink. "So what made you suspect that Alvior had thrown in with the Divisionists?" he asked, watching Renn.

Renn was quiet for a few moments, with a sad expression. "Looking back, I should have guessed sooner. I didn't even realize at first that Alvior had murdered Father. Made it look like an accident, but later, I could see that he'd arranged it." He knocked back the rest of the wine as if it were brandy, a gesture that told Cam quite a bit about how hard the years had been for his younger brother.

"You have to understand, after you and Carina...left, there was no one to take my part against Father—or Alvior." He turned his face in profile so that Cam could see the scar that sliced through his right eyebrow down onto his cheek. "Alvior gave me that one night when I got in his way. Must have been about twelve years old. Cracked me over the head with a pewter goblet for something that annoyed him. Father never said anything."

Cam felt old anger rise, but said nothing. Rhistiart looked down, silent as the brothers talked.

"I learned fast to stay out of Alvior's way. Spent as much time as I could out in the fields. Although I've got to say, all that has come in handy since Alvior ran away. At least I knew how the manor really operated. I even slept in the barn when I could, just to be out of his reach. But I was around enough to notice that something strange was going on after Father died.

"Alvior started getting visitors from across the sea. And he started bringing strangers to Brunnfen who weren't from around these parts. The men who came in boats looked highborn. Some of the other strangers, those who came on horseback, were ruffians. They never seemed to do anything but talk, so it wasn't as if he was entertaining them with wenching and dice."

Renn grinned ruefully. "One night, I decided to find out what was going on. They caught me eavesdropping. I guess Alvior could have made me 'disappear' but maybe he was afraid of getting caught after Father's death. So he threw me in the dungeon and locked me down there." He shrugged. "Once in a while he also remembered to feed me."

"And when Rhistiart helped me escape from the Divisionists, I told Donelan what I'd overheard: that Alvior was backing the traitors," Cam finished. "So Donelan's men came to Brunnfen, and they let you go."

Renn nodded. "If you think I'm skinny now, you should have seen me when they let me out of the dungeon. Pale as a *vayash moru* and skin and bones. I was scared to death that the king's men would assume I was on Alvior's side, but they heard me out and left me be."

"Any idea where Alvior went?"

Renn shook his head. "I asked the servants if they'd seen anything. One of the men said that Alvior headed down to the beach beneath the cliffs and that a boat with big sails left the inlet that day. There's nothing but islands off the coast until the other side of the sea, and I doubt he sailed toward Margolan or Eastmark, so I assumed he went across the sea."

Cam yawned and stretched. "Tonight, I want nothing so much as a soft bed. But tomorrow, will you show me Alvior's rooms?"

Renn nodded. "I thought you'd ask. Yes, I can show you.

And I'll take you down to the caves by the beach. We can't make it down and back tonight before dark, but I think Alvior's 'friends' had plans to return and I think Alvior was making ready for them."

"Now that's a cheery thought," Cam said, finishing off the last of his mulled wine. Beside him, Rhistiart looked as if he would fall asleep at any moment. "Let's get some sleep. Then I'd like to have a look around in the morning."

The next morning was clear and bright. Brunnfen was far enough north that although the sun was shining, even on a late summer day, there was a chill in the air. After a cold breakfast, Cam, Renn, and Rhistiart began the climb down the steep cliffs to the shallow beach along the sea. The spray from the waves was cold, and at low tide, the water was still a distance from the base of the cliffs. They reached the bottom without mishap, although Cam's bad leg was already starting to ache.

"Did you and Carina explore down here?" Renn asked as they picked their way through the rocks.

"Many times. Like you, we were happy to stay out of Alvior's way, and father minded Carina less when we were out of sight," Cam replied.

Renn jerked his head toward the cave openings that dotted the cliffside. "Come take a look over here."

Cam and Rhistiart followed Renn into the caves. Sconces were set into the rock, with torches awaiting a fire. Renn took down one of the torches, struck a spark to light it, and motioned for Cam and Rhistiart to follow him. The caves were cold and damp, and the passageway fit Renn and Rhistiart better than Cam, who had to turn sideways to make it through the narrow spots. The passage opened up into a large room. Renn's torch barely illuminated the space, but Cam could see that it was filled with boxes and supplies.

"I've been down here a number of times when I could steal away from the work," Renn said, making a slow tour of the room with his torch so that the others could see. "The boxes are full of armor and weapons. There are rooms like this in several of the other caves. That's just what I've found; I haven't gone a lot deeper because I haven't had that much time to explore."

The magnitude of Alvior's betrayal stunned Cam. "He was going to provision an army," Cam said quietly. "Against Donelan. Against his own king. The Divisionists were just a diversion. Alvior was playing them for fools while he assembled the real invasion, with help from...somewhere."

Cam turned to Renn. "Are Alvior's rooms as he left them?"

Renn nodded. "The king's men only seemed interested in Alvior himself. Far as I could tell, they didn't take any of his things." He paused. "Just so you know—Alvior moved into Father's rooms right after Father died."

Cam's eyes widened. "Father's rooms? Did you look in the secret room behind the wardrobe?"

Renn frowned. "What secret room?"

"There was a secret chamber that opened from a door in the back of the wardrobe in Father's room. Carina and I found it when we were little. I don't think Father ever used it. It was full of dusty old trunks and papers, and Carina and I pretended we were adventurers, discovering lost treasure." He smiled sadly at the memory. "We never talked about it because Father probably would have thrashed us. So I don't know if Alvior ever found it. But if he was brewing up a revolution...it would have been just the thing."

They made their way out of the cave with a renewed sense of urgency and climbed back up the cliffs before the tide came in. Cam led the way back into Brunnfen, up the stairs to the largest room in the manor house. Cam hesitated for a moment with his hand on the door knob. Although he knew his father was dead, a long-ingrained caution urged him to run. Cam drew a deep breath and pushed the door open.

The room was shadowy, even in daylight. Renn and Rhistiart lit candles, but they made a small improvement in the gloom. Brunnfen's windows were narrow slits, excellent for defense but poor for offering either light or view.

Cam looked around the room. The furnishings were the same as when his father had lived: a massive, four-poster bed hung with heavy bed curtains, an equally large desk and paintings of ships at sea. Wrought-iron candle stands and a large iron candelabrum would have made it possible to light the room well enough for reading or writing. The desk looked as if it had been rifled through, with papers strewn about.

"I did go through the desk after the king's men left," Renn said. "The papers were ordinary. Just accounts and such."

Cam nodded, chewing his lip as he thought. He headed for a door in the back that led to the valet's room and the large standing chest where Asmarr stored his finest court outfits. Letting memory guide him, Cam dropped to all fours, crawling to the back of the cabinet and feeling for a catch along the floor. A quiet *snick* answered his touch and Cam smiled. "Got it."

A panel swung open. The opening was large enough for a man's shoulders, but Cam had to shimmy to get his bulk through. "I guess I was a bit smaller the last time I did this," he grunted. Renn passed a lit candle to him, and then he and Rhistiart crawled through without a problem. Cam lifted the candle high and caught his breath.

A work desk had been assembled in the room and on it lay mortars and pestles, a scrying ball, and a number of bulging velvet pouches. The room smelled of herbs and candle wax. Along the walls were shelves filled with vials and jars, some of which held organs, severed fingers, and small animals suspended in a clear liquid. Yellowed bones were stacked along the wall; more lay on the desk.

"Alvior wasn't just planning an invasion," Cam said quietly. "He was working with a mage. A blood mage by the look of it." Another thought chilled him. "And if those bones mean what I think they do, maybe even a dark summoner." He looked toward the others as horror registered on their faces. "We may have ruined their plans to use Brunnfen, but they're out there, somewhere. And they'll come back."

5

Aidane fastened the ornate gold necklace and smoothed it on her chest. The necklace glittered against the red and orange silk of her form-fitting dress, nestling against her full breasts in a neckline designed to show off her assets. The client tonight was paying gold and promised a home secure from the intrusion of the Crone priests. Aidane's fingers trembled as she added gold cuffs to her wrists and a small, silver dagger hidden in the folds of her dress. Nargi priests were well known for their hatred of magic, and every client Aidane accepted was one more chance that the priests might catch up with her.

The client was paying gold for an evening with a ghost whore. Aidane did not want to be late.

She snatched her cloak from the peg and wrapped it around herself, concealing her dress. An ample hood hid her face. Her small apartment was comfortable by Nargi standards, with luxuries many could not afford. She did not have to share the room, and in truth, a roommate wasn't an option. Too great a chance for discovery, should the roommate report on the activities of her *serroquette* friend. Aidane's magic enabled her to eat well on a regular basis, to purchase the clothing and jewelry expected for a prosperous whore, and to pay a tight-lipped healer to fix her up when clients turned surly. She'd even been able to put a bit of gold away in a secret stash for hard times. It was as good as she could hope for, since long life wasn't likely to be an option.

Aidane locked the door behind her and made her way down the narrow stairs to the street. The rooming house smelled of burning meat and overcooked cabbage. The others who shared the building generally ignored Aidane, and she ignored them as well. Better that way. Aidane had clients enough to keep her fed, and more company from the ghosts who begged to be allowed to use her body than she needed. Solitude was the one luxury she couldn't purchase.

It wouldn't do to hire a carriage to take her all the way to the client's home; the driver might remember that he'd dropped off someone from this part of town near the home of a highborn magistrate. That could lead to questions, and in Nargi, questions never had good answers. Instead, Aidane would hire a carriage to take her as far as the marketplace, and from there, another carriage to the client's home.

"Where are you going?"

Aidane startled at the harsh voice. She looked up to see a man in the red robes of a Crone priest blocking her way. Her heart thudded in her throat. *He doesn't know. He can't see your clothing. It's just the usual night patrol.*

"Heading for the temple," she murmured, keeping her face averted. She hoped her voice was suitably respectful.

"Late for you to be out alone," the priest chided.

"I felt the need to pray," Aidane said quietly. "Please, I want to make my offering."

"Next time, go by daylight. Proper women aren't in the streets alone after dark."

"Yes, m'lord."

The priest turned away to shout at another passerby, and Aidane hurried away. After a long while, her heart stopped pounding and she said a prayer to the Dark Lady in gratitude for her safety. The priests despised *serroquettes*, male or female, and of the few other ghost whores Aidane had known, all but one had disappeared. That made Aidane's skills even more highly sought after, and enabled her to raise her fees. It also increased the odds that luck would turn against her.

Even at this time, the marketplace was busy. Torches lit the walkways and stalls that sprawled along the Kathkari Market, a tangle of pushcarts and tables covered with whatever goods might be had this week. The ascendance of the Crone priests under King Thaduc had made commerce a dangerous business, since edicts enlarged the list of forbidden items each week. Illicit goods, such as smoked fish from Principality, Tordassian brandy, or luxurious sweets from Dhasson, could still be had, of course, if the buyer had enough money and the right connections. Aidane shouldered her way through the crowd, ignoring the calls of the food vendors, although their bowls of noodles or skewers of chicken and beef smelled delicious.

She chanced a look around to make sure she was not being followed. It was difficult to know for certain in the bustle of the marketplace, but no one looked familiar. At the far end of the market, Aidane hailed another carriage, one with an enclosed passenger compartment, and breathed a sigh of relief as she settled into the cushioned seat.

By moonlight or by daylight, the city of Colsharti looked gray and lifeless. Nargi had always been conservative in its ways, some would say hidebound. But since Thaduc had forged his alliance with the Crone priests, the life had gone out of both the city and its people, who walked with their heads down, and usually with their cloaks up, as if skulking in broad daylight. Conversations had become guarded, and people now chose their words carefully, even among friends. Many public gatherings had been banned, so music and theater had become contraband, performed in cellars and in the caves beneath the city, constantly changing locations. Aidane fingered her necklace. Maybe soon she would have enough gold saved to buy her passage out of Nargi. Maybe soon...

M'lady, is it all arranged?

The voice sounded in Aidane's mind. The speaker was a ghost, a handsome man with dark hair and midnight-black eyes, the dead lover of Aidane's client.

It's arranged, Aidane answered silently.

You're certain she'll accept you? There was a hint of nervousness as Nattan, the ghost, replied.

She understood the offer.

Nattan hesitated. *Jendrie's taste didn't run to women. How...*

Aidane sighed. *It's just as we discussed. You said yourself that there are no male* serroquettes *to be found in Colsharti these days. When I'm alone with her, I'll give over my body to your control. You can do what you like together; Jendrie paid for two candlemarks' time.*

Nattan seemed embarrassed. *But you will know; you will see.*

Are you afraid you'll shock me? I've been a ghost whore since my moon days began. I've made couplings for ghosts of every taste and interest. You'd have to want something damn acrobatic to surprise me.

And I'll feel the coupling through your body?

Yes.

Nattan fidgeted. *It will be strange, coupling with Jendrie as a woman.*

Aidane's nerves got the better of her, making her patience thin. *It's up to you. If you'd rather, you can talk over tea—*

No. It just takes some getting used to. Perhaps there'll be opportunities for pleasure that are new in this arrangement. That's a good thing.

Serroquettes were just one more item of contraband in Nargi. Aidane fingered her necklace nervously, as if it were a good-luck charm. Every new appointment ran the risk of discovery by the priests, and with it the threat of torture, imprisonment, and death. Wealthy clients could usually buy their freedom. Poor clients, who had barely scrounged up the ghost whore's fee for a desperate reunion with a dead spouse or lover, often suffered the same fate as the *serroquette* should the priests learn of the liaison. And still, business was brisk.

If this goes well, when I can use you again?

Aidane hated the word "use" even as she had to admit it was accurate. *I accept one client each night. My nights are all taken for at least a month. Be cautious. You may be a ghost but Jendrie and I aren't dead yet and we'd like to keep it that way. Meet too often and someone will see, or Jendrie's husband will find out.*

Understood.

To Aidane's relief, Nattan said nothing more for the rest of the ride. She could still feel his presence dimly in the back of her mind. Silence gave her time to prepare. No matter how long she had been servicing clients, it took preparation to allow the ghost to fully inhabit her body. Usually, Aidane could lock herself away in a corner of her mind, resolutely ignoring what her body was doing until it was time to collect the fee. That worked most of the time, except when pain was part of the foreplay. Or when the lovers got into a quarrel that involved injury. Then, Aidane slammed back into consciousness, sometimes fighting with the ghost to share the body and protest rough treatment. And more than once, a determined ghost had tried to make the possession permanent. Fortunately, Aidane's magic had been strong enough, so far, to keep that from happening.

"Stop here," Aidane called out to the carriage driver as they reached the road that led to Jendrie's home.

"I can take you to the doorstep, m'lady," the driver said courteously.

"No, thank you. I can walk." She paused, reaching into a velvet purse for coin enough to pay the man. "Be back at this crossroads in two and a half candlemarks. Mind you don't stop and wait, just go up and down the road. I'll need a ride back to the city."

The carriage driver came around to open her door. Aidane made sure her cowl was covering her face so that he could not identify her. "Yes, m'lady," the driver said, helping her down. Aidane waited until the carriage had disappeared from sight before she began walking. Discretion was essential for a ghost whore, to protect both whore and client. Lanes to several manor homes led off of this stretch of road, so even if the carriage driver mentioned bringing a fare this way, he would have no idea where his passenger had gone.

Aidane paused at the gate to the large manor house. It wasn't the custom in Nargi to make an ostentatious show of wealth on the outside of a home. Better not to give the priests any reason to claim higher tribute or to covet one's property. Nargi's priests were infamous for bringing charges against even the rich and well-connected whose power or wealth might pose a threat to the iron control of the priesthood.

"Hurry," a voice called from the other side of the gate, which opened far enough for Aidane to slip through. "The mistress is waiting for you."

Aidane said nothing as she followed the servant up the long gravel carriageway. She kept her hood up. It was possible that the servant had no idea of the nature of Aidane's visit. That would be best. The less said, the better.

In Aidane's mind, she could feel Nattan's anticipation. He'd reconciled himself to the new arrangement, and the more he thought about it, the more urgent his lust became. Aidane tried not to guess at the nature of her clients' relationships with their dead lovers. For some, it was obvious that death had severed a deep, genuine love. Many of the others just missed a reliable lay, or found the novelty of sex by proxy to be titillating. Aidane and the other ghost whores promoted the fiction that they suffered memory loss after the ghost left them. While she fervently wished it were true, it wasn't, although the fiction pacified nervous clients and squeamish spirits. And it gave clients who later had second thoughts about the rendezvous less of a reason to hire one of Nargi's numerous and inexpensive assassins to eliminate a potential embarrassment.

"M'lady is this way." The servant led Aidane in through the kitchen door, down a darkened hallway. Perhaps Jendrie had dismissed the other servants for the night; the corridors were empty. They climbed up the servants' steps from the kitchen, then went through a narrow passageway intended for ladies in waiting and kitchen staff, before stopping at a door. The servant knocked four quick times, and the door opened. A woman stood in silhouette in the doorway.

"That will be all, Priscilla. Mind you say nothing of this to anyone or I'll have you beaten."

"As you wish, m'lady."

The servant fled, and the woman gestured for Aidane to enter. "Take off your cloak. I wish to see you."

Aidane did as Jendrie bid her, letting the cloak fall to the floor. Jendrie eyed her with a combination of suspicion and lust. "How do I know you can channel Nattan's spirit? Maybe you're just a good actress."

Aidane met Jendrie's eyes with an insolence the woman did not expect. "You know my reputation or you wouldn't have sought me out. Once he possesses me, you'll know. His gestures, his way of speaking, his way of pleasuring you... all will be as they were. Only the body has changed."

"And you'll remember nothing?"

"Nothing, m'lady."

"Very well." Jendrie stepped closer, and Aidane could smell wine on her breath. Apparently the encounter had unnerved her patron just as it had made Nattan's ghost fidgety. "Let's begin."

"First, my coin, if you please." Aidane's gaze did not falter. "Sometimes, my leaving is rushed. Best to handle business first."

An ironic smile touched the corners of Jendrie's mouth. As she turned to take a coin from a purse on the desk, Aidane got a good look at her. Jendrie was tall and slender. Her coppery skin showed Nargi blood, while her startlingly blue eyes hinted at a mixed heritage, perhaps Margolense or Dhassonian. Her chestnut hair was loose around her shoulders, and Aidane imagined that Jendrie had let it down for her lover, since the long pins and gem-studded combs that most highborn women used to bind their hair lay discarded on a stand. A black satin robe, another piece of contraband, clung to Jendrie's curves. Jendrie handed Aidane the coin and then loosed the belt of her robe, letting it fall away. She wore nothing underneath.

"I want Nattan," she whispered seductively, and reached out to stroke Aidane's cheek. "Bring him to me."

Aidane resisted the urge to shy away from Jendrie's touch as she put the coin safely in her purse. She reached out for her magic, letting it fill her, and called out to Nattan. The transition was always unpleasant as the ghost's spirit forced its way into her body, crowding out her own being. Aidane trembled as Nattan's spirit filled her, and she could see in Jendrie's eyes that Jendrie found it arousing. Aidane scurried to the far corner of her mind, to her hiding place, but not quickly enough to block out the depth of Nattan's hunger. A voice that was not her own spoke from her lips, as Jendrie began to unfasten the brooch and belt that held Aidane's dress together and Aidane's own hands, now Nattan's, fumbled with the unfamiliar clothing.

Aidane reached her refuge and slammed the mental door. The years had perfected the ability to block out the moans and pleasantries even as it deadened her awareness of pleasure and release. Chanting helped. Aidane chanted a series of long poems from the ancient tales, willing herself to pay no attention to the uses made of her body or the unfamiliar voice that spoke from her lips. On occasion, sudden pain broke her concentration as Jendrie's sharp fingernails drew blood. For that reason, Aidane preferred serving male clients or women who had lost female lovers. She was likely to sustain less unintentional damage that way.

Finally, it was over. In her mental hiding place, Aidane retained a sense of the passage of time, a necessary survival technique. The two candlemarks were ending, and Aidane needed to regain herself in order to leave before they were discovered. She ventured out of her sanctuary, but still not within Nattan's awareness. Her body lay entwined with Jendrie's on the broad bed. It seemed both Nattan and Jendrie had discovered that the novelty of the pairing brought new satisfaction. Nattan was talking, stroking Jendrie's tousled, dark hair.

"What of Zafon?"

Jendrie's lip twisted. "He's gone to court for a fortnight. He suspects nothing."

Aidane could feel Nattan's apprehension. "That's what you said before I died. But somehow, Zafon found out."

Oh, great, Aidane thought, feeling panic rise. *Nattan's not just her dead lover; he's her murdered lover. Funny how no one mentioned that. Time to get out of here—now!*

Before Aidane could force Nattan out of her consciousness, a door slammed open. She felt Nattan's terror at the sight of a tall, heavily built man in the doorway, and there was no mistaking the rage in the man's eyes.

"Zafon, no!" Jendrie screamed. She tried to scurry out of the way, but Zafon moved quickly, grabbing Jendrie by her long, slender neck. She wore nothing but her jewelry, which rang like bells as he shook her, closing his large hand around her throat until Jendrie's face grew red and she wheezed for air.

"Whore," Zafon spat, throwing Jendrie to the floor, where she lay sobbing.

Run! Move! Aidane tried to fling Nattan's consciousness out of the way to take back her own body, but the ghost was frozen with fear. Aidane watched helplessly as Zafon returned his attention to the bed. He took in Aidane's necklace and the heap of clothing that lay at the foot of the bed, and his face mottled with rage.

"Ghost whore," he hissed, as if his anger had robbed him of the breath to speak. "It's that good-for-nothing artist, I wager."

Aidane gave up on pushing Nattan completely away, but she finally got him to roll from the bed, barely missing Zafon's grasp.

"Didn't you learn anything when they killed you? They assured me it was painful. Said you shrieked like a stuck pig when they cut off your balls and that you didn't stop screaming until they slit your whore-spawned throat." A gleam came into Zafon's eyes. "But you came back. So I'll just have to kill you again."

Aidane tried to run, but without Nattan out of the way, she was clumsy, tripping over the rug. Zafon grabbed her wrist, twisting her arm behind her. Aidane screamed, and in her mind, Nattan whimpered, nearly beyond sanity with fear. On the floor, Jendrie quivered, still huddled on her knees, face down.

"Look at me, Jendrie!" Zafon roared. "I may not be able to kill you without risking your father's hired blades, but I can kill your lovers. This time, you get to watch." He pushed Aidane toward where Jendrie cowered. "Look at me, or I'll tie you to the bedpost and make you watch."

Jendrie raised her head. Tears streaked down her cheeks, which were already mottling with the bruises from the choking. Her eyes were no longer confident and lively. They had gone dead, paralyzed with fear. She was crying hard enough that she gasped for air, and sobs racked her body.

Aidane's heart pounded. Nattan's ghost fled. He left her suddenly enough that it felt as if he had ripped his spirit free, tearing along her magic and leaving her, for a moment, magically blind. She expected Zafon to draw a blade, thought that he would plunge it into her heart. Instead, Zafon's huge fist slammed into the side of her face, knocking teeth loose and sending her reeling. Blow after blow fell, and his heavy boots kicked hard into her stomach or slammed their soles down on her fingers. Aidane had felt many ghosts leave her body, but now it was her own soul that seemed to hover, gauzelike, in her mind, its grasp fading. Blood choked her as she tried to scream, but nothing appeased Zafon's rage.

I'm dying. She could feel her heart slowing. It hurt so much to breathe. Zafon lifted his large foot over her chest and cast a triumphant look at Jendrie, who clung to the bedsheet, gray-faced and terrified. "When I've gotten rid of the body, you'd better be waiting for me between those sheets, by damn," he growled. "I paid enough dowry for you to buy a houseful of whores, and I'll have value for my coin."

His boot slammed down, and Aidane was swallowed up by blackness.

Gradually, Aidane became aware of a rocking motion. *I must be dead. Perhaps this is what it feels like when a spirit crosses the Gray Sea.*

She lay face down on a pile of refuse. As consciousness returned, so did pain. Aidane felt as if she was watching from outside herself, not as she did when she hid during her clients' couplings, but in an odd way, from a distance. She was still naked, and the cold she felt had less to do with the night air than with the certainty that life was fading. She was in the back of a wagon, and the driver was pushing the horses to a full gallop down a road that made the wagon jostle hard enough that Aidane slipped in and out of awareness.

Finally, the wagon stopped. Zafon came around and grabbed her by the ankles, flinging her to the side of the road with a curse. Too weak to cry out, Aidane lay where she landed as the wagon rattled away. *Will I bleed to death before the cold takes me, or will the wild dogs finish what Zafon started?* It wouldn't be long. Dreams and voices came to her, and ghosts pressed all around her, waiting. She had nothing to offer them now, but still, they came. Some of the spirits taunted her, and others tried to force themselves into her dying body for any chance to live again. Still others just watched, sad-eyed and silent, as if her flickering soul were a candle and their gray spirits the moths.

After a while, footsteps sounded along the road. "What have we here?" a man said. His foot nudged her over, and she fell onto her back, too spent to make any effort to cover her nakedness.

"Not much left of her, is there?" his companion replied. Aidane's vision was blurry, but from what she could make out, the two men were dressed all in black, wearing neither the robes of the Crone priests nor the uniforms of the king's soldiers.

"Take her. She'll do," the first man said.

The second man lifted Aidane gingerly, less to keep from hurting her, she guessed, than to avoid soiling his cloak. He did not put her into a wagon as she expected, but instead, the two men veered from the road down a trail into the darkness of the forest. Branches stung as they slapped against Aidane's bare skin, and brambles tore at her. She shivered with cold, and the shivering made her injuries hurt more. She lost all sense of time. Even the ghosts fled.

Finally, they slowed. In the moonlight, Aidane could see the entrance to a cave. One of the men lit a torch, and then they began to wind their way down rocky passages. Sharp rocks skinned Aidane's knees and shoulders. Aidane was beyond fear, sure that death would come soon. Even if her new captors wished to inflict more pain, their amusement would not last long. She knew that. It comforted her. No more pain. No more ghosts. No more clients like Jendrie.

"Put her in there."

The man set Aidane down in a cage made with iron bars. "She's not a biter; that's her own blood. And if she was a shifter, I reckon she'd have made the change and bitten us. Doesn't look like she's got fight left in her."

"Do as I say."

With a shrug, the man turned a key in the lock. The first man pressed his face against the bars with an unpleasant smile. "Don't spill any more of that precious blood now, darlin'. We're going to need it for the Moon Feast." With that, he turned, and the two men left the chamber.

Aidane managed to shift, just a bit, to look around. It hurt to move much, but she could see other cages, and in them, huddled shapes. In the cage next to her, a man lay with a stake through his chest. He was as pale as a corpse and he did not breathe, but his face was turned in her direction and she could tell that there was consciousness in his eyes.

A groan sounded from another cage. Aidane mustered the energy to move far enough to see. A naked man lay curled in pain, arrows protruding from several places along his body. Aidane's eyes widened. That many arrows should have killed a mortal. Then she recalled her captor's comment about "shifters" and "biters." She knew little of either, but she had heard tell that both *vyrkin* and *vayash moru* could withstand injuries beyond a mortal's endurance.

The naked man seemed to sense her gaze. He turned to look at her and moved his leg to cover himself. His violet eyes seemed to see right through her. "Why are you here?" His voice was tight with pain. "You're mortal. What do they want from you?"

"Blood," Aidane managed through swollen lips, barely above a whisper. "My blood."

It occurred to Aidane that she was naked, and in the next moment, that she was too badly injured to feel shame. The man in the cage drew a labored breath.

"Sacrifice. They want you for a sacrifice. To Shanthadura."

Shanthadura. A name used to frighten children, spoken only in whispers. The Destroyer. The Great Darkness.

"You've heard of Her?" the *vyrkin* asked.

"She's not real," Aidane replied, her voice shaking with the strain of talking.

Those violet eyes locked her gaze. "Oh, yes, She's real. And we're all here to feed Her so Her disciples can let Her rise once more."

6

"Is there anything I can fetch for you, m'lady?"

Kiara, Queen of Margolan, looked up at the servant who waited anxiously in the doorway. "No, thank you. That will be all."

The door closed, and Kiara's attention returned to the baby in her arms. Cwynn looked so peaceful when he was sleeping, but Kiara had already learned how loudly the new prince could cry when he was hungry. Kiara's auburn hair spilled down, unbound, to brush against Cwynn's downy scalp. His skin was several shades lighter than Kiara's tawny hue, a combination of Kiara's Isencroft and Eastmark heritage and Tris's Margolan blood.

Kiara stroked Cwynn's dusky fingertips. "You carry the blood of three kingdoms, little one," Kiara murmured. "Are you heir to your father's magic? How can so many fates rest on one small child?"

She nestled him closer, rocking him gently, watching his chest rise and fall. In the shadows along the wall, she could see the dim glow of two of the palace's ghosts. Ula was a long-dead nursemaid to the children of one of Margolan's former kings. She had never left Shekerishet, even after her death, and she continued to look after generations of new princes and princesses. Tris had told her that he remembered Ula's ghost standing over his bed when he was a boy, and the soft sound of her humming, something only he could hear.

Seanna had been handmaid to Margolan's queens for over two hundred years. Seanna had welcomed Kiara and been a ghostly companion, making Kiara's transition to a new home in a new kingdom less lonely. Kiara was glad for the company, and she found the ghost's presence comforting.

The door opened, and this time, it was Tris who entered. "You finally got him to sleep?" Tris whispered.

Kiara nodded, and Tris came closer, careful to move without noise. He looked down at Cwynn, and then at Kiara.

"Can you put him down and get some sleep? Have one of the servants hold him. Lady knows, none of us have slept much these past nights!"

Kiara sighed. "I know. But I've just gotten him quiet." She watched Tris and frowned. "There's something on your mind."

Tris withdrew a packet from his doublet and handed it to her, untying the ribbon that bound it so Kiara could read the letter inside. "This arrived by messenger today from your father."

Kiara caught her breath, and then froze as Cwynn stretched in her arms at her sudden movement. "Is he all right?"

Tris shrugged. "I didn't read it."

Kiara's gaze scanned the familiar handwriting. King Donelan of Isencroft wrote with a bold stroke, pressing firmly enough that his quill sometimes punctured the parchment.

Kiara, my dear—

By the time this reaches you, your young prince will have been born. I pray to the Lady that both you and he are in good health. Please, take care. My seer has read mixed omens, and I don't know what to make of her portents. I asked her to read the runes for the child's fortune, and the runes refused to speak. I know little of magic, but I have never had the bones be silent.

I hope that Tris with his magic will be better able to discern these meanings.

Don't dwell overmuch on the signs and omens. Celebrate the coming of your first child. I know you've had a difficult pregnancy during extraordinarily difficult times. Much the same was your mother's fate, but she rejoiced in your birth and loved you from the first time she laid eyes on you, as did I. I trust that soon you'll have one of the court artists make a sketch you can send to me, so that I can see the boy for myself.

Your letter asked me to give you news of Isencroft and not hold back on account of your condition. I know my daughter, and fear if I were to do otherwise, you might arrive on horseback despite the birth, so I'll be candid.

I don't remember a time so bleak as these days. This year's harvest was only marginally better than the last. More people will be hungry, and with the hardship Margolan is enduring, I know Tris has no surplus grain to send this year. I had implored Staden in Principality and Kalcen in Eastmark to send grain if they had any to spare, but they may not send wagons until the plague in Margolan has run its course.

The Divisionists have scattered, but we haven't completely broken them, and grumblings about food and plague make fertile ground for unrest. I received a vayash moru *messenger from Dark Haven a few weeks ago from Cam. He is on his way back to Aberponte via Brunnfen. Cam intended to see to the lands now that they fall to him, and to find out more about Alvior's treachery. If it is true that Alvior left in a great ship across the Northern Sea, I also fear that we have not seen the last of him. Whether it's the regent magic or just an old man's intuition, I believe we'll see war ere long. My dreams are dark.*

Tice and Allestyr are well, and I keep them busy handling my affairs and running the castle. I'm well-recovered from my sickness of last year, and the hunt was good this year. We hunted more than usual to cull the herd. One bright spot is that we won't lack for venison.

I'm anxious for Cam to return to Isencroft. I value his counsel and rest easier knowing that he's at my back. I console myself with the thought that Isencroft has endured dark days before, and that we are a resilient people. I hear of Margolan's troubles, and I grieve that you and Tris have come to your throne in such turbulent times.

Plague has not yet taken hold in Isencroft, but such things are just a matter of time. We can't possibly police the entire border, and refugees fleeing Margolan are sure to bring the sickness with them sooner or later. We're preparing as best we can.

I trust that you've heard from Carina, so I won't repeat her letter at length except to say that she's well and quite ready for her twins to be born.

I pray for Chenne's favor on your child, and know that he'll make a fine king someday. Please give my greeting to Tris, and encourage him. The weight of the crown is great.

I miss you. Send word when you can, and remember Isencroft in your offerings to the Lady.

With love

Kiara sighed and set the letter aside.

"Bad news?" Tris asked, coming back to her side from the window.

"Nothing more than the usual, but that's enough." She stroked Cwynn's wispy hair and the baby stirred contentedly at her touch. "Some things I knew from Carina's last letter, about Cam being recovered enough to travel, and that she's feeling well despite the twins. But Father was honest in his other news, and it's not good." She handed the letter to Tris and was silent as he read it.

"Your father is one of the shrewdest kings in the history of the Winter Kingdoms," Tris said when he had finished the letter. "If anyone can guide Isencroft through stormy times, it's Donelan."

Kiara nodded. "Maybe I just have a better idea now what the crown really means. When Father was sick, I ruled from behind the throne for months, with Tice and Allestyr to help. That was hard enough, but now that I'm queen in fact as well as function, I understand even more why Father often seemed distracted, and why he took to the hunt so hardily when he was free from his duties."

Tris leaned down to kiss her head. "These times will pass. You'll see. They'll be just a bad memory by the time it's Cwynn's time to rule."

Kiara turned away. "If it ever is." She paused, and looked down at the sleeping baby. "He looks so perfect, but there are times when he wakes in a terror, eyes wide and screaming, as if he's seen horrors. He won't be comforted when that happens, no matter who holds him or what we do. When the fit takes him, he screams for candlemarks. Thank goodness for the servants!"

"Perhaps it's poor digestion. If the healers can't give you an answer, ask the cooks and the serving girls. They've got babes of their own and they must have ways to quiet them."

Kiara looked toward the empty fireplace as if she might see an answer in its depths. "Perhaps. But I think there's more to it than his digestion. Ula and Seanna can quiet him when no one else can reach him. He watches Ula as if he can hear her, and I swear he can feel Seanna's touch, although she isn't solid enough to hold him. Could he have your power so early?"

Tris shrugged. "I don't sense power in him at all. Not that I'd expect to—he's far too young. But when I touch him with my magic, he feels different somehow. It's not what I feel from people without magic, or what I sense in other mages. It's as if he's blank to me. And I've set wardings around these rooms. If any ghosts or *dimonns* tried to enter, I'd know. Perhaps you're seeing more in his tempers than what's there."

"Perhaps." She was silent for a moment, and then she worked up the nerve to say what had been on her mind all morning. "We need to think about having another one—"

Tris turned toward her, eyes wide. "You can't be serious!"

"Completely."

"No. Absolutely not. It's too soon. You won't have your strength back."

"Aren't I a better judge of that?"

"No. You're far too likely to do the brave thing for the good of the throne."

Kiara saw real concern in his eyes. "A second heir might ease the tension in Isencroft, if we had one son who could take the crown in Margolan and one who could become king in Isencroft. The idea of a joint throne fuels the Divisionists. And it's been fodder for people like Curane, who don't like sharing the Margolan throne with Isencroft."

"Curane is dead. The plague's the danger now, and it doesn't care who's king." Tris knelt beside her chair and met her eyes. "I nearly lost both of you the night you gave birth. I don't ever want to come that close to losing you again. You had a hard time of it, almost from the time you got pregnant. I don't want to risk it."

Kiara smiled and leaned her head against his shoulder. "I love you for that. But as you've said so often, kings don't get the choices other men have. Especially if...if something isn't right with Cwynn, then there needs to be a second heir, just to continue a joint throne."

Tris touched her cheek reassuringly. "You're borrowing trouble. Cwynn's growing well, and I've heard you complain that he has a healthy appetite." He sobered. "I know that what you're saying is logical. My head agrees with you, but my heart doesn't, not yet. Please. Let's see what the next months bring. The choices may be clearer then, if we have any choices at all."

A quiet rap on the door ended the conversation. Tris went to answer it, as Cwynn stretched and Kiara moved to quiet the sleeping baby. Ban Soterius stood in the doorway. Even when not dressed for battle, everything about Soterius marked him as a soldier, from his stance to his dark brown hair, short-cropped for a helm.

"I'm sorry to interrupt, Tris, but we've got a problem." Ban Soterius, now Margolan's youngest general, had been Captain of the Guard the night King Bricen was murdered. Along with Harrtuck the guard and Carroway the bard, Soterius had helped Tris escape with his life from the coup that claimed the rest of his family. Soterius and Carroway had been childhood friends of Tris's, and along with Harrtuck, they went willingly into exile to protect Tris. When Tris launched the campaign to take back Margolan's throne from Jared the Usurper, Soterius had rallied an army from those who had fled Jared's depredations or deserted Jared's corrupt army. His courage had earned him the rank of general, and his friendship with Tris placed him among the king's most trusted advisors.

Tris let himself out of the room quietly. "What's wrong now?"

Soterius sighed. "We've just gotten word of an attack on a village a candlemark's ride south of the city."

Tris frowned. "Who?"

"A better question might be 'what.'" Soterius's face was grim. "The patrols discovered it when they found a boy stumbling down the road, covered in blood. I heard the account from the soldiers who saw the boy themselves. They were pretty shaken up about it. According to the boy, something came out of the old barrow near the village and went on a rampage."

"Rogue *vayash moru*?"

Soterius shook his head. "Not likely. For one thing, the boy said it wasn't solid. He said it was a shadow that changed shape, but it was real enough to flay flesh from bone and to rip heads from bodies." He paused. "When it was daylight, the soldiers investigated. They found the village as the boy said. Everyone was dead."

"And the boy?"

"After that night, he hasn't said another word. The healers tried to treat him, but the wounds are festering. He's going to die."

"Where is he?"

Soterius gestured. "Come with me."

Two of Tris's bodyguards fell in behind them as they quickly descended the steps. They left the large, grand entranceway to the palace Shekerishet and crossed through the bailey to the guard tower. The sun was just setting. "We didn't want to bring him into the palace for fear of contagion," Soterius explained. Harrtuck, now Captain of the Guards in Soterius's stead, met them at the tower door.

"I thought you'd want to see this," Harrtuck said, but his raspy voice sounded shaken. "I pity the lad."

Tris glanced over his shoulder toward Dugan, one of his bodyguards. "Find Mikhail. He'll have risen by now. Bring him. I'd like him to see this. And send Esme to me." Dugan took off toward the palace. Tris returned his attention to Soterius. "You've had Esme look at the boy?"

"Esme says it's not something her magic can heal."

Prepared for the worst, Tris followed Soterius into one of the rooms usually used as a guard's bedchamber. He caught his breath at the sight of a still, small form on the bed. A young boy in his middling years lay pale against the sheets. His eyes were tightly closed, as if against nightmares only he could see. Esme had cleaned the boy's wounds, but blood seeped through bandages that covered his arms and chest, and a nasty gash sliced across one cheek.

"You wished to see me?" Mikhail's soundless approach made Tris startle, although he knew the *vayash moru* seneschal could move quickly and without noise. Mikhail was one of Lord Gabriel's brood, on loan for as long as Tris required his service. Since the *vayash moru* were immortal, Tris guessed that meant his own mortal lifetime.

"What do you make of him?" Tris said with a nod toward the boy on the bed.

Mikhail moved forward silently and bent over the boy. Tris hoped that the *vayash moru*'s heightened senses might pick up something mortals could not. Mikhail frowned and looked up. "This is bad." He met Tris's gaze. "You know that *vayash moru* did not do this."

"How can you be certain?"

Mikhail looked back toward the boy. "For one thing, he has his blood. The marks are wrong—claws, for starters. But not *vyrkin*, either. And there's a residue of dark magic." He looked up. "Bogwaithe?"

Tris nodded. "Or *dimonn*."

Tris moved around Soterius to sit beside the boy, who had still not opened his eyes. Tris stretched out a hand and lightly touched the boy's shoulder.

"You're not real. You're not real. You're not real," the boy chanted under his breath in the heavy accent of the Margolan farm country.

Tris closed his eyes and called for his magic. He felt the power rise, filling him. Tris raised wards of protection around the room, reinforcing the safeguards he had already placed around the castle. When the room was warded, Tris turned his attention back to the boy.

He could feel the boy's pain and terror. Just from his touch on the boy's shoulder, images flared into Tris's mind, carried by the magic. He could hear the screams of the villagers and smelled fresh blood, along with the stench of entrails. In the torchlight of the village night, men, women, and children ran for their lives from the black shape that rose from beneath the barrow. That dark presence changed from horror to horror as it moved. In one glance, it seemed to be the shadow of a shrouded skeleton, its face lost to the blackness of its cowl. In the next breath, it was the shape of a two-legged beast, and then the impossibly huge, long-armed outline of a featureless man, with hands that grasped and tore.

Tris's magic thrummed with the boy's fear as his Summoning power read from the child's soul. He heard the running footsteps as villagers ran for their lives, and he felt an icy chill as the darkness passed by him. Tris winced as the boy's memories supplied a vision of the dark thing lashing out at him, claws tearing down through skin and cloth. And then, abruptly, the thing left him, gliding off to run the rest of the villagers to ground. Tris pulled back from the contact, but he could hear the boy's screams echoing in his head.

As clearly as Tris could feel the boy's terror, he felt the poison the attacker left behind. *Esme can't heal this. It's not just poison and not just magic.* Dimonns *leave their own mark.* Tris reached out with his magic toward the thin, blue-white strand of light that was the boy's soul. The *dimonn's* poison wasn't just in the flesh or blood, but in the soul itself, like a growing rot. Tris brought his power to bear on the darkness that stained the strand of light, willing his magic to cast out the shadows. Even for a summoner of Tris's power, such a working took a tremendous amount of energy. Gradually, the shadows faded and the blue-white strand glowed more brightly, unsullied by the *dimonn's* touch. Tris withdrew his magic gently and looked up to see Esme watching him closely.

"I would like very much to know how you did that," the healer said, a smile touching the corner of her lips.

"If I could explain it in words, I'd tell you." Tris could hear the tiredness that colored his voice. Power always came at a price, and although Tris had learned over the last two years to wield powerful magic, such workings took a toll.

The boy's eyes snapped open. "Who are you?"

"He's your king, lad," Soterius said quietly. "You're safe."

The boy eyed Tris warily. "I must be fevered."

Tris gently took the boy's hand. "What's your name?"

"Evan of Treganowan."

"I've seen your memories, Evan," Tris said quietly. "What attacked your village was a *dimonn*. Have you heard the term?"

Evan nodded, eyes wide. "It was something evil, that's for sure."

"I'm going to have to put it right, and I need your help," Tris said.

"My help? For the king?"

Tris managed a smile. "Yes. I need you to remember, where did the *dimonn* rise?"

Evan's eyes darkened. "From the foot of the barrows outside the village."

"Are you certain?"

"Aye. Saw it when I went to gather firewood."

Tris thought for a moment. "Has anything disturbed the barrow?"

Evan gave him a frightened look. "How did you know?" His sudden movement made a silver talisman slip into view beneath his ruined shirt. Tris reached down and lifted it into the light. It was the mark of the Lady, wrought in silver, and by the look of it, very old.

"Where did you find this?"

Evan slumped back into the bed. "I didn't disturb the barrow, if that's what you're thinking. But two nights ago, when the moon was dark, something did. The next morning, when I went to gather wood, I saw that someone had dug into the barrow. I was curious, so I looked closer. There was a pile of rocks to one side, a lot of them carved with markings. What was left looked like a doorway into the barrow, with stone doorposts and more of those funny marks."

"And the necklace?"

"It was in the pile of rocks. I meant to give it to my mum. She likes—liked shiny things." His voice caught as he corrected himself.

"Did you go into the barrow?"

"I'm not crazy!" Evan suddenly remembered where he was. "M'lord," he added hastily.

"Smart boy," Tris said. "I have a feeling that necklace saved your life. It's been touched by old magic, very old." He looked up at Soterius and the others. "Whoever or whatever disturbed the barrow also weakened its protections. The runes Evan saw were part of those wardings, and so was the talisman, I'm betting. That *dimonn* didn't get out by accident."

"The black robes," Evan murmured.

"What did you say?"

"The night the moon was dark, my brother said he saw two strangers on the road outside the village. That's odd, because we don't get many outsiders our way. Said they wore black robes. They didn't stop and they didn't speak to anyone, so I didn't think of it again."

"Did your brother say anything else about the men?" Tris asked.

Evan thought for a moment. "He said he didn't like their look. He didn't see them up close, but he thought one man wore a necklace made of bones."

Tris and Soterius exchanged glances. "Shanthadura followers," Soterius muttered.

"Sounds likely," Tris replied. He stood and looked to Esme. "The poison is gone, but it will take a few days before he feels better. Since he can't go home, let's see about finding him a place here in the castle." He didn't say it aloud, but since the *dimonn* had marked the boy once, Tris preferred to keep him within the wardings, to prevent the *dimonn* from returning to finish what it had started.

"Call for Coalan," Tris continued. His valet, Soterius's sixteen-year-old nephew, would be the perfect person to help Evan. Like Evan, Coalan had also lost his family to violence, but in his case, it had been Jared's soldiers and not *dimonns* who were responsible for the slaughter. "Have Coalan sit with him until Evan's feeling better." He met Esme's eyes. "Get whatever you need to fix him up."

"Yes, m'lord."

Soterius and Harrtuck fell into step beside Tris as they left the guard tower. "That story about an amulet from a tomb remind you of anyone?" Soterius murmured.

Tris glanced at him. "Yeah. Jonmarc." Long before he had become Dark Haven's brigand lord, Jonmarc Vahanian had been a blacksmith's apprentice in a poor Borderlands village, hired by a stranger to retrieve an amulet from one of the cliffside tombs. That night, magicked beasts overran the village, slaughtering everyone except Jonmarc, who was wearing the amulet during the battle. The scar that ran from Jonmarc's ear down below his collar was a permanent reminder of that fight.

"Only it was a blood mage who wanted the amulet then. Foor Arontala," Soterius replied.

Tris shrugged. "The way I see it, Arontala's blood magic isn't that different from what the Shanthadurists are doing. The question is... what do they want from the barrows?"

"I have this awful feeling you're going to feel the need

to ride out there and take a look for yourself," Soterius said, resignation in his voice.

Tris gave a lopsided grin. "Of course."

A small group of heavily armed soldiers rode out from Shekerishet with Tris and Soterius the next morning. Sister Fallon also rode with them, and Beyral the rune scryer, along with Esme, the king's healer. Although the morning was bright, the group rode in silence, alert for signs of danger. After a candlemark's ride, they arrived at the crossroads just beyond the village lane.

"Can you feel it?" Tris said to Fallon.

She nodded. "There's power that shouldn't be here. It feels wrong."

Tris nodded. "Just as well it's daylight."

If they had doubted Evan's word, the stench of rotting bodies quickly proved the truth of the boy's tale. The villagers' bodies, many of them torn to shreds, lay strewn across the village green. Nothing else appeared to be touched, verifying that the murders had not been the work of raiders.

Tris nudged his horse on, past the carnage and toward the path that led from the village into the forest. Soterius and two of the guards led the way, with Fallon and Tris in the middle, followed by three more soldiers. Tris appreciated Soterius's attempt to protect him, but if the *dimonn* manifested, the soldiers were unlikely to be able to hold it off.

They had timed their arrival for just after the sun's highest point, since the netherworld was at its closest at noon and midnight. *Dimonns* were among Tris's least favorite supernatural foes, and he had the scars to justify his opinion. After a short ride, they reached the barrow.

The barrow was a mound covered with sod. If someone hadn't looked closely, it might have passed as a hill, and many of the ancient barrows were assumed to be part of the natural landscape by those who lived in their shadow. Tris knew otherwise. Barrows like these dotted the landscape of the Winter Kingdoms. Some were just the resting place of long-dead warriors and warlords, men who lived and fought before the kingdoms had come into being. Other barrows held the remains of something else, and while Tris was not sure what that something was, the legends said it wasn't human.

Those barrows had been thought to be so dangerous that the nomadic Sworn patrolled them, making their circuit from the Northern Sea on Margolan's far border down across Dhasson to Nargi. Tris had not met the Sworn, but as he dismounted from his horse and approached the desecrated barrow, arranging a meeting with one of their warriors suddenly jumped to the top of his list of things to do.

Tris's mage sense prickled a warning the closer he got to the barrow. He heard nothing unusual with his ears, but on another level, it seemed as if voices whispered just beyond hearing range. He did not need to recognize their words to sense the malevolence.

"I need you and the men to step back," Tris said to Soterius. "Protect Esme."

"We're here to keep you in one piece," Soterius said levelly, meeting Tris's gaze.

"I appreciate that. But if a *dimonn*'s what we're really up against, it won't care about swords. Magic's the only thing that can turn it."

"We've vowed our lives to keep you safe."

"Then honor that vow by stepping back. If I'm distracted by worrying about protecting you, I'm that much more likely to make a fatal mistake."

Soterius yielded, but his dislike for the order was clear in his face. "Fall back!"

When the soldiers had stepped back a dozen paces, Tris joined Fallon in walking a circle around the barrow, using his drawn sword as an athame as they raised wardings for protection. Or, more precisely, to protect the soldiers and anyone on the other side of the warding from what was inside it with him and the two mages. When they finished, Tris kept his sword in hand, although he knew it was unlikely to deter whatever dwelled within the barrow.

"Look here." Fallon bent over a pile of rubble. Beyral knelt next to the stones, and Tris could see that her hands were working in the complex motions of a spell.

Beyral's magic made the runes on the broken pieces of stone glow. "Someone set sigils of protection over the entrance to the barrow," Fallon said quietly. "These are old—very old."

"The Sworn?"

Fallon frowned. "I don't think so. I've come across the barrows they patrol on occasion and their magic feels completely different. No, I don't think this is one of theirs."

"Can we seal it back up and put protections back into place?"

Fallon and Beyral exchanged glances. "If it were the two of us alone, I'd say no. Whoever did this the first time was a powerful mage. But your magic is stronger—and you're a summoner. I really don't want to think about anything you can't bottle up."

"Let's get started," Tris said, with an anxious eye toward the sky. Although late-summer afternoons seemed to last forever, Tris knew that strong magic required time, and he would prefer to finish the working long before the sun began to set.

Tris had just lifted the first of the sigil stones into his hands when he felt a rush of frigid air. A black shadow spread from the gaping hole in the barrow's side, growing like a bloodstain.

Beyral began to chant, while Fallon and Tris stood shoulder to shoulder, blocking the shadow's way. Tris had given Evan's talisman to Fallon, and its protection gave her more freedom to move.

"*Lethyrashem!*" Fallon spoke the banishment spell as Tris gathered his power for the first salvo. The *dimonn* fell back momentarily, and then surged forward once more. Magic arced between Tris's hands and a blinding flare of light streaked toward the growing shadow. The thing shrieked, and the odor of burned, rotted meat filled the air.

The *dimonn* twisted, evading the worst of the blast, and this time it was Beyral who sent a curtain of flame, cutting off the *dimonn* as it lunged for Fallon. Tris anticipated its next move, and his sword-athame drew an opalescent scrim between himself and the *dimonn*.

"We can't contain it forever—any great ideas?" Tris shouted.

"If you can get it to back down, Beyral and I can seal the opening with runes," Fallon replied.

What are you? Tris stretched out his magic toward the shadow.

I am hunger. The *dimonn*'s voice sounded like a hundred screams in Tris's mind.

Who loosed you?

Those who would be my master.

Why have you come?

To consume everything.

"Wrong answer," Tris said between gritted teeth. To make the next magic work, he would have to drop his shielding. That would make it a contest to see whether he could be faster than the *dimonn*.

In one breath, Tris dropped the coruscating power that shielded him from the *dimonn*. It rushed toward him, and the *dimonn* slashed at him, and one clawed arm sliced through the chain mail that protected Tris's arm and shoulder. He could feel the *dimonn*'s hunger for blood, for life, for power. The fresh blood drove the *dimonn* into a frenzy. Tris fought vertigo as he ignored the pain, and he saw his opportunity. Tris met the *dimonn* with the full brunt of his power, drawing on the magic of the Flow, his own life force, and on the fire within that pumped the bright red blood from his wounds. Everything else seemed to dim as Tris poured his power into forcing the *dimonn* back into the darkness of the barrow. Distantly, he could hear Fallon's spell-casting and Beyral's chanting, and beyond the wardings, the shouts of his soldiers.

Tris shut it all out, everything except the screeching wail of the *dimonn* as his power forced it backward. He could feel the old magic of the barrow, the sundered charms, and the broken spells. The old power buoyed him, feeding back into his magic.

"Ready, Tris!" Fallon shouted.

Tris charged forward with a cry, and a wave of power roiled up around him, rising from the barrow itself. The *dimonn* clawed at the sod, its talons gouging into the dirt as the magic forced it back from the edge of daylight into the darkness of the tomb. Beyral and Fallon ran past Tris, each carrying part of the stone lintel that had once capped the barrow entrance. They pushed the broken stone into the hole that had been dug into the mound, and their chants raised the dark runes on the stonework into fiery lettering. The *dimonn* gave one last shriek from the depths of the mound, and Fallon and Beyral brought down the rest of the marked stones, burying the talisman Evan had found in the center of the stone sigils.

Warily, Tris let the power flow out of him and gasped as the pain of the gashes on his shoulder fully registered. He did not drop the outer warding until he had helped Beyral and Fallon completely seal the barrow entrance. Together, they stood and made one last working over the mound, incorporating magic to deter any who might think to repeat the desecration.

"You're hurt." Fallon looked at Tris with alarm, and her gaze followed the bloody trail from his shoulder to his ribs.

"I've felt better," Tris said, shaking from the expenditure of power. Magic usually left him with a headache, and the severity of the pain depended on the difficulty of the working. A reaction headache was already beginning to pound behind his temples, but he guessed that the fever he felt had more to do with the *dimonn*'s poison.

Tris eased himself to the ground. Esme ran to him and began to tend his shoulder as the guards formed a protective ring around them.

"Dammit, Tris! You should have let us in to help," Soterius swore, giving the injury a worried glance.

"It went through the chain mail. The only reason it didn't take my arm was because my magic was holding it back," Tris said tiredly. "Your soldiers wouldn't have stood a chance."

"Can you heal him?" Soterius said, looking to Esme.

Esme nodded. "Yes, but it's going to hurt like hell." She glanced at Fallon and Beyral. "I'll help them once I get Tris patched up."

Tris lay back into the dry grass. Esme removed what was left of his chain mail. The *dimonn*'s claws had sliced through the heavy metal rings as cleanly as a sword. Already, the wound was beginning to putrefy. Tris could smell it. He concentrated his own power on containing the poison. He could feel it beginning to flow through his blood, feel his arm and shoulder growing feverish. Drained from the battle, Tris marshaled his magic, drawing on his life force. If the *dimonn*'s poison reached that blue-white thread as it had with Evan, there would be no summoner to save Tris's life.

Tris felt the poison war with Esme's magic. The cuts had been deep, and the poison was strong. While Tris had used his magic many times to help heal others, he had rarely turned the power inward. He didn't need Esme to tell him that his life depended upon finding a way to do just that. Tris could feel his heart struggling to beat. It was getting harder to breathe.

Tris focused his magic on the putrefying wound. *I have the power to breathe life into the dead, although it is forbidden. Perhaps dead flesh is just dead flesh.* Tris called his summoning magic to him and concentrated on the flesh of his shoulder. He could feel the death spreading, and he met that death with magic, willing the necrotizing skin to live and forcing the blue-white light of his life thread into skin and tissue. He fought back a scream at the pain as his body warred against his spirit and his power. Esme was amplifying his magic, channeling it into the most damaged places.

"It's working, Tris," Esme urged. "But it's not gone yet."

With a cry of pain, Tris forced blood and spirit back into the blackening flesh. He felt death yield to him, and with its surrender, the sullied skin and muscle began to thrum once more with blood and life. In moments, the wound was cleansed. Four raw gashes still laid open the left side of his arm and chest nearly to the bone, but they were clean of rot and free of poison. Tris swallowed hard and sank back against the ground, barely conscious.

"I'll take it from here," Esme said, bending close to his ear. "You're safe now."

"I really don't want to explain this to Kiara," Soterius muttered, kneeling next to Tris on the other side. "I don't think she'll take it well."

"She's used to...this sort of thing," Tris managed. He meant to say more, but Esme's healing magic swept over him like a warm blanket, taking with it both pain and consciousness.

7

"I fail to see how this is any of our concern." Astasia leaned back in her chair, letting her long, chestnut-colored hair fall across her shoulders, spilling down over full breasts barely hidden by her revealing neckline. The *vayash moru*'s pale skin was a sharp contrast to the deep burgundy of her gown. Astasia met Jonmarc's eyes with a look that combined both seduction and malice.

"It's your concern because you're the Blood Council, dammit!" Jonmarc glared at Astasia. Once, being the only mortal in a room of *vayash moru* might have tempered his comments. Now, a year after he had come to Dark Haven as its lord, he had fought and bled for its residents, living and undead. The insurrection he'd quelled that winter had set him directly against two of the Blood Council's members, Uri and Astasia, at peril of his life. He still had a scar from two puncture wounds at the base of his throat, where Malesh, one of Uri's renegade *vayash moru*, had tried unsuccessfully to kill him. Surviving that attack had made Jonmarc a legend, as had returning alive from making Istra's Bargain, a pledge to forfeit his soul in exchange for the death of his enemy. Having stared down both the goddess and Malesh, Jonmarc found his fear of the undead was considerably diminished.

"My brood has no quarrel with the Durim," Astasia said blithely.

"Then you are a fool." Riqua wheeled on Astasia. "The Dark Gift is no protection against their torches. They hunted me when I lived, and I hid from them when I was first brought across. No more. I will fight." In life, Riqua had been the wife of a wealthy merchant, and that sensibility still served her. She was a handsome woman in her mid-fifties, with upswept, dark blonde hair. Her gown was of the most current fashion favored at court, and the expensive jewelry that glittered at her throat and on her wrists was a testimony that undeath had been favorable for building wealth.

"Of late, you seem ready to battle anyone," Astasia purred.

Riqua's scorn was evident on her face. "I'm not ashamed that my brood fought alongside Lord Gabriel's to defeat Malesh. We preserved the Truce with mortals to protect ourselves. I paid a price for that; half my brood was destroyed in the fighting. You might not have dirtied your hands with battle, but I recognized many of your brood among those who fought for Malesh."

"So?" Astasia pouted. "It's the way of things. Uri's fledge started the war. Mine just played along. Immortality without conflict is...boring."

"You brought our kind to the edge of destruction because you were bored?" Riqua hissed. "You were a stupid, empty-headed whore in life and you haven't learned anything in death to improve on that."

Astasia started from her seat, and Jonmarc thought she might attack Riqua, but just then, Gabriel rose to his feet. He fixed Astasia with a cold glare, and she sat down. *She's afraid of him*, Jonmarc thought, suppressing a smile. He knew just how formidable Gabriel could be. Astasia might be willful and utterly self-centered, but if she recognized Gabriel's power, she wasn't quite as stupid as Riqua supposed.

"One war is behind us," Gabriel said. When he was certain Astasia was silenced, he turned his gaze toward the other members of the Blood Council, the ruling body whose word was law to the *vayash moru* in much of the Winter Kingdoms. "Now, another threat has risen. The question is: What will we do about it?"

Gabriel's cold gaze went first to the Council's chairman, Rafe. Though dead for centuries, Rafe still had the look of a priest or scholar. He had the ebony skin of an Eastmark noble and eyes that were almost black. Although he'd been in his early thirties when he'd been brought across, his hair had grayed to a sand color. "You're certain the Durim are behind this?"

"Does being dead affect your hearing?" Jonmarc growled. "I just took a strike force of *vayash moru* and mortals into the caves to burn out a group of Durim. It took a mage and a hell of a fight to get out of there in one piece. They were draining *vayash moru* and slaughtering *vyrkin*. I've got a manor house full of *vayash moru* and *vyrkin* refugees. The war has already started."

"You're good at burning things, aren't you?" Uri tented his fingers over his chest. He had the olive skin and dark features of a Trevath or Nargi native, and even centuries after his death, he still had the air of a card sharp and two-*skrivven* hustler.

Jonmarc met his eyes. "When I have to be, yes."

Uri made a show of sighing, a completely artificial gesture since he no longer had to breathe. "As much as it pains me, I actually agree with you for once." Uri toyed with the heavy gold rings on his fingers. "The Durim's threat is real. Like Riqua, I also remember when the followers of Shanthadura drove us from our homes and then from our crypts. I have no desire to see their ilk return to power." His expression darkened. "It was plague that brought them to the fore, long ago. Lady knows, I have no love for the Crone priests, but they are nothing compared to the Durim." He leaned forward, looking past Astasia toward Rafe. "We must do something."

Rafe frowned. "What would you have us do? We've only barely restored the Truce. The people of Dark Haven may suffer the *Lord* of Dark Haven to lead his guards against other mortals, but if *we* begin to strike the living, they'll all turn against us."

"Leave the Durim to Jonmarc and King Staden's men," Gabriel countered. "Our own kind needs our help. Riqua and I have been funneling supplies and funds to help the Ghost Carriage." He met Uri's dark eyes. "Kolin has led dozens of *vayash moru* and *vyrkin* out of Nargi and Trevath to safety in Dark Haven. As plague spreads, the need becomes more desperate. Even in those areas where the Durim have not yet gained power, as the mortals die with the plague, they fear and hate us because we're untouched. And the burnings begin."

A shadow seemed to pass over Uri's face. For once, all bluster was gone. "Unlike Jonmarc, I did not get out of Nargi alive. I swore I would never return."

"You've done business there, through intermediaries," Gabriel replied. "Kolin needs money, horses, safe houses. He needs connections who have no love for either the Crone priests or the Durim."

Uri gave a short, sharp laugh. "Honor among thieves, is that what you're expecting?" His eyes darkened. "There are a few of my associates who have their own reasons to wish to see the Durim become nothing but a bad memory. The Crone priests are bad enough.

"To a point, fear is profitable. It keeps order. But when people are terrified, they stop spending money, stop hiring whores, stop betting their gold. Bad for business." Uri touched the heavy gold bracelets that hung from his wrist. "I have names I can give Kolin, and I can change his *skrivven* to Nargi coin. But he should remember that my contacts have no love for me—or him—

because he is *vayash moru*. They tolerate me because I make them a profit. They will help Kolin only so long as it protects their interests."

"Thank you," Gabriel said. "It's gotten bad enough that even a *dimonn*'s bargain looks good."

Uri clapped his hands and gave a deep belly laugh. "Is that what you think of me? A *dimonn*'s bargain. That's rich. I'll take that as a compliment."

"I see no benefit in bringing more *vayash moru* into our territory," Astasia said. She could be beautiful when she wished. Her looks and body had brought her wealth and position as a consort to rich old men, until one of her suitors brought her across to make her a more permanent possession. Like Uri, it was rumored that she had eventually destroyed her maker. Jonmarc looked at her pale blue eyes, and he did not doubt that she was capable of doing anything to preserve her interests.

"Will these newcomers respect the Council? Must we take them into our broods, knowing nothing about their makers? Will Old Ones arise to challenge us?" She crossed her arms across her bosom. "What's in it for us? The mortals in Dark Haven tolerated us—before Malesh's war—better than in many places. They put up with us because they know they still outnumber us. If they fear that we're growing in strength, will they still observe the Truce? Maybe not—and maybe they're right to doubt. There is, after all, only so much blood to go around."

"Astasia is correct that as new *vayash moru* come to Dark Haven, the Council must be the ultimate law," Gabriel said. Jonmarc noticed that Gabriel avoided looking at Astasia directly.

"It would be best if we could replenish our broods by accepting refugee *vayash moru* instead of turning mortals," Riqua said. From her expression, Jonmarc guessed that it galled Riqua to agree with Astasia in any way. "Both methods have risks. Without broods of sufficient strength, we lack the strength to hold our seats on the Council. Turning mortals—given the situation—could lead to reprisals. But accepting strangers into our broods can be dangerous, even if we know their makers. Our power over our broods must be ruthless and absolute. Otherwise, some of these newcomers will see an opportunity to better their station at our expense."

"Then you see my point." Astasia's voice was a cool purr.

"Much as it pains me, on this, we agree in principle even if our means may differ," Riqua replied.

"With the Durim's power growing, you'll also need to keep a close eye on your broods," Jonmarc said. "The Durim are opportunists. They'll go after lone *vayash moru* who make an easy target. They've also been going after the mortal families of the *vayash moru*."

"What do you propose?" Rafe asked. There was an edge to his voice.

Jonmarc kept his expression neutral. "Secure your day crypts. Alert your mortal family members and arm them so they can protect themselves. Your people are in danger if their families can be used against them. Don't take unnecessary risks."

Rafe leaned forward. "We're predators. We don't hide." His eye-teeth showed plainly, something Jonmarc knew was intentional.

He met Rafe's eyes. Jonmarc knew it disquieted Rafe that the *vayash moru* could not use his glamour or compulsion against Jonmarc's natural resistance. "Until we defeat the Durim, you can hide or you can burn. It's your choice."

"That went well." Jonmarc and Gabriel rode away from the meeting at Rafe's villa toward Wolvenskorn, Gabriel's manor.

Gabriel gave him a bemused look. "Oh?"

Jonmarc shrugged. "Any time I leave the Blood Council alive, it's a good day."

Gabriel chuckled. "You have an interesting way of looking at things."

"Riqua is solidly on our side. We knew that going in. Rafe doesn't like it, but he sees the logic. Uri's actually scared. For once, I think he might do what he's supposed to do. That leaves Astasia."

"She's a formidable enemy. And she hates you."

"Coming from Astasia, that almost counts as a character reference."

Gabriel gave him a wary smile. "Don't underestimate her. She earned everything in life—and after death—by being ruthless. If she sees an opportunity in the current situation to advance her position, she'll take it."

Jonmarc glanced sideways at him. "Astasia is the Council's problem. I've got my hands full with the Durim and the refugees."

"I'll make sure Kolin learns of the Council's support when he gets back from Nargi," Gabriel replied. He fell silent. Jonmarc glanced in his direction.

"What's bothering you?"

Gabriel frowned. "I share Riqua's sentiments about the point Astasia made. Gathering the *vayash moru* in Dark Haven may enable us to save our kind. In plagues past, retaliation from the mortals nearly wiped out the *vayash moru* in Trevath and Nargi. All of the kingdoms have had their day hunting us, some more recently than others."

"On the other hand, gathering everyone in one place not only makes for more family squabbles, it gives your enemies a central place to strike, and a reason to rally the locals."

"Exactly."

"I don't see many alternatives." The night was cool and Jonmarc shivered despite his traveling cloak.

"Neither do I. But I've always believed there was a reason

why the *vayash moru* are spread out across the kingdoms. Death changes everything and nothing. The Dark Gift gives us speed and strength and immunity to the things that killed us as mortals. Immortality provides perspective and time to reflect. On the other hand, greed, lust, and vengeance don't require a heartbeat. Grievances nursed over centuries have a way of flaring into conflict. Dark Haven will be a tinderbox full of frightened mortals and threatened immortals. All it will take is a spark to set it ablaze."

They reached Wolvenskorn, Gabriel's manor, just before midnight. Wolvenskorn's oldest sections were built back when the Winter Kingdoms were ruled by independent warlords, before the monarchies were established. Three levels of tall, sharply sloping peaks made of wood and stone thrust skyward. The oldest section was daub and wattle with a sod roof that sloped down to meet the forest soil. A tall, slim cupola ringed by carved monsters crowned the manor.

Grotesques and gargoyles watched from the peaks. Runes and sigils were carved into the doorposts and sills. Jonmarc doubted their function was decorative. Carved panels on the wooden sections of the building hinted at some of its history. Overlapping shingles covered the lowest portions. Although only one of the pillars was visible from the coachway, Jonmarc knew that thousand-year-old stone monoliths ringed Wolvenskorn, a remnant of ancient times. Though the makers of the stone pillars had died long ago, the enclosure still possessed powerful magic.

Jonmarc and Gabriel dismounted and handed over their reins to waiting groomsmen. Sior, one of the ranking *vyrkin*, was waiting for them. "You appear to be intact," Sior noted with a raised eyebrow.

Jonmarc gave a lopsided grin. "The Blood Council was as charming as ever."

"Is the ceremony on schedule?" Gabriel glanced toward the trail that led into the forest.

Sior nodded. "Vigulf and the others are heading to the grotto. You're just in time."

Sior took a torch from one of the sconces in front of the manor house and Jonmarc followed him down the forest path. Jonmarc was certain the torch was for his benefit, since neither Sior nor Gabriel needed the extra light. He guessed that although he could not see them, Gabriel's *vayash moru* were patrolling the outskirts of the area to make certain that there would be no interruptions.

"How did the negotiations go?" Jonmarc asked Sior quietly.

Sior sighed. "It was predictably complicated. Some of the descendants of our older, most established packs feel threatened. But the numbers don't lie. We lost three quarters of our males of breeding age in the war with Malesh. And we had barely enough females to replenish the pack and care for the pups before the war. When we lost more to the war, the pack became endangered. The elders can squabble over bloodlines all they like, but we must accept the newcomers or face extinction."

"I'm less worried about the elders than the females," Jonmarc observed dryly. "What did they have to say?"

Sior chuckled. "Spoken like a married man. What would you expect?"

"I'd expect them to be choosy and aloof, but when push comes to shove, they'll do what's right for their pups. My money is on the females."

"You'd have made a good wolf," Sior replied. "Our packs are extended families, each one headed by a top hunter. Unlike animal wolves, the male and female share the duty to protect the young. In human form, they'll share the work of a farm or craft, just like mortals. And in some pairs, the female is the more deadly hunter."

"That doesn't surprise me at all."

Sior gave him a grin. "I thought you'd understand. So the elders debated territory and power and bloodlines for several candlemarks, until the four top hunter-females had enough of it. Together, they have twelve pups, and half of those are females with no likely males for partners. Two of the females were widowed in the war, as were over half of our pack females." He gave a grim laugh. "Kella, our top huntress, invoked the ancient right of females to choose their mates. She'd already rallied all the other females, including the mates of the elders."

"So she handed them their balls on a plate."

"An interesting image, but accurate. Kella and the widowed huntresses had already chosen from among the new males. They extracted a vow of *vyrgild* from the other single males." He glanced at Jonmarc. "Are you familiar with the term?" Jonmarc shook his head. "It means blood oath. In exchange for acceptance into our extended pack, the new males forswear their right to challenge for a leadership role, on pain of death. Their children will be full pack members who can lead if they're able, but it keeps the pack stable for now. It's something the elders might have actually thought of themselves if they hadn't been so busy marking their territory, figuratively speaking."

They veered from the path through what seemed to Jonmarc to be unbroken forest. Even with the torch, it was difficult for Jonmarc to keep his footing as they moved through the dense brush. Sior and Gabriel did not seem to have any trouble, moving with the grace of a predator. They came to a cave opening that was partially obscured by vegetation. As they drew nearer, Jonmarc could see that the scrub plants had been arranged to appear as if they were blocking the opening, but, in fact, a narrow trail led behind them. Sior motioned for Gabriel and Jonmarc to follow him, and as they headed into the caverns, Jonmarc could hear singing in the clipped, tonal language that seemed to be the speech of wolves adapted to humans.

The cave path gradually widened and became a true corridor. Jonmarc glanced around as they walked down a torchlit hallway carved into the rock. Runes and paintings adorned the walls. Some appeared to have been placed for protection, while others seemed to tell the story of the Dark Haven *vyrkin*, or perhaps of all *vyrkin* in the Winter Kingdoms.

The corridor opened into a series of large chambers. These chambers had been decorated with carvings, paint, and embedded precious stones and metals. It was clear that they had entered a place of high ritual, and Jonmarc wondered whether or not these caves connected to the crypts below Wolvenskorn. A glance around the chamber revealed skulls—both human and wolflike—stacked or placed near every wall.

Vigulf, the *vyrkin* shaman, stood in the center of the largest chamber. He was a powerfully built, older man with a trim, gray beard and deep-set eyes. Tonight, he wore his shamanic robes, a richly woven cloak embroidered with symbols that seemed to change and move although always just beyond the ability to see them clearly. He carried a wooden staff set with the carved head of a wolf. The wolf's mouth was open as if to strike, and its eyes were rubies.

Six couples stood hand in hand in the center of the room. They might be the couples who were about to wed, but to Jonmarc's eye, they looked nervous. None of the brides or grooms appeared to be older than their mid-twenties, and one couple looked to be in their late teens. Jonmarc recognized the women as belonging to the local families of *vyrkin*, but the betrothed young men were unfamiliar. He did recognize the faces of the few *vyrkin* males who stood alone around the edge of the room, and there was no mistaking the animosity in their mood.

"If you have unmarried men, why not marry within the local packs?" Jonmarc murmured to Sior.

Sior glanced over the crowd. "The single men who are left are all too closely related to the single females. Brothers, half-brothers, first cousins. The war forced us to do what would have become inevitable in a few years: seek out new blood. But whether we did it out of necessity or out of choice, some of the males would have resented the intrusion."

That was an understatement, Jonmarc thought. Several of the men along the wall looked like they were spoiling for a fight. The only question, Jonmarc thought, was whether the brawl happened during or after the ceremony.

He'd wondered whether the *vyrkin* married in human form or in their wolf form. It appeared they at least planned to begin the ceremony on two legs. The women wore dark green robes. The men were bare-chested, with dark pants. All of the participants had bare feet. Each wore a chain with a single silver disk representing the full moon.

Vigulf stepped into the center of the chamber. "Welcome, honored pack," he said, looking to the *vyrkin* who surrounded him. He looked toward the skulls along the wall. "Greetings, esteemed ancestors." His gaze fell on Jonmarc and Gabriel. "And welcome, honored guests. Tonight we join more than the lives of the individuals who stand before us. We join together the present and the future, and from the loss of the past we weave the promise for tomorrow. Tonight, we strengthen the pack by your joining," he said solemnly to the nervous young couples who stood in front of him.

Vigulf began to chant in the clipped, tonal language of the *vyrkin*. Although Jonmarc had no idea of the words, he guessed the meaning clearly enough. Vigulf was hallowing the space. But as Vigulf chanted, Jonmarc felt the air in the cave grow colder. Wraiths began to stream into the cavern from the passageways that led into darkness and to rise from the stacked skulls along the wall. Not quite solid but no mere illusion, the wraiths brushed past Jonmarc with a cold, moist feeling that made the hair on the back of his neck rise. He'd grown accustomed to ghosts after a year on the road with Tris Drayke, and Dark Haven had its share of resident and visible spirits. But these spirits felt different. Some of the spirits had the shape of men and women, while elsewhere ghost wolves glided through the assemblage. A few of the revenants had no real shape at all, and some manifested as a faint green glow.

The spirits apparently were expected. They moved among the crowd, gradually gathering around the betrothed couples. Whether the ghosts were direct ancestors or just spirits from the pack, Jonmarc had no way of knowing. When the ghosts were quiet, Vigulf stepped forward along with an assistant. He approached the first couple and removed a long rope tied with objects from the bag of ritual items his assistant carried. Jonmarc was close enough to see that the rope looked like felted fur or hair and that the objects knotted into it were bits of bone, tooth, and claw.

The first couple looked to be no older than their late teens. The girl had long, dark brown hair and a pretty, heart-shaped face. Her groom was a tall, thin young man with lank brown hair that fell into his face. He looked scared. There was something different about him, Jonmarc thought, whether it was his features or a slightly lighter hue to his complexion, but Jonmarc guessed that the young man was one of the pack outsiders Sior had mentioned. When Vigulf stepped toward the couple, one of the men who had been standing along the back of the chamber edged forward, making his way to the front of the crowd. One glance told Jonmarc that the man was closely related to the bride, a brother, most likely. He did not look pleased.

Vigulf withdrew a knife from his belt and took the first young woman's hand, turning it face up. She flinched as he drew a

113

thin cut down her palm. The cut beaded with blood. Vigulf lifted the woman's palm and solemnly gave it to the young man who stood beside her. The groom murmured something in the *vyrkin* language and bent his head, licking the cut clean. Vigulf repeated the cutting ritual with the young man's hand, and the woman did likewise. Then Vigulf took the rope and wrapped their hands together, raising and lowering his staff four times. The spirits began to stir, passing not just around the newly wed couple but ghosting through their bodies. Vigulf repeated the ritual with each of the couples until all six pairs had been joined.

The gathered *vyrkin* began to chant. While the chanting had a definite rhythm, it was unlike any human speech Jonmarc had heard. It seemed as if the entire assemblage was breathing as one, and although Jonmarc possessed no magic of his own, he could feel the power rising all around him.

A figure appeared from the depths of one of the corridors. Jonmarc was uncertain whether the figure was real or another spirit. It was taller than a man and wraith thin. It wore a mask over its head that looked like the head of a large, black wolf with eyes that glowed in the firelight. Its garment was made of many-hued wolf skins, some that looked recent and some that appeared quite old. The figure stopped just at the edge between light and darkness, and the room fell silent.

"I bless you, my children." The voice that came from the figure sent a chill down Jonmarc's back. Whatever—whoever—the thing was, the sound that came from its throat was not entirely human. The spirits glided across the cavern chamber to mass around the gaunt figure, and the *vyrkin* bowed deeply. Following suit, so did Gabriel and Jonmarc, although Jonmarc never took his eyes from the shadowed visitor. "Restore the pack. Replenish the blood. Remember our way."

Jonmarc blinked and the figure vanished.

The figure's sudden departure seemed to trigger something

within the pack. Several of the *vyrkin* began to shift, changing into their wolf forms. But as the first couple turned around, a cry came from the crowd and the man Jonmarc guessed to be the bride's brother launched himself at the groom, tackling the younger man and crashing to the ground.

Jonmarc started forward to break up the fight, but Gabriel caught his arm and gave a warning shake of the head. Vigulf stepped toward the two men who were struggling on the floor, and Jonmarc expected the shaman to intercede. Instead, he raised his staff and gave a deep-throated cry that sounded more wolf than human.

Like a blast of winter air, the spirits came rushing toward the struggling pair on the floor. They swarmed around the attacker, lifting him into the air although he was a muscular man. The spirits seemed to be entering the attacker's body through his mouth, eyes, and ears, and from the silent scream that formed on the man's face, it was obviously not a gentle possession.

Three of the *vyrkin* who were still in human form rushed forward to drag the injured groom away from his attacker. The bride stood transfixed, looking in horror between her wounded husband and the punishment her brother endured for the attack.

"What the Wolf Father has blessed, no one may challenge," Vigulf warned. "Harm to one is harm to the pack. You must be made to remember."

As abruptly as the spirits had seized the attacker, they now departed, streaming from his mouth. The man's body twitched and his eyes were wide with terror. As the spirits rushed from him, he grew paler, finally collapsing on the ground. Sior tugged at Jonmarc's sleeve as the rest of the assemblage began to file silently from the room, following the narrow pathway up to the forest.

No one spoke until they reached a clearing where a meal had been set out on large tables, which Jonmarc guessed had been brought from the manor house. That the menu consisted of nearly raw meat did not surprise him. To one side, Jonmarc saw a table by itself. It was set with a plate of food, a goblet, and a large hunk of bread. Dozens of candles glittered atop the table. There was no chair. "An offering to the ancestors, who are honored guests at the feast," Sior murmured from just behind Jonmarc, following his gaze and guessing at his thoughts. Jonmarc followed Gabriel and Sior to places that had been set for them. Conversation resumed and the gathering regained a festive air, although Jonmarc did not see any of the newly married couples, nor was there a table set for them.

"What will happen to him?" Jonmarc asked Sior.

Sior frowned. "Eljan didn't like his sister marrying someone outside of our pack. Vigulf tried to reason with him. What he did endangered the pack, because we need new members in order to survive."

"Will Vigulf kill him?"

Sior met Jonmarc's eyes. "No, we're already too few. But he'll be punished."

Jonmarc remembered the terrified look on the man's face and did not doubt that a repeat of the attack was unlikely. "And what about the newlyweds? Where are they?"

Sior's expression softened to a knowing grin. "They'll celebrate privately."

The night was mostly spent before Jonmarc and Gabriel returned to Wolvenskorn. Torches blazed at the entrance and candles gleamed in the windows. Between the posturing of the Blood Council and the tension of the *vyrkin* weddings, Jonmarc was tired and ready to rest. He followed Gabriel into the manor and they walked into Gabriel's well-appointed study. Books and scrolls filled shelves that went from floor to ceiling. The library was worth a fortune, and Jonmarc wagered that few kings could boast of so large a collection. Gabriel poured a brandy for

Jonmarc and a goblet of goat's blood for himself and motioned for Jonmarc to take a seat in one of the large leather chairs that sat in front of the now-darkened fireplace.

"So you expect Kolin back from Nargi...when?" Gabriel asked.

Jonmarc took a sip of the brandy and let it burn its way down his throat. "Depends on how thick the patrols are, and how many safe houses Kolin needs to use along the way. They don't dare travel openly in Nargi, and it's gotten to be more of a problem getting across Dhasson, Kolin says. From what I've heard, King Harrol tries to be neutral when it comes to the *vayash moru*, but all that really means is that he doesn't organize purges. He also doesn't go after the Durim or the occasional lords who do order a purge. But I would expect Kolin within a few weeks."

Gabriel nodded, sampling the blood in his goblet. "I had hoped for a better showing from the Council tonight. Uri can actually be a help to Kolin and the Ghost Carriage. I think Rafe will support us as well. He plays the ascetic, but he's a very wealthy man."

"And Astasia?"

Gabriel's expression hardened as he finished his drink. "This is a dangerous time for her to be playing games. Leave her to me."

8

"Daddy, wake up!"

Jair Rothlandorn groaned and tried to roll over.

"Wake up, Daddy!" The voice was persistent, close to his ear. Jair opened his eyes. A small face framed in dark, ringlet curls stared back at him only inches away. His son, Kenver, had the same amber eyes as his mother and the Sworn. His golden skin was a lighter cast, somewhere in between Talwyn's tawny hue and Jair's pale complexion, although by the end of the Ride, Jair would be nearly as dark as Talwyn. Kenver's face was a mixture of Jair's and Talwyn's features, and right now, Kenver's expression was pure joy.

"Mommy, Mommy. Daddy woke up!"

Jair took a deep breath and wrapped his arms around the boy, gathering Kenver's small frame against him. He breathed in the scent of his hair, hair that smelled of sun and horse and wood smoke. At three years old, Kenver had no thought for his heritage, that he was by birth an heir to the throne of Dhasson, and by blood an heir to the magic of his mother and the chieftainship of the Sworn. Ignoring the pain of his freshly healed wounds, Jair tightened his grip and wiggled his fingers, tickling Kenver under his arm. The boy shrieked with delighted giggles.

"I'm glad to see you're feeling better." Talwyn stood in the doorway. Jair kissed the top of Kenver's head and released the boy, who scampered off. Jair held out his hand to Talwyn and drew her to the side of the bed. He sat up and winced.

"Much better, considering the last thing I remember feeling was mostly dead." He put his arm around his wife and pulled her toward him, into a kiss that let her know just how much he had missed her these past six months.

Talwyn's amber eyes sparkled as she drew away. Her hair was dark and straight like the rest of her people's, and it framed a rectangular face that was strikingly beautiful but not at all the delicate prettiness favored in the Dhasson court. Talwyn's arms were strong as they wrapped around him, lean and toned from long days of riding and from training with the long, heavy *stelian* swords. Around her neck hung a variety of charms with polished rock, bits of metal, and bone on a thin cord woven from hair and leather. The charms spoke of Talwyn's status as *cheira*, or shaman, and of her duty as next in line to be chieftain of the Sworn. One of the charms was from Jair, a betrothal token given years ago, the mark of the Lady set in a silver circle.

"You heal quickly," Talwyn murmured, clasping Jair's hand. The stylized tattoo of dark ink that circled one side of his wrist completed the circle around hers, matching perfectly. Each mated couple among the Sworn had a unique marking, one that was made up of elements signifying both families' heritage. Kenver had a matching tattoo that circled his right bicep, marking him as their child.

"With help." Jair gingerly fingered the newly healed skin on his arm where the *dimonn* had raked him with its claws. The cuts were almost completely healed, leaving thin, dark scars, a permanent reminder of his battle. His fever was completely gone, assuring him that the *dimonn*'s poison had been cleansed from his system. "Thank you."

119

Talwyn's expression grew serious. "That was too close. We almost didn't make it in time."

"What about Emil and Mihei?"

"Emil is healing, but we nearly lost him. It will be awhile before he is ready to fight again. Mihei is badly drained, but rest will cure that. Now you know why I sent them to ride with you. The roads have been more dangerous of late."

"I noticed." Jair looked around himself. He was in one of the tents the Sworn called home. It was a round structure with wooden poles covered with sturdy canvas. Its roof was fanlike, also made from wood and canvas. It unfolded to form a circular, sloping top that was secured to the base with leather straps. Jair knew from experience that the entire tent could be struck or set in little more than a candlemark. Within the tent, colorful cloths hung from floor to ceiling, separating the sleeping chamber from the sitting and dining area. Jair closed his eyes and took a deep breath. The canvas smelled of the spices typical of the nomadic group's cooking, and of Talwyn's incense, and of fresh meadow grass. Despite the battle of the day before, something within Jair relaxed. Here, more than any other place, he was at home.

"How did I get here?" Jair looked chagrined. "I guess I passed out when we got to the inn."

Talwyn suppressed a smile. "You made it up the stairs," she offered helpfully. "After that, the healers took care of you and Emil and Mihei, and then gave you something so you'd sleep and heal. The next morning, we loaded you into a wagon and brought you to the camp. If you feel groggy, it's because the elixir has just worn off."

"How long did I sleep?"

"A full day."

Talwyn took his hand and drew him over to plates of food on a low table in the center of the public area of the tent. The inner walls of the tent were marked with runes and symbols.

Some told the history of the Sworn. Others gave the narrative of Talwyn's family, a long and proud lineage among the nomadic warriors. And some of the runes were for protection, invoked by Talwyn when she worked her shamanic magic.

"We must be fairly close to towns," Jair guessed as he filled a large piece of thin bread with roasted vegetables and meat flavored with the piquant spices the Sworn preferred. "It's goat meat instead of rabbit."

Talwyn settled beside him, crossing her legs under her. Kenver scrambled over to sit between them and filled his own slice of bread nearly larger than his mouth. "We're still a good distance from any settlement, but this year, there are more goats roaming free," Talwyn said. "Their owners died of the plague and the goats broke out of their pastures. The same is true for sheep and there are hogs rooting through the forest. Good for eating, bad for Margolan in general."

"What of the barrows?" Jair asked. He finished his food quickly. Not for the first time, he wondered what accident of birth had placed him in the glittering Dhasson palace when his heart and soul seemed at home with the nomadic Sworn.

"Several of the ones we've visited recently have been desecrated," Talwyn said. She handed Jair a leather wineskin. "Some more than others. At one or two, we've found markings and some shallow digging, as if someone were trying to work magic for which they didn't have the power. We've been able to put those right fairly easily. But the last one—"

"What happened?" Jair laid the wineskin aside and drew Kenver onto his lap, reveling in the closeness of his family after the half-year absence his court duties had forced upon him.

"Someone at the nearest barrow had a better idea of what they were doing," Talwyn said darkly. She glanced to Kenver, a signal for Jair that the boy shouldn't hear what would be said next.

"Have you gotten any better with your bolas?" Jair asked Kenver.

The boy beamed at him. "Lots better. Want to see?"

Jair grinned. "Of course I do. Let me finish talking with your mother and then I'll be out. Go ahead and practice." Delighted, Kenver ran from the tent.

Talwyn watched to make certain the boy had gone. She lowered her voice, just a bit. "The barrow we've camped near has been vandalized by someone doing blood magic. They did enough damage that the spells binding the tomb have been weakened. Tonight, I need to walk the smoke to gain wisdom on how best to reseal the barrow. Tomorrow night, I'll do the working." She looked up at Jair. "I'd like you with me, both nights."

Jair nodded solemnly. "You know I'll be there." He thought for a moment. "Do you think the disturbers of the barrows are organized? Father doesn't hold much with meddling in the ways of the *vayash moru*, but ever since I went back to Margolan for Tris's wedding, I've seen how important it is to rule both the living and the undead. Tris connected me with the *vayash moru* leaders in Dhasson, and through them, I've heard that with the plague, some people are turning back to the old ways, to human sacrifice and blood magic to appease Shanthadura and the Shrouded Ones. Do you think that could be behind the barrow desecrations?"

Talwyn shivered although the day was warm. "The Sworn remembers the cult of the Shrouded Ones. Those were very dark days. It's been hundreds of years since anyone has worked their rites—at least, that we've heard about. But the smokewalkers will know. I'll ask."

Late that night, after the Sworn had gathered for dinner to greet Jair and welcome him back to the Ride, Jair and Talwyn headed toward the ceremonial tent. They were joined by Pevre, who was Talwyn's father and the Sworn's chieftain. Pevre was a large, strongly built man. He was esteemed among his people for both his leadership and his ability with a sword, but now, as Jair and Talwyn entered into the ritual tent, it was Pevre's mystical connection to past generations of the Sworn that was foremost in Jair's mind.

The chamber had been prepared. As they entered, one of the Sworn warriors handed a cup filled with a clear blue elixir to each of them, then stepped outside to guard the entrance. Jair took a deep breath and swallowed the elixir. It seemed to sharpen his senses immediately, even as it gave him the feeling that he was floating within his own body, untethered to the physical world. Three pillows sat next to a small brazier in the center of the tent, and in front of it, a series of small cups filled with sacred herbs that would help open the passage to the spirit world.

The ceremonial tent was large enough to hold all of the adults in the Sworn. The walls of the tent were painted in more pictures and runes. Bells hung from a central support, and on the other side of the tent, bits of colored glass, polished stone, and reflective metal glittered in the firelight where they were suspended as a warding against evil. Along the back wall, a small altar acknowledged the ancestors, whom the Sworn believed continued the Ride for eternity, aiding from beyond the mortal world in maintaining their watch over the barrows and the Dread who dwelt within them.

"Are you ready?" Talwyn's voice was level. Jair nodded, although he had no idea what tonight's ritual entailed.

Pevre began to chant. The language of the Sworn was heavy with consonants, a language that almost seemed more growled than spoken. It was far different from the languages of the seven kingdoms, or from Common, the language spoken by traders. Some said the Sworn's language was older, while other tales said it took its origins far south, beyond the Winter Kingdoms, from peoples now long gone. It had taken Jair years to master it, but now he followed the chant in what had become his second native tongue.

"Spirits of those who have gone before, come to the gathering. Walk with us on the paths of smoke. Let us see with your eyes, and counsel us with your wisdom. We are the people of the Ride. We are the guardians of the barrows. We are the watchers of the Dread. We are the protectors. We are the Sworn." Pevre raised a ceremonial knife and sliced a gash in his forearm. He held his arm over the brazier so that drops of the fresh blood fell into the coals, hissing. Pevre took herbs from the first of the cups next to the fire and dropped it onto the fire. Pungent smoke rose, filling the tent with the smell of absinthe.

Pevre passed the obsidian-bladed knife to Talwyn. Talwyn rose onto her knees and spread her arms wide. Her head fell back, exposing her throat and chest to the cloud of smoke. She raised her head and brought her hands in, palms up, as she looked toward the opening in the tent roof through which the smoke slowly spiraled.

"Travelers who have made the journey, walk with me, fathers of my father, mothers of my mother, bone of my bone, I call you. I want to walk the paths of smoke with you tonight. Accept me into your company." Talwyn raised the flat of the knife to her lips and kissed it, and then drew the point down the palm of her left hand. She let drops of the blood hiss on the brazier coals, and then added herbs from the second cup to the fire. This time, the smoke rose with the scent of cinnamon, mingled with holly and dandelion.

The knife passed to Jair. He had none of Talwyn's shamanic gifts, nor Pevre's second sight. But the blood of kings flowed in his veins, a powerful and ancient magic. Bound to Talwyn by oath, sex, and magic, Jair's presence was essential for the working of the night's ritual. As Talwyn had taught him, Jair focused his attention on the ancestral altar.

"Warriors of the Sworn, aid your people. Seers of my tribe, bring us your visions. Souls of our honored dead, we bid you welcome." Jair slashed the blade down his left thumb, opening a cut that bled freely into the coals. With his other hand, Jair dropped another handful of the ritual herbs into the fire. Smoke rose that smelled of sweetgrass and anise.

The smoke grew thicker, dense with the smell of blood and herbs. It hung in a heavy layer within the tent and as Jair watched, the haze began to move. Jair thought he glimpsed barely formed images in the smoke, faces or forms almost perceived and then gone. Along the wall, the bells chimed.

The elixir made Jair feel light within his body. The smoke beckoned his spirit to walk the ghostly pathways that stretched out before them. Jair took another deep breath and felt a shift, as if a part of him had left his body behind. Embraced by the smoke, Jair could see Talwyn and Pevre standing next to him, not in physical form but as if they, like he, were made of the smoke itself.

Figures stepped out of the cloud of smoke that filled the tent. Two of the men were dressed like chiefs of the past. They moved to stand one on each side of Pevre, and they walked with him into the smoke, where he disappeared from Jair's view. A man and a woman came for Talwyn. They both wore the robes of a tribal shaman, and the woman wore a necklace that had an animal skull at its center. Talwyn held out her hands to them, and they, too, vanished into the smoke.

Jair felt an otherworldly calm settle over him as he awaited his spirit guides. After a moment, two warriors appeared out of the cloud. They were gray like the smoke, as was Jair's spirit form, but when they offered him their hands in greeting, the touch felt solid and warm. Jair had not heard the spirit guides speak to either Pevre or Talwyn, but the taller of the two spirit warriors met his eyes and spoke to him in a low, strong voice. "Walk with us, and we will show you what we have seen."

Jair nodded, uncertain whether he would be able to answer them, and he let the warriors guide him. The smoke closed around them, but a new vista opened up, and it seemed to Jair that they were walking among the hillsides of Margolan in the desolate countryside where barrows stood. He had no way to know whether they were still within the ceremonial tent or whether his spirit guides had taken him far beyond its canvas walls. They passed over the road without any sound of footsteps, and though Jair could see wind blowing the branches of the trees around them, he did not feel a breeze on his skin. The landscape seemed drained of all color, but the details were crisp, as if everything were washed by moonlight.

Jair followed his warrior spirits to a large barrow. He saw the wardings that were set by the Sworn long ago, protections most passersby would not notice, like the four oak trees planted at the quarters and the holly bushes planted at the cross quarters. High on the trunks of those trees, runes were cut deep into the bark. Belladonna, basil, and cowslip were planted around the barrow and over its mound to strengthen the magic. But as Jair approached with his spirit guides, he could see that something was terribly wrong.

The holly had been knocked down, and the trees viciously slashed. Where the bushes or the trees were too sturdy to fall, counter-runes had been carved into the bark to negate the magic. Bits of hellebore and black willow were strewn around and over the mound to cancel out the protective plants. A hole had been hacked into the side of the barrow, and above it was a rough wooden door frame. From the top of the frame hung the butchered body of a goat. Blood from the offering pooled at the entrance to the hole. In this spirit realm, Jair could feel the

126

hidden energies roiling, and beyond them, a powerful dark presence that was hungry and searching.

"Who did this?" Jair asked his spirit guides.

The taller of the two men led them backward, and it looked as if everything around them moved in reverse with them, from the direction of the wind to the motion of the moon overhead. The barrow was now untouched. Jair and his guides watched as four men in black robes approached the barrow. One of the men lifted his arms and his hands began to move with the spell he cast as another of his companions withdrew a live rat from a bag and impaled it with a large knife into the ground at his feet. Jair watched as the four men carried out the desecrations he had seen, ending with the offering of the goat. Their heavy cowls hid their faces, but in the moonlight, Jair glimpsed the amulet that hung from a chain around one man's neck, and he glimpsed the same amulet on the silver cuff of another. It was the three-bone charm, sacred to the Shrouded Ones, Peyhta, Konost, and Shanthadura.

Jair started toward the figures. Both of his spirit guides drew their *stelians* and blocked his way.

"Let me stop them!"

"What you see has already happened. It cannot be undone," the shorter warrior said. "We show you what has already come to pass."

They stood alone now in the shadow of the desecrated barrow. "Can the damage be repaired?" Jair asked, keeping a worried eye on the darkness that stretched down from the large hole hacked into the barrow's side.

"If your shaman has the power," the tall warrior replied. "This is but one barrow among many. But beware, blood calls blood."

With a roar, something dark streaked from the opening. It blotted out the moonlight where it passed, stretching out like the flow of a black river. The two spirit guards moved to block it, and the taller guard turned to Jair.

"Return to your body. It knows you're still alive. Go back among the living and it can't follow."

Jair fled into the smoke, hoping that he could find the path back to rejoin his body. Suddenly, he found himself in the ceremonial tent again, facing his body. Jair couldn't tell whether Pevre and Talwyn had returned to themselves or whether they, also, faced danger in the paths of smoke. He ran at himself, and as his smoke spirit passed through his living flesh, his body jolted awake from its trance. Moments later, he saw Pevre and then Talwyn rejoin themselves as well. Talwyn took a final handful of herbs from the last of the containers, and the strong smell of rosemary and clove sealed the working. Talwyn shook her head as if to clear it, and then bowed toward the brazier before she stood. Jair and Pevre climbed to their feet beside her. The two guards opened the tent flap and a cool night breeze dissipated the last of the smoke.

Judging by the position of the moon, the ritual had taken several candlemarks. Talwyn motioned for Jair and Pevre to follow her back to their tent. Kenver was asleep on his mat. She poured wine for each of them and then brought out a tray of sliced apples, mint, and cheese to ground them once more in the world of the living. After they had eaten and finished the wine, Jair looked to Talwyn and Pevre.

"What did you see?"

Talwyn drew a deep breath. "I walked with the shamans to understand the binding of the barrow, long ago. They showed me how the protections were made, and how to re-bind the wardings."

Pevre drained the last from his leather cup and laid it aside. "I walked with the chiefs to the last time the Dread were in the world. They're neither good nor evil, but their power is far greater than ours. We wake them at our peril. They serve us best watching the gateways to the abyss."

Talwyn turned to Jair. "And you?"

Jair nodded. "I didn't have nearly the adventure you did. I probably saw only a week or so ago, when the barrow was desecrated. But there's no doubt: The Durim are the ones who broke the wardings, although I don't know what they thought it would do or what they were after." He shivered. "Even so, something bad nearly got out. The spirit warriors blocked it, and they said if I returned to my body that whatever it was had no power over me, but it was like a large, solid, black shadow and it felt evil."

Pevre looked thoughtful. "There are worse things than *dimonns*," he said quietly. "The old stories say that, long ago, monsters walked the world. Things that look like the magicked beasts you've fought," he said with a nod toward Jair. "But worse. Much worse. In those days, it didn't take a blood mage to conjure the monsters, and they preyed on all living things." He poured another draught of wine and settled back to continue the story. Jair guessed it was for his benefit, since he was certain Talwyn knew the old tales as well as her father.

"Long ago, the Shrouded Ones ruled the night. Peyhta, the Soul Eater, Konost, the Guide of Dead Souls, and Shanthadura, the Destroyer. They called the monsters and the monsters did their bidding. Some of the monsters were beasts. Some were like the shadow you describe. Some were *dimonns*, but *dimonns* with much greater power than those that find their way to the world today."

"How were they defeated?" Jair asked, leaning forward.

"The Shrouded Ones are the Old Gods, as are the animal spirits: the predator-cat Stawar God in Eastmark, the Wolf God of the *vyrkin*, the Bear God of Trevath, and the Eagle God, still the patron of the Sworn. They were worshipped here long before the Winter Kingdoms were formed, when there were just bands of tribes wandering these lands, and later, when the first warlords began to bind those tribes into fiefdoms. But raiders came from the east and from the south. They worshipped a new goddess, one with eight faces. The Sacred Lady." Pevre paused.

"The Light Aspects of the Sacred Lady—the Mother, the Childe, Chenne the Warrior, and the Lover—took the animal gods as their consorts. But the Dark Aspects—Sinha the Crone, Athira the Whore, Istra, the Dark Lady, and Nameless, the Formless One—fought the Shrouded Ones. Through their mages and shamans, they broke the power of the Shrouded Ones," Pevre said. "Athira lured the Shrouded Ones to their downfall, and Sinha bound their monsters and sent them to the Abyss. Nameless scoured most of the followers of the Shrouded Ones from the lands. Istra called to the Dread to guard the Abyss, and she charged her best warriors to become the Sworn protectors of the barrows, to guard the Dread and keep the wardings."

"But Nameless didn't destroy all of the followers of the Shrouded Ones," Talwyn added. "For centuries, in the far country, or up in the mountains, there were those who remembered the old ways and kept their rituals secret. Each time plague or famine would rise, the followers of Shanthadura, the Durim, would come to the fore again. And when the dark times passed, they would disappear once more. And now, plague, war, and famine have swept across the Winter Kingdoms. And like the pox, the Durim return to shed more blood."

Jair sat in silence, letting the story sink in. "What do the Durim think will happen if they free whatever is down in the Abyss?"

Pevre shrugged. "We don't know for certain. They won't tell their secrets, and no one leaves the cult of Shanthadura alive. But I suspect their motives are simple. They would turn the monsters on their enemies and reinstate the worship of the Shrouded Ones." He met Jair's eyes. "And if that day comes, the Winter Kingdoms will fall into darkness. I've heard stories from some of the old *vayash moru* about how the Black Robes terrorized the people, about the human sacrifices and the ritual deaths. We can't allow those times to return."

"What now?" Jair looked from Talwyn to Pevre. "Can we renew the warding that was broken on the barrow they desecrated?"

Talwyn avoided his eyes. "Yes."

"Yes...but?" Jair probed, getting the feeling that he was not going to like the full answer.

"I have to spirit walk into the barrow. My magic isn't strong enough by itself to reinstate the wardings. I have to ask the Dread for help."

"They're neutral in this, right?" Jair asked, fearing for Talwyn's safety. "You'll be able to return when you're through?"

Talwyn took a deep breath. "I'll need an anchor. I'm not a summoner, so my soul doesn't actually leave my body, but my consciousness—my spirit—does. Sometimes, when the spirit walks, it can lose its way, especially in the dark places. Normally, I'd ask Father to anchor me, but I need him to work some of the wardings." She reached out to take Jair's hand. "We're oath-bound. You can anchor me. I'll see the light of your spirit to find my way back to my body."

"And if you can't?"

Talwyn looked away again. "Then my body remains, but without consciousness. It will sleep without waking until it dies from hunger or thirst, but my spirit will be lost."

"I don't like this," Jair said, looking from Talwyn to Pevre. "Surely there's another way."

"There's no other choice," Pevre said, and his tone gave Jair to know that Pevre did not like Talwyn's plan, either.

Jair could see in Talwyn's eyes that she understood the risk, to herself, to the Sworn, and to the Winter Kingdoms should she fail. And Jair knew that he could not refuse her, even though his fear for her chilled him to the bone. "Then you know I'll be your anchor. You knew before you asked."

Talwyn gave him a wan smile. "I believed you would do what must be done."

The moon was rising as Talwyn, Pevre, and Jair went to the barrows. With them went four of the Sworn's warriors, to assure that the working would be uninterrupted. Jair knew that tonight, the *stelian* that hung from his belt would be useless. Tonight's battle would be decided by Talwyn's magic and the cooperation—or lack thereof—of the Dread.

He watched nervously as Talwyn and Pevre made their preparations. Magic was widely practiced in Dhasson, but unlike his cousin, Tris Drayke, Jair had no magical power of his own. He hoped, and feared, that Kenver would inherit his mother's power. His own lack of magic left Jair feeling helpless as the others prepared for the confrontation. Talwyn wore the robes that were a mark of her role as shaman and as the daughter—and heir—of the chief. They were woven in rich shades of ochre, sepia, and hues of green, the colors of the ground and the plants from which the Sworn called their power. Embroidered into the robes were symbols and runes as well as a complex pattern that seemed to brighten and dim with every breath Talwyn took.

Pevre, also, was dressed to work magic. Tonight, he wore the ceremonial regalia of a Sworn chieftain, and the mantle of a shaman. A breastplate of leather set with runes in carved bone and precious stones covered his chest and back. Leather vambraces set with silver covered his forearms. A tunic woven in shades of blue, green, and brown extended beneath his breastplate, matching his trews, and a mantle that matched the robe Talwyn wore lay across Pevre's shoulders. From his belt hung tokens of favor from the Consort Spirits: the claw of a stawar, the eyetooth of a bear, a charm made with the fur of a wolf, and two wing feathers from an eagle.

Jair came dressed to fight. He wore the leather battle armor of the Sworn warriors, and his *stelian* hung close by his side, along with an array of knives and throwing blades sheathed in a baldric across his chest. On his right hand, he wore the signet ring of the heir to the throne of Dhasson, and on his left palm, the tattoo that marked him as one of the *trinnen*. Though he would have been well-armed for any mortal battle, tonight, Jair felt at a decided disadvantage.

Talwyn raised her arms to signal that she was ready to begin the working. Pevre began a steady rhythmic beat on the hand drum he had carried from the village. Talwyn started to chant in the language of the Sworn, and Jair followed along, swaying to the rhythm of her words.

"Faces of the Sacred Lady, turn to me. I am your daughter. Honored dead, protect me. We are kin. Consorts, I ask you to accompany me. Spirits of the Dread, permit me to enter." As Talwyn spoke, her form began to shimmer. And as she called to the spirits, a mist rose from the land around her, and as Jair watched, shapes began to appear in the mist, only to vanish like smoke a moment later. Jair thought he glimpsed the ghosts of Sworn warriors, still bearing their death wounds, and the wizened faces of long-dead ancestors. The figure of a woman with long, black hair turned to face Jair, and for an instant, he thought he had come face-to-face with Istra, the Dark Lady. The image vanished as quickly as it came, and Jair saw new shapes coalesce in the mist. Beside Talwyn were a bear, a large wolf, and a large, black predatory cat that was as big as the wolf. Jair recognized it as a stawar, one of the most feared hunters of the Eastern plains. Talwyn took a deep breath, and her robes fell away, leaving her skyclad. From the mist above her head, the figure of an eagle landed on her outstretched forearm.

Talwyn's body collapsed atop her discarded robes, and a spirit image stepped away from her still form. The spirit image gave one glance back toward Jair and then moved to the crude doorway the Black Robes had erected over the hole they had dug into the side of the barrow. Darkness extended down into the tomb. Talwyn's spirit image paused at the entrance and she bowed, and then her lips moved, but Jair could not hear her words. Accompanied by the spirits of the Consorts, Talwyn vanished into the darkness.

"How will I know if she needs me?" Jair asked, when Pevre slowed his drumming.

"You'll know. It's not unlike the bond between a healer and his assistant. It's your life energy that her spirit will follow back to you and back to her body."

Jair looked toward the place where Talwyn's body lay crumpled and still surrounded by her robes. Everything in him wanted to run to her and gather her into his arms, but both Talwyn and Pevre had warned him to disturb nothing. Instead, he stared into the darkness of the shaft Talwyn had entered, straining to see a glow or a wisp that might give him any hint of what was going on.

Jair felt suddenly off balance, as if someone had shoved him hard from the side. He opened his eyes, and everything around him changed as quickly as if tapestries with a different landscape had been unfurled all around him. Distantly, he heard Pevre's voice.

"Steady, lad. Talwyn's drawn you into the bond. You see what she sees. Watch, and do nothing."

Pevre's warning was easier heard than followed. Through the bond, Jair felt Talwyn's fear as she and the spirit guides wound their way deeper into the barrow. The path led through complete darkness, and a mortal might have had to crawl to follow the winding, mazelike passageway. More than once, the path dropped away into air, as if whoever had made the barrows for the Dread anticipated mortal tomb raiders and set traps for them. Talwyn and her spirit guides continued, unimpeded.

A growing feeling of uneasiness seized Jair, like the wind before a storm. His skin prickled with fear, and he felt the hair on the back of his neck stand up. Talwyn was afraid, but Jair felt her muster her courage to press forward. The darkness became oppressive, suffocating, as if the shadows themselves had mass. Jair felt Talwyn and her spirit guides stop.

"Show yourselves!" Talwyn's voice rang out in the darkness. "I've come to restore the wardings. I can't do it without your help."

Before Talwyn spoke, Jair thought the darkness of the barrow was absolute. But as he watched through Talwyn's eyes, the darkness grew even blacker, but this time, Jair knew that the Dread moved in the shadows. Through Talwyn, Jair could feel the gaze of the ancient watchers, and a shiver of power ran through him. Whoever—whatever—the Dread were, they had not been human in a very long time.

"Blood has awakened what long slumbered," a sonorous voice rumbled from the sentient shadows. "Our task has become more difficult."

"We hunt the ones who disturbed your rest, the ones who shed blood to awaken what you guard. But I can't do the magic to seal the barrow again by myself. I don't have your power. Will you work with me?"

"You are not the only one who seeks our help," the rumbling voice replied. "For a thousand years, we have remained below, to guard the abyss. We have not meddled in your ways. Now, new powers have arisen, and they would court us. What do you know of this?"

"New powers? The Durim?"

"No. The Durim do as they are bid. Distant power, drenched in blood. It calls to us, but it truly seeks those whom we guard."

"I know nothing of these 'new powers,'" Talwyn replied. "But if they seek to awaken the monsters of the Abyss, then surely, they are the enemy of the Sworn."

"Perhaps." The voice echoed through the deep places of the barrow and Jair shivered. The tone of the disembodied voice said as much as its words. While the Dread had been buried with their prisoners for centuries, whether or not they chose to remain so was up to the Dread. For the first time, Jair realized that the wardings had no power over the Dread themselves, serving only to keep mortals from entering the barrows and to keep the monsters sealed in the Abyss from escaping. Now, Jair shared Talwyn's realization that should the Dread choose to walk again among mortals, no power in the Winter Kingdoms could stop them.

In the distant shadows, Jair heard whispers of other voices, and farther beyond, the muted snarls of horrors he did not wish to see. As if the Dread had conferred among themselves, the rumbling voice suddenly returned.

"We will help you, daughter of the Sworn. But heed this warning: We keep our own counsel. A great darkness is coming. We have not yet determined how—or whether—we will act. Do not presume to know our mind."

Talwyn clasped her hands in front of her and bowed to the spirits. "Thank you, guardians. I will bear your warning."

"Leave us now. When you rejoin your body, you will have the knowledge and the power you need to ward the barrow. Do not come to us again unless we summon you."

Jair shook off the trance and looked up. Talwyn's spirit image and her guides were making their way toward them through the mist. The spirit-Talwyn stood before her crumpled body, and then stepped into the form, raising it around her. Talwyn blinked and took a deep breath. Her amber eyes glowed with power, and the spirit guides moved beside her as she walked toward still staring out to sea. "Do you think that was

d. "I don't know. A lot of the servants just
hile Alvior might have harmed one or two, I
led them all. You knew him. He was miserable.
ts went back to their farms or families rather
im. Hell, if I'd had anywhere else to go, I'd
."

that, too."

nd on Cam's shoulder. "It's time to stop apolo-
ou couldn't control, Cam. From what you've
ina had your hands full staying alive. And look
hampion. Carina helped to put Tris Drayke
throne. None of that would have happened if
. Truth is, I could have run away if I'd really
." He chuckled. "Probably could have learned
something useful. But I didn't, and that was
o stop apologizing. The important thing is,

ck from the sea to the cairn. "I have to leave

I know." He grinned. "Now tell me the truth—
ng. Your bride-to-be is waiting." He paused.
ne. While you and Rhistiart were out riding
enger came from the palace. Brought you a
ing and a sealed envelope that looked like a
. I meant to tell you at breakfast this morning
the desk in the study." He paused. "So…
y of the manor like? Don't tell me she's one
doll aristocrats."

rn to laugh. "Rhosyn? Hardly. Oh, she's got
curves that would stop a runaway wagon in
can also carry a full sack of hops without

the barrows. She spoke in a language Jair had never heard, and the words seemed impossible to fix in his mind, as if it was not given for mortals to remember them. The hole in the side of the barrow filled in; no, Jair thought, it *healed* as if the soil and rock were sinew and skin.

Pevre was the first to move. He began to beat his hand drum in rhythm with the strange chant that Talwyn sang. Jair felt fatigue wash over him, and he realized that Talwyn had begun to draw from his energy to sustain herself as she worked the magic. Linked to Talwyn, Jair felt energy crackle around him as if lightning had struck at close range. The pull from Talwyn was stronger now, and her face was set with fierce concentration. Jair had only rarely seen Talwyn work this level of magic. He could not shake off a primal fear of the power that consumed her and the steady pull that drew from his own life force.

Linked to Talwyn, Jair saw the barrow begin to glisten, and he realized that he was seeing the magic as Talwyn saw it. Honeyed strands of power wove around the barrow, glowing brighter as they crossed and reinforced each other. Jair could feel the hum of Talwyn's power and the echo of old, strong magic as the power of the Dread reinforced what Talwyn did. Caught up in the link, Jair felt the damage to the barrow as if it were a physical injury, and he sensed the relief of the land and the Dread as it was restored. Gradually, the mist around them began to thin. One by one, the spirit guides that had accompanied Talwyn into the barrow walked into the mist and disappeared. Talwyn staggered, and Jair glanced to Pevre, who nodded that it was safe to go to her. Jair grabbed Talwyn's robe and gathered her into his arms as she began to collapse, completely spent.

"Did you see?" Talwyn murmured.

"I saw," Jair replied. "You were amazing."

"Then you heard…the warning?"

Jair nodded. "I heard. And we'll figure out what to make of it later. Right now, I want to get you home and let you rest." He wrapped her robes around her as if dressing a small child.

Talwyn nodded, but her head fell forward as if she were too exhausted to hold it up. Pevre joined them as they walked back to their horses, and he took Talwyn from Jair until Jair could swing up to the saddle. On the short ride back to the camp, Talwyn nestled against Jair as her horse followed behind them.

Jair was glad that Kenver had already gone to sleep. Talwyn was pale and her breathing seemed shallow. He carried her into the tent and set her on the bed. Talwyn reached out to take his hand.

"Thank you," she murmured.

"I just stood there," Jair said, managing a smile. "You did all the hard work."

"You did more than you know. You sustained me." Talwyn's voice was distant and sleepy. Jair brushed the dark hair back from her face and brought her a cup of wine and a few slices of apple.

"Sleep now. We'll talk with Pevre in the morning. I don't know what to make of the warning the Dread gave you, but among the three of us, we'll figure it out. For starters, it seems like the kind of thing Tris should know about. I'm sure I can get a message to him."

Talwyn's eyes fluttered closed. "Stay with me," she murmured.

Jair leaned down to kiss her forehead. "Always, m'lady."

"We buried her unde
Cam stopped just a f
Beneath it lay a cair
and Father didn't seer
keeper, and we burie
We made sure it wa

Cam looked at hi

A pained express
quickly after you an
of it."

"I'm sorry I wasr

Renn's laugh wa
Alvior's. Not your
think Mother woul
out of her when Fa

"What happened

Renn looked fro
hilltop, Cam could
"He stayed on for a
that he didn't lik
Brunnfen to go liv

Cam nodded,
the real reason?

Renn shrugg
vanished—and
don't think he ki
I think the serva
than deal with
have joined ther

"I'm sorry fo

Renn laid a ha
gizing for what
said, you and Ca
at you, King's
on the Margolan
you'd stayed her
set my mind to i
to be a tinker, o
my own fault. S
you came back."

Cam looked b
again, you know.

Renn nodded.
it's not just the k
"Which reminds
the fields, a mes
packet from the
lady's handwritin
and forgot. It's c
what's the new la
of those porcelai

It was Cam's t
a pretty face and
its tracks, but she

straining. She's got the only pedigree I value—she's the daughter of the head of the local Brewers Guild." He looked toward Brunnfen and sobered. "What she'd make of this place, I don't know."

"Rhistiart said that she's a spitfire. And he said her father offered you a place at the brewery if you decided to stop soldiering." Renn looked to Cam expectantly. "Would you take it?"

Cam shrugged. "There was a long time when I thought that would be a perfect job when I got too busted up to soldier. But from what Rhistiart and I saw of the grain crop, and from the unofficial survey we made of alehouses in town," he added, clearing his throat, "I think that a good brewery would do well here. It couldn't brew worse than the cow piss they sell for ale down in the village."

Renn laughed. "You've tried the local brew then?"

Cam made a face. "The pond scum that the Divisionists gave me to drink wasn't as bad as that 'ale.' Actually, that's where Rhistiart is right now. I sent him to scout for a good location to build a pub in town and to do some investigating about the local Merchants Guild." He looked at Renn conspiratorially. "The ale-brewing business wouldn't be such a bad way to refill Brunnfen's coffers, either. If Rhosyn could get her father to loan us a brew master, I'm sure Donelan would give us the title of 'king's favorite ale.' And a tavern makes money year-round—rain, snow, or shine."

"All joking aside, I'd love for you and Rhosyn to settle here—and Rhistiart, too."

"You know, for a guy who was on the run a few months ago, Rhistiart's luck just keeps getting better and better," Cam replied. "A *vayash moru* silversmith in Dark Haven gave him an offer as an apprentice, and now, he's on his way to becoming manager of an alehouse. Plus, I wouldn't put it past Donelan to offer him a silversmith position at the palace. Getting captured by the Divisionists was the best thing that ever happened to him."

Cam sobered and grew silent, watching the tall grass blow in the wind beside the cairn. "I'm sorry that Mother didn't live to find out that Carina and I ended up all right. And I'm so sorry that she won't see her granddaughters."

"Carina is having twin girls?" Renn grinned broadly. "When you said twins, I assumed a boy and a girl, like you and Carina. Yes, you're right. Mother would have loved that." He grew pensive. "You know, there were years when I was angry at everyone after you left. I was angry at Mother for abandoning me and leaving me on my own with Father and Alvior. I was angry at Father and Alvior, and I was angry that you and Carina didn't take me with you."

Cam glanced sideways at him. "You were a little young to sign up as a merc. Hell, if I hadn't been half the size of a mountain, they wouldn't have believed it when I lied about my age."

"I didn't say it made sense. I just said I was angry." Renn sighed. "I spent a lot of time out here, talking to Mother. And while I can't see spirits like your friend King Drayke, I don't really think she ever left Brunnfen. Sometimes, I can sense her in the manor house. It's particularly strong on the balcony in her room. She would stand there, just staring out at the horizon. I always thought she was hoping she'd see you coming home."

"You don't know how often Carina and I thought about it," Cam replied. "Carina's first love was a mercenary, Ric. Ric and his older brother, Gregor, ran the merc outfit we signed on with. Ric once offered to lay siege to Brunnfen to avenge Carina."

"Really? What happened?"

The memory made Cam smile. "It was a very nice idea, except that we were based in Principality and we couldn't figure out how to get the mercs to Isencroft without accidentally starting a war with Margolan." He grew wistful. "And then Ric died in a border skirmish and Carina nearly died trying to save him. That's how I ended up at the palace, you know. The Sisterhood took Carina to see if they could heal her. She went too deep when she tried to save Ric's life and it was like she couldn't find her way back. I didn't know what to do. Gregor was furious that Carina couldn't save Ric, and he threw us out. I had nowhere to go—again. I knew that we were distant cousins to the king, so I rode to the palace. One day, I just showed up on Donelan's doorstep and claimed a blood-bond right to serve him."

Renn's eyes were wide. "What did he do?"

"Donelan came thumping down the stairs to see what was going on, and he recognized me right away as Father's son. Seems he'd heard about what Father did and didn't like it. So he took me in and put me in the Veigonn, his personal guard."

The manor house tower tolled tenth bells. "I'd better get back and see that the supplies I ordered came in, or we'll be eating nothing but parsnips and beets," Renn said with a glance over his shoulder. "Are you coming?"

Cam shook his head. "I'll be up. I want to stay for a while longer."

"Don't wait too long—I can't promise how much lunch will be left if you're slow!"

Cam waited until Renn had climbed back up the rocky foot-path to the manor before he walked a few steps to a patch of wildflowers and picked a handful. He returned to lay them atop the cairn, and bent to retrieve a small rock, which he added to the rest of the pile. Cam laid a hand on the rock tomb and closed his eyes.

"I don't know whether or not you're still here," he said quietly. "If you are, I know the dead can hear the living. I'm sorry for the grief I caused you. Sorry I wasn't here to protect Renn. Sorry I couldn't stand up to Alvior—or Father. I want you to know: Carina and I never stopped thinking about you. We wrote letters, but I guess Alvior or Father made sure they didn't get through. If you can hear me, then I just want to tell you that everything's all right. And Carina and I love you."

An unseasonably cool breeze tousled Cam's unruly curls. For a few seconds, he thought he saw something shimmer in the air, although the day was not warm enough to see heat rise from the ground. There was no sound, but in that instant, Cam felt a warmth and comfort slip over him, there and gone, that made him suspect that his comments had been heard. He did not try to choke back the tears that streamed down his face. And if the ghost saw, Cam was certain that she understood.

When he had regained his composure, Cam walked back to the trail that led from the manor down to the shore. He turned away from Brunnfen and found himself heading down the path he had taken so often as a boy. Then, like now, he found consolation in the sound of the waves and the fresh spray. His thoughts were a jumble as he walked. When he shook himself out of his brooding, Cam found himself far down the rocky beach, at the base of the cliff that formed Brunnfen's foundation. He looked out across the water toward the long dock where Asmarr, his father, had kept the boat he loved to take out onto the bay for fishing. Farther out, the bay was quite deep, but silt had filled in along the coastline, and so the pier extended far out from shore. Years ago, large ships could lay anchor in the inlet, and rumor had it that the first lords of Brunnfen had been smugglers. It would be difficult for more than a couple of small boats to come into shore now.

Movement on the pier caught Cam's eye, and although the day was warm, Cam felt his blood turn to ice. Standing on the dock was his father's ghost.

Cam's eyes widened and he felt his heart begin to thud. Asmarr did not seem to see him. Cam watched as his father went through the motions of untying a boat, although there was no boat moored on the dock. Suddenly, Asmarr's ghost staggered, falling backward as if he had been pushed by an unseen hand. Before the ghost could catch his balance, he staggered again, clutching his head before collapsing. Unseen hands rolled the body off the pier and into the water. Cam watched in horror and remembered something. Asmarr couldn't swim.

Before Cam could gather his thoughts, the air around him began to stir, and he felt a touch on his shoulder. He spun around to find Asmarr staring at him. The ghost on the dock had been translucent. But the apparition that stood in front of Cam might have passed for a living man had Cam not known that his father was dead. Asmarr's face was set in a determined glower, and he reached out with both hands, giving Cam a hard shove toward the pier.

Cam tried to step around the ghost. "I didn't come back here to fight you, Father. You're dead. It's over."

Asmarr blocked his path, shoving him again down the beach. Cam felt his anger rise.

"You're dead. Your favorite son, Alvior, murdered you. And you still can't let it go, can you? You can't accept that I'm back, when you hated me and Carina just for being what we were. Well, I'm not leaving. You threw me out once. You're not running me off again."

Asmarr's expression darkened, and the ghost seemed to grow in size, becoming more solid. A hail of rocks suddenly flew through the air at Cam, pelting him from the direction of the path. Cam spotted a second trail at the far end of the beach. It was on the other side of the dock, but it was the only way back to the manor without winding through the caves. As another shower of rocks flew toward him, Cam began to sprint to the second path.

Rocks struck him on the shoulders and back, and Cam

realized that Asmarr's fury had not abated. The rocks came from the inland side of the beach, and Cam found himself being driven toward the water.

"It's not enough that Mother died, you want to kill me, too?" Cam shouted. He was sore where the rocks had struck him, and he could feel blood running down the side of his head.

Asmarr's ghost launched itself at Cam, moving to block his escape. Cam drew his sword and brought the blade down with a killing slice that would have cleaved a living man from shoulder to hip. The blade passed harmlessly through the ghost's form. Cam swung at Asmarr, and it felt as if his fist hit something solid, though not quite human. Dropping his sword, Cam began to pummel the ghost, all the while realizing that Asmarr was, slowly but surely, forcing him down the pier. He wondered if Asmarr meant to push him into the water, and if that happened, whether the ghost could hold him under. He didn't want to find out.

The Divisionists did their best to drown me. Goddess! I have no desire to die like that at Father's hand.

Cam rained blow after blow down on the ghost, but Asmarr's expression was determined. If the ghost felt the punches, it gave no sign, although Cam knew they would have felled a mortal. Broad-shouldered and ham-fisted, Cam had held his own in enough bar fights and battles to know how to throw a punch. In life, Asmarr could never have withstood Cam's strikes. Now, Cam knew he was losing the fight.

Near the end of the pier, Asmarr's eyes glinted with something akin to madness. Cam suddenly felt as if someone had thrown a boulder at him, as an invisible force pushed him to his knees. He was sweating hard, fighting the ghost's power, as he fell to all fours on the dock. Something forced his head down, so that his gaze went into the water.

And then Cam knew. Asmarr wasn't trying to kill him.

Asmarr was warning him.

Someone had dredged the inlet.

"I see! Get the hell off me!"

Immediately, the ghost released him. Cam gasped for breath as the force that had held him down disappeared. Cam staggered to his feet. "You never had any tact when you were alive," he grumbled, straightening his shirt. "Why should I be surprised that you have none now that you're dead?" For the first time, as he looked around the inlet, he saw something that had not been there before. He looked back at the ghost.

"What are those posts sunk into the rock?"

Asmarr's ghost pointed out to sea.

Cam frowned. "They're meant to moor boats—a lot of them. That's it, isn't it?"

Asmarr nodded.

Cam looked down the cliffs at the long line of posts, and then out to sea. "He wouldn't need that many to tether small boats from supply ships." The only reason was one that made Cam shudder. "Men. The boats wouldn't be for cargo. They'd be carrying troops from larger ships beyond the inlet. Alvior intended Brunnfen to be a staging area for an invasion."

Asmarr stood a few paces away. A pained expression had replaced the dogged determination of a few minutes before, and it was the closest thing Cam had ever seen to remorse on his father's face.

"Alvior did this?"

The ghost nodded.

"He meant to bring a fleet here to challenge the king?"

Again, Asmarr's ghost nodded.

Cam let out a creatively obscene curse and stood staring at the water, his hands on his hips.

"That probably means he's coming back, doesn't it?" Cam began to pace on the pier. "It's late summer, so he's got a few months until the ice starts to build. It's already been close to seven months since he disappeared. So the question is, will he strike before winter or wait until spring?"

Asmarr pointed to the trees, and brought his hands down through the air, fingers moving.

"He's coming back when the leaves fall," Cam said. "Damn! I wish Tris Drayke were here to interpret. I hate guessing games." He bit his lip as he thought. "Maybe we can make it expensive for him."

He looked up to see Asmarr watching him. "Will you let me pass now that I've seen what you wanted to show me?"

Asmarr nodded. Cam shouldered past the ghost, and then stopped. He turned back. "Thank you," he said quietly. "I don't imagine you're pleased that I came back. I suppose you showed me this because, despite throwing Carina and me out of the manor, you were always loyal to Donelan. But whether you like it or not, I won't be run out of Brunnfen again. I'll stay or leave on my terms this time." He grinned. "And I just might be able to get Tris to visit and send you to the Lady if you don't agree to cooperate. Understand?"

Asmarr did not move, but his eyes gave Cam to believe that the ghost did hear him. "Good. Now you can go back to haunting the bay if you'd like. I've got work to do."

Cam sprinted back up the trail toward Brunnfen. His head was spinning, both from the encounter with his father's ghost and from the new evidence of Alvior's further treachery. Brunnfen loomed high above him, dark and forbidding on its perch above the Northern Sea.

Asmarr's ghost wasn't the first to haunt Brunnfen, and it wasn't likely to be the last. Cam slowed as he crossed the threshold. Portraits of long-dead—but not really departed—ancestors seemed to glare down at him, sharing his father's disapproval. It had taken him years to understand that not everyone's family history was quite as tragic or blood-soaked as the tales of the lords of Brunnfen.

Grandfather Gierolf, who had gone mad and murdered a dozen servants and his own wife believing himself beset by *dimonns*. Great-grandmother Nessa, who had immolated herself and her children in a rage over her husband's infidelity. Asmarr's brother, Raynor, who murdered his eldest son in a blind rage over spoiled wine. A great-uncle who had locked an unfaithful wife away in an oubliette beneath the lowest wine cellar. Insanity and violence were the heritage of Brunnfen's heirs. Cam had never felt the weight of his heritage so oppressively as he did now.

"M'lord, lunch is ready." Haulden, the steward, was one of the servants Renn had cajoled into returning to the manor.

"Where's Renn?"

"He ate quickly and said he needed to see to accounts in town. Said to tell you he'd probably spend the night at the inn and be back late tomorrow." Haulden took in Cam's disheveled appearance. "Is there something wrong?"

"How many able-bodied men do we have on the manor grounds? Men who could do hard work."

Haulden thought for a moment. "Not so many as when your father ran the holding. Counting the men who are in the fields, about three dozen. A few more, if you take the older boys from the stable."

"Unless you want Alvior back in charge, get me every man with a strong back you can find. Tell them to bring chains and axes."

Haulden's eyes widened. "You intend to fight?"

"I intend to change the rules of Alvior's game. When he comes back with his ships, we'll have a surprise waiting for him."

* * *

"What in the name of the Eight Faces do you think you're doing?" Renn's voice carried across the water. Cam and three other men were shirtless in the late-summer heat, putting their combined strength into shoving a huge tree stump from a raft into the harbor.

"Stopping Alvior from coming back," Cam grunted.

Renn ran out on the pier until he was across from where the raft floated. "Who told you he was coming back?"

"Father—or at least, his ghost."

Renn looked from Cam to the flurry of activity. Along the forest's edge, men felled trees and loaded them into wagons. Near the water's edge, teams of men bound the trunks together into spiked balls, with as many limbs as possible protruding to snag unwary navigators. Horses and a brace of oxen dragged the snares to the water. From the end of the pier, two men fed a heavy chain down to others who dove into the inlet's chilly waters. Along the beach, the stablehands were busy fashioning barricades from smaller trees and thorned bushes. There were even men on the roof of Brunnfen, hauling logs by pulleys up to a flat area. Barely visible at the edge of the beach stood Asmarr's ghost, watching.

"What are you building on the roof of the manor house?" Renn shouted to Cam.

"A watchtower. We'll keep it manned at all times, change it out in shifts. If boats approach, whoever's up there will show a lantern and ring a bell. We'll send a rider out to Captain Lange. He's based at the outpost about a candlemark's ride from here. They'll be the first reinforcements."

"And you know Lange will come—why?"

"Because Cam asked me." The voice came from behind Renn, who turned sharply to see a broad-shouldered man with a fighter's build coming up behind him.

Cam's raft drew up alongside the pier and Cam hopped

off. "Renn, meet Captain Lange. Lange, this is my brother, Renn."

Lange extended his hand to Renn, who shook it dubiously. "Dammit, Cam. I leave for a day and you tear the place apart," Renn said.

"I sent a rider down to warn Lange yesterday morning, as soon as I realized what Alvior had done," Cam said, using a rag to mop the sweat that matted his hair against his head. "We've been on a campaign or two together in the past."

"Or three or four," Lange added dryly. "It's not every day the King's Champion sends a rider to see if you can free up a few men to keep a foreign navy from landing in your own backyard."

Cam grinned. "So Lange came, and he brought a couple dozen of his men with him. Together with the servants, we've done a decent job of snaring the harbor and making the beach unfriendly. Which means that if Alvior and his friends do come back, they'll be hung up on the snares or stuck at the mouth to the bay, where we can hammer away at him with the trebuchets Captain Lange is so helpfully going to provide."

"Damn," Renn said again. He paused and looked back at Cam. "Wait a second... *Father* told you about Alvior?"

Both Renn and Lange listened intently as Cam recounted his struggle with the ghost. When he was done, Renn shook his head.

"I'd meant to warn you not to come down to the beach alone. I'd seen Father's ghost once, but I got my ass out of there before he had the chance to get closer, and I've been wearing an amulet ever since then to keep ghosts away." Renn pulled a silver pendant from beneath his shirt. "Knowing Father, I figured that he wouldn't let being dead get in the way of a good beating. I'm sorry. If I'd been braver, I might have had the warning sooner."

Cam snorted. "I'd have run for it myself if he hadn't been throwing so many damn rocks at my head. Don't blame yourself. Father was his usual, charming self. He's angry that Alvior betrayed him, and maybe that Alvior betrayed the king. That doesn't mean Father's sorry about what he did to either of us." He gave an unpleasant smile. "But if Alvior does come back, I hope he gets close enough for Father to throw a couple of big rocks at his head, just for good measure." He paused. "What do you know about the posts sunk into the rock?"

Renn shrugged. "Don't know for sure, but I'll tell you my suspicions. They weren't here when Father was alive. They suddenly appeared about the time Alvior started to get his 'visitors.' At first, there were just a few, and I figured they were for those ships. All the others were put in while I was locked in the dungeon. I've asked among the servants, but the men who sank the posts for Alvior either fled or disappeared."

"Father seemed to agree with me, that they had to be for invading ships."

Renn nodded. "That's my guess."

"Lange's offered to post some men here at Brunnfen to protect you," Cam added.

"From Father?"

Cam shook his head. "Now that we have more of an idea of what Alvior is planning, I've got to get back to Aberponte and warn Donelan. I can get there as fast as any messenger. It's bad enough that Alvior has a dark mage—maybe even a dark summoner—on his side. Whoever's backing him has some kind of navy or Alvior wouldn't have gone to all the trouble to prepare the bay. The next move is going to be big, and unfortunately, Brunnfen's going to be right on the front line."

Cam paused and met Renn's eyes. "It's your choice. I'm not going to billet troops in your home without your consent. But I'd really like you to consider it."

Renn looked from Lange to Cam. "Alvior's the one who threw me in the dungeon and starved me, remember? Billet all the troops you want—only mind that they bring their own food, because we don't have that much to spare." He grinned. "Think you can get that alehouse of yours started before you leave? Soldiers like their ale, after all."

"I'll see what I can do about that." He sobered. "Thank you, Renn. For everything. I'm sorry that I have to leave."

Renn shrugged. "You're the King's Champion. And at least you're not leaving me on my own. Alvior was none too popular in the village. I would be surprised if we couldn't round up a militia if we put out the word that he might be back. Folks out here aren't sophisticated, but they're loyal to the king. And they don't like strangers."

"When Donelan hears about it, he might send a regiment or two to back you up. I'm starting to wonder what else is going on, and whether this is bigger than just Alvior." Cam rubbed the stump of his severed finger, the one he lost to the Divisionists. "When I was captured by the Divisionists, Ruggs and Leather John said Alvior had been paying their bills. But Alvior didn't have the money to build a navy. So my question is…Whose navy is it? I'd like to know that."

"Before we fight them," added Lange.

10

Aidane drifted in and out of consciousness, waiting to die.

Suddenly, the doors to the chamber slammed open. Aidane's heart began to pound. Whatever her captors planned for her, it would not be an easy or painless death. Battered as she was, Aidane was aware enough to feel fear.

"Get the cages open. Take everyone. We'll sort it out later." The speaker was a tall man with straw-blond hair and blue eyes. Half a dozen men swarmed into the chamber, and with them was another man in brown robes. The robed man's hood fell back. He was from Nargi and, by the rune necklace at his throat, a mage.

"Stand back from the doors, if you're able," the leader warned. Green light flared from the mage's hands. The metal cages glowed for a moment, and then the bars became a dull gray and the cage doors swung open of their own accord.

The men began to heft the injured prisoners into their arms. Others helped the prisoners who could stand get to their feet. One of the men stood in the doorway to Aidane's cell.

"We've got a problem."

The man who seemed to be the leader came to stand beside him. "Mortal?"

The other man nodded. "Well?"

Aidane could barely turn toward the two men, even though she knew they debated her fate. Stay or leave, it would be over soon, whether or not the black-robed Durim returned. It was like a coin toss with no winner. King's head, die now. King's crest, die later.

"Bring her."

Aidane could not bite back a moan as one of the men wrapped her in a cloak and gathered her into his arms, although she supposed he was being gentle. They seemed to fly up the stairs and into the cool night air. They were flying, just at treetop level. Aidane supposed it was the kind of vision the dying are said to see. If so, it calmed her. She had often wondered what the world looked like to the birds, to the sparrows and the crows that could fly away from Nargi and its problems, creatures of the air. On the ground beneath them, Aidane glimpsed men moving quickly, dragging bodies. She managed a thin smile. She was still dying, but the Black Robes had died first. Perhaps the Goddess did have a sense of humor, albeit bleak.

Aidane lost track of time. The sense of flying was peaceful, and if it turned out that her rescuer carried her spirit across the Gray Sea, well, so be it. She hadn't counted on long life. The late summer's night was cool, and Aidane could hear the chirps and croaks of night creatures. Finally, they slowed and then seemed to hover. Her rescuer landed gently, carrying her as if she were weightless. Even on the ground, the man who carried her moved with unnatural grace. Or perhaps, Aidane thought, the shock of her wounds just deadened the pain from his movements.

One of the other men gestured from the doorway for them to hurry. They entered the ruins of an old barn, then went down a set of stairs carved into the rock beneath and through a winding passage.

"Set her down." The command came from the blond man.

Aidane struggled to focus her eyes. His looks were average. He had a thin build, and now that she got a good look at him, Aidane could see that he was quite pale. *He's not from Nargi*, she thought. *But he just might be* vayash moru. The leader's blond hair was caught back in a queue, but even with it hidden, he couldn't have passed by day as a Nargi, although Aidane realized that the man was speaking Nargi without an accent. Then she met his eyes, and her vision seemed to swim. In his place, she saw a shorter man, with the dark hair and features of a Nargi native. She blinked and the vision was gone. She'd heard that *vayash moru* could hide themselves in plain sight to mortals who could not resist their glamour. Now, she understood.

"Who are you?" The man looked at her, and Aidane knew he was deciding her fate.

"Someone with really bad luck." Aidane's words were slurred through her swollen lips.

To her surprise, the blond man laughed. He glanced over to the far side of the room and waved for a short, squat man to join them. "Varren is a healer. Let's see if he can earn his keep."

Varren looked up to the blond man for direction. "Put her right, if you can," the blond man said. "If you can't, end her pain. We can't stay here long, and we've got a long road ahead."

As Varren inspected her wounds, Aidane tried to keep her eyes focused well enough to look around. Varren looked to be the only mortal, other than herself, among the group. Even the mage looked to be *vayash moru*.

The chamber was smoky and torchlit, like the tunnels beneath the city. It smelled of soot and sweat and old blood. The wounded *vayash moru* and *vyrkin* Aidane had seen in the cells were being tended, and all looked to be healing faster than she could hope to. The *vayash moru* who had a stake through his heart gave a cry as one of the others pulled the stake free, but to Aidane's surprise, the wounded man staggered to his feet moments later, looking shaky but functional.

Varren was muttering to himself as he made note of the gashes and broken bones, but he said nothing directly to Aidane. As she watched, the man who had carried her hurried over from where he had been talking with several other *vayash moru* to find the leader.

"You're healing her?" He gave a jerk of his head toward Aidane.

"I want to know her story, Zhan. Why was a mortal in one of their cells? There might be more to her than we know."

It was obvious that her rescuer, Zhan, did not share the leader's opinion. "She was there to be a sacrifice. Fresh, human blood. She'll slow us down. She can't heal like the others. We can't afford to get caught."

The leader's face hardened. "It's my mission. I decide."

Zhan took a step back and made a slight, stiff bow. "My apologies. Of course."

When Varren finally completed his examination, the leader appeared beside him, although Aidane hadn't seen the *vayash moru* move. "Well?"

Varren shrugged. "Whoever beat her up meant to kill her, but fortunately, he wasn't very good at it. Broken bones, punctured lung, blood loss. She'll probably lose a couple of teeth. She's a stubborn thing, or she'd be dead by now. And she's tougher than she looks."

"How long until we can move?"

"A candlemark. I've already healed the lung, and I've set the bones to healing, although it'll take some time. There's some internal bleeding from the bruises. I'd say whoever hurt her did most of his damage with his boots. That's what takes a little longer to put right."

"Understood. I just want to get her across the river."

"Aye. Let me get to work."

Varren turned his attention back to Aidane, and this time, he met her eyes. "I know you heard all that. So I'll make you a deal. I'm going to stop the pain, and you're going to use whatever magic you have to speed the healing. I know what you are. Open yourself to the ghosts and let them fill you. It won't hurt as much, and the energy will help you heal. I'll make sure no one overstays his welcome. Trust me."

Aidane could only nod. It was taking too much energy to keep up her shielding against the ghosts. They had found her, and once again, they clustered around her. Varren lifted Aidane's head and dropped a bitter liquid into her mouth. She swallowed, and she felt the elixir burn down her throat. Almost immediately, warmth radiated through her body, blunting the pain. She relaxed, and the ghosts rushed in. Aidane gave herself up to Varren and the ghosts, beyond caring whether she lived or died.

She awoke in darkness. The stale smell of the caves was gone. Instead, Aidane smelled the loam and leaves of a forest. A light rain was falling. She shivered. "Be still. Stay quiet." It was the voice of her rescuer, Zhan, the Nargi *vayash moru*.

"Where are we?" Aidane whispered.

"Nearly to the river. There's a patrol ahead."

Surely the *vayash moru* could fight a mortal patrol, Aidane thought. Then again, leaving a trail of bodies would make it that much harder for them to return to free others, and by the looks of the group, they weren't new at their game.

Before Aidane could reply, Zhan was slammed backward as a dark figure sprang from the shadows. "Captain! Captain! We've got runners! Over here!"

Zhan sprang toward his attacker with a growl, eye-teeth bared. Four more attackers seemed to appear from nowhere, and in the

dim light, Aidane realized their betrayal. The attackers were
vayash moru.

Aidane scrambled out of the way, amazed her body had
healed enough to permit her to move. Whether it was the
healing elixir, Varren's magic, or sheer self-preservation,
Aidane found that she could stand on her own, and she pressed
back into the shadow of a huge oak, although she knew that
its canopy could not hide her from undead attackers.

Across the clearing, she could hear the *vayash moru* leader
swearing fluently in several languages. Swords clanged and
blades swished through the air, moving fast enough to be just
a blur in the moonlight. Not too far distant, Aidane heard the
pounding of feet as the mortals, alerted by the traitors, came
running.

They'd been betrayed by *vayash moru*, but not by any of
those who had rescued her. No, these *vayash moru* were
newcomers, and by the way the fight was going, their betrayers
weren't doing well at holding their own.

Just then, an arrow slammed into the trunk of the tree beside
her, narrowly missing her shoulder. Aidane bit back a cry of
surprise and ducked, running for new cover. More arrows flew,
and one of her *vayash moru* rescuers fell as the shaft took him
through the heart. He crumbled to dust before he reached the
ground.

"*Rethniris,*" the *vayash moru* leader snarled, bearing down
on one of their attackers with a two-handed sword press that
would have felled a mortal just in its savage strength. Aidane
had heard the term. It meant "blood traitor," someone who
betrayed their essence. And from the look on the *vayash moru*
leader's face, he held it to be a killing offense.

All around her, swords clanged and arrows flew. Only eight
vayash moru had been part of the rescue team, counting the
healer. Three had fallen in the attack. Of the four *vayash moru*

traitors, only one was standing, and as Aidane watched, the *vayash moru* leader disarmed his opponent and went for the kill barehanded, tearing the traitor's head from his body and throwing it with deadly accuracy at the nearest archer.

I can help. It was a ghost's voice, and in her mind, Aidane could see the spirit clearly. She was a beautiful Nargi woman with dark, straight hair and luminous eyes.

How?

The soldiers got lucky. They weren't looking for you. They're posted at the village near here. That's where I died. Where we all did.

There were several ghosts now, all young women. *We were married or betrothed to those beasts, and they killed us for our dowries or in their drunken rage. Give us our vengeance. Let us fill you, and we'll call them to their deaths. We'll lend you our strength.*

Aidane hesitated, just a moment.

Or do you want to be captured again? the first ghost asked.

Take me.

Aidane stiffened and arched as the first ghost filled her. It was rougher than usual, but Aidane opened herself without reservation. She saw the ghost's memories of a thick-set Nargi soldier, a captain, and as the ghost filled her, Aidane remembered the spirit's death at her lover's hands as if it were her own. Aidane drew a deep breath and smoothed her hands down over her body, as if the ghost were reassuring itself that it had form. *Let's get them.*

Aidane took a step forward, yielding her will to the ghost. The *vayash moru* leader looked at her in alarm. "What the hell are you doing? Get back!"

Aidane kept going. "Varn! You worthless son of a cheap whore! You murdered me for my father's money. Come here, I've got a little something for you." Aidane felt the ghost controlling her movements, and she let herself sashay into the dim moonlight that filtered through the trees. "Varn! You bastard son of a goat! Dung eater! Show yourself." Aidane's movements were both seductive and threatening, and she knew that the ghost's possession was so complete that even her facial expressions were not her own.

"Sathrie? Sathrie? Is that you? But you're dead—"

The mortal captain stood transfixed, staring at the shadow that had become his murdered lover. A moment's hesitation was all it took for one of the *vayash moru* to send a sword scything toward the captain at shoulder height, taking his head clean from his shoulders. Blood was still pumping from the stump of his neck as his body collapsed to the ground.

Sathrie's ghost fled Aidane's body, and another spirit filled her so quickly that Aidane nearly passed out. Aidane ran for the shadows, only to reappear elsewhere in the glade. "Theddan! You limp-hung rat eater! You were too cheap to hire a healer and you let me die from the pox." Aidane's whole stance had changed. Where the last ghost had moved with the seductive grace of a dancer, this new ghost stood with hands on her hips, leaning forward, strident as an angry scullery maid.

"Be gone! I paid to have you buried," a voice came from the forest. The hail of arrows lessened.

"Not deep enough, you lice-ridden thief. Come taste my maggots. Lie in my grave with me, lover."

A man cried out, and the cry ended in a strangled groan. Aidane could feel the ghost's satisfaction as it fled her body. This time, more than one ghost forced their way into her consciousness, and the voices that poured from her throat changed from breath to breath.

"Venaddon! Do you remember me? You buried me behind the barn."

"Jakertan! It's Nesha. Warm me. My grave is so cold."

"Mathan! Come to your sweet, dead Tallie. I'm waiting for you."

All around Aidane, battle raged, but sustained by the ghosts, Aidane moved steadily toward her prey, arms outstretched, sure that her expression carried all the malice she could feel radiating from the ghosts that filled her. The men dropped their weapons and fled, run quickly to ground by the *vayash moru*. In moments, the glade was silent once more. Satisfied with their vengeance, the ghosts slipped one by one from Aidane's consciousness, and she sank to a seat on the trunk of a fallen tree.

The leader of the *vayash moru* stood in front of her, his blue eyes wide. "What are you?"

Without the support of the ghosts, Aidane once more felt the fatigue of her injuries. "I'm a *serroquette*. A ghost whore." It was cold satisfaction to realize that she had actually managed to startle a *vayash moru*.

"Kolin, we've got to get moving." Zhan laid a hand on the blond leader's shoulder.

Kolin nodded, and spared one more glance toward Aidane, as if he wasn't quite sure what to say. Then he turned abruptly and motioned for the others to follow. "Let's get out of here."

For the remainder of the trip, the *vayash moru* seemed to treat her with a combination of curiosity and disdain. Aidane was too exhausted to care, so long as she made it to the other shore of the Nu River alive. She felt a pang of regret at leaving behind the gold coins she had hidden, the passage money she'd been saving. And she had no idea what kind of payment, if any, her unlikely rescuers would demand or whether, after her performance in the glade, they would count being rid of her payment enough.

"Almost there." Kolin hunched in the cover of tall grass on the river's bank. The water of the Nu flowed swift and dark. "Wait for the clouds to cover the moon, and then go. I don't care where you land, but we rendezvous at Jolie's Place."

For a moment, terror gripped Aidane as she stared at the cold water of the Nu River. She had never learned to swim. Then one of the *vayash moru* stepped up behind her and viselike arms encircled her chest. Clouds darkened the moon, and in a breath, Aidane's feet left the ground. In just moments, they came to land on the other bank, and as she stepped away from her protector, she realized it was Kolin, the *vayash moru* leader.

"That was some show you put on back there," Kolin said. From his tone, Aidane was still uncertain what the *vayash moru* thought about the diversion. *Leave it to me to spook the undead*, she thought dryly.

"I'm not much good with a sword, at least, not as myself," Aidane replied. Now that she stood on dry land on the Margolan side of the river, the energy of the fight seemed to rush from her body and she felt light-headed and weak.

"I'll keep that in mind," Kolin replied. Aidane's head spun, and she fell. Kolin cursed as Aidane collapsed, and only his *vayash moru* reflexes enabled him to catch her before she hit the ground.

"You're more bother than I bargained for," he muttered, scooping her up as he started the climb toward a large, well-lit building that sat on the shore of the river.

"If you go back, I can pay you...I have gold hidden..."

Kolin's face hardened. "I don't take pay."

"Sorry. I didn't mean—"

"Forget it. But up here, let me do the talking. Jolie's usually good with whomever we bring across, but I don't know what she'll make of you."

"That's the whorehouse on the other side of the river," Aidane said weakly.

"Yeah."

"Drown me now."

163

Kolin chuckled. "That good, huh? How about you leave Jolie to me."

Jolie's Place was a large wooden building, part of which was cantilevered off a hillside near the riverbank. Kolin motioned for the others to follow him, and he climbed a set of twisting, wooden stairs toward a rear door. Lights were on inside the building, but for a tavern and bawdy house, the building was strangely quiet.

"Jolie? Astir? Open up. It's me, Kolin."

The late-summer's night was cool. Aidane shivered. They waited for what seemed like a long time in silence until the door opened. A dark-haired *vayash moru* opened the door.

"Thanks, Astir," Kolin said, shouldering past with Aidane. The others followed. Kolin set Aidane down on a bench. She looked around. They were in a back room and, by the looks of it, it was the off-duty sitting room and dining area for the tavern's staff. A wide fireplace sat unused at one end. Their group quickly filled the empty benches around several tables.

"What's going on? Everything's pretty quiet tonight."

Just then, a door at the other end of the room opened. "Kolin! Varren! Thank the Lady you arrived safely. I was worried." A tall red-haired woman swept into the room. "Astir! Let's get them some food. Goat's blood for the *vayash moru*, and take some of the sausage and cheese for the others." The woman who Aidane assumed was Jolie moved with grace, gesturing flamboyantly as she spoke. It would be impossible to overlook Jolie. Though Aidane guessed her to be in her middle years, Jolie was trim with a generous bosom, and the cut of her crimson dress accentuated her curves. The dress was fashionable and could have come from any of the high courts. Gold bracelets stacked up both arms, glittering in the candlelight, and the gold and gems in her earrings seemed to dance in the light. Perfume clung to her, heavy and sweet, like incense. Whatever kind of house Jolie ran, it was a profitable one.

Jolie gathered Kolin into her arms, planting a kiss on both cheeks. "I worry about you, Kolin. These raids are dangerous. Even Jonmarc almost didn't get out of Nargi alive." She shook her head and sighed. "Ah, but you're here, and that's what's important. And Jonmarc? He's well?"

Kolin smiled, taking Jolie's hands in his. "He's managed to stay out of trouble for a couple of months, which is a record for him. Carina's feeling well, although it's not too much longer until the twins come."

"Which is another reason I'm going to Dark Haven," Jolie announced. Her voice was deep and throaty, sounding of strong liquor, and her consonants softened into a blur that gave Aidane to guess that Jolie spoke the river patois of smugglers and traders, perhaps as a native tongue. From the surprise on Kolin's face, Jolie's comment was obviously the first he had heard of these plans.

"You're going to Dark Haven?"

Jolie nodded, and her fiery, shoulder-length hair bobbed, catching the light. "We're nearly packed. I was expecting you to come after this run, and since you'll be heading back to Dark Haven, we're going with you."

Kolin looked utterly perplexed. "You're closing Jolie's Place? But you even have the endorsement of King Martris, after you gave him shelter when he went back to fight Jared."

Jolie chuckled. "Can you imagine that on a plaque? 'King's Favorite Brothel.'" She sighed. "It's not government trouble. It's the plague. No one's traveling. They're afraid to go out at night, afraid to be in gatherings, afraid to leave their homes. Whether it's ill magic or ill humours, no one goes about anymore. Even the soldiers aren't stopping like they used to. People are afraid. It's bad for business."

Astir came and stood beside Jolie, casually putting his arm around her waist. Jolie leaned against him for a moment. It was clear to Aidane that the two were a couple, though Jolie seemed to be mortal. "Anyhow, there's no one else I'd trust more than you to guide us across Dhasson," Jolie continued. "We'll close up the Place, and when the plague passes, well, perhaps we'll return. Until then, I've a mind to set up in Dark Haven."

Kolin chuckled. "And have you discussed this with Dark Haven's lord?"

Jolie laughed, a full-bodied, earthy sound that spoke of a zest for life. "Do you think he'll turn me away at the border, *cheche*? Jonmarc is the son I never had." She paused. "Actually, we did discuss it a bit, when Maynard Linton and I went up to Dark Haven for Jonmarc and Carina's wedding. Maynard had already made arrangements for his caravan to move their base to Dark Haven. Now, with the plague, there's not much call for caravans and fairs, either. I have some coin put away, enough to buy a new place and set it up. And you know my girls are just as sweet on *vayash moru* and *vyrkin* as they are on mortals."

"You're the best, Jolie."

"Damn straight."

Some of the joviality faded from Jolie's eyes as she spied Aidane. "Who's this, Kolin? She's not your usual passenger."

Kolin stepped back, and Jolie moved to stand in front of Aidane. Aidane gathered the shreds of her self-respect along with the hem of the borrowed cloak and met Jolie's eyes. Jolie stared at her in silence, taking in the fading bruises, the cloak that barely covered her nakedness, and the jewelry that hadn't been torn off in the beating or lost fleeing the Durim.

"She's a—" Kolin began.

"I know what she is." Jolie's voice was flat.

"I didn't intend to cause trouble," Aidane said, squaring her shoulders. "I can be gone in the morning."

"The Durim had her," Kolin said from behind Jolie. "She'd been beaten and left for dead. The Black Robes took her for a sacrifice. She was in the cages, along with our people, when we attacked."

"I've never had her kind in my house. Not sure I want one now."

"I didn't come to work," Aidane said, lifting her chin defiantly. "I just wanted to keep on breathing."

"Her...'gift'...helped us get out of an ambush," Kolin said. "If you've any question as to whether or not it's genuine, the spirits that spoke to her in the glade were real enough."

Suspicion and skepticism glittered in Jolie's light-brown eyes. "What do you say for yourself, girl?"

"My name is Aidane."

The corner of Jolie's red-tinged lips quirked upward, but it was not a smile. "Aidane, *serroquette*s often think themselves better than common whores. What do you think?"

Aidane forced herself to meet Jolie's eyes. "I think a whore is a whore. I had no choice in the matter. The spirits took me and I did as I was bid. Why others choose this life, I don't know. But the end result is the same."

"Spirits or no, most had little more choice, if any, than you," Jolie said. "And in my house, there is no shame. We're entertainers, companions, and confidants. My girls come of their own will and stay of their own will. And when they will it, they leave, with a purse and skills if they choose to do something else. Most who claim to be *serroquette*s are frauds. They beggar the desperate and the grieving. If you're what you claim to be, there's comfort to give in that."

Jolie sighed. "Margolan's not a good place for us right now. Kolin vouches for you. I won't object if you want to travel with us. On the road, you see people as they are. If I like what I see, I'll make a place for you."

"Thank you," Aidane said raggedly.

The vibrancy seemed to return to Jolie's face as she turned back to Kolin. "Well now, that's settled. When are you planning to head for Dhasson?"

If Kolin was taken aback by the sudden shift of subject, he did not show it. "The *vayash moru* are healed, but some of the *vyrkin* could use a day's more rest. Since we're not hunted in Margolan—at least, not yet—there's no hurry. When will your people be ready to travel?"

"We'll be packed by sunset tomorrow," Astir answered. "And don't fear—we travel light. The girls will take only what they can carry themselves. I've arranged for some of the local *vayash moru* to watch the place while we're gone." He frowned. "Although while King Martris would never sanction it, there have been incidents between mortals and *vayash moru*, even in Margolan, that worry me. When people start to die of plague, they look for someone to blame. And we are, always, among the usual suspects. So I'm none too sorry to spend some time in Dark Haven, and none too sure our friends here will be able to carry out their charge."

Kolin grimaced. "Even in Dark Haven, there have been... incidents. Jonmarc's intervened himself, as has King Staden's guard. But nowhere is ever truly safe for our kind."

"Or mine," Jolie agreed, taking Astir's hand.

They seemed to have forgotten all about Aidane for a time, which suited her fine. She watched the conversation, trying to understand the companions she now found herself among. It was clear that Kolin and Jolie were of long acquaintance, though there did not appear to be anything more than friendship between them. Jolie was a formidable presence, but despite her cool reception, Aidane found herself trusting Jolie. *At least I know where I stand with her.* In Nargi, *serroquettes* were outlaws by definition, which precluded them from working in the brothels and taverns where the other whores made their way. Technically, the Crone priests disapproved of any sold sex, but they were receptive to bribes. But while the priests were willing to ignore the common strumpets and streetwalkers, the presence of magic in a *serroquette*'s favors was too much to overlook.

She'd take a cut of my pay, but on the other hand, I have a feeling Jolie might also watch my back, Aidane thought. Or at least, Jolie's hired muscle—much of it *vayash moru* by the look of it—would keep danger to a minimum. It could be worth a percentage, especially if protection included reining in the drunks and angry patrons who so often dealt with their women with their fists.

"Here, try these on. Jolie sent them."

Aidane startled and looked up. A dark-haired young woman stood in front of her. The woman was close to her own age, just a bit over twenty summers old, Aidane guessed. She had the coloring of a Margolan native and wore a plain linen shift. Her long, brown hair was tied up in a functional braid. Although Aidane surmised that she was one of Jolie's girls, the young woman wore no makeup or jewelry tonight, and she had a hurried look.

"Thank you," Aidane said, accepting the pieces of clothing.

"It's not fancy, but we won't be dressing like peacocks on the road," the young woman said. "I'm Cefra. Jolie thought I might have an extra shift that would fit you. We do look to be about the same size, though you're bigger on the top."

Aidane smiled. "That's kind of you. I'm afraid I left Nargi with nothing."

Cefra led Aidane to a small closet and waited outside as Aidane changed. "Is it true that you're a ghost whore? I've never met one before. Thought it might just be stories made up to get more coin for a lay, if you know what I mean."

Aidane found that Cefra's shift fit her, albeit snugly in the bosom. She smiled as Cefra motioned for her to use the pitcher and basin that sat on a stand just outside the closet, and Cefra handed Aidane a towel to help her clean up.

"Yes, I'm a ghost whore, and yes, it's real—at least for me. That's what got me in so much trouble. A client wanted to be reunited with a dead lover, and we got caught by her husband." Aidane grimaced, touching the wet cloth lightly to the still-painful bruise on her cheek. "No one told me that was how the dead lover got so dead."

"You might find yourself popular in Dark Haven," Cefra observed.

"Why's that?"

Cefra shrugged. "I'd guess that *vayash moru* have outlived lots of lovers. Should be more than a few who're of a mind to see someone again, after a century or two."

Aidane had to admit that she felt much better in clean clothes and with fresh water splashed on her face. When she turned back, Cefra pushed a small plate of sausage, cheese, and bread toward her, along with a mug of ale. "I doubt you'll want goat's blood like Kolin and the others," Cefra said.

After the pain and terror of the last few days, Aidane had barely realized how famished she was. She gobbled the food quickly, and found that the ale was much better than the contraband spirits in Nargi.

Cefra stayed, and Aidane had to admit it was nice to have company. She still wasn't sure of her reception from Kolin and the *vayash moru*, and Aidane had been alone in Nargi for quite a while. "Have you worked for Jolie long?" Aidane finally asked after she had finished her food.

Cefra thought for a moment. "About two years, I guess. When Jared the Usurper, pox take his soul, was on the throne, his guards raided my village. They took grain and women when we had no coin to give for second taxes. After that, I wasn't quite as marriageable as before," she said with a grimace. "And the guards had killed most of the young men in the village anyhow." She straightened her back. "So I went out on my own and found that while a serving wench might keep food in her belly and a roof over her head, favors went further to putting coin in my purse."

"How did you find Jolie?"

Cefra shrugged. "Oddly enough, my story isn't too different from yours. I was roughed up by a customer who threw me out on the street to die. When I woke up, I was here. Jolie runs a tight business, but she tends to find her girls among the cast-offs and she does her best to give us choices we never had."

"What's this place usually like?" Aidane ate as Cefra regaled her with tales of what Jolie's Place had been like before the plague.

"Even when Jared the Usurper took the throne, we had business," Cefra sighed. "You know, don't you, that King Martris and Jonmarc Vahanian took shelter here when they came back to fight Jared? It was right before I came here, but I've heard about it." She grinned conspiratorially. "Jolie even got invited to King Martris's wedding because she gave him sanctuary. Imagine!" She shook her head in amazement. "So if Jolie says we're welcome in Dark Haven, I believe it."

Aidane finished chewing and took a drink of ale, hoping it would relax her sore muscles. Thanks to Varren's healings, her injuries were nearly gone.

"You don't mind leaving?"

"Margolan's gotten scary. I heard that in Ghorbal, so many people died of plague that there wasn't anyone well enough to bury the dead, and they just stacked the bodies in the street or left them lie where they had died. Even our regular customers aren't coming in anymore. And it's true that there've been attacks—on *vayash moru*, on whores, and on minstrels. People blame the plague on folks who travel, like the minstrels, and on the ones they never liked anyhow, like us and the *vayash moru.*"

Aidane pushed the empty dish away and managed a tired smile. "Thank you, Cefra. You've been very kind."

Cefra blushed and looked away. "Oh, it's nothing. And if you're not of a mind to sleep on the benches in here, there's a spare room upstairs. One of our girls lit out of here a few weeks back, didn't say why or where she was going. Figure she got scared of the plague, like the customers. But it means there's a bed upstairs, at least for tonight, and you can sort through the clothes and such she left behind. You might find some things to suit you."

The unexpected generosity surprised Aidane, but hard as she tried, she couldn't figure out why Cefra would have cause to lie. "Thank you," Aidane said, unaccustomed to the kindness. She followed Cefra up the back stairs, too weary to look for hidden motives.

11

Tris Drayke stood on the balcony outside his rooms. He felt the sun on his face and tried to relax. Thanks to Esme, his shoulder, arm, and chest were nearly healed from the *dimonn*'s attack. His dogs clustered around him. The two large wolfhounds were nearly tall enough to see over the carved stone railing. Content to press up against Tris's leg was the ghost of a large, black mastiff. Tris let his hand fall to pet the dogs as his thoughts strayed. With a small brush of magic, even the mastiff felt his touch, and the big dog's ghost leaned harder against him, a weight that would have caused Tris to change his footing had the dog been solid.

Cwynn had had a hard night, and even with the help of Kiara's nurses and nannies, the young prince's agitation was taking a toll. Tris blinked a couple of times and sipped a cup of *kerif*, wishing the bitter drink could do more to keep him awake. Cerise, Kiara's healer, had assured both Tris and Kiara that such things were not uncommon with a young baby, but the last time Tris remembered feeling so bone-achingly tired had been in the aftermath of a pitched battle.

Tris heard a knock at his door and turned. Out of old habit, one hand fell close to the pommel of his sword, even here, at home. Coalan, his valet, poked his head through the doorway.

"Uncle Ban's here to see you. Should I send him in?"

Tris relaxed and nodded, then finished the rest of his *kerif*. The dogs followed him inside. They sprawled in the sunlight that warmed the floor just inside the balcony, with the mastiff's ghost curling up next to the two living dogs, just as he had often done in life.

Coalan stepped aside to allow Ban Soterius to enter.

"Rough night?" Soterius said with an appraising glance. Soterius and Coalan were old friends of Tris's, and their friendship was one of the few remaining ties Tris had to a time before Margolan's troubles began, and before he had shouldered the burden of the crown.

Tris chuckled. "Just wait until you and Alle have a baby of your own. But not right away—please! One of us should be awake to defend the kingdom."

Soterius grinned. "I'm still adjusting to being a married man. I have a mind to wait as long as I can before we add to the family." His grin widened. "Although don't mention that to Alle, please. She may have other plans."

Tris sank into a chair near the cold fireplace and motioned for Soterius to join him. "What are you hearing from the barracks?"

Soterius shrugged. "Not a day goes by that one of the men doesn't hear from someone back home about the plague. And it's not just folks taking sick. The trading villages are starved for business since the caravans aren't traveling and even the minstrels are staying close to home. Between Jared running the farmers off their land and last spring's rains, planting got a late start. The crops are in the fields, but now there aren't enough men in a lot of the villages to harvest them."

Tris closed his eyes and let his head sink back against the cushions. "Can the soldiers help? At least for the farms near garrisons and within a day or two of the palace? How about the *vayash moru*? It would mean night harvesting, but Margolan

174

can't afford another hungry winter, and we'll have one if we leave crops in the fields."

"Most of the villages are already heavily relying on their *vayash moru* family members to care for the sick, bury the dead, and help where they can with the farming. There aren't that many of the *vayash moru*—fewer since Jared went after them, but they're starting to trickle back, although the incidents don't help."

"Tell me about the 'incidents.'"

Soterius stretched his legs. He was tall, but still a hand's breadth shorter than Tris, and muscular. His brown hair was cut short for a helm, and his dark eyes hinted at a keen intelligence. "It's not so much about our Margolan *vayash moru* as it is the refugees. They're coming over the border from Trevath and even from Nargi, although why any *vayash moru* would stay in either of those kingdoms is beyond me, given how the Crone priests treat them."

"Family," Tris replied tiredly. "They stay for their families, or because it's home. It's not so different from why the living put up with terrible conditions rather than leave. It's home."

Soterius sighed. "Yeah, well, I guess both of us know a thing or two about that, don't we? Anyhow, I've taken several dozen of the *vayash moru* and *vyrkin* refugees to Huntwood. You remember Danne, Coalan's father?"

Tris nodded. "Danne was married to your sister." When Jared's troops murdered Soterius's family because of Lord Soterius's loyalty to Tris's father, only Danne, Coalan, and one loyal servant had survived.

"Danne is rebuilding Huntwood. It's slow going. Jared's men made a real mess of it. But the walls have been repaired and it's got part of a roof again. The *vayash moru* and *vyrkin* are helping, and they've got the forest to keep themselves in deer meat and blood. It helps that Huntwood is out in the country. Fewer people around to get it into their heads that the *vayash moru* have something to do with the plague.

"We've also got as many of them as we can over at Glynnmoor, Carroway's family house. When he and Macaria get back from Dark Haven, they'll have a lot of company, but at least the old manor house is livable again. And the rest of the refugees are on Lady Eadoin's lands at Brightmoor. For now, we've been able to keep them out of the way, so that the villagers don't get frightened about a sudden influx of undead and shapeshifters. You know how that goes—every time a goat goes missing, someone blames it on a *vayash moru*."

Tris nodded again, tiredly. "But there are still incidents."

Soterius took a long breath. "Yes. Mostly over on the eastern side of Margolan. It's been hit the hardest with the plague. And it had more of the farms that lay fallow this season with no one to work them. The violence doesn't seem organized. Someone burns out a crypt here or there, tries to burn out a den of *vyrkin* somewhere else. What worries me aren't the locals so much as the Durim."

Tris opened his eyes and sat forward, reluctantly alert. "Tell me."

Soterius shrugged. "One of the garrisons out toward Ghorbal said they've had problems with tombs being looted, even a couple of the old barrows. At first, they thought it might be locals down on their luck, looking for a bit of gold to pawn. But there were some weird things that made the garrison leader look twice. Slaughtered goats and chickens, odd runes, and a couple of young girls gone missing. Then one night, they caught some men in black robes in the process of trying to hack their way into an old tomb. Put up an awful fight. Even used some magic. Fortunately, that particular garrison has its own battle mage. We think the Black Robes are Shanthadura followers, but they're not talking."

Tris smiled thinly. "Put them in magical bonds and have them sent to me."

"I thought you'd say that."

Tris pushed out of his chair and began to pace. The dogs roused at his movement, and while the wolfhounds soon stretched back out, the mastiff padded over to pace beside him. "No one's tried to revive the cult of Shanthadura in over three hundred years. Now, it's springing up everywhere. You saw what happened in the village, with the boy and that *dimonn* in the barrow. Now imagine that kind of thing happening across Margolan, across the Winter Kingdoms."

Soterius glanced up sharply. "What makes you say that?"

Tris walked to his desk and picked up three pieces of folded parchment. He handed them to Soterius. "Those have all come via messenger over the last few days. One came by *vayash moru* last night from Jonmarc. They're seeing a lot of the same kind of 'incidents' even in Dark Haven—and he's gone up against those Black Robes himself. He's positive they're Durim, and he says Gabriel and some of the other Old Ones who actually remember when Shanthadura was worshipped are not too happy about seeing the cult revived.

"Then I got another note from my cousin, Jair. You know Jair."

Soterius nodded. "He's your Uncle Harrol's son. Next in line for the Dhasson throne. He was at your wedding. Not too bad with a sword, as I recall."

"You could say that. Under an old agreement, he spends about half of the year riding with the Sworn."

Soterius let out a low whistle. "Really? The Sworn are a spooky bunch. I tried to recruit them during the Rebellion to fight against Jared, but they said they had bigger monsters to worry about, and I had my hands full, so I didn't ask questions."

"The Sworn don't get involved in the usual squabbles—even

something like the war against Jared. They're the keepers of the barrows, and it's their job to make sure what's buried in those barrows stays buried."

"You're a summoner. Isn't that your job?"

Tris gave a wan smile. "I've never messed with the things that live in those barrows, and I don't want to. Whatever's down there has been buried for over a thousand years, and it's nasty enough to have another set of guardians, the Dread, to make sure it doesn't rise."

"I thought the Dread were just fairy tales to keep children from wandering off."

Tris shook his head. "They're real. I try to steer clear of the barrows because when I get too close, I can feel...something... is down there. Whatever it is, it's old and powerful, and it seems to sense when I'm near. So until I can find out more from Fallon and the Sisterhood, or Royster and his library, I give the barrows wide clearance. But according to Jair, the Sworn are seeing the same kind of attacks you're describing. And in at least one case, the attacks came too damn close to weakening the barriers." He ran a hand across his eyes. "We really don't want what's down there getting loose."

"There's a third letter here."

Tris leaned against the mantel. "That came from Cam, and he must have messengers riding in shifts to get it here in only two weeks. Cam went back to his family's holding at Brunnfen to clean up the mess his traitor brother left behind. He's certain that his brother Alvior had some kind of connection to a blood mage—maybe even a dark summoner." He watched Soterius's face. "And Cam thinks whoever it is will try to invade Isencroft."

Soterius's eyes widened. "A dark summoner? Can you tell if he's right?"

"Not completely."

"I don't like the sound of that, Tris. I really don't."

Tris clasped his hands behind his back and began to pace once more. "Ever since we returned from the Battle of Lochlanimar, I've felt edgy. I tried to tell myself it was battle fatigue, or even some nervousness about the birth, but it's something else. The magic is wrong."

Soterius shifted in his chair to watch Tris as the other paced. "I thought you and Carina fixed the Flow during the battle."

Tris shrugged. "There are many rivers of energy in the world. The one that we fixed was the Flow that runs from the far north country in the east down through southern Margolan and beyond. But there are others. Fallon once told me there are at least three major energy rivers that run through Margolan and into Isencroft—and even the Sisterhood isn't completely certain where the offshoots and tributaries, for lack of a better word, run.

"The closest of those energy rivers is the Northern Flow. It runs from the Northern Sea, along the Nu River, and down into Dhasson and Nargi." Tris gave a pointed glance back to Soterius. "And not too surprisingly, the line of barrows that the Sworn patrol run right along that course."

"Oh really?"

"There's another Flow that also comes from beneath the Northern Sea and veers westward, into Isencroft. Several of the old palaces were actually built along one energy river or another. Cerise told me she's almost certain Aberponte in Isencroft is built on a Flow. I think the palace in Eastmark may be as well. But Shekerishet wasn't built for magic; it was built as a fortress. So we're between the Flows, but not on top of one."

"They obviously weren't expecting a Summoner-King," Soterius observed dryly.

"Maybe not. But the point is, while we're not right atop one of the Flows, there's enough 'leftover' magic that I can feel it. I never realized that was what I was drawing from, until Fallon explained it. But lately, the Flows have felt sluggish. It's hard to put magic into words, but if you've ever seen a stream that's gotten fouled with leaves and silt, it doesn't run right. That's sort of what the magic feels like. Fouled. Not broken apart and wild like the Flow underneath Lochlanimar. But wrong."

"You said that blood magic damaged the Flow," Soterius said slowly, thinking as he spoke. "Wouldn't a dark summoner also damage the magic?"

Tris grimaced. "I don't know. The last dark summoner we know about was Lemuel, but when he became the Obsidian King, he was also using blood magic. In that case, they weren't able to heal the Flow when it got out of hand and, as a result, we got the Blasted Lands, a place that's magically unstable and too dangerous for anything mortal to live."

"So you're saying that you might not sense a dark summoner just by the Flow?"

"That's what Fallon tells me."

Tris could tell from Soterius's expression that the other was calculating possibilities. "So is there any way to find out whether or not Cam's right before we've got trouble on the northern shore? Because I really, really don't want to take an army up against someone who's as powerful as you are, only on the other side."

Neither do I, Tris thought. "According to Fallon, we have a couple of options."

"I'm all ears."

Tris grinned. "Good, because I'm counting on your help. And the first person I need to go see is Alyzza."

Soterius stared at him. "The old hedge witch?"

"Actually, according to Fallon, Alyzza's had a hard time of it since she helped Carroway and Carina muster up a riot on the night we fought Jared. Fallon says Alyzza's come 'unstuck.' She's lost her bearings in time and place, and she sees visions and carries on conversations with thin air."

"I seem to recall someone else who can see visions and talk to thin air, but you're quite sane."

Tris rolled his eyes. "In my case, there's a ghost in that thin air. According to Fallon, no one's been able to confirm that Alyzza is really talking to anyone. She's up at Vistimar, in the citadel of the Sisterhood."

"I didn't think you and the Sisterhood were getting along so well these days."

Tris shrugged. "Landis didn't want her mages to take sides during the war. She thinks mages should be above that sort of thing. And she wasn't too happy about Fallon and the others going rogue and defying her. But...I *am* the king. And maybe more important for Landis, she still respects Grandmother's memory."

"Your grandmother earned that respect," Soterius replied. "I remember Bava K'aa. Even when we were children, although she was always kind to me, there was something about her that seemed too powerful to just be someone's grandmother."

Tris chuckled. Bava K'aa had been the most powerful summoner of her age. "She led the battle in the Mage Wars to defeat the Obsidian King the last time he rose, before Arontala tried to summon him. I only ever thought of her as a grandmother, but Fallon tells me that every king in the Winter Kingdoms recognized her power."

"Vistimar is a place of the damned, Tris," Soterius said quietly, returning to the subject. "The people in there are more than just insane; they're dangerous. I've heard stories that might even curl your hair, and I know you've looked into the Abyss itself."

"The old legends say that madness is a touch of the Goddess," Tris replied. "But Alyzza was one of Grandmother's inner circle. It was the war with the Obsidian King that drove her mad. She's the only one alive that I know of who actually went up against a real dark summoner."

"You're mage-heir to their power, aren't you? Bava K'aa and

181

Lemuel?" Soterius said quietly. A mage once known as Lemuel who had been possessed by an ancient, malevolent spirit, the spirit of the Obsidian King. But until the night Tris had won back the throne, he had not known that Lemuel was his grandfather, something Bava K'aa had managed to hide from nearly everyone. Defeating the Obsidian King a second time had freed Lemuel's spirit and had provided Tris with a frighteningly clear picture of just how dangerously wrong magic could go when misused. Tris vowed not to make the same mistakes. He, Kiara, Soterius, and Fallon were the only ones who knew the secret.

Tris nodded. "They were the two greatest summoners of their age. I've always wondered why, when there were times that had more than one summoner, I should be the only one now." He met Soterius's eyes. "Maybe I'm not."

That night, five cloaked men left the city without attracting notice. Their horses bore no livery. A cold rain was falling, and so no one wondered why their hoods covered their heads, obscuring their faces. If the bulges under their cloaks suggested that they were well armed, the guards at the gate did not think it their business to ask why. Tris, Soterius, and Mikhail rode to Vistimar, accompanied by two soldiers Soterius had personally chosen for the task.

In the shadows along the road, Tris could sense a dozen *vyrkin*, who provided silent reinforcements. He did not expect trouble on the road between Shekerishet and Vistimar, but Soterius and Mikhail had argued strenuously against riding with less protection, and Tris had reluctantly agreed. For most of the way, they rode in silence. The rain grew heavier, then lightened, but never stopped completely. It made the two-candlemark ride unpleasant, even though the autumn night was warm. Mud splashed as high as the horses' bellies, and Tris fidgeted as the rain made his cloak cling to his shoulders and arms.

Finally, they reached Vistimar's entrance. Tris lowered his hood and the startled gatekeeper dropped his keys twice in his hurry to unchain the madhouse's massive iron gates. The *vyrkin* took up positions around Vistimar's entrance. Tris and Soterius led the others into the compound, and the heavy gates clanked shut behind them. The chain rattled ominously as the gatekeeper secured the gates, and while Tris knew that a blast of his magic would be more than sufficient to free them if need be, uneasiness prickled at the back of his mind.

Tris stopped his horse a few paces inside the gates.

"What's the matter?" Soterius asked as his horse shuffled and pawed.

"There are wardings in place. Since this is a social call, I'd rather not blast through them."

"What do we do, ring the bell?"

"I think we've been noticed," Tris replied, inclining his head toward a brown-robed figure who was making its way toward them through the rain.

Tris swung down from his horse, and so did Soterius and Mikhail, though the others remained on their mounts. "The night's greetings to you, Sister," Tris said. He pushed back his hood again, so that his face was plain.

The Sister closed her eyes and raised her hands, palm out, and Tris knew she was sensing his power, confirming his identity. She opened her eyes and looked from Tris to the men who rode with him. "What brings the king to such a place on this miserable night?" Her voice was scratchy with age, but neutral.

"I've come to visit an old friend," Tris replied. "Alyzza."

"You've come at a bad time."

"Perhaps. Might we discuss this out of the rain?"

Grudgingly, the Sister raised her hands once more, and Tris felt the invisible wardings fall. She motioned for them to move forward, although the horses shied and tried to sidle away. When they had moved a dozen paces, Tris felt the wardings snap back into place. He touched the wardings with his power, and they flared. They were well set, and it would take a considerable amount of power to break them, Tris thought. While he did not doubt that he could muster the magic to do so, being encircled by shields that were not his own increased his wariness.

The Sister led them to Vistimar's entrance and motioned for them to tether their horses in a nearby copse of trees. By moonlight, Vistimar looked like the stuff of nightmares. It was an old building, and Tris guessed that it had once been a fortress for a local garrison. He stretched out his mage senses and realized that the stonework was much older than he had first suspected. Vistimar was older than the line of Margolan's kings, dating back to a time when warlords fought over wild lands that knew no sovereign. The thick stone of its walls had been chosen for defense, not for looks. It hunkered like a large, blocky beast against the night sky.

Tris stretched out his magic. Though they heard nothing but the sound of the rain, Tris could sense a restlessness inside Vistimar that had more to do with madness than it did the weather. Vistimar's residents were uneasy.

They followed the Sister up the wide, front steps to a heavy oaken door bound with iron strips and studded with hobnails. The Sister gestured, and Tris felt the brush of her magic. From the other side of the door, they could hear the clunk of iron bolts drawing back and mechanical locks releasing. Vistimar might once have been built to keep unwanted visitors out, but now its formidable defenses appeared to be arrayed to keep its unwilling residents in.

Two servants appeared to take the men's cloaks. If the Sister noted that beneath their plain cloaks Tris and the others were armed well enough for battle, she said nothing. She turned to Tris, and in the light of the entranceway candles, he had the first clear look at her features. She was in her middle years and looked to have some Isencroft blood. Her long hair had streaks of gray through it, and her skin had been roughened by the sun. But her dark eyes were clear and bright, and Tris could sense her magic swirling around her like a mantle of power. This was a mage he didn't know, although her brown robes marked her as one of the Sisterhood, a community of elite mages that Tris's grandmother, Bava K'aa, had once led.

"What brings you out to Vistimar on such a night, my king?"

"I need to see Alyzza. I assume you know which of your residents that is?"

Before the Sister could answer, the night air filled with cries. They came from far back in Vistimar's corridors, and they seemed to echo from every corner of the ancient stone building. Some sounded like screams of terror, while others, wails of pain. High-pitched keens sounded like nothing that came from a human throat. The two soldiers flinched at the noise. Tris saw that Mikhail was examining the entrance hall carefully, using his heightened senses.

"Alyzza has not been well," the Sister said. "Forgive me, I haven't introduced myself. I'm Sister Rosta."

"As you've noted, Sister Rosta, it's a bad night to be about. I have an important matter that requires me to talk with Alyzza."

"Of course, Your Majesty. But she's not as she was when you last saw her." Rosta's voice dropped, and Tris had to listen hard to hear her above the wailing. "Alyzza was once a very powerful sorceress, and a friend of your esteemed grandmother. But the battle against the Obsidian King broke her mind, and she was never quite...fully sane...after that."

"She had moments of clarity. I've seen her quite lucid," Tris countered.

Rosta nodded. "The madness came and went. The Sisterhood tried to heal her, and when her affliction did not respond to our efforts, we attempted to shelter her for her own safety, and that of others. Of late, the madness hasn't left her."

185

"Tell me what her madness is like."

Rosta looked away and pursed her lips, thinking. "Sister Landis thinks that Alyzza is reliving her youth and the Mage War. Terrors wake her in the night. She begs for salt to ward her room, and she drives herself to collapse warding her room over and over." Rosta shook her head. "She's in no danger here. These walls have withstood sieges for one thousand years, and we have spelled them stone by stone. Nothing can get in."

Tris nodded, although he was disinclined to take Rosta's word for the security of Vistimar's wardings. *No warding is perfect, and there's always something that has more power than you think it does.* "What else?"

Rosta frowned. "She's arranged all of her furniture to barricade the northern wall of her room. And we discovered that she's been stealing small objects and hiding them in her room— worthless things, but she's got a whole pile of odds and ends that she's carved with symbols and strewn around the room."

"What kind of symbols?"

Rosta met his eyes, and Tris knew that in this at least, she was telling the truth. "No one knows. We've called in our best rune scryers. We've consulted the old texts. They don't match anything we can find. Lately, she's taken to making blood charms."

Tris raised an eyebrow. "Where does she get the blood?"

Rosta's gaze was level. "It's her own. She cuts herself. It's a fearsome thing, m'lord. On the nights when the frenzy takes her, she dances until her clothes are soaked with sweat. She chants and sings, but no one can figure out what she's saying. We've tried to tie her to her bed—for her own safety, to stop the cutting—but she can still summon strong magic, and every time, she's ripped the shrouds from around her arms and left them in pieces."

Another scream echoed down Vistimar's halls. "Your residents don't sound happy tonight, Rosta," Tris said evenly.

Rosta sighed, and Tris could see exhaustion in the lines around her eyes. "You'll judge us harshly by tonight, m'lord. I can't blame you. It wasn't always so. Vistimar is haunted by the restless dead. That's true. There are wretched souls who have never left these walls, and some dark spirits that torment the vulnerable. But in the last few months, it seems as if all the poor souls here are troubled. Have you watched dogs before a storm, turning and fussing? Or horses, when a killing wind is coming? It's like that, as if they feel something on the night air or hear something on the breeze. All the Sisters have tried to use their magic to quiet them, but it's no use. Whatever it is, it's not for the sane to hear."

Tris looked around the room. Once, Vistimar might have been a wealthy warlord's prize, but now, evidence of decay was everywhere. The old castle had a dank, musty smell. Rosta was correct about restless spirits. Tris could sense them, and he knew that they felt his power and recognized it for what it was. Already, he could feel them gathering like moths to a flame.

Tris opened his mage sight. On the Plains of Spirit, Tris could see dozens of spirits. As his power focused, the spirits moved toward him, and he could see them in their human forms, with their death wounds. Some had been hanged and others stabbed. More than one had died from a fall. How many of the deaths were self-inflicted, Tris did not know at first sight, but given the uneasiness of the ghosts, he was quite sure that most had died by their own hand.

"Why do you trouble the living?" Tris added another surge of power, assuring that Rosta and the others could see the assemblage as he saw them.

"This is our home," an old man whose neck bore the mark of a noose spoke. The noose had been badly made, and it was clear that he had died by strangulation and not from the snap of his neck.

"Then stay in peace, and leave the living alone."

The strangled man's ghost made a deep bow. "You mistake me, m'lord. We seek to warn them."

"About what?"

The ghosts pressed closer around him. Tris felt their agitation. No, it was more than that. Fear. Few things retained the power to make the dead fearful. Most feared the coming of one of the Dark Aspects of the Sacred Lady. That was the most common reason Tris had found for spirits refusing to go to their rest. Others wanted to remain near loved ones, or just lingered out of a fascination with the everyday drama of life. A few were confused about whether or not they were truly dead. And more than a few were bound by the trauma of their deaths to a place or time. Those were the ghosts who appeared on the anniversary of their death or seemed doomed to reenact their final moments for eternity. And while Tris's powers as a summoner were strong, he had learned the hard way that it took an enormous expenditure of power to banish a ghost who did not want to go, and it was not within his power to release a ghost from its self-imposed reenactment until it had made its peace.

No matter the reason that these ghosts remained at Vistimar, tonight they shared something in common. They were terrified.

"What do the dead fear?"

The strangled man's bulging eyes fixed Tris with a steady gaze. "We fear the North Winds, m'lord. On them comes the Hollowing."

"Hollowing?"

The strangled man nodded, bobbing his blood-bruised face. "Darkness rides the North Winds, Hollowing soul from spirit like marrow from bone. We have heard the cries of the spirits who were extinguished, like the flame blown from a wick. We fear the judgment of the Lady, m'lord, but we fear the Hollowing more."

"If I add my protection to Vistimar's wardings, will you agree to leave the living in peace?"

The strangled man looked to the other spirits. Their faces held a terror Tris had rarely seen among the dead. "Your power is great, but it may not hold against the North Winds. Can you save us from the Hollowing?"

"Who brings the Hollowing? By whose power does it come?"

The strangled man considered the question. "We don't know. But we've felt it like a stain at the edge of the Plains of Spirit. Can't you sense it, Summoner?"

Tris stretched out his power beyond the gathering of spirits. Space and time on the Plains of Spirit did not correspond exactly to the mortal world. In the Nether, it was difficult for Tris to judge distance or place. But in the distance, Tris saw a darkness he had glimpsed before. More solid than a shadow, "stain" was the right word for it, and it sent a cold shiver through Tris. His power moved cautiously forward, but the darkness receded, rolling back like the tide and disappearing into the Nether. It left behind a residue, an unknown signature of magic, powerful and evil.

"I sense it," Tris replied. He began to weave a warding of his own, both in the Plains of Spirit and around Vistimar itself. If Rosta thought to interfere, she said nothing. Tris felt for the wardings the Sisters had placed around the madhouse and added his own signature of power, his own protections. In his mage sight, the new wardings shone like a coruscating barrier, gossamer thin, yet powerful.

The spirits felt Tris's magic and began to calm. What remained was their usual level of agitation, but not the fever pitch of frenzy.

"Thank you, m'lord," said the strangled man. "Our duty is complete. We have delivered our warning."

"I'm grateful for your warning," Tris replied, gathering his power to fully return to the realm of the living. "Will you be sentinels for me? For the living?"

The strangled man looked to the others and nodded. "Yes, m'lord. We will watch."

The spirits drifted away and Tris released his power, returning completely to himself. Rosta was watching him carefully, and in her eyes, Tris saw a mixture of admiration and caution. The two soldiers who had accompanied them looked pale but stood their ground. Soterius and Mikhail, who had seen Tris work powerful magic many times before, looked disquieted but not surprised. "Well?" Tris asked. "I made sure you could hear what the spirits had to say."

"It's certainly disturbing," Mikhail replied thoughtfully. "But consistent with some of the comments I've heard among the *vyrkin* and *vayash moru*. There's an edginess, a feeling that a storm is coming."

Rosta nodded. "It's been discussed among the Sisters, unofficially. Sister Landis will not speak of it. But the magic feels... wrong. And there is a feeling like when the wind changes before a squall that something unseen is coming."

Tris met Rosta's eyes. "Take me to Alyzza."

Rosta led Tris down a long, shadowed corridor. Mikhail and Soterius followed a few paces back, and behind them, the soldiers. Tris wasn't sure whether Soterius had insisted that they follow out of any real belief that they could be of help, or whether after the confrontation with the spirits, no one really wanted to remain behind.

Tris could sense that the level of agitation had dropped among the residents, but there was an odd discordance in the magic that he sensed around him, as if each of the residents was playing a different instrument at once, and all of them off-key.

"We have over seventy-five mages here, all hopelessly mad,"

Rosta said as they walked. "And if they are at Vistimar, they have some type of magic that makes them a threat without control of their powers."

"How many of your residents have come within the last year?" Tris asked. He had to increase his shielding to keep the magical noise from distracting him.

Rosta paused to think. "Interesting you should ask. Fifteen of our residents were committed to our care over the last year or so. That's more in a short span than we had seen in a while— since Jared the Usurper carried out his attacks against mages. Without a war, we often get only a handful of damaged mages each year, and most of them have just gradually declined from eccentric to unstable."

"Is there anything different about the new residents?" Tris pressed.

Rosta nodded. "They're more agitated than usual, and more self-destructive. We've had more suicides than usual." She looked abashed. "I know Your Majesty must be judging us harshly. Our resources are few, but we do try to do our best for the poor souls given to our care. No Sister is forced to come here to serve. We come of our own will, and we would protect our charges with our lives."

Tris nodded. "I didn't come to judge you. I can tell that what you say is true, and I commend you for your work. Is there anything else about the newcomers? Anything at all?"

Rosta frowned as she thought. "They were all once mages of power. I know Alyzza has passed herself off as a hedge witch for close to fifty years, but in her prime, during the Mage Wars, she was a fearsome sorceress."

"What broke her mind?"

Rosta drew a deep breath. "Have you ever heard musicians tune their instruments to a bell or chime?" When Tris nodded, she continued. "Those of us who work among the afflicted have a theory, although please don't speak of it to Landis. She doesn't like what she can't prove."

"You have my word."

Rosta dropped her voice. "You know how bells of different sizes produce different sounds? Well, we think—but we can't prove—that magic is like those bells. For some, the power is like a gong, while for others it might be like a delicate chime. I've heard it whispered that Alyzza's magic was 'attuned' to the power of the Obsidian King, and that the backlash from his destruction damaged her." She paused as if she were debating whether to say more. Finally, she gathered her courage. "We think that those who have gone mad in this recent group all heard the same pitch, for want of a better word. We think that's why they're still so addled. Their magic is resonating with something that literally frightened them out of their wits."

They stopped in front of a door. All of the rooms down the corridor had heavy wooden doors braced with iron. This door was solid iron. "We've had to put Alyzza in this room because it's the most secure in the whole fortress. The windows are warded so that nothing can enter or leave except light. Her furnishings are minimal, to keep her from hurting herself." Rosta motioned for Tris to come to one side of the door. She raised her hand and spoke a word of power. The stone wall became transparent. Inside, Tris could see a figure swaying and dancing, arms upraised.

"She's quiet at the moment," Rosta said. "But she dances or paces all day long. She barely sleeps. It's mania. I wanted you to prepare yourself."

Tris nodded. "I'm ready."

Rosta gestured for the others to stand back from the door. "I'd suggest that you raise your wardings. When you're ready, I'll drop the magic that binds the door long enough for you to enter. I have to raise the magic again when you're inside. I'll keep watch on you while you're with her. When you're ready to leave, come to the door, but make sure Alyzza keeps her distance." She paused. "M'lord, I realize that you think of Alyzza as a friend. But I beg of you, be wary. She's not as you last saw her."

Tris raised his wardings and waited. The magic that bound the door shifted, and the door opened for him of its own accord.

"Come in, come in. It's time, you know." Alyzza's gravelly voice was a sing-song chant. She had a threadbare shawl wrapped around her body and head, and her feet danced to music only she could hear. She did not turn.

From the back, Alyzza looked gaunt and frail. She had been stooped before, but now the hunch was more apparent. Where she had been well fed, now her skin hung like crêpe on her bones. "It's time, it's time," she sang, almost to herself. Swaying to the rhythm, Alyzza turned to face Tris. Her face looked as wizened as an old corpse, and her eyes were bright with madness. But in those eyes, Tris saw a glimmer of recognition, and something else. Fear.

"Ah, yes, you've come."

Tris slowly took a few steps into the room. "Do you recognize me, Alyzza? It's me, Tris Drayke."

It had been only two years since Tris had fled for his life from Jared's coup. Tris, Soterius, Carroway, and another friend, Harrtuck, had tried to elude Jared's guards by hiring on as tent riggers with Maynard Linton's caravan on their way to safety outside Margolan's borders. Alyzza, then a hedge witch traveling with the caravan, had been the first to recognize Tris's newly woken magic, powers Tris did not understand and could not control. Alyzza and Carina had been his first teachers as he struggled to keep his power from destroying him. And it had been Alyzza who one night had put a blade against his throat, determined that he should prove himself to her rather than let a new dark summoner rise again.

Alyzza hummed a tune and swayed towards him, looking like

an animated corpse. "The king, the king, all hail the king," she sang. "Let warriors tall and maidens all attend, all hail the king." The words were to a popular song, long a tavern favorite, but the melody had been replaced by a discordant sing-song that sent a chill down Tris's spine.

Tris met Alyzza's eyes. Fire and fear burned in equal measure, and with them, a canny intelligence. "What do you see, Alyzza? What frightens you?"

"Fie!" Alyzza's outburst startled Tris. "I will not speak ill of the damned, lest we meet, and soon." Words to a play this time, a drama that local bards often performed at festivals. A play popular among taverngoers for its lurid enactment of corpses drawn from their graves by a dark mage.

"Where would the damned meet, if not by moonlight?" Tris ventured, remembering a line from the play. Alyzza's eyes lit up with recognition, and a gap-toothed smile spread across her face.

"Walk not by moonlight, m'lord, or risk your soul. There be corpses in the copses, and *dimonns* by the wayside. On such a night, keep salt and iron at hand." Alyzza's voice had become conspiratorial, though her words were still those of the play. Tris glanced around Alyzza's sparse room. All along the walls lay a fine white powder of salt. Runes were scratched into the stone walls, darkened with what Tris guessed was blood, from the ruined fingernails and scabbed fingers of Alyzza's hands. A circle had been drawn on the stone floor in what appeared to be charcoal, and a braid of rags had been added to it as a charmed mat. At the quarters and cross-quarters lay bits of slag iron. Salt and iron—two of the most basic charms to ward off evil.

Tris racked his brain for memories of the tavern play. It had been a long time since he'd seen it. Carroway could probably recite the entire play from memory, but he was far away, healing his damaged hand in Dark Haven. Tris gambled on his memory

194

and remembered another line. "The Wild Host comes on the north wind. But 'tis souls, not stags, that come to the hunting horn. Hide yourself away."

Alyzza's face shone with recognition. Tris felt as if they were sharing an elaborate code. "Where will you hide, when Nameless sounds Her horn? Where will your soul take its refuge? Would there were a summoner to hide my soul away."

Tris drew a sharp breath. He had forgotten that line. The stories of Nameless, the eighth Aspect of the Sacred Lady, told of the Goddess in her guise as the Formless One riding the cold autumn winds through the countryside, harvesting souls. Tris had heard it said that many villagers would not be abroad by night in the weeks around the Feast of the Departed for fear of hearing Nameless's horn and being called to her hunting party of the damned.

"I'm that summoner, Alyzza," Tris said, meeting Alyzza's eyes. "I have the power to protect you. Tell me what you see."

"I see, I see, a far, far sea. The sea we all must cross. Gray and cold, dark and deep. Across that sea there comes a ship, a ship. A ship that comes for me."

Cam's note said that Alvior sailed away in a strange ship across the Northern Sea. Cam thinks Alvior's coming back across the sea with his dark mage. Alyzza may be mad, but she's mad as a dancing spider.

"You hear a bell I can't hear, Alyzza," Tris said evenly. "Let me listen with you. I won't hurt you. Let me listen *through* you."

Alyzza exhaled in a hiss. "I would not take that road, m'lad, though all the gold be mine. Not king, nor queen, nor beggar fool return from that dark lane." A song again, about a desperate man's date with Death.

"The bells, Alyzza. Let me hear the bells."

Reluctantly, Alyzza stretched out a gnarled hand. Despite her madness, she stopped just shy of Tris's wardings without touching them, giving him to know that she saw the magical protection and knew it for what it was.

Without dropping his wardings, Tris projected his magic across the shield to touch Alyzza's outstretched palm. Tris drew them both onto the Plains of Spirit, anchoring Alyzza with his power. Tris could sense the power that Alyzza's magic still commanded, although that power had become as gnarled as her bony hands. Tris extended his spirit, and as Alyzza dropped her own battered and ragged shielding, Tris let his power brush against her mind.

Immediately, he heard it. The sound was low and distant, like a rumble of thunder or the crash of a rock slide. But this sound was as much unlike those sounds as it was similar. Deep and vibrating, the sound waxed and waned. At its loudest, it crowded out thought, but at its softest, it hovered menacingly at the threshold of hearing, threatening to return. Carroway had once told Tris that there were certain chords that could produce madness if sounded incessantly. Tris had heard of torturers who used particular sounds to increase the pain of their victims. Until now, Tris had believed that the sounds of battle were the most damnable, along with the dying screams of men. But something in that distant rumble resonated with primal terror deep in Tris's mind. It supplanted reason and training, and all vestiges of modern civilization, a warning to the animal core at its most basic. Channeled through Alyzza, Tris heard the reverberating sound, felt it amplified through her terror and her tangled power. It was all he could do not to tear free and scream.

Alyzza suddenly launched herself at him. His shields held, but Alyzza reached as if to grip and hold his head close to hers, hanging on though the magic of his wardings burned.

"It comes," she shrieked, as if she were trying to shout over the low, damnable sound. "A key. A bridge. A voyager. It comes for these."

"Who? What key? Which bridge?"

But as abruptly as Alyzza had thrown herself toward him, she drew back. For an instant, her eyes were unclouded. "Protect the bridge, Tris. Protect the bridge."

Like a curtain, the madness descended once more. Alyzza's hands fell to her ragged skirt and she curtsied as she began to dance. "Oh, will you walk a space with me, a pace with me, or two or three. Oh, will you walk a pace with me for now, the sun is setting." It was a child's rhyme this time, and Alyzza's voice was reedy and high, like a deranged young girl. "Oh hush, my love and don't you fear, or shed a tear, or two or three. Oh hush, my love, and don't you fear, for I the fire am setting." Alyzza's voice grew by turns louder and softer, and she turned away from Tris as if she had forgotten he was there. He watched her for a moment, and then walked to the door, making sure that he did not turn his back on Alyzza. Until Rosta opened the door, Tris did not realize he had been holding his breath.

"You see, she is quite mad," Rosta said as she closed the door behind Tris, setting the wardings back in place.

"I felt it, Rosta. The resonance. You were right. There's something out there, something she's attuned to—and probably the others, too. Goddess help me, if I had that in my head all the time, I'd be as mad as she is."

The guards took up their places outside the door as Rosta gestured for Tris, Soterius, and Mikhail to follow her into a small parlor. Its furnishings were threadbare and hard used, but at the moment, Tris welcomed the chance to sit down. His encounter had left him shaken, and he wondered if it showed. As if Rosta guessed his thoughts, she went to a cabinet and withdrew a bottle of Cartelasian brandy, pouring Tris a generous portion and offering some to the others as well. Soterius accepted the drink. Even Mikhail looked uneasy.

Rosta and the others listened as Tris recounted his exchange with Alyzza. At the end, Tris looked to Rosta and Mikhail. "What do you make of it?"

Rosta thought for a while before she replied. "I don't know what the 'bells' are that you heard, unless it's the reverberation of immensely strong magic. Some mages are able to see halos of energy around people, and they say we each glow a different color and that our colors change or fade depending on many things. If some mages can 'glow,' perhaps others have a sound to their magic, although I've never heard of such a thing."

Mikhail nodded. "You may be immune to it as a summoner, but most mortals get an uneasy sensation near places where the undead dwell—both *vayash moru* and other immortals." He paused. "My point is, just the presence of the magic that sustains us seems to 'resonate'—to use your word—with mortals on a level that's often below thought. They don't know why they're uneasy; they just are. Something makes them avoid an area, for no apparent reason. It's stronger for some than others, and a few are either immune or are able to block it out. I'm thinking about Jonmarc Vahanian in the latter case, a mortal surrounded by undead all of the time."

"There are mages of minor power—hedge-witch-quality magic—who can sense the presence of spirits year-round, not just on Haunts, but they can't summon them," Tris mused. "I've spoken with several. Some of them are quite attuned to restless spirits, places where energies remain disturbed after a massacre, things like that. They also say it's a disquieting feeling, almost like a hum, that alerts them.

"We had a genius of a scientist who built our war machines at the Battle of Lochlanimar last winter," Tris said thoughtfully. "Wivvers. He makes all kinds of contraptions and tries to figure out how magic—and other things—work. Wivvers explained to us how particular noises, like the banging of drums or very shrill pipes, can make glass shatter or whole walls collapse. Perhaps that's something like the 'resonance' Alyzza hears, and maybe only some mages are attuned to it."

He sighed. "I had a first-hand experience with just how powerful the Flow really is when Carina and I healed one of the energy rivers. I saw it as light, but perhaps others 'hear' it."

"Well, if it drives mages mad, then we're fortunate you can't hear it," Soterius said. "And I'm the last one to speculate about how magic works, not having a speck of it in my bones. But the possibility remains that something is coming from across the sea—and it's not friendly." He looked at Tris. "You fought Foor Arontala and won. You defeated the Obsidian King's spirit. And I saw the magic you did at Lochlanimar—you're much stronger now than you were then. Do you doubt that you could fight whatever this is?"

Tris swirled his brandy and stared at the golden liquid. "Only a fool never doubts," he murmured. He looked up. "You know as well as I do that I very nearly died fighting the Obsidian King. And from what I remember—and the scars I have to prove it—I defeated Curane's mages and his Elemental by the skin of my teeth." He shrugged. "That's the thing about magic; you aren't always sure what you're up against until you're in the thick of it."

Rosta sat back in her chair and sipped the brandy she had poured for herself. "There's another problem. Landis still wants the Sisterhood to be apart from 'mundane concerns.' She's no different than when she denied you assistance for the war last year. She wouldn't be willing to provide any further training, and to be honest, I can't think of another mage alive today who can harness more power than you already can."

"Thanks, but that's rather disquieting in itself," Tris said with a grimace. "Because what I know about magic has been learned one battle at a time, the hard way."

Soterius smiled. "I happen to remember Jonmarc saying something like that about sword fighting, when he was trying to sharpen our skills back in the caravan. He said he'd learned everything he knew one battle at a time. He's right. Some things really can't be taught. If you survive the education, you get to keep the skill."

"Which might also account for the fact that there are so few very old mages of great power," Tris observed. "Trial and error has its peril."

"Alyzza is the last of the mages who played a key role in the Mage Wars fifty years ago," Rosta said. "But you might see what the Library at Westmarch has regarding that period."

Tris nodded. "I've already sent a messenger to Royster at Westmarch with a request that he come to Shekerishet and bring as much as he can carry regarding the Mage Wars." He leaned forward. "Which raises the next question: What do you know of the Dread?"

Rosta did not conceal a shiver. "Why do you ask?"

Tris told her about the messages he had received. Rosta's expression grew worried. "The Dread haven't walked abroad in a thousand years. Their power was greater than a mage like the Obsidian King, as was the power of the things they guard. If someone seeks to awaken what slumbers in the Abyss, then dark times are truly upon us."

"I know nothing but legends and tales told to frighten children out of the forest," Tris replied. "I need more than that. Especially if we do face a dark summoner, I need to know which side the Dread will choose."

"The Dread have always chosen their own side," Rosta said, and she made the sign of the Goddess in warding. "But there is a way you might find what you seek." She looked at Tris. "You're a summoner. Call to the bones of your fathers. Their spirits will speak to you."

"I've never called spirits that old. I don't even know where to find their tombs."

Rosta smiled. "Now *that* I can help with." She rose and gestured for Tris to follow her over to one of the large shelves of books that lined the parlor's walls. Rosta ran her hand along the spines of the books on one shelf until she found the leather-bound volume she wanted. The book was thick, with a heavy cover of handworked leather and gold leaf. Its pages were fragile and yellow with age. Rosta carried the heavy volume to a desk and opened it carefully, searching for the right page.

"Here," she said finally.

Tris looked at the page over Rosta's shoulder. At first glance, it was a long genealogy with a series of names of fathers and firstborn sons. "One thousand years ago, Margolan didn't exist as a kingdom," Rosta said. "It was wild territory, divided up among tribal chieftains and warlords. The old Cartelasian Empire never established a firm foothold in most of Margolan. They got as far as Eastern Margolan and were driven back." She glanced at Tris. "Some say the Dread had a hand in that.

"There's not much left from that long ago," Rosta said. "Even these genealogies were passed down by bards from memory for centuries before someone finally wrote them down. But the bards took great pride in remembering the genealogies perfectly, so much so that when there were legal disputes over inheritances or properties, a bard's word was law regarding family line."

Tris looked down the yellowed page at line after line of careful script. In many places, the ink was almost too faint to read. The centuries rolled back as he traced backward the family line. "Wait, that says Marlan the Gold. He was the first real king of Margolan," Tris said, eyes widening.

Rosta shrugged. "He's far enough back that 'king' is probably not quite as accurate as 'chieftain,' but you're right. Marlan the Gold is remembered for driving back the Cartelasian Empire and proclaiming that all the territory was Marlan the Gold's land, hence the name, Margolan."

"Are you certain there was no magic in his line?" Tris asked, peering closer at the list of names. "Look here. Hadenrul the Great. He was the king who defeated the last great uprising of the Shanthadura followers over three hundred years ago." He looked at Rosta. "Those are both impressive victories for men who you say had no magic."

Rosta nodded. "They weren't known as mages in the stories that have been passed down, but who knows? Sometimes, men and women who used powerful magic long ago were thought to be particularly blessed by the Goddess. There have been many times when it wasn't wise to admit to being a mage."

"Marlan the Gold and Hadenrul the Great were both in Father's lineage," Tris said.

"And so, your kin. Even if they weren't, as king you have the right to consult the ancient dead for their advice. Your claim on them is even stronger since their blood is yours."

"How do we know they haven't both gone to their rest with the Lady long ago? After all, Grandmother and Lemuel both asked me to make their passage for them. That's why I can't just ask their advice."

Rosta shrugged again. "You won't know until you call for them. According to this book, Marlan the Gold was buried beneath what is now the Shrine to the Mother and Childe. And while no one seems to know exactly what happened to all of Hadenrul's body, legend has it that one of his chief advisors—probably a mage himself—brought Hadenrul's skull, breastbone, and the bones of his right hand to the same shrine." She looked at Tris. "There were hundreds of years separating their deaths, yet a devoted follower carried part of Hadenrul's remains to lie in the same tomb as Marlan's. Why? I don't think it's any coincidence that those were the bones that were taken."

"Why?" Soterius asked.

To Tris's surprise, it was Mikhail who answered. "There are

old beliefs that say a man's essence is stronger in some parts of the body than others. The skull rules thought, the breastbone, heart. And the right hand, will. There is some truth to that. There is more than one reason those who seek to destroy *vayash moru* take the head and heart."

"What if whoever took Hadenrul's bones to the shrine did it so that his spirit would be available to future kings?" Soterius mused. He looked at Tris. "Didn't you say that King Argus's spirit stayed in the crypt beneath Westmarch to guard a sword?"

Tris nodded. "I had to fight him for it, and prove my magic worthy in battle before he yielded. And then he also went to the Lady, so that's one more person who fought the Obsidian King who can't be asked for help."

Rosta finished her brandy and laid her goblet aside. "The night is late, m'lord. Vistimar's hospitality is sparse but sincere, and while our suppers aren't what you're used to at the palace, we have an excellent cook whose portions are more than ample. You're welcome to stay the night, and in the morning, you can plan your journey to the Shrine to the Mother and Childe." She looked to Mikhail. "There are crypts beneath Vistimar where no light can reach. You won't be disturbed if you take your refuge here until next sunset."

Tris smiled. "Thank you. We'd be grateful for the hospitality." He glanced toward Soterius. "And I think that soon we'll make a little family visit to the Shrine."

12

This night, the Sworn rode to battle. Jair rode with them, ready to fight. To his right was the leader of the *trinnen*, Alin. Talwyn was to his left, armed for magic and for battle. Pevre led them, and the insignia worked into his leather armor made it clear that he was a chief and a warrior. With them rode more than twenty Sworn warriors. Emil and Mihei, the warriors who had been wounded with Jair on the journey from Dhasson, were with them, fully recuperated. Each of the warriors carried at least one *stelian*, and many, like Jair, had a variety of wicked-looking blades on baldrics across their chests, as well as a two-handed blade in a back sheath. Despite an array of weapons that would have been ample in pitched battle, tonight, Jair felt unarmed. He fingered the new amulet at his throat nervously. Talwyn had given each of the Sworn fighters a charm that she said would ward them against the Black Robes' magic. Although Jair had the utmost faith in Talwyn's power, he found it difficult to put his trust completely in a talisman to protect him. For that, he relied on his *stelian*.

A man stepped into the moonlit path ahead of them, and Pevre motioned for them to halt. The scout moved into the moonlight, letting them be certain of his identity, before venturing closer. He made a quick bow toward Pevre and Talwyn before turning toward Alin.

"It's as we thought. The Durim are massed near the barrow."

Alin nodded. "How many?"

"Equal numbers, perhaps more."

"Are there captives?"

"We counted two. A woman and a man. They had also brought a goat and a chicken."

A mirthless smile touched Alin's lips. "Sounds like they were worried about running out of blood."

They were still a distance from the barrow; half a candlemark on foot, Jair guessed, and less than that on horseback. Alin motioned to the soldiers behind them, and half of them slipped down from their horses to tether their mounts among the trees. Pevre was among them. Jair and Talwyn remained on their horses.

"Pevre will signal Talwyn when we're close," Alin said quietly. "Mihei will come with us. We may need his talents to help conceal our approach." The land mage inclined his head in acknowledgment. "With luck, we'll strike before the Black Robes can work any real magic or properly ward themselves." He made the sign of the Goddess in blessing. "May the Lady's favor ride with you."

With that hushed blessing, Alin and his fighters melted into the night. Though Jair had mastered much of the Sworn's lore, he still could not move as silently as the best of the warriors, despite years of practice. On the other hand, courtiers in Dhasson often noted his silent approach. But tonight, there was no room for error, and so Jair willingly stayed with those on horseback.

Jair had his *stelian* in hand, as did the rest of the riders, prepared to fight. Finally, a distracted look crossed Talwyn's face just an instant before she smiled with grim purpose.

"They're in place. Let's ride."

Talwyn and Mihei timed their magic so that a brilliant flare of light burst from both sides of the assault in unison. As the riders and the foot soldiers attacked, Jair could hear both mages chanting the counterspell to weaken or destroy the Black Robes' warding.

The woman captive screamed. Jair could see that the goat and the chicken had already been sacrificed. The man lay on an unlit pyre, unmoving. Their attack appeared to have interrupted several of the Black Robes who were digging into the side of the barrow.

The autumn night felt thick with power. Though Jair had no magic of his own, he knew the tingle of it against his skin. Talwyn and Mihei blocked a blast of the Black Robes' mage, and the sky lit in an arc of white light. But a prickle at the back of Jair's neck told him that more magic was in play.

"What was that?" Alin held his *stelian* in hand, watching the night around them. Jair had just the barest glimpse of movement, like a shadow among the trees.

A cry went up from the foot soldiers, who surged forward as Talwyn and Mihei forced down the Black Robes' warding. Alin ordered the horsemen forward, riding from the cover of the forest to attack the Durim's flank.

Magic crackled in the air as Talwyn and Mihei battled the Shanthadurists' wardings. If the Sworn had grown more alert to the barrows desecrators, then the black-robed Durim had obviously learned to anticipate an attack. A red-tinged dome of power encompassed the Durim's ritual area and the barrow. The warding was translucent; it looked as if a red haze hung in the air. Inside the dome, where the Durim's black-robed priests had begun digging into the side of the barrow, they had erected what looked like a wooden door frame around the hole. The lintels and cross piece were marked with bloody sigils, and a slaughtered goat hung by its legs so that blood dripped into the freshly turned soil. A dead chicken hung beside the goat, and around the base of the door frame were dark objects that looked from a distance to be severed body parts. A woman knelt beside the door frame, bound to the rough wood. She sobbed hoarsely, as if she were too terrified to scream.

The man lay still on the unlit pyre. Bundles of grain lay around the base of the pyre like offerings. Above the pyre, one of the Black Robes lifted a pitcher of what appeared to be oil and poured it over the man's body. Over the pyre was a scaffold with three large wheels made from dried cornstalks, one for each of the Shrouded Ones. The Durim priest lit the wheels and they began to spin, sending arcs of flame and sparks into the night air and lighting the oil to set the pyre aflame.

Talwyn and Mihei sent a blast of golden power simultaneously, and the red-tinged warding flared brightly, glowing blood red. The wheels of flame inside made the red warding pulse like a heart. Mihei beat a rhythm on a hand drum, and his chanting followed Talwyn's as they sent wave after wave of golden light against the warding.

Emil's band of soldiers was ready to attack the moment the wardings fell. Alin ordered the horsemen into position. Jair threw up his arm to shield his eyes as the light grew brighter and brighter. Inside the red dome, the female captive screamed in terror.

With a blinding flash, the red light flared and disappeared. The Durim's mage, one of the Black Robes, collapsed to the ground, and as Talwyn's power reached him, his robes began to smoke and then burst into flames. For a moment, the entire clearing was bathed in a golden light like sunset. Emil's foot soldiers let out a battle cry and began their run toward the Black Robes. There were a dozen of the Shanthadura priests in the clearing, as well as the dead mage. Three of them drew long, wickedly curved and serrated blades ready to meet the Sworn's challenge. The other two continued with their ritual, chanting in a language Jair did not recognize.

Jair kicked his horse into a gallop, riding into the fray. The Black Robes were vicious fighters, buying time to complete the ritual.

One of the Black Robes advanced on the captive woman, even as the night rang with the clash of swords and the pounding of hooves. He raised a large *damashqi* dagger overhead, ready to strike as the woman gave a terrified, piercing scream. Jair rode his horse straight for the man, leaping at the last moment over the sobbing woman to ride down the Durim priest. His *stelian* sang through the air, taking the Durim's head off, and it fell still covered by the man's black cowl.

A bolt of red lightning flashed from the hand of one of the Black Robes, catching one of the riders square in the chest and knocking him from his mount with a smoking hole in his ribs.

Talwyn and Mihei were in the front lines of the battle, and Jair realized that Mihei was working defensive magic while Talwyn turned her power against each of the Durim in turn.

Jair rallied the horsemen for another salvo. But before he could give the order to ride, shadows rushed toward them from the forest. Jair's eyes widened. *Dimonns?* he wondered, even as he readied his sword to strike. Whatever they were, if they passed the line of mounted soldiers, this new dark power would have a clear shot at Talwyn's back. Jair reined in his horse and readied himself to face a new enemy.

"Hold your positions!" Jair shouted as the dark shapes passed over them. Men swung at the shapes with their swords, but their blades passed through them with no apparent effect.

The horses changed footing restlessly. Jair was sure that their mounts could see whatever loomed in the trees. The autumn night was suddenly cold, and Jair fought a feeling of fear that urged him to flee. By the looks on the faces of his fellow soldiers, they felt it, too.

Screams rent the darkness. They came from the shapes in the

forest, and rose high and frenzied above the panicked shouts of the two captives. The screams were followed by a deep, rumbling laughter that was cold and menacing.

"Hold your place!" Alin shouted. "They're not *dimonns*. They're ghosts."

A hail of rocks came from the shadows that slipped among the trees. They struck men and horses with force, and bounced against Jair's shield hard enough to send a shock through his shield arm.

Behind him, Jair could hear the sounds of battle as the foot soldiers engaged the Black Robes. But as much as he wanted to take part in the fight, exposing their flank and their mages to the darkness from the forest seemed a bad idea, especially now that their disembodied attackers proved themselves able to draw blood.

In the moonlight, Jair saw shapes among the shadows. The oppressive sense that something awful was about to happen grew stronger, as did the primal urge to flee. The wailing from the shadowed shapes became louder. In a rush of cold wind, the shadows became blade-thin, rushing at them from the forest to streak among them and *through* them.

Jair cried out as a dead coldness passed through his body, making his heart seize as if it would stop altogether. For an instant, Jair could not breathe and his terror was complete. Then the coldness vanished, but not before Jair's horse reared in utter panic, nearly bucking Jair from his saddle.

The dark shapes circled them, and the soldiers positioned themselves in a line, facing outward, creating a barrier between the forest and the battle. The shapes grew more solid, stalking them now from the shadows. Whatever the shapes were now, they had the form of men, though their eyes burned like fire. Some had features, and others were like a starless night cut in the shape of a man. The shapes stretched and contorted as if to prove that they were not bound by the constraints on living men. One of the shadow shapes stretched out its arm toward Jair, and the clawed hand moved toward him, though the arm grew impossibly long. The entire shape slowly elongated, growing gaunt and huge, menacing in its reach.

By the cries of the men around him, Jair knew he was not the only one to be terrified by the apparitions. He struggled to keep control of his frightened horse. Maneuvering as best he could to evade the outstretched hand, Jair was mindful not to expose his back.

The shadows seemed to grow thicker and more solid. This time, the shapes that passed among them felt cold and firm. One of the warriors screamed as he was abruptly pulled from his saddle and flung to the ground. Alin, sword already swinging, charged toward the shadows. Solid as they had seemed as they passed him, his blade made no contact, though it disappeared into blackness. Unseen hands shoved Alin backward. Jair charged forward on horseback, only to have his horse rear, eyes wide with panic. Shadows swarmed over the soldier on the ground, and it looked to Jair as if they slipped into his mouth and nose, slipped underneath his skin. The downed soldier gave a terrified shriek.

Darkness poured like blood from the soldier's eyes, ears, mouth, and nose, and when the darkness cleared, the man lay unmoving on the ground.

Alin had regained his feet and was advancing slowly, *stelian* upraised. "What the hell are we fighting?"

Before Jair could answer, more of the shrieking shapes swooped from the forest. There was nowhere to run, and Jair had no intention of abandoning their line and opening their companions to a second enemy. Anger filled him, and Jair shouted a battle cry with all his might. He ran at the blackness, leaping over the body of his fallen comrade, and he realized something as he hit the ground.

The dead soldier was not wearing Talwyn's charm.

Shapes rushed him, and utter coldness filled his body as the darkness slipped beneath his skin. Cold hands touched him, grabbing at his arms and legs. It was hard to breathe. His lungs felt as if he had gulped frozen air, and there was a weight on his chest. Jair staggered and fell to his knees. Spirits slipped against and through his skin like hundreds of blades. Jair reached beneath his tunic and touched the talisman as the darkness closed around him. The talisman flared with a blue light. As the glow grew brighter, the darkness drew back, rushing away from him. He gasped for breath, clutching the amulet, which was now almost too bright to see.

"Use your amulet!" Jair shouted.

Suddenly, the glade was filled with light. Blue-white light streamed from the amulets of the soldiers, which they held out in front of them to drive back the darkness. Jair realized all of the men were now on foot. They closed ranks, shoulder to shoulder, holding the amulets out in front of them. One step at a time, in unison, they advanced on the darkness, forcing it back into the forest.

"We can hold them back, but for how long?" Alin shouted. "It's a standoff."

Just then, a golden glow like sudden dawn flared between them and the shadows. A clear, bell-like chime seemed to sound from everywhere and nowhere. Screams rose from the darkness, but where the shadows had shrieked before to terrify their victims, now the cries that came from the darkness sounded of pain and terror.

The shadows fled into the tree line. Alin, Jair, and the others did not take their eyes from the edge of the forest until they were certain the shadows were gone. Only then did Jair turn to see Talwyn behind them, her arms upraised, face turned toward the sky, lips moving in a chant. Another blast of the golden glow streamed along the floor of the forest, beneath the lowest branches. It illuminated the forest floor like daylight, showing it to be clear of threat.

Talwyn lowered her arms and fell silent. Jair wondered if the others could see how much it drained Talwyn to work her magic. He could see the strain in her eyes, though he said nothing.

"Thank you," Alin said, and his voice was not entirely steady. "What were those things?"

Talwyn's lips pressed together in a thin line. "The restless dead. The blood magic of the Black Robes calls many things to its power. Restless and malicious spirits are hungry for warmth. And while they don't have the power of *dimonns*, you see that they're dangerous, nonetheless."

"Gather the wounded," Alin ordered. Out of the soldiers who had ridden with them, three had been injured during the encounter with the spirits. Several needed to bind up gashes before they would be ready to ride, and the healers came forward to tend them. More than one man cast wary glances toward the forest, expecting the spirits to return, as the healers bent to their work.

"You did well to hold the spirits here," Talwyn said. "The Black Robes put up quite a fight. Their mage was more powerful than I expected, and it kept Mihei and me busy, so it's good that we didn't have the malicious dead to worry about as well." She looked back toward the barrows.

"We took some casualties until we were able to strike down their mage. No one's dead, but our healers will be busy for a while."

"And the Black Robes?" Jair asked.

Talwyn sighed. "One died in the battle. That was their mage. Seven died fighting. We took the other four for judgment. They had already killed the man they took prisoner. The woman will need a mind healer. And from the preparations they'd made for the ritual, they'd obviously killed some other people. We had more body parts than bodies," she said with a grimace.

"You're certain they're Durim? Were they trying to open the barrow?" Alin pressed.

Talwyn looked tired, and Jair could hear the fatigue in her voice. "Yes, they're definitely Durim. We collected enough of their trappings to tell that they're part of the cult of Shanthadura. And from everything we found, we're betting they thought their power was stronger now because it's the eve of the Moon Feast."

They were walking within the area that had been inside the red dome. Jair could see scorch marks on the ground where the powers had clashed. The pyre still burned, and the air was heavy with the stench of burning flesh. The three cornstalk wheels had burned to cinders. Jair's boot kicked something, and he looked down, bending for a better view. A human figure made from corn husks lay near his boot, and as Jair looked around the area, he saw others like it. Some were painted with symbols, while others had been dyed in colors. Many of the figures had been maimed, missing limbs or heads, or pierced through with nails. The wind shifted, carrying away the noxious odor of the pyre, and Jair caught the strong smell of camphor, rosemary, and thyme.

"Talwyn, have a look." Jair motioned for her to see. Talwyn knelt next to the pile of figures Jair had made.

She let her hands hover above the poppets for a moment, and Jair knew she was sensing for magic. Then she opened her eyes and began to gingerly handle the figures, turning them and frowning as she looked at the symbols.

"This gives me a whole new perspective on those spirits you fought," Talwyn said, sitting back on her haunches. "We assumed the Durim called them to attack you. But I don't think that's what happened. This is going to sound really strange, but I think you actually saved those spirits."

Jair looked at her in utter confusion. "How do you figure that?"

Talwyn held up the corn husk figure in her hand. It was a reddish brown, and Jair bet the coloring came from blood. The figure had been struck through with a wooden nail. "The Durim weren't content with the people and animals they killed. They were trying to raise real power here, and they wanted more sacrifices. These dolls are symbolic sacrifices. That's why they've been 'killed' in effigy." She looked around the battlefield in horror. "By the Dark Lady! It's true what the old stories say about Shanthadura's followers. Their appetite for blood is never sated."

"Where did the spirits come in?"

Talwyn looked toward the now-quiet forest. "They would have become sacrifices, too. It's the Moon Feast tomorrow. We celebrate the harvest from the crops in the fields. But there are old stories about another harvest that used to be held, long ago, before the ways of the Sacred Lady came to these lands." She looked to Jair and met his eyes. "They called it the 'soul harvest.'"

"What's a 'soul harvest'?"

Talwyn's eyes took on a faraway look. "The stories say that the Shanthadura priests—the Black Robes—would cull the herds, taking out the sick, the old, and the lame. Those animals would be eaten, or offered as sacrifices. But they would do the same among the people, reducing the number of mouths to be fed over the winter. Those people became sacrifices, too. There would be bonfires, and sometimes, a huge effigy of Shanthadura, made of cornstalks and branches, and in its belly, some of the people would be burned alive." She swallowed, then went on. "The Black Robes used that blood magic to bind the spirits of the dead. They called it a 'soul harvest.' They drew on the power of the souls to feed their own power, destroying the souls and robbing them of their rest. The weak souls they destroyed, but the stronger souls escaped them. Those they caught and couldn't destroy they 'hollowed.' They left them like disembodied *ashtenerath*, wandering, mindless, out of control. They became like minor *dimonns*, tortured things that preyed on the living." She shivered, and Jair put his arm around her shoulders.

"So those spirits we fought were actually being called to their destruction? The Black Robes would have hollowed them?"

Talwyn nodded. "That's my guess."

Jair looked around the battlefield. Emil and Alin's men had carried away the Sworn's wounded and had stacked the bodies of the dead Shanthadura priests in a row. The survivors were bound and hobbled and thrown over their horses. Talwyn looked up sharply.

"Don't burn the Black Robes or the corn figures!" Talwyn rose and strode over to where Alin froze, midmotion, just about to throw the body he had hefted onto the pyre.

"But *Cheira* Talwyn—"

Talwyn shook her head. "The pyre's been spelled. If we add bodies, we feed the sacrifice. Send two men to bring lye from the soap maker. Go to the village if you must. These were blood mages, so we'd best also assure that they don't rise with the new moon."

"M'lady, they're dead."

Talwyn met Alin's eyes. "Some blood mages have the ability to bind or project their souls so that something of them exists, even after death. It's not a full summoner's power, thank the Lady, but I don't want to meet these particular Black Robes again."

"What do you want us to do, *Cheira* Talwyn?"

"Remove the head, breastbone, and right hand. Cover those with lye and let the lye eat them," Talwyn directed. "What remains of the bodies, we'll use to placate the spirits of the barrow. If anything remains of the Black Robes after that, I'll leave it to the Dread to deal with them."

"What about the captives?" Jair asked with a nod toward the sullen Durim priests who were bound and kneeling.

Talwyn's eyes grew cold. "We will take them for judgment before the Consort Spirits. They chose this night because the spirit world is closer. They're about to find out just how close it is."

Only a few candlemarks remained before dawn by the time the Sworn warriors returned to camp. Talwyn, Pevre, and Jair knew the night's work was still not over. Jair oversaw hurried preparation to bring the four captive Durim priests to judgment as Talwyn and Pevre readied for the working.

Though the bells of a distant village sounded the third candlemark of the morning, all but the children of the Sworn filed silently into the common tent. A fire burned in the center, and incense smelled of sandalwood and juniper. At the four quarters of the compass, gemstones hung from the roof supports, flickering in the firelight with the colors of orange chalcedony, jade-blue aventurine, green peridot, and yellow citrine, one for each of the Light Aspects of the Sacred Lady. At the cross quarters hung bloodstone, garnet, iron, and salt—tribute and wardings for the Dark Aspects.

Tonight, it would not be the Aspects that judged the Black Robes. For a high working such as this, the Sworn relied on the four Consort Spirits. A drum beat a solemn rhythm as the people of the Sworn assembled. Jair, Emil, Alin, and one of the other *trinnen* warriors escorted the captives into the gathering space and forced them to kneel in a line facing the center fire. The four warriors were clad in black, with cloth head wraps of black fabric that covered all but their eyes. Their large *stelian* blades glimmered silver in the firelight. They were present to keep the peace, but they would not be the agents of the Consorts' judgment this night.

When the prisoners were in position, the drum began a different rhythm. The crowd stirred for a first look at the figures entering the round tent. Four beings with the bodies of humans and head-dresses like the heads of animals entered silently. Their robes were the colors of the Moon Feast, red, gold, yellow, and orange, honoring both the moon and the harvest. One figure wore the head of a bear. Another wore the head of a stawar, the great dark-furred cat that roamed the Eastmark wilds. The third wore the face of a wolf with glistening black eyes. And the fourth looked like an eagle with a sharp, hooked bill. Talwyn, Pevre, Mihei, and Estan, a senior healer, wore the costumes but something about their manner made Jair wonder how much of each Consort's powers the ritual participants took on.

Incense hung heavy in the air, and the firelight danced from the warding stones to cast a shifting pattern of light on the walls. Jair fought the shiver that coursed down his back as the murals painted on the canvas walls seemed to move.

The four prisoners each wore a silver charm that kept them from wielding their magic. Their black robes had been confiscated, leaving only men in loincloths who looked ordinary and defeated. Outnumbered, bound, and stripped of their power, they awaited the judgments of the Consorts with sullen glares.

The eagle figure stepped forward. Jair knew it to be Talwyn, but the figure spoke in a voice unlike hers, shrill, like the cry of a raptor. "Black Robes, Durim, priests of the Shrouded Ones, of Shanthadura, you have brought blood magic among us. You desecrated the barrows of the Ancients, and you committed human sacrifice, in fact and effigy. What do you say for yourself, here in the Judgment, that we might hear your plea?"

The four prisoners remained silent, glaring up at their judges defiantly.

"If you will not speak, then we will let your spirits speak for you," the Bear Consort rumbled. The figure raised its arms, with palms out and fingers spread. The air seemed to resonate with magic. One of the helpers poured a mixture of herbs into the fire that stretched between the Consort judges and the accused, creating a cloud of smoke that smelled of spice and pine. Four shapes appeared in the smoke, and the crowd murmured as it became plain that the shapes were those of the prisoners' smoke walkers.

It was the Stawar Aspect who spoke next, its voice a low growl. "For whom did you sacrifice?"

The smoke images of the prisoners lacked the defiance of their counterparts. "We serve Shanthadura."

"And for what reason did you violate the barrow?"

"We must awaken the Ancient Dead."

"Why do you seek this?"

"He Who Calls Us ordered it. We are to make ready. His legions will sweep across the land, bathing it in blood and awakening the old ways. Everything will be swept away, and from that chaos, Shanthadura will rise once more, making new."

"Who is this who calls you?"

"He is called many names. We know him as Cataclysm, and he is the right hand of Shanthadura."

"Did you call the Restless Dead?"

"We called them for the soul harvest. We must feed the Ancients."

"And did you call the *dimonns*? What of them?"

"They have been bound inside the barrows for centuries. They hunger. Shanthadura welcomes their blood offerings. We fear nothing from them."

"Have you attacked *vyrkin* and *vayash moru*?"

"Their blood is a potent sacrifice, filled with the Wild Song and the Dark Gift. Our mistress covets their blood."

The four Consorts turned toward each other, and though they said nothing, it looked to Jair as if they conferred. Finally, the Eagle being turned back toward the assemblage.

"You have murdered the living and desecrated the places of the sacred dead. You have made sacrifices of the *vyrkin* and the *vayash moru*, who are favored by the Dark Lady. And you have hollowed the souls of the Restless Dead, which is an abomination. For your crimes, you must be destroyed."

The smoke walking spirits showed their disdain. "We welcome death. Our deaths feed Shanthadura. We have no fear of it."

"Your judgment is up to the Consorts," the Eagle Consort replied.

The drums began to beat faster, and the smoke was heavy with power. The figures of the four Consort Spirits seemed to waver. Three men and a woman wore the costumes of the Aspects, but the smoke figures that emerged were of the animal Aspects. From Pevre's costumed form came the smoke walker of a great bear. An eagle flew free from Talwyn's form, as if it launched from atop her shoulder. They were joined by the powerfully muscled figure of a stawar, with its large paws and sleek head, and the figure of a huge gray wolf. The smoke walkers of the prisoners disappeared, and for the first time, Jair saw fear in the captives' faces. One of the prisoners tried to rise to his feet to flee, but a guard gave him a shove that forced him back to his knees.

In unison, the four figures raised their heads. The stawar was first to strike. With a growl, the large cat sprang at one of the prisoners, passing completely through the man's body to emerge with a very real heart clenched between its jaws. With a look of astonishment, the Durim priest swayed and fell backward.

The bear lumbered toward its prisoner, rearing to rake its huge smoke claws down the man's chest. Deep gashes tore across the prisoner's body, deep enough that his organs spilled from his belly. The wolf passed through the fire as if the flames were not there, launching itself toward its prisoner and clamping its strong jaws around the man's neck, tearing through his throat and bone. The last Consort was a huge eagle. Its wingspan was as wide as the bodies of the four prisoners. With a shrill cry, the eagle brought one taloned foot down on the skull of the last doomed man, and with one sharp movement, clenched its claws so that they penetrated bone, crushing the head within its grasp.

The smoke wavered, and the spirit walkers of the Consorts dissipated, leaving behind only smoke and the mauled bodies of the condemned men.

Through it all, the drumbeats had never faltered. Now, indifferent to the stirring of the crowd, the four Consort figures turned and filed from the tent, followed by Jair and the other guardians. By the time Jair reached the outside, Talwyn and the others had vanished.

"I've seen that done only once before," Alin said quietly as he walked beside Jair back to the tent that was the headquarters of the *trinnen* and the barracks for those among the elite warriors who were not married. "I don't know how Talwyn and Pevre and the others do that, and I don't think I want to know."

As often as he'd seen Talwyn work her shaman's gift, Jair found it both wondrous and unsettling. He tried not to think too hard about the fact that the woman he held in his arms at night was also able to be the direct channel of the spirits of the Consorts and the Lady's Aspects. How the power worked, he didn't know, and he doubted Talwyn could explain it to him. From what he gathered, even among those with a shaman's gift, training was more by example than it was something that could be reduced to words.

"I'm happy to stick to my swords," Jair replied. "Swords are simple." But he knew as he said it that it wasn't completely true. Swords were indeed simple, but wars never were. And if the boasts of the Black Robes were correct, then war was coming, and it would be anything but simple.

* * *

The morning of the Moon Feast dawned clear and bright. And although Jair knew that Talwyn and Pevre had to be exhausted from the battle and from the working of the previous night, they were ready for the festival to begin when the sun was high in the sky.

"How do they celebrate in Valiquet?" Talwyn teased as they watched Kenver compete with the other boys at bolas throwing.

"The way they celebrate everything—with a feast and chamber music," Jair said, feigning an exaggerated yawn.

"Perhaps when you become king, you can liven it up for them," Talwyn replied.

Despite how tired he was from the events of the night before, Jair laughed. "I can just picture Lord Scovitt and Lord Janev competing at goat herding."

"Oh, but surely the palace bakes a meal to rival ours." Talwyn's grin showed how much she enjoyed needling Jair about the other half of his life. "After all, how can roasted goat compare to the delicacies they must cook for you every feast night?"

Jair took in a deep breath. The smell of roasting goat mingled with the scent of cooked leeks and onions. A groaning board of the first fruits and vegetables of the harvest would be served tonight around huge bonfires that would light the night, offered to the living, the guardian spirits of the ancestors, the Dread in the barrows, and to the Lady and her Consorts. Mead would flow freely, and the afternoon belonged to the young men in games of skill. The night was for the bards and storytellers, who would recount legends of long-ago warriors and great chieftains, and tell of the magic and victories of revered shamans. It would be a day and night of feasting, with handfastings encouraged to begin a new cycle of birth in the spring. Jair felt more at home here, among the Sworn, than he ever felt amid Valiquet's opulence.

"Actually, the palace cook makes a passably fair roasted

goat," Jair replied, pulling himself from his thoughts. "Although venison is more favored at court. Most of the nobility prefers wine to mead, and the spices take more after the western fashion—bland, compared to what we use here."

Talwyn took his arm. She and Pevre had completed their official morning duties to begin the festival, and when darkness fell, she and Pevre would usher in the night in the traditional way, by setting a large, tarred wagon wheel aflame and rolling it down a path on the highest hill in recognition of the setting sun and the coming shorter days of winter. "Do you think Kenver will win with his bolas?"

Jair chuckled. "He's got good aim for his age. Give him time. From the dents he's put in the hitching post, I'd say he's been practicing."

Talwyn laughed, and her long dark hair fell around her face, framing it and making her amber eyes gleam. The festival robes she wore indicated her rank as *cheira* and shaman, but without the formality of her ceremonial regalia. And when she laughed, Jair saw a rare glimpse of the beautiful young woman unburdened from her position and responsibilities.

"This is my favorite time of year," Talwyn said, resting her head against Jair's shoulder. "First of all, you're on the Ride with us. But I love the autumn weather and the harvest foods. I don't even mind the winter if the harvest has been good. And I'll admit that as much as I enjoy Winterstide, the Moon Feast and the Feast of the Departed are two of my favorite festivals."

A question crossed Jair's mind, something he had wondered from the events of the night before, but he pushed it away, unwilling to spoil the mood. Talwyn noticed the shift and gave him a questioning look.

"What is it?"

Jair frowned. "Just something I heard last night. We didn't really get a chance to talk after the tribunal."

Talwyn's mood sobered. "Sorry about that. There are rituals to follow after a working like that to ground yourself back in this realm, and offerings to be made. By the time I came back to the tent, you and Kenver were both fast asleep."

Jair leaned over to kiss the top of her head. "It's not that—I know you have obligations. But when one of the Black Robes was rambling, he talked about a war and chaos. Did that make any sense to you?"

Talwyn sighed and withdrew her arm, walking a few steps ahead. "Unfortunately, it does."

"That doesn't sound good."

Talwyn looked out across the camp. Children's laughter echoed with the sound of singing and the thunder of hoofbeats as young men raced their horses in the distance. "There are legends about how the world was made, very ancient stories. According to the legends, the world has been made and unmade several times. The Dark Aspect of the Formless One is chaos, where worlds are torn apart and new worlds are born. She's neither good nor evil—she just *is*. But Shanthadura and the Shrouded Ones embraced the chaos. They revered the power to destroy, but not to create. That was one of the main reasons why some of the kings like Hadenrul the Great worked so hard to supplant the cult of Shanthadura with worship of the Sacred Lady. You can just imagine what it would be like with the Black Robes running around with the power to do real damage."

"Where does the war come in?"

Talwyn walked slowly, and she held out her hand to Jair. "The old stories talk about the World Cycle that moves much like the year. Everything is new in the spring, it blossoms in the summer, it bears fruit in autumn, and it lies barren and dead in winter, only to begin again. The stories say the World Cycle begins and ends in a great war, the War of Unmaking. That's what the Black Robe was talking about. To the blood mages and the dark summoners and the worshippers of Shanthadura who draw their power from death, it's the ultimate source of energy, the destruction of everything. For those who worship the Lady and her Consorts, the focus is on rebirth and the power of creation." She met Jair's eyes. "As you can see, it's another point of contention between the two sides."

"Do you believe him? That there's a dark master out there who is going to usher in the War of Unmaking?"

Talwyn shrugged. "The sages warn us against trying to predict such things. Worrying about the War of Unmaking is a lot like fearing your own death. It comes whether you fear it or not, but you miss out on all the living up to that point."

"But could it be true this time? So many things are happening. The Durim and the Black Robes bringing back the cult of Shanthadura after hundreds of years. The desecration of the barrows. And now this power that's rising. Could it be true?"

Talwyn shivered, although the day was warm. "I don't know, Jair. I don't know. Those are exactly the things that the old stories say happened before the last War of Unmaking. And does it change anything? Do we sit by and let this dark power— whatever it is—rise? Maybe it's not the War of Unmaking. Maybe it's just one more man with too much power. Maybe the War of Unmaking is just a legend, a story that's been made of old wars all added together and given a good dramatic twist by some long-ago bard." She met Jair's eyes. "It doesn't really matter. If the Black Robes are right and there's a darkness rising, then I have to fight. The Sworn will defend, so long as we have breath."

Jair took her hand in both of his. "Where you ride, I ride. That's why I asked. Because I think war is coming, and when it comes, I plan to fight."

13

"Make them stop stealing our dead!"

The red-faced man leaned across the table, and his body trembled with his shout.

On the other side of the table, Lord Jonmarc Vahanian passed a hand across his eyes. There were many duties that came with the title and land holdings that Jonmarc enjoyed. Holding court was not one of them. "Sit down before I put you down," Jonmarc growled. The red-faced man looked startled, but he pulled back and took his chair.

"Now, let's start at the beginning," Jonmarc said tiredly. As lord of the manor, he was the final arbiter of disputes, petty and otherwise. While the Blood Council dealt with disagreements between *vayash moru*, and the *vyrkin* handled their problems among themselves, dealings between mortals or between a mortal and either a *vayash moru* or a *vyrkin* fell to the lord of the manor to arbitrate. The irony of the once-brigand Lord of Dark Haven now handing down judgment was not lost on Jonmarc. "Why do you think your dead are missing and what makes you think anyone took them?"

"They bloody well didn't walk off all by themselves," the man retorted.

Jonmarc fixed him with a glance. "Want to rephrase that?

Dark Haven has more dead men walking than anywhere else I've ever been."

The florid-faced man glanced at Gabriel, who stood behind Jonmarc, and reined in his temper. "These dead aren't biters."

"And you're certain of that how?"

The man sighed. By his clothes and his manner, Jonmarc guessed him to be a farmer. Beside him sat another man, likely a tinker or tradesman, Jonmarc thought. Probably a newcomer to the area, and thus automatically under suspicion. The yellow-haired tinker looked bewildered and indignant. Things like walking dead were out of the men's experience, and some days, Jonmarc wished they were out of his, as well. But a year spent with Tris Drayke and another year as Lord of Dark Haven had altered a good many of his theories about life, death, and after-life. "Because our dead stayed dead, until he came," the farmer said, with a glare toward the tinker.

Jonmarc glanced at Sakwi, who had agreed to attend the tribunal should any need for magic arise. "Can you tell if he's a blood mage or a summoner?" Jonmarc asked Sakwi.

Sakwi moved closer to the tinker, who drew back in his chair fearfully. Though Sakwi's specialty was land magic, Jonmarc had learned enough about mages from recent experience to know that, regardless of their expertise, they could sense another's magic. Sakwi held out his hands, palms out, and closed his deep-set, brown eyes, losing himself in thought for a moment. Then he opened his eyes and shook his head. "No. No magic at all, in fact. Just a charm around his neck that isn't worth its tin."

The tinker relaxed, but only for a moment. The farmer was again on his feet. "I don't care what your hocus says. Someone is stealing our dead!"

"You've said that twice now, without explaining it," Jonmarc said, with a dangerous undercurrent in his voice that was not lost on the farmer, who remembered himself and sat back down. "If someone's robbing tombs, then we need to look for a thief. Do you bury your dead with gold or jewelry?" The question was logical, but the hard-scrabble look of the farmer made Jonmarc doubt that the man or his neighbors had a gold coin among them, let alone treasures to waste on the dead.

"You're not hearing me," the farmer said, straining for control. "No one's stealing the pots and charms we buried with the bodies. They're still in the graves. It's the bodies that are gone. Someone's torn up our burial grounds."

"Is it just the newly dead who've gone missing?"

The farmer shook his head. "They're gone, but they're not the only ones. We have a crypt that the whole village uses. It's dug into the caves. We've used it for generations. My sister's husband was killed last week when his horse bolted. Broke his neck. We washed the body, and the women prepared it with herbs and honey, as we do all our dead. When we'd mourned him, we wrapped him in a shroud and carried him into the tomb. But when his widow went back two days later to bring a soul offering, the crypt had been opened. His body was gone—windings and all—and so were the other bodies in the newest chamber." He swallowed hard. "You can excuse my sister for not taking a complete count when she realized what had happened."

"So you don't know how many bodies are gone?"

The farmer shook his head. "No. But three weeks before my sister's husband died, an old woman in the village died of the cough. And then last month, one of the Rimmin boys drowned in the creek. Their bodies should have been in the crypt—but they weren't, and neither were the bodies from the three we lost to consumption over the summer."

Jonmarc exchanged puzzled glances with Gabriel. "Do your people know anything about this?"

Gabriel shook his head. "I can assure you no one of my brood has made any new fledglings. I'd be willing to wager that Riqua's family hasn't, either. I can't say for certain about the other *vayash moru* broods, but what the man described doesn't sound right for a *vayash moru* rising."

"Could the bodies have been taken by animals?" Jonmarc asked. "The herbs and honey used to preserve them might smell like food."

The farmer looked appalled. "We're not stupid, m'lord. The crypt seals tightly."

Jonmarc felt a headache beginning to grow. "I didn't mean to imply that you were stupid," he said carefully, "but people forget things in their grief. Is it possible that someone forgot to close the crypt?"

The farmer shook his head. "We were all there when the body was laid to rest. We helped to seal the door. It was closed."

"How difficult is it to open the door?"

"I'm not a small man, m'lord, and I can't open it by myself. It was made heavy enough to require two men, to stop tomb robbers and vandals." He paused. "There is one other thing, m'lord. The dead weren't carried off. They walked."

Jonmarc had been slumped in his chair. Now he sat up and leaned forward. "Walked?"

The farmer nodded, wide-eyed. "My eldest son saw it. Ran home babbling about wights, but at the time, we just thought a trick of the moonlight spooked him."

"Is he with you?"

The farmer turned and summoned a young man from the back of the room. This was the last judgment of the day, and the room was otherwise empty of onlookers. The farmer's son bore a strong family resemblance, with a wide face and a strong jaw and an unruly shock of straight, brown hair that stuck out at odd angles. The boy looked to be about sixteen summers old, old enough to testify in court as a man.

"Tell us what you saw," Jonmarc said.

The boy spoke without looking up. "I wasn't supposed to be out that night. But I'd slipped out to see Molly Rimmin. We'd agreed to meet up in a clearing that's just out of view of the village."

"You always meet your girlfriends in the burying grounds?"

The boy winced. "We weren't actually in the burying grounds, but the crypts aren't far from there. We'd been...busy...for a while, when I heard a noise, like something crashing through the underbrush. I was scared that it might be wolves."

"If it had been wolves, you wouldn't have heard them until they were on you," Sior, the representative for the *vyrkin*, spoke from his place behind Jonmarc. The boy blushed scarlet.

"We didn't have all our clothes on," he admitted in a mumble. "I didn't want to die naked, and I was trying to put my pants back on when I saw them."

"Who?"

"I saw the dead. I know my own uncle. And I knew he was dead. But there he was, and behind him were others. I didn't stop to count. I grabbed Molly and what clothes we could gather and we ran."

"What did they look like?" Jonmarc pressed.

The boy made an impatient expression. "They looked like themselves, only dead."

Jonmarc shook his head and silently counted to ten. "Was there anything unusual about how they moved?"

The boy shook his head in frustration. "Did you not hear me? They were dead and they were walking—that's damn unusual where I come from!"

The farmer cuffed the boy on the side of the head. "You forget yourself. That's the lord you be talking to."

"Sorry," the boy mumbled, looking down.

"I once saw a dead body able to move when a ghost possessed

it," Jonmarc said. Even now, the memory sent a chill down his back. "Is the area around the crypt haunted?"

The farmer shrugged. "No more than any burying ground. We have our ghosts, like all villages. Our ancestors lie in there. They stay with us."

Jonmarc struggled to make himself understood. "Do you have any bad ghosts? Ones who throw things or try to hurt people? Anyone who was murdered and looking for revenge?"

The farmer thought for a moment and shook his head. "Old man Velnost hung himself in his barn a few years back, and he soured the milk when his wife remarried, but our ghosts are quiet folk, like they were when they were alive. I don't imagine my sister's husband was happy about dying, but he wasn't the sort to trouble the living."

"Has anyone other than the tinker come to your village lately?" Sakwi's question was unexpected, and everyone turned to look at the land mage.

The farmer thought for a moment. "Just the two holy men who blessed the village."

Sakwi and Gabriel both stepped closer, and Jonmarc leaned forward until he was nearly eye-to-eye with the farmer. "What holy men?"

"They came two days after I did," the tinker spoke up, eager to clear his name. "I was staying at the inn, trading odd jobs for my room and board. Not much coin to be made as a tinker these days, with the plague and all. The inn was pretty empty, which is why I remember. Folks aren't going from place to place anymore, and they don't welcome those who do. I knew the innkeeper from my last travels, so he took me in, but I think he would have turned these two away if they hadn't been scholars."

"Why did he think they were scholars?" It was Gabriel who spoke. The *vayash moru* had moved close enough to meet the tinker's eyes. Jonmarc guessed that Gabriel was using the compulsion *vayash moru* could use on most mortals to enable the tinker to tell his story more coherently. While Jonmarc was better able than most to resist that compulsion, he understood its power.

The tinker's eyes widened just a bit, and Jonmarc was certain Gabriel was nudging the man to examine his memories closely. "They carried satchels with them that looked heavy. The innkeeper asked what was in them, and they told him it was books. They said they were going to see the Sisterhood, and the innkeeper stopped asking questions." He made the sign of the Lady to ward off evil. "We don't have anything to do with the likes of them."

Sakwi looked lost in concentration, but he roused himself from his thoughts. "What did these 'scholars' look like?"

The tinker frowned. "They were plain-dressed and clean-shaven. Couldn't see much of their clothing under the black robes they wore."

"Black robes," Jonmarc repeated, feeling his heart sink. What he'd assumed had been petty tomb robbing or a prank had just taken a turn into serious business. "You're certain the robes were black?"

The tinker nodded vigorously. "Black as night, m'lord. That didn't strike me as odd, but this did: For scholars, they paid their fare in gold."

"Whose gold?"

"That's the other thing that was strange," the tinker said. "The innkeeper didn't recognize the coin. It was gold, no doubt about it, but strange looking. When he asked them, they said it was an old coin that had been in their citadel's treasury."

Jonmarc pressed his fingers to his temples, trying to stop the headache that was now throbbing. "Great. Just great. Walking dead, Black Robes, and a coin no one can recognize." He felt the

231

weight of a long day that was just about to get much longer. "I don't know where your dead have gone to, but I've got a good idea who took them. We need to see the crypt, and I'd like to know whether your innkeeper still has that coin. Will you take us to your village?"

The farmer and the tinker exchanged glances. The animosity between them had been exchanged for a sense of foreboding that Jonmarc could read clearly in their faces. "Yes, m'lord. We would be honored."

Jonmarc looked to Gabriel, Sior, and Sakwi. "I think you need to see this, too."

Gabriel nodded. "Clearly so."

It took half a candlemark on horseback to reach the village. Synten, the farmer, led the way, followed by the tinker, Val. It was a small farming village, perhaps only three dozen homes, and Jonmarc was willing to bet gold that all of the inhabitants were related by blood or marriage. It was the kind of village that dotted the countryside across Dark Haven and Principality, not so different from the village where Jonmarc had grown up. The inn probably also doubled as the village bakery, Jonmarc guessed as they rode into town. Unlike the larger taverns that, in better times, did a brisk business along major roadways, the inn looked as poor as the village.

Val the tinker led them into the inn. Everything about it was small, cramped, and hard used. In his smuggling days, Jonmarc had stayed in many inns like this one, and he could guess that its ale was watered, its food middling at best, and its mattresses buggy. The innkeeper was a wan-faced man with a sallow complexion. He looked up as the newcomers entered, but his eyes held no welcome.

"What brings you out here?" he asked, his voice carefully neutral. Jonmarc was certain the man had spotted Gabriel as a *vayash moru* and Sakwi as a mage, and while it was less likely for him to guess that Sior was *vyrkin*, it was clear that the innkeeper was wary of strangers.

"This is Lord Vahanian," Val introduced. "He's come about the ... problem."

Fear flashed in the innkeeper's eyes for a moment before he locked down his expression once more. "Honored to meet you, m'lord, and your friends," he said with a glance toward Sakwi and the others.

"He's interested in the two men who came here a couple of weeks ago. The ones in the black robes."

The innkeeper made the sign of the Lady in warding. "Pox take them! Wouldn't have let them in if I'd known they were hocuses. Had to whitewash the room to be rid of their markings, and my dog went missing when they left. Sprinkled salt all around the room they used, and salt's not cheap, but my wife says nothing less will cast out *dimonns*."

Jonmarc asked the innkeeper to lead them to the room, and the man did so, reluctantly. It was a small room, barely large enough for a bed. As the innkeeper said, it had been freshly whitewashed, both floor and ceiling. Despite the clean appearance, Jonmarc shuddered. An ominous feeling clung to the room. It seemed unseasonably cold, and he wondered if something about the runes had called ghosts. Whatever it was gave him an instinctive urge to flee. Neither Gabriel nor Sior seemed to be affected, but Sakwi looked both thoughtful and concerned.

"What did the runes look like?" Sakwi asked.

The innkeeper's eyes widened. "I did my best not to look at them."

"It's important," Jonmarc said, fixing the man with a glare. "If you want to find your dead, we need your help."

The innkeeper grimaced, and then sighed. "All right. What do you need?"

Sakwi motioned for him to come to the hearth, and he handed

233

him a half-burnt stick. "Can you draw the runes you saw on the hearthstone?"

"I can try."

They watched in silence as the innkeeper struggled to trace the runes that he had seen. Finally, he sat back on his heels. "That's the best I can do. They seemed to move when I looked directly at them, and although I should remember what they looked like, they're blurry in my mind."

Sakwi nodded. "They weren't meant to be read by anyone who wasn't a mage. Thank you, this will do." He hunkered down next to the hearth as the innkeeper scrambled away as if the runes might burn him.

"What do you make of them?" Jonmarc asked.

Sakwi's lips moved silently as his hands made warding gestures. Finally, he looked up. "Someone did blood magic in this room."

"I can smell traces of blood, even over the whitewash," Gabriel said. "I'm betting Sior can, too." Sior nodded.

"I don't recognize all of the runes. Rune magic isn't my gift," Sakwi continued. "But the runes I do recognize are words like 'destroy,' 'destroyed,' 'destroyer.'"

"Shanthadura," Jonmarc murmured. Sakwi nodded.

"Yes, I believe they stand for the name. I think that whatever magic was done here called to the dead."

"Were they summoners?"

Sakwi frowned. "I don't sense that strong a magical resonance. It's not the same kind of signature as Tris's power. No, this feels like blood magic, although it's strong. Remember, a blood mage can animate a corpse, but can't force a soul back into the body. Blood mages can also draw ghosts to them, but they can't call specific spirits like a summoner can, or give them their final rest."

"So there are ghosts? I thought I felt something."

"Oh, yes," Sakwi, Gabriel, and Sior all spoke at once. The innkeeper paled.

"Can you get rid of them?" he asked, his defiance replaced by desperation. "We've got enough trouble getting guests to stay as it is without ghosts running them off."

Sakwi did not answer immediately. He took pinches of several herbs from the pouches on his belt and mixed them in his palm, then sprinkled them over the runes the innkeeper had drawn. He bade the innkeeper to bring him water and salt, which the man returned with promptly. Sakwi muttered under his breath as he sprinkled salt over the hearth, and then made small gestures of warding over the basin of water. Finally, he poured the water over the hearth, washing away the markings. When he was finished, he stood.

"I didn't think it wise to leave the runes. Such things, even badly copied, have power." He glanced around the room toward the corners of the ceiling, places that looked empty to Jonmarc but that seemed to hold Sakwi's attention. "Yes, whatever was done here called spirits, and I don't think they're pleased." He thought for a moment. "As I said, my gift is land magic, not summoning. But I will do what I can."

Sakwi threw open the window and door, and checked to assure that the chimney was clear. Then he lit a fire in the fireplace. The night was too warm for a fire, and the hearth looked as if it had not been used in months, but it was stocked with wood and kindling, and the fire caught quickly. They stood back as Sakwi gathered items from his pouches. On a small nightstand, he laid out a disk of amber and a pendant of onyx. He drew wolfsbane leaves, dried witchberry, and sticklewort from his pouches, and sprinkled them with a few drops of an oil that smelled strongly of juniper. Then he carefully gathered the mixture and threw it into the fire, making a gesture of warding as he did so.

"Go in peace. You are released. Go in peace," he murmured.

The air around them stirred. There was no sound, no other movement, but all at once, it felt to Jonmarc as if an oppressive weight had been lifted. The air had a heaviness, like a gathering storm, but in that moment, the sense of foreboding vanished.

"I can't send them to their rest," Sakwi said, stifling another bout of coughing, "but I could free them from this place. They'll most likely return to wherever they came from, if they lack the will or ability to cross over to the Lady."

The innkeeper, Val, and Synten stared at Sakwi in a combination of respect and fear. For Synten's son, the look was complete panic. Val the tinker was the first to regain his composure.

"Do you still have the coin they gave you?" Val asked the innkeeper. "The gold one?"

The innkeeper spit and ground the spittle with his heel in a gesture of warding. "Buried it, I did. Don't want no more of the bad luck they brought. What do you want with the likes of them?" His eyes narrowed.

"We've come to find out what happened to your dead," Jonmarc replied. His annoyance with the innkeeper's thinly veiled hostility was clear in his voice. "Can you find the coin?"

A tug-of-war of emotion crossed the innkeeper's face. On one hand, Jonmarc was quite sure the man resented being bothered, and it was clear that, for a man in his business, he didn't like newcomers. At the same time, he wasn't quite ready to disobey a direct order from his lord. "Follow me," he said, and led them out the back door.

The coin was buried beneath a large oak tree. Grains of salt clung to the dirt, and Jonmarc guessed the man had taken as many precautions as he could to ward against evil. *At least he didn't throw it down the well.* The man handed it over to Jonmarc as if the coin would bite, and Jonmarc held the coin up in the moonlight.

"It's not Principality gold, that's for sure," Jonmarc murmured.

"It didn't come from any of the Winter Kingdoms," Gabriel said, his voice unusually quiet. Jonmarc turned to him, and saw concern in Gabriel's eyes.

"You've seen it before?"

Gabriel nodded. "I've seen coins with those markings, yes. A very long time ago. And either the Black Robes were telling the truth about it coming from an ancient stash of treasure, or we have a very big problem." He met Jonmarc's gaze. "The last time I saw a coin like this was when I was mortal, over four hundred years ago. Men brought them from across the Northern Sea when they came, first as traders, and then as invaders."

"Why would Black Robes have gold from across the Northern Sea? The Durim are following the old ways, but they're from here in the Winter Kingdoms. None of the Black Robes we've fought gave any indication of being from somewhere else."

Gabriel shrugged. "We didn't stop to interrogate them before we killed them. We weren't looking for outsiders. Or perhaps someone from outside has found common cause with the Durim."

"I really don't like what you're suggesting," Jonmarc replied. "Especially when it comes to the walking dead."

They thanked the innkeeper for his trouble and paid him in Principality gold the equivalent of one night's lodging. That seemed to improve the man's mood, although he didn't offer them ale in the bargain.

"I can take you to the crypts now," Synten said. His son blanched, and it was clear that the young man did not want to go, and equally clear that his fear of the dead came second to his fear of his father. Synten and his son stopped at their small, thatched house long enough to gather torches, which they lit. Gabriel and Sior refused to carry torches, and Jonmarc knew both could see better by moonlight than most mortals could see in the day. Sakwi wanted his hands free for magic. Jonmarc took a torch, but he also unsheathed his sword, keeping it at the ready. Synten gave the sword a nervous glance, and then motioned for them to follow him.

Sakwi walked in the lead along with Synten and his son. Although the mage said little to avoid panicking the farmer, Jonmarc was certain that the land mage was using his power to sense for traces of magic.

Jonmarc followed. No one had claimed that the missing dead were dangerous, but he had found over the years that it was much easier to negotiate with a sword in hand. Sior and Gabriel followed, but they each took a meandering route that often left the path. Both the *vayash moru* and the *vyrkin* had heightened senses, and Jonmarc wondered what, if anything, they were picking up from the trek through the fields. But if either of them sensed anything amiss on the short walk from the village, they said nothing.

"There," Synten said, pointing. They had walked along the edge of several fields that were almost ready for harvest. The ground rose on the other side of the fields, and Jonmarc could see several squat, stone buildings set into the hillside. It was grassy and open from the edge of the fields to the crypts, though forest edged the entire area. Jonmarc scanned the tree line for danger, but saw nothing.

"Where were you and where were the dead?" Jonmarc asked, turning to Synten's son.

The young man blushed scarlet. "Molly and me were over there, around the bend of the trees," he said, leading the way. If his trysting place had been a secret before, it was no longer. The set of Synten's jaw told Jonmarc that the farmer would have a few choice words with his son in private, later.

They followed the young man around a copse of trees. The village and part of the fields were now out of the line of sight. "We'd made a place in the grass over there," the young man said, licking his dry lips nervously. "We weren't looking at the crypts. No reason to pay them any mind." He paled at the recollection. "We heard something coming through the woods. Making an awful racket. Sticks cracking, leaves rustling. I grabbed a stone and got up, thinking it might be a wolf, or a pack of dogs. But it was my uncle. My dead uncle."

"How did he look?" Sakwi probed.

"He looked dead!" The young man's voice was close to panic.

"Did he recognize you?"

The young man calmed enough to think for a moment. "I don't think so. Mind, we got out of there quickly! I didn't stick around to ask questions. But he looked blank, dazed. And he moved oddly, stiffly. Like one of those puppets on strings that the traveling bards had at the inn one time. Only there warn't no strings, and no puppet master."

"Not one you could see," Sakwi murmured. The land mage moved away from them and began to walk slowly along the tree line. He was slightly built, and in his brown robes, he blended in among the trees. He stopped for a moment as a violent coughing fit racked his thin body, but he held up a hand to forestall help. "It's nothing. Nothing," he protested, and took a wad of herbs from a pouch beneath his belt to put beneath his tongue. In a few moments, the coughing ceased and Sakwi continued walking.

Gabriel and Sior followed him at a distance. "There are footprints here," Sior said. "They smell of the dead. Many scents. Perhaps a dozen."

"Not fresh dead," Gabriel added. "There's more than scent here. There're bits of flesh and grave clothes in the grass and on the twigs. If they'd arisen as *vayash moru*, that would not be so." A note of relief was in his voice. "No, *vayash moru* didn't do this. If the old dead had really been brought across, they would have risen within the first few nights after their burial. And they wouldn't rise in a group. That's not our way."

Sakwi continued his walk toward the crypt in silence. Jonmarc, Synten, and the young man followed. Even at a distance, Jonmarc could see that the crypt had been sealed.

"You closed the crypt?" he asked.

Synten nodded. "When he rushed in babbling like an idiot," he said with a nod toward his son, "I had to go. My wife begged me to stay home; it was growing dark. But if Midri really had risen from his tomb, well, I needed to see for myself. So I brought out my neighbors, and we took our torches and scythes. There wasn't anyone in sight when we got here, but the crypt was open. That's why we thought someone had stolen the bodies. I figured my son just saw them being carried off and lost his head."

"I need to enter the crypt." Sakwi's voice startled them. The land mage stood near the crypt door, running his hands along the entrance without touching the stone. "I want to see how it was disturbed."

Gabriel and Sior moved the heavy door easily, using their preternatural strength. The door was as large and thick as Synten had said, and Jonmarc had no doubt that two men would struggle against its weight unless they were quite strong. Jonmarc and Gabriel ventured in first. Having a torch in an unfamiliar crypt made Jonmarc just slightly more comfortable; in the unlikely event that the tomb robbers had been *vayash moru*, the torch would deter an attack. And just in case anything still lurked within the tomb, Gabriel's *vayash moru* reflexes were a good defense.

As Synten said, the first room of the crypt was empty. Bits of torn shroud littered the floor. While the entrance to the crypt was made of cut and fitted stones, it was clearly designed to fit the entrance of a natural cave. Flat spaces had been carved into the rock, wide enough to lay a body. The niches were empty, but along the ground, the tokens left behind by grieving loved ones remained. Clay pots, strings of beads, homemade toys, or well-worn hunting gear lay undisturbed, although the bodies of the people for whom the gifts had been meant were gone.

"Look there," Sakwi said quietly, pointing. Crudely drawn onto the walls of the crypt were the same runes they had seen at the inn.

"Well, that makes it pretty certain that either the Black Robes from the inn were here, or their friends were," Jonmarc said.

They moved through the first room and into the next. The crypt smelled of death and moldering cloth, but there was a cold air that told Jonmarc that the passageway eventually led into caves below. "How large is this crypt?"

"It's very old," the farmer replied. "My family has worked this land for five generations, and all our dead are buried here. The same is true of my neighbors, who share the crypt. No one goes into the lowest levels; they were filled with bodies long ago. But my father told me once that there are thirty-two rooms. Eight faces of the Sacred Lady, times four for the Light Aspects. A good number to settle the dead."

"Do the caves go beyond the crypt?"

Synten frowned. "I haven't explored them, but I've heard it said that when the crypt was made, the men blocked up the back to keep out the rats and scavengers."

Gabriel raised his face to the stirring of cold air. "The passage is no longer blocked." He vanished before anyone saw him move, and returned a few moments later. "The tomb is empty. There are runes like these all along the passageways. I found where stones once blocked off the rest of the caves. They've been removed."

"And the grave offerings? Are they gone, too?"

Gabriel shook his head. "Everything else is in its place. In the lower levels, where Synten says no one has gone in years, there were fresh footsteps in the dust. They led back into the caves, beyond where it was blocked."

"So the dead that I saw were only part of it?" Synten's son was wide-eyed, and his voice cracked with terror. "You mean that the rest are wandering around somewhere, down in the caves?"

"My guess is that whatever animated them drew them to it along the easiest route. The newly dead close to the door came out that way, and the older dead went towards the back." Sakwi looked thoughtful. "Or perhaps, they were all meant to go to the caves, and those in the front didn't respond properly." He looked up at the others. "It would take a powerful blood mage to move so many bodies, but remember, they're puppets, not capable of thought."

"They're still dead and moving. That makes them a problem." Jonmarc's jaw clenched. "What I want to know is, why? Why did the Black Robes want the bodies? From what you say, they wouldn't be easy to use in battle. If they can't think for themselves and they can't move without magic, then someone has to move them, right? It would take a lot of mages—and a lot of magic—to operate that many 'puppets' in any kind of battle, and I can't imagine they'd move with any skill."

"They wouldn't need skill if terror would do," Gabriel replied quietly. "Soldiers are leery to strike down the bodies of their kin. And while you've become somewhat accustomed to the dead and the undead, many mortals are not so calm about such things."

Skilled or not, dozens of puppet-dead would create chaos on a battlefield, Jonmarc knew. They would also spark panicked riots in any city. "I don't get it," Jonmarc said, shaking his head. "This seems big for the Black Robes that we've fought. Until now, they've taken people, *vayash moru*, and *vyrkin* for the blood they need for their magic. They've disturbed the barrows, but that made sense if they were trying to draw on old magic. But these dead aren't special. They weren't mages. They didn't have any magic. What do they gain from stealing the bodies? And why go to the trouble to use magic to make them walk? Why not just tear down the rocks at the back of the caves and carry them out?"

Sakwi met his eyes. "Find out who gave the Black Robes their gold, and you might find your answers."

The ride back to Dark Haven went by quickly. The night was cool, and a nip in the air warned that colder weather would come soon. The exchange in the village was troubling, and Jonmarc knew that, come daylight, he would be back at the crypts with as many mages as he could find, hoping to track either the missing dead or the blood mages who troubled their rest. But even the *vayash moru* counseled caution in the darkness, and Jonmarc wasn't of a mind to argue.

"*Skrivven* for your thoughts," Sakwi said from beside him.

Jonmarc smiled. "Looking forward to a good Moon Feast dinner, to tell you the truth. Carina put Carroway in charge this year, and so I won't be surprised if we have a celebration worthy of the palace."

Sakwi chuckled. "It would be nice to end the evening on a happier note. Did you know that Carina asked me in to have a look at Carroway's hand? It's much improved; perhaps Macaria can persuade him to play tonight."

"He's lucky. I've seen men stabbed through the hand before, and most of them never got back enough movement to play an instrument. Some of them were lucky to hold a knife or make a fist."

Sakwi shrugged. "While most people would say it was worth it to save the heir to the Margolan throne at any cost, it would be a great shame to lose so fine a bard as Carroway. Even when you were all outlaws, he gave the best performances I've ever seen."

Jonmarc chuckled. "And more than once, he earned the coin to keep us fed and get us a place to sleep when we were trying to stay out of Jared's dungeon. I won't argue with you—he's talented, and it would be nice to see him get patched back up."

"Of course, a good meal never hurts. Fresh bread, candied squash, baked early apples," Sakwi mused. "Corn and roasted chicken and a blueberry cobbler if we're lucky." He sighed, smiling. "Ah yes, it's good to be visiting a manor on a feast day," he said with a grin.

"You're out of luck if you were hoping to see the same kind of spectacle they put on in Principality City," Jonmarc replied. "No burning cornstalk men in Dark Haven."

"Why not?"

"Because in other times, when the *vayash moru* weren't so well received, such burnings usually involved one of our number, staked through the heart and wrapped with dry leaves and branches and set to burning." Gabriel had ridden up alongside them, and the look in his eyes gave Jonmarc to guess that the other had seen such things done.

"You mean when Shanthadura was worshipped."

Gabriel nodded. "The rituals date from then, but whenever the *vayash moru* become feared or hated, someone remembers the old ways. Worship of the old gods is just an excuse for hatreds long nurtured."

"Not this time," Jonmarc said, setting his jaw. "Not if I can help it."

Dark Haven was alight with candles when they arrived. An offering of cider and freshly baked bread lay within a protective circle drawn in the center of the courtyard around a great oak tree ringed by candles. A silver disk hung suspended from the oak, in honor of Istra, the Dark Lady, the patron Aspect of Dark Haven and the protector of outcasts and *vayash moru*. The manor house windows glowed, and even at a distance, Jonmarc could

244

hear music and voices. Games of chance and cards were especially favored this holiday, and Jonmarc was certain the festivities had not waited for them to begin. Despite the conversation, his mood lightened. Tomorrow be damned; tonight he would celebrate. He'd spent too long on battlefields to miss an opportunity to enjoy a feast. The next battle would come soon enough.

Carina was waiting for him. She stood, framed in the doorway, watching as Jonmarc and the others gave their horses to servants to tether and headed for the broad stone stairs. Her gown of yellow and orange made the green of her eyes even more striking. Now, her expression was tense.

"I was worried when you were late."

Jonmarc took her in his arms and kissed the top of her head, brushing back her short, dark hair. "Unexpected complications," he said. Her swollen belly made it difficult to hold her close, and he let his hand fall protectively to her abdomen. It was a reminder that new responsibilities lay ahead, and an even greater obligation to keep those who depended on him safe from harm.

He took Carina's hand, forcing himself to smile and pushing the dark thoughts from his mind, at least for a few candlemarks. "I want to see what kind of a celebration you and Carroway have cooked up."

Carina smiled, although Jonmarc doubted she would forget to ask for details of his trip later, when they could speak in private. "If I didn't know better, I'd guess that most of the village is here. We did our best to make sure there's food enough for all of the refugees. Some of the *vyrkin* brought in additional deer, so there's plenty of meat and an ample supply of blood for the *vayash moru*."

Gabriel and Sakwi followed them into the large dining room. Candles glittered overhead in the large candelabras, and the torches along the walls banished the autumn chill. Carroway and Macaria had gathered the local musicians from the village pub and had obviously been rehearsing new material, because the crowd was clapping, dancing, and cheering. Carroway sat in the second row, unusual for the Margolan court's master bard, who preferred the visibility of center stage. Then Jonmarc realized that in the second row, no one had a clear view of his left hand, or how nimbly his fingers moved across the lute's strings. Carroway's head was bowed in concentration, and his long, dark hair obscured his face, but once, Jonmarc caught a glimpse that told him whatever precision Carroway wrested from his healing hand was not painless.

"It's the first time Macaria and I have gotten him to perform for more than a small audience in the pub," Carina whispered, as if she guessed his thoughts. "Although I've persuaded him to play for the refugees and he does quite well then. I think he's more focused on their pain than his own when he plays while I'm healing. He might not have Macaria's magic, but Lady Bright, he's still the most talented musician I've ever heard."

"And maybe the first bard to save a kingdom." Jonmarc chuckled.

"Jonmarc!"

Jonmarc looked up to see Berry hurrying toward him. Although Carina had persuaded Berry to dress for the occasion, she looked more like the daughter of a well-to-do merchant than a princess. Berry's auburn hair was loose, though it retained a wave from the tight braid that kept it out of her way as she helped Carina with the refugees. Her dress was in shades of orange and brown in keeping with the holiday, but devoid of the gemstones and pearls that glittered in the gowns Jonmarc had seen her wear in the palace.

"Carina made me dress up." Berry gave a joking pout. "Do you have any idea how often I have to wear gowns like this back home? They're heavy and hot and the corset hurts when I sit down."

Carina laughed. "I promised your father I'd keep you in practice. What will he say if we return a hoyden instead of a princess?"

"He knows me. He won't blame you. He could never keep Mother in hand, either. That was one of the things he loved about her."

"You look beautiful," Carina said, reaching out to plump one of Berry's sleeves.

Berry gave a decidedly unladylike snort. "The only thing this much cloth is good for is hiding my blades." She shifted, just a bit, and the steel of a throwing knife glittered in the candle-light. The set of knives had been a gift from Carroway, who had taught her how to throw during the long nights the group had spent on the road fleeing Jared's soldiers.

"Someday, you're going to make a very interesting queen." Jonmarc's voice was serious, but a smile tugged at the corner of his mouth.

Berry rolled her eyes. "I hope it's not until I'm old. Old and gray and wrinkled. Maybe Father can be brought across by a *vayash moru* and live forever, and I'll never have to suffer through those interminable Council of Nobles meetings."

"From your lips to the Lady's ear," Carina murmured.

Just as quickly, Berry's mood shifted as the musicians took up a popular dance tune. "That's the song I asked Carroway to play for me! Got to go." She blew an exaggerated kiss to Jonmarc and headed back through the crowd to find a place in the circle dance that was just forming. Jonmarc could see Laisren and Lisette among the couples who were dancing, and even Sister Taru had joined the circle. Riqua and many of her *vayash moru* "family" were present, as were most of Gabriel's brood and Sior's pack of *vyrkin*. Rafe and Uri stood near the far end of the room, deep in conversation. Jonmarc had been as surprised that Uri came to the feast as he was certain that Astasia would not deign to visit. But the fact that four of the Blood Council were in attendance was a positive sign, and Jonmarc was determined not to spoil the evening with concerns that could wait until morning.

Despite the plague, the resurgence of the Black Robes, and the coming winter, spirits seemed high, and Jonmarc let out a long breath, aware of how tight his shoulders were, as if he was anticipating danger. He looked around the room. Carina and Carroway had done an excellent job organizing the feast. One table along the back of the room held an assortment of bread sculptures. There were intricate braids and bread formed in the shape of sheaves of wheat and corn shocks, to thank the Lady for the harvest thus far and petition for good weather to gather the remaining crops. He could smell spiced cider simmering on the hearth, and large dishes offered guests a bounty of fruit compotes, roasted squash, and potatoes, along with a roasted deer and plump baked chickens.

"How is the harvest going?" Gabriel had moved silently to stand beside Jonmarc.

"Very well, considering. Neirin keeps the harvest teams circulating from farm to farm, or to the vineyards, depending on who's got crops ready to gather. Sior's brought all the *vyrkin* who don't have pups to care for to help, and with the assistance we've gotten from your brood and Riqua's brood, we can harvest day and night, so we might stay a jump ahead of the rains this year."

Gabriel nodded. "Some good luck is overdue. Between the wars in Margolan, the refugees, and the plague, we don't need a poor harvest as well."

"Even Maynard Linton's caravan pitched in, since they're effectively stranded here until the plague runs its course. They've been helping press the grapes and make mash for the ale, and lending a hand mending fences and fishing nets, that kind of thing."

"Speaking of whom…" Gabriel said with a nod toward the crowd.

"Jonmarc, m'boy. Good to see you!" Maynard Linton was a short, round man whose coppery tan spoke of seasons spent out of doors. He bustled through the revelers with a wide grin on his face. "Damn fine celebration. Damn fine!" He clapped Jonmarc on the shoulder and gave Carina a kiss on the cheek.

"Glad you could make it, Maynard." Jonmarc could not resist a grin. Maynard Linton had taught Jonmarc how to make his way on the river as a smuggler years ago, and they had maintained an on-again, off-again business relationship that profitably trod just this side of legality. When Jonmarc accepted the title of Lord of Dark Haven, he had extended an invitation for Linton's caravan to winter with him. It was good business for both of them, since it supplied Linton with a safe place to rest off-season, and it gave Dark Haven's village and *vayash moru* craftsmen and distillers a way to sell their wares to the Winter Kingdoms when the caravan headed south in the spring.

Linton snorted. "Make it? No place I'd rather be, what with the pox and the Black Robes loose. Did I tell you that when we go south next season, we'll have a troupe of *vayash moru* performers? Carroway made some introductions, seeing as how you and Tris and Carina and he could all speak firsthand for the caravan and all. Course they can only perform at night, but that makes them a rare spectacle that commands a premium admission fee," he said and chuckled.

"Which, of course, you'll be sharing with the performers," Gabriel finished with a pointed gaze.

"Of course, of course. Just good business to keep the performers happy. Wouldn't do to make them famous and have them bribed away by another caravan," Linton said hurriedly.

"Uh-huh. I've never known you to split profits with anyone less than sixty-forty." Jonmarc folded his arms.

Linton rolled his eyes. "By the Whore! Must you give up all my secrets! Yes, yes, I agreed to a fifty-fifty split. Only keep it down, or the dancers and jugglers will demand a bigger percentage and you'll drive me out of business."

Linton's outburst managed to make Gabriel chuckle. "You don't think Carroway's thought of that?"

Linton glanced toward the musicians with a look of horror that Jonmarc suspected was only partially falsified for their benefit. "You don't really think—"

Jonmarc shrugged. "I learned a long time ago not to underestimate Carroway. Not after the first time I saw him throw a dagger and peg a slaver between the shoulders, anyhow."

"Fie!" Linton made the sign of the Lady in warding. "Don't even mention that word around me." Linton's former caravan had been attacked by slavers hired by Jared the Usurper to hunt for Tris Drayke. Tris and his friends had barely escaped with their lives, and Linton had needed two years to rebuild. "On the bright side, between the plague and new management in Margolan, the slavers seem to have gone out of business. For now." He sobered. "Course, it's the Black Robes a body has to watch for now."

Jonmarc and Gabriel exchanged glances. "What do you hear?" Jonmarc asked.

Linton dropped his voice, so their conversation did not carry. "There's talk along the river that the Black Robes are behind the people who've been disappearing. Heard that in Nargi, they're working with the Crone priests to hunt *vayash moru*. Dhasson's never held with that sort of thing, but can't say that King Harrol will send his army out to stop it, either. Bad for business. Bad all the way around, if you ask me." He shrugged. "Ah well, no need to talk shop when there's ale to be drunk. Did I tell you that you give a damn fine party, Jonmarc? Damn fine." And with that, Linton bustled away toward the barrels of ale.

"Did I mention that Maynard was quite open to the idea of helping the Ghost Carriage spirit *vayash moru* and *vyrkin* out of trouble spots?" Gabriel said. The musicians struck up a lively tune that had Carina tapping her toe and swaying to the music.

"Oh?"

"Says that being a legitimate businessman is too stressful, and he wants to smuggle something to keep his hand in and his skills sharp." Gabriel smiled, and his long eye-teeth showed, just a bit. "That's part of the reason for the new *vayash moru* and *vyrkin* entertainers. Of course, Riqua and I have promised to make some introductions for him in return, introductions that will give him the stawar's share of the Noorish rug market and some of the best Principality gemstones."

"Of course."

Carina had just tugged on Jonmarc's hand to lead him to the dance floor when Neirin hurried in, scanning the crowd until he spotted them. By the look on the grounds manager's face, there was trouble.

"There's someone here to see you."

Jonmarc spread his hands to indicate the crowded room. "There are several hundred people here to see me, or at least to drink my ale."

"It's Captain Gellyr. And he's got a visitor with him from the palace."

The sense of foreboding Jonmarc had managed to dispel returned, and his smile vanished. "Please handle the formalities for me," he said to Carina, with a glance to Gabriel as well. "Let me see what's going on."

He followed Neirin to the manor's entrance hall. Captain Gellyr was the commander of King Staden's garrison at Jannistorp. Jonmarc's previous interactions with the captain had been cordial, and Gellyr had been helpful in quelling unrest when a rogue *vayash moru* had violated the Truce, but it was highly unusual for him to show up unannounced at Dark Haven. Gellyr's companion wore a traveling cloak, and at a glance, Jonmarc knew it for military issue. Boots, pants, and sword marked the other as a ranking officer, and Jonmarc felt any hope dim that this might be just a social call.

"Lord Vahanian." Gellyr's voice was friendly but businesslike. "Good feast to you." Gellyr was a large man, taller than Jonmarc, and perhaps a decade older, with enough scars on his face and hands that it was clear his rank had been earned the hard way. Though he wore no armor this night, his blond hair was cut short for a helm, and his manner would have marked him as a soldier in any crowd. The man beside him stood stiffly, and though the entrance hall was warm, he had made no move to remove his cowl.

Jonmarc nodded warily. "And to you." He shook Gellyr's hand, mentally noting that since neither of them had drawn a blade, it was going well so far. "If it's the Moon Feast that's brought you to Dark Haven, you're welcome to join us. There's ale enough for all."

Gellyr shook his head. "Unfortunately, I'm here on king's business. May we speak to you in private?"

Jonmarc led them to Neirin's office and lit the torches, then closed the door. "Now, what made Staden send you all the way out here on a festival night?"

Gellyr looked at his companion. "You'll have to ask the general. I'm just the guide tonight."

The man beside Gellyr lowered his cowl. He was a dark-haired man with intelligent, brown eyes and a hard line to his mouth. "So good to see you again, *Lord* Vahanian." The venom in the man's voice matched a deadly glint in his eyes.

"Gregor." Jonmarc kept his hand away from his sword, but he was glad there was enough space between him and his guests to give him a chance to draw his blade if need be. "Don't you have prisoners to bully?"

"I see the wound to your shoulder healed. Pity."

"I'm surprised you kept your commission, since the last time you managed to throw both Martris Drayke and your own princess in the dungeon."

Anger flashed in Gregor's eyes, telling Jonmarc that the error might not have gone completely unpunished. "I had my orders. King Staden didn't say why he wanted your group, only to detain you and bring you to the city. I don't question a direct order."

"Understanding is different from questioning, *General*."

Gellyr cleared his throat uncomfortably. Gregor glared at Jonmarc and took a deep breath. "King Staden sent me with this." He reached slowly beneath his cloak, keeping his eyes on Jonmarc's sword at all times, and produced a sealed parchment. Gregor handed it to Gellyr, who handed it to Jonmarc. "Staden's taken ill with the plague. He wrote this the night before I left, and by morning, he had lost consciousness. Despite what the healers have done for him, he may not survive." Beneath Gregor's anger, Jonmarc heard a note of sorrow.

"That parchment is his signed decree, in case anybody missed your investiture ceremony, making it clear that you are Princess Berwyn's Champion," Gregor said bitterly. "If he dies, it's your responsibility to escort the princess to the palace and see that she's safe until she can be crowned."

Jonmarc broke the seal and read down through the formal document. Staden's royal seal at the bottom left no doubt as to the letter's authenticity. "I'm sorry about Staden's health. Do you want me to call Berry?"

Gregor seemed to wince at the princess's nickname. "Not yet. Wait and see. But the king wanted you to be prepared for the worst." He paused. "The sickness came on him quickly. Just a fortnight ago, he and King Kalcen met aboard a ship at sea for two full days, working out an accord. We know they made agreements, and that a group from Eastmark is supposed to come to Principality soon to complete the pact, but Staden took ill before he was ready to tell anyone what commitments he'd made. If anything happens to him, the princess will have to pick up the pieces."

A hard glint came into his eyes. "You know, even in Principality City we hear about the legendary healer, Lady Vahanian. Staden gave specific instructions for her to remain here, at Dark Haven. He said it was too late for anyone to help him, but I wonder." Gregor's thin lips twisted to a sneer. "After all, she let my brother die."

Jonmarc struggled to keep his hand clear of the pommel of his sword. "Trying to heal Ric nearly killed Carina. That was almost ten years ago. Tris Drayke summoned Ric's ghost. Ric forgave her."

"Well, I haven't." He paused. "Then again, your reputation's reached the palace, too. Perhaps you deserve each other. A smuggler-lord and a fraud healer. Perhaps the plague will take her and give me my long overdue vengeance."

Jonmarc didn't bother with his sword. His right arm swung hard, connecting his fist with Gregor's jaw before Gregor moved for his blade. Months of training against *vayash moru* opponents gave Jonmarc an edge in speed that few, if any, mortal opponents could match. Before Gellyr could move to break them apart, Jonmarc landed two more blows, easily dodging Gregor's punches. He slammed Gregor against the wall and had a dagger drawn against Gregor's throat.

"I don't give a damn what you think. Carina's my wife. No one speaks about her like that."

Gregor spat blood from a split lip and laughed. "Princess Berwyn thinks you're quite the hero. What would she think if she saw you now?"

"I'd think you were an ass, Gregor." The voice came from

the doorway. Berry stood framed in the entranceway, and her eyes glinted with anger.

"Your Highness." Gellyr dropped to one knee. Jonmarc released Gregor and watched him warily as Gregor slumped more than bowed.

"Father sends you with a message, and this is how you represent the crown?"

"Your Highness, I did not mean—"

Berry made a disdainful gesture. All the coquettishness she had shown in the festival was gone, and everything in her manner left no doubt that she had been raised to rule. "I know exactly what you meant. I heard you from outside the door. Carina told me there were visitors from the palace."

"You weren't supposed to know."

Berry's fists were balled at her sides. "Not supposed to know my father is dying? Not supposed to prepare myself to take the crown if he doesn't recover?"

Gregor flinched. "He didn't want to worry you."

"He's my father. But he's also the king. Not worrying me is a luxury we can't afford."

"He forbade you to return to the palace until...until he recovers or dies. He was adamant, m'lady. He does not want you to contract plague."

Jonmarc could see the struggle on Berry's face. "And as much as I want to go, that's not a luxury we can afford, either. I will stay at Dark Haven...until we know how he fares." She stepped closer to Gregor and Jonmarc stepped back.

"General, I command you to look at me."

Gregor lifted his face. His lip was split. One eye was beginning to purple, and there was a small cut on his neck where Jonmarc's blade had drawn blood.

"Jonmarc risked his life for me time and again. He rescued me from the slavers. He protected me on the road. He earned

255

the right to be my Champion. He bears that title by order of the king. To question that is to question the king." Berry had drawn herself up to her full height. Her voice, her words, and her bearing were unmistakably royal. Two years ago, Berry's acting skills had saved her life, keeping the slavers from realizing just what a valuable prisoner they had taken. Now, Jonmarc realized how carefully Berry intentionally hid her upbringing to fit in at Dark Haven and to pass among the refugees without drawing attention to herself.

"I understand, Your Highness."

"Here's something else to understand, General. Lady Carina is a gifted healer. She told us what happened to your brother. I'm sorry for your loss. But she is a favorite of the king's and of mine. You will not speak ill of her. And"—Berry paused for emphasis—"if letting the past go is too difficult for you, I can see about having you reassigned."

"There is no need for that, Your Highness. I understand."

Berry's gaze was unyielding. "I hope so, General." She drew a deep breath, and for an instant, Jonmarc could see the worry beneath her control. She turned to Jonmarc. "Neirin's brought food for them and readied rooms so they can stay, since it's late. But after this display, I wouldn't fault you if they're unwelcome."

"They can stay." Jonmarc resheathed his knife. "Just keep him the hell away from Carina."

Berry held out her arm for Jonmarc to escort her, and he suppressed a smile at a gesture he knew was solely for Gregor's benefit. After they had left Neirin's office and were out of earshot, Berry took a deep breath. The fight and formality seemed to leave her, and she looked like a worried young girl.

"Do you think it's true? Do you think he'll die?"

Jonmarc winced at the despair he heard in her voice. She threw her arms around him and he held her close as though she were a frightened child. "Your father earned his reputation for stubbornness. He doesn't give up easily. Even when I was just a merc, I heard stories about how he faced down raiders and fought off challengers to the throne. He's tough."

Berry struggled not to cry. "I saw how Mother's death last year affected him. I don't know how much of that fight he still has with her gone."

Jonmarc tipped Berry's chin up to look him in the eyes. "He has you. I'm just getting used to the idea of being a father, but I know I'd battle the Formless One herself for Carina and my girls. Don't borrow trouble."

Berry sniffed back tears and wiped at her cheek with the back of her hand. "Thank you," she said, stepping back. "For everything." She met Jonmarc's gaze. "I'm glad you're my Champion."

Jonmarc managed a lopsided grin. "I'll try to stop beating up your generals."

That got a laugh from Berry, though tears glistened in her eyes. "I haven't quite forgiven Gregor for the way he treated us when he threw us in the dungeon. But Father forgave him because he has a good record on the battlefield. We might need him. I think he'll watch his tongue after this—if you didn't break his jaw."

Jonmarc rubbed his own bruised knuckles. "I wasn't trying to, but then again, my last few fights have been with *vayash moru*. They don't break as easily, so I've gotten in the habit of hitting harder."

Berry sobered. "If we go back to the palace, I'd like you to bring Laisren, too. I know Gabriel will need to help Carina here at the manor, but I'd like you to have someone else you trust completely, and I've heard enough to know Laisren understands both court and the army."

Jonmarc frowned. "Are you expecting a challenge?"

Berry shrugged. "Under normal circumstances, no. But look

around. These aren't normal circumstances, not with the plague and a lean harvest and the Black Robes kidnapping victims for Shanthadura. Now we find out Father's made commitments to Eastmark and we don't know what promises he made. It's just a feeling I've had for a while now, like there's a storm coming. I was hoping I was wrong, but now, with Father ill—"

Jonmarc laid his hand on her shoulder. "As Carina tells me all the time, don't fight the battle until it's time." He forced a smile, although he was certain it did not fully reach his eyes. "I can still hear music playing. Carroway's counting on his best patron to appreciate his performance. And I know Carina asked the cook to make the apple tart you like so much. So why don't you go have some before it's all gone?"

Berry mustered a wan smile. "Thank you. That sounds perfect. Maybe the wassail won't be gone, either." She stretched up on tiptoe to kiss Jonmarc on the cheek. "And don't worry, I won't tell Carina about Gregor. No need to open old wounds."

"Thanks, Berry."

"I'll have them pour a brandy for you, so hurry back!"

Jonmarc watched her go and he took a deep breath. Down the corridor, he could hear Neirin leading Gellyr and Gregor to their rooms for the night. Principality had managed to remain remarkably stable given the chaos that had been Margolan's lot over the last few years. Staden's reputation as a fair ruler with a firm hand had a lot to do with that. It was a bad time for the crown to pass to a young, untested heir, even one as bright and strong-willed as Berry. Despite the feast night and his own visions of the Dark Lady, it was not Jonmarc's custom to pray. But just in case, before he returned to the feasting, Jonmarc lit a candle in Istra's chapel beneath Dark Haven, for the health and soul of King Staden.

14

"I don't know how you get used to just riding up to the castle gates as if you owned the place." Rhistiart rode alongside Cam. It was market day in the palace city, and down the long road that led to Aberponte, vendors cajoled and bargained with passersby to purchase all types of foods, housewares, and jewelry. Cam and Rhistiart maneuvered their horses carefully through the throng as children ran across their path and shoppers bumped and jostled their way through the crowd.

"Every now and then, I wonder at it myself," Cam admitted. "You've seen Brunnfen. It's hardly the center of the aristocratic world in Isencroft. 'Backwater' doesn't seem to quite cover it. That used to stick in Alvior's craw. The few times he went to court with Father, he came home fuming because he wasn't dressed properly and he was ashamed. That didn't go over well with Father. He was more practical. It didn't matter to him whether he had the latest fashions or not. That's probably one reason he and Donelan got on so well."

They rode in silence the rest of the way. Cam kept trying to imagine just how he would break the enormity of Alvior's betrayal to Donelan, and he hoped the king would maintain his usual practicality in his response. After all the blows he'd taken from his older brother over the years, Cam had no desire to bear the brunt of the king's wrath for Alvior's treachery. Rhistiart seemed to sense Cam's mood and, for once, kept his songs and stories to himself.

They passed the lower guards with a cheerful greeting from the soldiers who recognized Cam and welcomed him back. Stable hands ran to take their reins as they reached the courtyard. Cam headed for the broad palace steps, and turned to see Rhistiart standing still.

"I thought I'd see to our bags," Rhistiart said nervously.

Cam glanced around the bustling courtyard. "There are servants for that."

Rhistiart swallowed nervously. "What are squires for?"

Cam sighed and grabbed the reluctant silversmith by the arm. "Oh, no you don't. You're an eyewitness to what we found at Brunnfen. I want someone to back me up. I'd rather Isencroft not prepare for war on my word alone."

"War? Nobody said anything about war," Rhistiart protested as Cam prodded him toward the steps. "This isn't really what I had in mind."

"You wanted an adventure. Well, we're right in the middle of one, and from what we saw at Brunnfen, it's a lot scarier than Leather John and his Divisionists. If Alvior really does come back across the Northern Sea, I guarantee you he'll have more than a few dozen malcontents with him."

Cam strode off through Aberponte's corridors, greeted and waved on by the guards and servants who recognized him. Rhistiart ran behind him, making halfhearted objections that Cam ignored. Cam finally stopped at the entrance to the king's private chambers. Rhistiart hung back as Cam spoke quietly to the two guards at the doors. One of them disappeared inside, and Cam waited, drawing a deep breath to ready himself.

The double doors flew open. "Cam! You're back! Thank Chenne. You look well. Come in, come in. How's that leg doing?"

King Donelan stood in the doorway. Though he was not dressed for formal court, one glance would have told anyone who wondered that this was Isencroft's king. Donelan was a bear of a man, tall, broad-shouldered, and barrel-chested. He'd earned a reputation for reckless courage on the battlefield as a young man, and for a bottomless zeal for life as he aged that included a love of fine brandy and good hunting. The brocade doublet in rich tones of brown and gold accentuated hair that showed few signs of gray though Donelan was well into his fifth decade. His grin was genuine, as was the energy with which he embraced Cam like a long-absent son.

Cam smiled and motioned for Rhistiart to follow him into the king's chambers, paying no heed as Rhistiart looked around himself, wide-eyed. "Leg's much improved, thanks to Carina. I've got a thick letter in my bags for you. She made me promise to give it to you right away. And of course, she sends her love." Cam chuckled. "I hope she delivers those twins on time, because she's already as big as a house with two more months to go. But everything you've heard about how her healing magic has grown is true. She healed the rift in the Flow, and she can mind heal. Oh, and she can also reduce the pain of injuries to *vayash moru* and *vyrkin*."

Donelan shook his head in amazement. "Truly? I thought such tales grew in the telling. And what of Jonmarc?"

"Up to his ass in trouble of one sort or another, as usual. If it's not an uprising among rogue *vayash moru*, it's undead refugees afraid of retribution for the plague or the mortal residents who are cranky about all the new *vayash moru* and *vyrkin*."

Donelan uncorked a decanter of brandy and poured a generous amount for Cam. Rhistiart had stepped back to stand along the wall, for once as still and silent as the paintings. "I've got Allestyr working on a banquet in your honor," Donelan continued, pausing to take a drink from his glass and give a sigh of contentment at the fine liquor. "Would have done it before this, but you were too banged up to enjoy it." He gave Cam a knowing look. "I took the liberty of having him contact the head of the Brewers Guild. Your last letter indicated that you and that spitfire of a girl—"

"Rhosyn."

Donelan made a gesture as if he recognized the name, and then went on. "Yes, yes. So you're still planning on marrying the girl?"

Cam swallowed wrong and began to cough, startled at the turn of conversation. "Yes, we are. I mean, I am."

"Good, good. I'll do the honors myself. We can do it right before the banquet, give you two things to celebrate."

Cam could only nod. Behind him, Rhistiart was chuckling from the shadows. "Oh, you've brought the silversmith back with you?" Donelan said, casting a glance to where Rhistiart was doing his best to be inconspicuous. "Good for you. He can help Allestyr pull the whole thing together. How did he like Brunnfen?"

Cam was used to Donelan's abrupt changes in direction, but he was certain that the rapidly switching subjects were making Rhistiart's head spin. "Actually, that's one of the reasons I brought Rhistiart with me to the palace today. I have some more bad news for you from Brunnfen."

Donelan frowned. "Renn's well? They're far enough north that the plague hasn't reached them, I hope."

Cam shook his head. "No, no. But I'm afraid there's evidence that Alvior's treason goes further than we first thought." He paused. "We've seen evidence that I think shows Alvior means to return with an invasion fleet."

Donelan's mood changed as quickly as his topics of conversation. "Then we'd best have a few other people hear this," he said, all joviality gone from his voice. He leaned outside the door and spoke to the guards. When he returned, his face was serious. "I'd like the head of the Veigonn in on this, as well as General Vinian. If war's coming, they need to know."

Cam felt nearly as nervous as Rhistiart looked as they waited. But before long, both Wilym, the head of the elite Veigonn, Donelan's private guard, and General Vinian arrived. Donelan motioned for them to join him in chairs near the fireplace, where a banked fire kept the chill away. Donelan insisted that Rhistiart also step forward to assist in the telling of the tale, and he forced a generous portion of brandy into Rhistiart's hand, which was visibly shaking.

Donelan, Wilym, and Vinian listened in silence as Cam recounted what they had found at Brunnfen. Rhistiart corroborated Cam's story, as well as vouching for Renn's ignorance of Alvior's betrayal and Cam's brother's willingness to do anything to help capture Alvior and prevent his return to Brunnfen. Throughout the telling, Donelan's expression grew dark and his eyes flashed with anger. When Cam and Rhistiart finished their tale, Donelan sprang from his chair.

"By the Whore! If Alvior wants war, then he'll find it here." He glanced at Wilym. "I'll write to Tris Drayke in Margolan, to Staden in Principality and Kalcen in Eastmark. Their kingdoms border on the Northern Sea. They'd best know what's brewing. We have no idea whether this invasion of Alvior's would just target Isencroft, or whether it's the entire coastline that's at risk. I want riders ready at dawn to ride as hard as they can with the letters. The others need to be warned."

General Vinian looked to Cam. "You have no idea of Alvior's timetable?"

"If he intends to bring ships into Brunnfen's harbor, then he'll have to come before winter. What I gathered from Father's ghost gave me to think it would be sometime in the fall."

Vinian looked to Wilym. "That doesn't leave us much time,

especially if we're to field an army and ready ourselves for an invasion fleet."

"I've always been one to keep my feet solidly on dry ground," Cam said. "But what of Isencroft's navy? Can it hold off an invasion?"

Vinian shrugged. "It's been a long time since we've had cause to worry. The kingdoms on the far side of the Northern Sea have kept to themselves for over a hundred years. Long ago, Eristan the explorer brought back ships with silver, gems, and furs from Temnotta, the Midnight Land. There were a few attempts to exchange ambassadors, but the king of Temnotta grew suspicious. He was afraid that Eristan would return with warships to take Temnotta's riches. So the king closed the borders, and for generations, foreign ships have been refused entry." Vinian rubbed his chin as he thought.

"Of course, that king would be long dead. We've had little information from Temnotta, and most of it can't be verified. But what we've heard from traders who were allowed entry and from *vayash moru* who have come through Temnotta is that the succession was uncertain and that there was tension between rival aristocratic families. Several of the men in line for the throne died under suspicious circumstances. There's very little known about the new king except that he's fairly young—perhaps thirty summers at most—and that he comes from a noble family with strong ties to the military. We don't even have a name."

"What of the Northern Raiders? Where do they come in?" Cam asked, accepting a second drink when Donelan offered the decanter.

"The Northern Raiders have been at odds with Temnotta more than they've been aligned," Wilym replied, swirling the dark brandy in his glass. "The Raiders hold the outer islands, and to the best of our knowledge, they owe fealty to no king. They're a loose alliance of warlords who are just as likely to be fighting each other as anyone else, and they've usually been more interested in looting and carrying off prisoners than they have been in conquering territory."

"I'd heard it said that the raids came more often long ago, before Isencroft was a kingdom," Cam mused. "And that in those days, the Raiders sometimes stayed behind to trade or farm. There are rumors, in the coastal towns at least, that many a family had mixed blood with Raiders who traded more than trinkets and fur."

Wilym nodded. "And the rumors are probably true. But the Raiders alone wouldn't pose a threat to Isencroft, not without a navy behind them. Or at least they wouldn't be a challenge to the king, but they might make a mess of the villages and rural areas until we could get soldiers out to take care of it."

Cam sighed. "At least we're rid of the Divisionists."

Wilym and Vinian exchanged a glance that made Cam's heart sink. "Not totally," Wilym said. "You took out the head of their organization, but there's still anger among the rabble about Kiara's marriage to Martris Drayke, and now that their child's been born, it makes the idea of a joint throne even more ominous. We think the Divisionists have gone underground. We're not counting them out yet."

"Do you think they've still got ties to Alvior's treason?"

Vinian shrugged. "Who knows? We've had years of poor harvests, and now, the plague. People are angry, and they blame the king. They don't think about whether or not he could fix what ails them, but he's in charge, so to their thinking, it must be his fault. I think Alvior was always using the Divisionists as pawns. They were just to draw off the army's attention from the real threat. If Alvior really was in league with Temnotta, then he was never worried about the joint throne. He had plans all along to be Temnotta's puppet king himself."

"Was either group said to use magic? What we found at Brunnfen was a workshop for a mage."

To Cam's surprise, Wilym nodded, and his expression was solemn. "The legends say that Temnotta had many powerful mages, the Volshe. It was rumored that the kings of Temnotta ruled at the pleasure of the Volshe, and that it was the Volshe, not the kings, that cut off trade with the Winter Kingdoms, for fear their secrets might be stolen."

"Do the legends say what kind of mages the Volshe were?"

Again, Wilym nodded. "The legends talk about blood magic, and about mages that could create horrors to punish their enemies. That's consistent with the few stories we've gotten from the *vayash moru*, and what little our agents have been able to confirm."

Cam finished his drink. It did little to calm him. "So the idea of a dark summoner coming from across the Northern Sea isn't unthinkable."

"No," Vinian answered. "Unfortunately, it's not unthinkable at all."

By ninth bells, the fear of war was replaced by a very different kind of fear. Cam shifted from foot to foot as Rhistiart fussed over Cam's uniform jacket and adjusted the new medal pinned there to let it hang straight. "Stand still! Sweet Chenne, if you've got nerves like a cat, how do you manage going to battle?"

Cam could feel himself beginning to sweat, although the night was cool. "Battle is one thing. This is my wedding. There's no comparison."

Rhistiart chuckled. "I wouldn't know myself, but I've heard it said that both are forms of warfare."

They waited in a small parlor just off Donelan's private quarters. It was a room Cam had visited many times when he and the king had spent pleasant evenings playing dice or swapping tall tales over a bottle of brandy. Cam tried to remember a time when he'd felt quite as nervous and couldn't think of one. "I imagine there's a back door if you've changed your mind," Rhistiart said with a grin.

"No, no. Rhosyn's everything I ever wanted in a woman," Cam replied, aware that his voice was not entirely steady. "I love her hair. I love her curves. I love her laugh."

"And you love my daddy's ale." They turned to see Rhosyn in the doorway. Rhosyn's unruly red hair was swept up and secured by a golden mesh. Her gown was in Isencroft's traditional colors of flame, sacred to the Warrior Aspect, Chenne. Red silk, edged with a border of orange, made Rhosyn's pale skin glow. The silk hugged her ample curves and Cam swallowed hard as he felt his body react appreciatively.

"Yes, I love your daddy's ale, but that's beside the point," Cam said, moving to take Rhosyn's hand. "I'm sorry I couldn't stop on the way to the palace. I had news for Donelan that couldn't wait."

Rhosyn sighed. "Always business." She gave an exaggerated sigh. "Since it was for the king, I guess I can forgive you." She grinned as Cam drew her close for a kiss. When they moved apart, she gave an appraising look to Cam's newly healed leg. "How did it heal?"

In answer, Cam walked from one side of the room to the other. The limp was noticeable, but not pronounced. "Do I meet your approval? After all, no one buys a horse without checking to see if it's lame."

Rhosyn shook her head, as if she guessed that Cam's humor hid a very real fear that she might reject him. "Cam of Cairnrach! You know I'd have you even if you were gimping along with a wooden peg. And here I was, hoping that your sister might knock some sense into that thick head of yours!"

Cam laughed. "Carina's been trying to do that for years.

If you ever figure out how, you'll have to promise to let her know."

Rhosyn took Cam's hand, and beneath the banter he could see nervousness in her eyes. She smoothed her skirts with her free hand. "You should have seen the look on Father's face when a messenger came from the palace with an invitation from the king. Father'd been thinking all along that we'd have the wedding down at the tavern. After all," she said with a sly smile, "it's one of your favorite spots. He'd already insisted that I spend a small fortune on the dress and he'd had his jacket made special for the occasion. He didn't want it said you were marrying below your station."

Cam frowned. "You know I'm not concerned with things like that."

"Some are. Father didn't want to embarrass you. But he never expected that the king himself would marry us."

"You've met Donelan before, when I was sick. Is he that fearsome?"

Rhosyn's eyes were wide. "He's the king, isn't he? That's plenty fearsome."

Cam squeezed her hand. "I'm glad it didn't scare you off."

Rhosyn tossed her head. "Takes more than the king to scare me away from you, Cam of Cairnrach. I'm made of sterner stuff than that!"

Just then, the door opened and Donelan swept into the room. Despite her protestations a moment before, Rhosyn paled enough that Cam feared she might swoon. Donelan seemed oblivious. Behind Donelan trailed Allestyr, the seneschal. Rhistiart stepped back, and Cam knew that the silversmith probably would have found an excuse to bolt from the room had Cam not expressly asked that he stay as a witness.

"We've got a roomful of guests ready for a banquet downstairs," Donelan said. "Let's get you two married so there's even more reason to celebrate." He peered at Rhosyn as if it were the first time he had looked closely at her. "Let me see you, girl." Rhosyn was trembling, but she put on a good face and stepped forward. Donelan stroked his chin.

"I assume that you've seen this great ox when he's well into his cups," Donelan said. "I'd hate to think you didn't know what you were getting into."

Rhosyn drew a deep breath and straightened her shoulders. "I've helped him stagger into the guest room to sleep off many a feast night, and on occasion, I've heard him sing and lived to tell about it. There's no one who'll do but him."

Donelan nodded and looked at Cam. "She's got enough fire in her belly to keep you in line, m'boy," he said, and Cam heard the humor beneath Donelan's sober expression. "She just might finish what Carina started and make you presentable after all."

"It's a risk I'm willing to take, Your Majesty," Cam replied.

Donelan clapped them both on the shoulder. His huge hand nearly staggered Rhosyn, but she managed to keep her feet. "Excellent. Well then, let's get on with it." Allestyr handed an ermine stole to Donelan, as Cam and Rhosyn clasped their right hands together, facing one another. Donelan wrapped the stole four times around their hands. A large pendant of the dragon seal of Isencroft hung from a heavy chain around Donelan's neck. He raised the pendant and touched it to his lips, and then removed the chain and draped it over the stole.

"Cam of Cairnrach, Lord of Brunnfen, and Rhosyn, daughter of Elkhart of the Brewers Guild. Be it known that from this day on, you are joined as man and wife by order of Donelan, King of Isencroft, witnessed this day by Allestyr and Rhistiart. May your days be long and may all the faces of the Lady smile upon you." Donelan reclaimed his pendant and unwound the mantle from around their hands. Only then did Cam realize he had been holding his breath.

Donelan leaned forward and planted a kiss on Rhosyn's cheek before the astonished girl had the chance to react. The king turned to Cam with a rakish grin. "There's time before the cook brings out the venison and the banquet gets under way for the two of you to greet each other properly. Do me proud and have a baby on the way before we're off to war."

With that, Donelan was gone, striding from the room without a backward glance. Allestyr followed, and Rhistiart paused just before he left the room. "I took the liberty of having the servants tidy up Cam's room to suit a lady's sensibilities," he said.

Rhosyn grinned, and punched Cam jokingly on the arm. "What ladies have you been having up to your room?"

Rhistiart glanced from Rhosyn to Cam, not sure whether the misunderstanding was deliberate. "M'lady, I readied his room with you in mind—"

Cam and Rhosyn both laughed, and Rhistiart relaxed, fleeing with a chagrined look on his face.

"Don't go getting ideas that I'm going to be one of those fancy court ladies," Rhosyn teased. "I'm from good, solid, common stock, and not ashamed of it."

Cam wrapped his arm around Rhosyn's waist. "I wouldn't have it any other way."

By eleventh bells, the feast was ready to begin. Cam was impressed by Allestyr's ability to put such a gathering together on short notice. Then again, Cam realized, it was the night before the Moon Feast, and Allestyr would have had nearly everything ready for the holiday. Cam squeezed Rhosyn's hand to reassure her as they entered. A cry went up from Wilym and the Veigonn in greeting, which was echoed by the guests, all of whom Cam recognized. He glanced at Rhosyn. Cam knew her well enough to know that the attention unsettled her, but Rhosyn had years of experience with crowds at the tavern. She squared her shoulders and smiled, and although she was nervous, the smile was genuine.

"A toast to Cam, Lord of Brunnfen, King's Champion, and his bride Rhosyn!" Wilym made the toast, raising his tankard high. Voices echoed the toast, adding ribald comments and shouting well wishes. One of the servants ran to fill goblets for both Cam and Rhosyn. Out of the corner of his eye, Cam spotted Rhistiart busily helping Allestyr and looking like he'd been managing palace events all his life.

"To Cam and his lady! Hear, hear!"

Musicians struck up a lively tune, and Rhosyn began to sway to the music as she sipped her ale. A burly man with wild, red hair shouldered his way through the crowd. He was broad-shouldered and wide-chested, with strong arms and hands broadened by work. Tonight, he wore a jacket of dark green brocade with puffed sleeves and gilt trim, and it took Cam a moment to recognize Elkhart, Rhosyn's father, since he had never in all his years seen the brewer dressed for court.

"Cam, Rhosyn, the Lady's blessings on you!" Elkhart said. He slapped Cam on the back hard enough to slosh the ale in Cam's tankard. "It's good to see you up and about, m'lad," he said with an appraising glance. "Last I'd heard, you looked as if you'd been ridden over by a tinker's caravan!"

Cam grinned ruefully. "I would have been in better shape had it only been a tinker's caravan. But thanks to the king's battle healer, Trygve, and my sister, Carina, they patched the worst of it up right."

Elkhart glanced down at Cam's feet. "Looks like you kept the leg, thank Chenne for that."

Cam nodded. "I understand I put both Trygve's and Carina's healing to the test. It's good to be back." He slipped his arm around Rhosyn's shoulders.

Elkhart looked at Rhosyn, and the burly man teared up.

"You're a beauty to rival any at court in that dress, my dear."
He sniffed back tears as Rhosyn beamed. Elkhart looked up at
Cam worriedly. "It's not true what I hear, that there may be war,
is it?"

Cam shifted uneasily, and Rhosyn looked to him with an
expression that mirrored Elkhart's concern. "There's a threat
from the north coming that we can't afford to ignore. But I pray
to the Lady that nothing comes of it, or that we put it right
quickly."

Elkhart nodded. "That's how it goes, isn't it? Ah, well.
Tonight, we celebrate." He managed a smile, although this time,
it did not entirely reach his eyes. "Eat. Drink. Make merry. You
deserve this night." He glanced over his shoulder to where the
ale was being poured, and was suddenly all business. "Wouldn't
do to run out of ale at the king's celebration, would it?" He
kissed Rhosyn on the cheek and ambled off through the crowd,
already giving orders to the men from the brewery.

"Moon Feast at Aberponte is one of my favorites," Cam said,
steering Rhosyn through the partygoers to where a groaning board
of food awaited. The scent of roasted venison, mutton, and duck
filled the room, along with the delicious aroma of onions, leeks,
and parsnips. Pies, cobblers, and trifles filled the air with the smell
of baked apples, raisins, and rum sauce. Cam sighed. There was
much he enjoyed about being the King's Champion, and the
palace food was worth every bit of danger he endured.

He steered Rhosyn to a balcony. "Look there," he said,
pointing. Bonfires flared in the courtyard, sending flames high
into the night sky. Lanterns in the shape of the moon's phases
hung from trees and from cords strung back and forth across
the open space. In the center of the courtyard, a large figure of
a man made from dried cornstalks and tree branches blazed.
The air was sweet with the smell of incense to the Sacred Lady
and of ritual herbs rising on the smoke. Festivalgoers carried

candle-lit lanterns on poles in the shape of the phases of the moon. The night sky was filled with paper lanterns lifted into the air by a fire within that carried them up to the clouds, and with them, the prayers of the people who released the lantern kites to the heavens.

"Tomorrow, there'll be jousting all day. We get to sit in the king's box to watch. I guarantee we'll have the best seats!"

Rhosyn laughed. "And are you one of the jousters?"

Cam shook his head. "I'm a foot soldier at heart, not cavalry. Wilym will joust as the King's Favorite. I can fight on horseback, but I much prefer to have the ground under my feet."

Along one side, eight women in white robes filed into the courtyard. The crowd parted like water for them.

"Who are they?" Rhosyn murmured in an awed voice.

Cam's eyes widened. "The Oracle and her attendants. This is very unusual. She doesn't come to the palace. Kings go to her." He touched Rhosyn's sleeve. "Let's go back inside. We'll know why the Oracle is here soon enough."

They had just filled their plates when a trumpet fanfare blared from the doorway. King Donelan swept into the room, attended by two members of the Veigonn and half a dozen pages and retainers. He stopped in the center of the room as the crowd quieted.

"Good Gentles, all," Donelan boomed. His voice filled the room and his forceful personality ensured that he had everyone's full attention. "Tonight we thank the Lady, Mother, Childe, Lover, and especially our patron, the Warrior Chenne, for the harvest to be gathered." One of his aides pressed a tankard into his right hand and a fresh loaf of bread into his left.

"We thank Her for the wine and ale that sustain us through the winter, and for the bread that feeds us. And we thank our Lady Chenne for the bounty of the hunters and the victory of the warriors. All praise to the Lady!"

Cheers erupted from the crowd and tankards rose into the air in salute. Donelan smiled, pleased with the crowd and the evening. But as quickly as the cheers had risen, the room suddenly fell silent as the white-cowled figures appeared in the doorway. Donelan turned slowly, and his eyes widened to see the newcomers.

"My lady Oracle," Donelan said, bowing. Everyone in the room also bowed. A few fell to their knees. The faces of the Oracle and her acolytes were hidden beneath their cowls. The Oracle moved to the front as her entourage parted.

"Donelan, son of Jendran, grandson of Talith, I bear a message from Our Lady Chenne."

Donelan took a step forward and spread his hands in a gesture of supplication. "M'lady, we did not anticipate the honor of your presence. I have no gift for you."

"The Lady desires no gift save your understanding." The Oracle's voice was clear, but if there was a face beneath the cowl, it was lost in shadow.

"Do you desire a private place to give your message? Is it for all to hear?"

"This is a true saying, one that touches all of Isencroft," the Oracle replied. "All may hear it."

"Speak, m'lady, and I will listen."

Even though the Oracle's face was hidden beneath her cowl, Cam had the feeling that Donelan's deference pleased her. Cam had heard Donelan express his doubts about the Oracle's wisdom on more than one occasion. Donelan was a man who preferred action and plain-spokenness. The Oracle's pronouncements were often vague and open to interpretation, making it difficult to take decisive action.

"Harsh winds blow from the north. Fire burns the edge of the sea. Old graves spill forth their bones and souls are torn from the Lady's embrace. Hear us, son of Jendran. Crowns will fall, and scepters pass to untested hands. All that has been will change. A War of Unmaking is now upon us. Even She of the Amber Eyes cannot see its end."

Donelan hesitated for a moment, and then did something Cam did not expect. The proud king knelt stiffly and bowed his head. "Oracle of My Lady Chenne, if I have displeased my goddess, then let Her vengeance fall on me and me alone. Do not bring a War of Unmaking on the Winter Kingdoms."

The Oracle glided closer to Donelan and laid her hand on his head. Or rather, something under her long, wide sleeve rested on the king's crown. No part of the body beneath the robe was exposed to view, and Cam shuddered, wondering whether or not the Oracle was even human.

"You have well pleased My Lady. The fault lies not in you, or in the crowns of Her kingdoms. There is a current, swift and cold, and it bears all away in its depths. As the moon moves through her phases, so our times move from full to dark. I bear the message that darkness rises. But take heart, Donelan, son of Jendran, darkness also passes."

With that, the Oracle and her entourage turned and left as swiftly and silently as they had come. Donelan rose, and for a moment, before his studied expression slipped back into place, Cam met Donelan's eyes and saw something there he had never seen before. Fear.

15

" *Serroquette*, I need you to bear a message for me."

Aidane gathered her cloak around her. It was autumn, and there was a nip in the air. The chill she felt at the moment had little to do with the weather. "I'm not taking clients," Aidane replied to the ghost that spoke to her from the edge of the forest. Something had drawn Aidane to wander away from their camp, and now she knew that it had been the spirit who called her. But after her last, nearly fatal assignation, Aidane was more than happy to comply with Jolie's edict that, on the road, none of the girls would take customers, so that the group could travel without incident.

"Please, hear me out." The spirit was a fine mist in the darkness, but as Aidane watched, the mist formed itself into the outline of a young woman. Aidane could see the ghost clearly in her mind. The woman was about her own age, just a few summers more than twenty years, and she wore a gown that looked to be several hundred years out of date. Her dress suggested that she had been merchant-born, neither peasant nor royal. Dark hair in curls framed the young woman's face. But it was the urgency in the woman's eyes that made Aidane listen.

Aidane sighed. "I'll hear you. But I'm not allowed to take clients now, even if I wanted to, which I don't."

"I want you to take a message to Kolin."

Aidane's eyebrows rose, as did her suspicions. "How do you know Kolin?"

The ghost stepped closer, and Aidane could see sorrow in the young woman's eyes. "My name is Elsbet. Two hundred and fifty years ago, Kolin and I were lovers. Haven't you noticed how sure he is traveling through this area? Every run, he returns here. Up on the hill, you'll find the ruins of his family's home. That's where he'll shelter the fugitives tonight. I've seen him come time and again, but I don't have the power on my own to contact him. Please, you have to help me."

It had been over two weeks since Kolin, Jolie, and the others had left Jolie's Place. The mortals in the group traveled by daylight, along a route they agreed upon each night. By nightfall, Kolin, Astir, and the *vayash moru* and *vyrkin* they had rescued out of Nargi caught up. By now, they were partway across Dhasson, northbound for Dark Haven in Principality. Each night, Kolin, Astir, and Jolie conferred in quiet tones about the next step of the journey. About three days after they had crossed the Nu River, they had met up with a group of four musicians and a peddler, all fleeing Margolan for the relative safety of Dark Haven.

Aidane glanced back at the group that sat around the fire. The musicians were playing softly. If they were practicing, it sounded good. Aidane suspected that they played to settle their own nerves, rather than to perform for their traveling companions. They were better than the usual tavern players, and Aidane liked their selection of songs. They had been friendly to Aidane without judging, or perhaps even knowing, what she was. The peddler was a solitary fellow. He'd offered to trade any of his wares for the chance to travel with the group, and he'd admitted that a few nights before meeting them he had been waylaid and robbed of his coin.

Jolie's girls were clustered together. They never seemed to lack for conversation, and while Cefra had invited Aidane to the circle and Aidane sometimes joined them, tonight she had been restless. Now, she knew why. She turned her attention back to the ghost.

"How do I know you're telling the truth?"

Elsbet's ghost spread her hands, palms up. "I can tell you about Kolin, but without asking him, you'd have no way to verify what I say. Let me tell you my tale, and you can decide."

Aidane nodded. "Go on."

Elsbet sighed. "Kolin's family owned the manor on the hill. My father was the most successful merchant in town. By the time I met Kolin, he had been a *vayash moru* for one hundred years. We met at a dance in the village and fell in love. His family had been highborn, but they had lost much of their money and standing. Kolin stayed to help with the estate. And although I was common-born, his relatives were kind to me." A shadow crossed her face. "My father was not happy that I was seeing Kolin. He thought it was wrong for us to be together, since I was mortal and Kolin was..."

"Dead."

Elsbet grimaced. "According to Father, yes. I refused to listen. Then Father got the idea to send me away, to make me live with my aunt near Valiquet. I was afraid that I'd never see Kolin again. We made plans to run away and be married." She raised her eyes to look at Aidane, as if she expected to find judgment in Aidane's expression. "Such things are legal in Dhasson, even if not everyone approves."

"I know." Aidane watched the ghost carefully. She'd heard the tales of many spirits who sought her services, and early in her vocation, she'd been lied to many times by ghosts who really wanted vengeance. More than once, those falsehoods had nearly gotten Aidane killed, and once, the ghost who possessed her had used Aidane to murder a faithless lover. But now, watching this ghost, Aidane heard nothing false in the story. "Go on."

Elsbet's expression grew sad. "I went home to gather my things. But my father found me, and he was drunk. He was angry that I had defied him, and even angrier that I was sleeping with a *vayash moru*. He beat me. I don't think he actually meant to kill me, but he did. I died before Kolin rose for the night. I was dead before he could try to bring me across."

Aidane could feel her heart pounding. "What happened?"

"When I didn't meet Kolin as we had planned, he came to look for me. I guess he thought my father had locked me in. He found me dead, and my father was just beginning to sober up and realize what he'd done." Her voice grew soft. "I knew Kolin to be gentle and kind, but that night, I truly understood what it meant to be *vayash moru*. It was as if he'd lost his mind with grief. He killed my father, and he carried my body up to the crypt on his family's land. I saw him grieving, but I didn't have the power to make myself heard to him." The ghost knelt and reached out to Aidane.

"Please, m'lady, I beg of you. It's been over two hundred years since I died. But every time Kolin passes this way, he comes to the crypt. He talks to me as if he knows my spirit remains. I know about how he travels to Nargi to free the *vayash moru* and *vyrkin*. I know that he serves Lady Riqua in Dark Haven, and that he holds a place of honor among his people. But, m'lady, every time he passes here, he brings gifts to me and places them beside my bones. He blames himself for my death."

Aidane realized she was holding her breath. "What do you want from me?"

"I want you to let me speak through you. I want to touch Kolin and tell him how sorry I am that I couldn't return to him." Elsbet's eyes were wide with sadness. "I want to take my rest in the Lady. My spirit is tired of wandering. But I won't go away and leave him alone again without saying good-bye. Please, m'lady, I can pay. There's a mound of jewels and gold that Kolin brought to me over the years. It lies beside my dust. Take it all. Only please, give me one last night with him. I beg of you."

"Why should Kolin trust me? I don't think he even likes me. I got rescued by accident."

Elsbet managed a sad smile. "I'll tell you what you need to say. He'll believe."

Aidane stared back at the group around the fire. Her welcome among Kolin's lieutenants had been grudging at best. But it had been Kolin who insisted that she be rescued along with the *vayash moru* and *vyrkin*, and it had been Kolin who had stood up to Jolie on her behalf. "I offered to pay him for rescuing me, and it made him angry," she said softly. "If he would accept that I carry your spirit, perhaps I can offer him payment that he would accept."

"Thank you, m'lady. Thank you."

Aidane wasn't at all sure that it would go as smoothly as Elsbet supposed. But she nodded. "Kolin will go up to the crypt a few candlemarks before dawn. Meet me here and we'll ... join. Then I'll let you guide me from there."

"As you wish, m'lady. I'll be waiting."

Aidane was deep in thought as she made her way back to camp. "There you are!" Cefra waved her over to a place on the log near the fire. "I thought you might get eaten by wolves. Didn't anyone tell you it's not healthy to wander alone at night?"

Aidane gave Cefra a reassuring smile that did not reach her eyes. "Just needed to clear my head."

Cefra pressed a flask into Aidane's hand. Even before she lifted it to her lips, Aidane could smell that it was river rum. "This'll clear your head just fine. We were just listening to Ed tell us his stories." She nodded toward the peddler, who gave a broad smile, and Aidane guessed that Ed had not only provided the rum but had a good bit of it himself.

"I was just tellin' the ladies about the time I took my wagon down to Valiquet, to the palace city," Ed said. He held his rum well, so that it gave just a slight slur to his words. Ed had the narrow, angular features of a Dhasson native, but his accent made Aidane suspect that he spent most of his time trading along the river, and that he probably spoke the river patois like a native.

"I did a good business in the city, fixing jewelry and trading new pots and pans and the like with the innkeepers and taverns." He gave a broad wink. "But the service that was most requested was repairing fidelity rings. You know what those are?" When his listeners shook their heads, Ed's smile broadened. "Well, now. Among the well-to-do in Valiquet, these fidelity rings were quite popular. They come apart like a puzzle, and they're the Crone's own to put right again. Men'll give them to their wives without tellin' the secret of how the puzzle's done. Then if she strays and takes off her ring, it falls apart and odds are that she won't be able to put it right. So he'll know she's been cattin' around."

Ed stretched. "Now fittin' pieces together is my specialty. I fix all kinds of things. So it turns out I have a talent for figuring out these fidelity rings, even though some of them are damned difficult." He beamed with false modesty. "Just a gift, I guess. Anyhow, after I'd done one or two, word got out among the ladyfolk, and every night, I'd have a couple of well-born ladies come looking for me round back of the tavern. I'd fix their rings, and they'd pay me well." He gave another wink. "Some even paid coin, if you take my meaning." The girls laughed at his joke, but Aidane's thoughts remained on Elsbet's tale.

"What happened?" Cefra asked, leaning forward.

Ed shrugged. "What do you think? Eventually, one of the husbands found out, and he came back with his friends. Nearly busted up the tavern, and I barely got down the road with my wagon in time. If they'd ridden me down on horseback, I might not have escaped, but I heard tell that the innkeeper settled them down by giving them free ale and food, and I managed to escape with my skin." He crossed his arms. "And they say a peddler's life is dull."

"What's the strangest thing that's ever happened to you?" It was Cefra asking, and Aidane wasn't sure whether her new friend was trying to flirt with Ed or just looking for a diversion.

Ed's eyes grew dark. "They say that truth is stranger than the wildest tale. 'Tis true, I fear. There's a caravan that passes through Dhasson every year. Now, lots of caravans pass through Dhasson, that's true. But this caravan wasn't as big as the one Maynard Linton runs. This was a nice size, with all kinds of traveling merchants, musicians, acrobats, jugglers, and fools. Of course, there was plenty of need for a peddler, and so I made it my business to set my meanderings so that I would cross their path. Lots of tin to mend, ale to drink, and sights to see.

"Well and good until a few months ago. They were going to make a loop through southern Margolan, and I told them that was a bad idea. Told them there was plague afoot down there. But they didn't listen." Ed shook his head. "I knew their route, and I meant to meet up with them again. That's when I got the scare of my life."

Cefra's eyes were wide, and even Aidane leaned forward to catch the tale. "What happened?" Cefra asked.

"I could tell before I ever got within shouting distance that there was something wrong," Ed said. "People didn't seem to be moving right. Jerkylike, as if they were stumbling. There were tents up, sort of, but not proper tents, as if a blind man who had never seen a tent tried to assemble one. I could hear

music, too. Always liked their musicians. But this time, everything was off-key, slow. Sent a chill down my back. And the
smell! I thought I'd come upon a charnel house in midsummer.
Then I saw that there was a pile of dead animals to the side of
the road." He shook his head. "Those were the wild beasts the
caravan used to charge people coin to see. Animals from all
over the Winter Kingdoms, and some from beyond." His expression was sorrowful. "Not only were they dead, but some of
them"—he swallowed before he could continue— "some of them
had been chewed on."

A gasp went up from Ed's listeners. Aidane looked hard at
him, trying to tell whether he was concocting the tale, but his
distress seemed genuine. "I turned around to run, and there was
Venn. Venn was one of the guards I was friendliest with. Drank
many a pint of ale with him, out behind the tents. Well, there
stands Venn, or what was left of him, Goddess rest his soul.
Lady true! I would have taken him for a corpse if he hadn't
been moving, although it was more shambling than walking.
His nose was eaten off, and his eyes were sunken back in his
head. He was covered with pox sores, and his skin was yellowish-
white. But his eyes. By the Whore! His eyes were mad. He
made a grunting noise and started after me, and I ran for all I
was worth."

"What happened to them?" Aidane couldn't help asking.

"*Ashtenerath*," one of the girls whispered, the word like a
curse. Ed nodded.

"That's the Lady's truth. Not dead, not really living, and
nothing but rage in his eyes. Corpses that don't know enough
to lie down and die, that don't have the peace of the dead." Ed's
eyes were wide with fear. "But there's worse. I've seen them
twice since." Ed glanced over his shoulder at the horizon, and
the fear in his eyes was real. "Saw them traveling all in a line,
like they used to, only it was a caravan of the damned. Horses

foaming at the mouths, bones jutting out everywhere, mad with fear. Musicians playing songs from the Abyss, songs for the dead. Even their wagons looked like they were rotting away. I guess they'll keep on going until they drop, one by one, in their tracks, or just rot into pieces." He shivered and wrapped his arms around himself. "Dark Lady take my soul! I don't ever want to see that sight again!"

Aidane turned to look for Kolin. She spotted him with Zhan and Varren. He moved to sit near Astir and Jolie. Two of the *vayash moru* who had been rescued from the Nargi stood guard, and Aidane was sure that the now-healed *vyrkin* were also prowling the woods, both to bring down game for their dinner and to assure that the camp would not be disturbed.

Aidane watched Kolin in the firelight. His blond hair was caught back in a queue. Now that she had a chance to study his features, she could see the Dhassonian bloodlines, with perhaps some Margolan heritage as well. He was dressed plainly, as they all were, to avoid attracting the attention of robbers, but even so, Kolin moved with assurance. She had no doubt that in life, Kolin had been highborn, even if his family had not been truly wealthy. From what Aidane had overheard, it was clear that, as a *vayash moru*, Kolin had attained a position of responsibility and respect among the undead and the *vyrkin*. Even Astir and Jolie deferred to him, though Jolie never gave ground without a fight.

Kolin seemed to sense that someone was watching him, and he turned. For just an instant, his eyes met Aidane's. He was curious, and distrustful. Aidane hurried to look away.

He knows what you are, the ghost murmured so that only Aidane could hear. *Perhaps it's crossed his mind that you could bring me to him, if only for this night. Even now, he's not so distant as he pretends.*

Aidane looked down at her hands. She thought she could feel

Kolin's gaze, even though she told herself she was imagining it. She did her best to shut out the sound of Ed's next story and strained to hear what Kolin and the others were saying.

"—nights are getting colder," Jolie said. "We're going north. We won't be able to sleep outside for too much longer."

"We have safe houses," Kolin replied.

"What of the new ones?" Astir asked. "The minstrels and the peddler. They're more than we expected."

Kolin glanced toward the group by the fire and shrugged. The musicians kept on playing, oblivious to the fact that their future was being discussed. "They're good cover. More eyes to keep watch, and a few more men to travel with, make it a little less obvious that we're moving the residents of a whorehouse to safety," he said, but Aidane could hear humor in his voice and knew Kolin was gently baiting Jolie.

Jolie sniffed. "You're just afraid that if word got out, we'd have so much business we wouldn't reach Dark Haven till winter. We're the most exciting thing that's passed this way, I wager."

Aidane heard Astir's rich, tenor laughter. "Give it up, Kolin. You know you can't win an argument with Jolie. You're lucky she agreed not to dress her little peacocks in all their finery, or we'd have a line of patrons following us every step of the way!"

"It's not the patrons that worry me; it's the Black Robes," Kolin said. "In Nargi, they seemed to single out whores to kidnap. There's more than one reason I'd like to travel without attracting attention."

"Do you think that's why the Nargi took Aidane?" It was Zhan speaking, and Aidane tensed, remembering that Kolin's lieutenant had not been happy about the order to bring her with them.

"Could be." Kolin paused, and Aidane was afraid to look up, for fear he was looking her way. "Though it might be as she said, that she was in the wrong place at the wrong time." He hesitated. "What do you make of her?" Aidane guessed that Kolin had turned to Jolie, and she tensed, fearing Jolie's reply.

"Don't know yet. She doesn't seem too taken with herself. That's unusual for a *serroquette*. I'd like to see her with the spirit on her, see if her 'gift' is real."

"It was real enough for the men we ambushed," Kolin replied. "The dead lovers got their revenge." His voice was flat, and it was impossible for Aidane to guess what Kolin was thinking.

After that, the talk among Kolin and the others turned back to planning the route ahead, and Aidane's attention returned to Ed the peddler's next story just as the pudgy, blond man reached the punch line. Aidane joined in the group's laughter, even though she hadn't heard a word of the story. Knowing what she had promised Elsbet's ghost, Aidane fidgeted until it was time to go to bed. She helped the other girls forage for pine boughs and make their bedrolls as comfortable as possible, with a wary glance skyward to see whether rain would wake them. Tonight, the sky was clear and the moon was bright.

Kolin and the *vayash moru* headed up the path toward the ruins of the house on the hill. The *vyrkin*, some as wolves and others in human form, stayed to guard the mortals. Ed eyed the *vyrkin* warily, but if he had misgivings, he said nothing. The four musicians packed up their instruments. The musicians were as odd a bunch as the rest of them, Aidane thought. Their outfits might have been fine enough to play in better taverns once, but now they were stained and torn from travel.

There were three men and a portly woman. One of the men seemed to belong with the woman; they were older than the others and had the most skill on the dulcimer and drone. A thin young man with shaggy, dark hair and a half-grown beard played the flute with skill. The fourth man, who looked barely out of his teens, carried an hourglass-shaped drum with markings that looked like runes. Tattoos on his arms and hands mirrored the markings on his drum. He got a faraway look in his eyes as he drummed, and his fingers flew in complex rhythms that sometimes stretched his companions' ability to keep up. The musicians were jovial company, but Aidane wondered what story they were hiding, and what details they preferred to keep to themselves.

This night, the elder musician, the drone player, caught up to Ed before the peddler left the circle around the fire. "A word about that caravan you saw, if you please."

Ed looked at him suspiciously, but did not pull away. The four minstrels exchanged glances. "We also saw your caravan of the damned." It was the older, portly musician who spoke. "My name's Cal. We had just closed up after playing at an inn long past midnight. It was just past second bells. We heard something like music, strange and jumbled. We went to look for it." Cal looked to the others, who nodded for him to go on.

"You can ask my wife, Nezra," he said with a tilt of his head toward the plump dulcimer player beside him. "We saw a caravan in the moonlight, outlined against the sky, shuffling and stumbling, just like you said. Some of them were groaning and moaning, and the horses whinnying in fear." He shivered.

"Bez over there, our drummer, and Thanal, the flute player, thought they'd be brave and get closer for a better look. Well, they got closer, all right. Almost had their arms ripped off when two of those…those…*things* came after them. Pulled their cloaks right off them. They didn't follow too long when Bez and Thanal ran away, as if they forgot what they were following. We saw the things that chased Bez and Thanal go back to the group, and they all started up again. 'Twas the Crone's own, if you ask me!"

The musicians looked from one to the other. "We thought perhaps there was something wrong with the ale, or that Istra's Fire was upon us, and we'd seen a vision. We haven't spoken of it to a soul until now."

Ed nodded. "We'd best keep an eye out. Their old route takes them through these parts, and I've no desire to see them again."

Aidane dawdled by the fire, intentionally letting the others wander off to bed. "Are you going to sleep?" Cefra asked, with a note of admonishment in her voice.

Aidane smiled. Cefra was the one among all her companions who was trying the hardest to reach out to her, and Aidane appreciated the gesture. "I'm not tired just yet," Aidane said, and it was not entirely a falsehood. "I think I'll watch the fire die down a bit."

Cefra looked at her as if she suspected more to the tale. "Just mind that you remember; not all the wolves out there belong to our group. It'd be a pity to be rescued just to get eaten."

Aidane chuckled. "I'll remember that. Really, go on. I won't be too long."

Cefra stretched. "I've had a good meal and enough river rum to take the chill off the night. I promise you, I'll be asleep as soon as I lie down, so don't trip over me and wake me!"

"I promise." Aidane watched Cefra go, and then settled down, hunching forward to watch the embers glow. Before too long, the camp was silent.

We should go now. Elsbet's voice held a note of excitement. Aidane pushed down her own uneasiness. Despite Elsbet's assurances, Aidane was not certain about how Kolin would receive her "gift." She rose, careful not to make noise, and she made her way toward the edge of the camp. If anyone saw her go, Aidane guessed that the two men on night watch assumed she had to relieve herself. No one called out to her, and no one moved to follow.

Inside the darkness of the forest, Aidane took a deep breath. She could sense Elsbet's ghost nearby. Aidane closed her eyes and opened herself to the possession. Elsbet's ghost slipped into her, and Aidane felt the familiar lurch as she gave over her body to the ghost's control. Suddenly, the shadows seemed less dark and the forest less frightening. Aidane felt Elsbet's excitement, which rose as they made their way through the forest. Elsbet knew the terrain, and she found a path that Aidane would have overlooked. It was long overgrown, as if no one living now bothered to visit the ruined house on the hill. Aidane prepared to lock herself in the corner of her mind where she hid during assignations, but Elsbet's ghost kept chattering to her, telling her about how it was long ago, when Elsbet was alive and Kolin was newly dead.

Both the wolves and the *vyrkin* seemed to give Aidane room. If the *vyrkin* wondered why one of their company was heading toward the crypt, something about her tonight kept them from coming closer. Elsbet knew the way, and she led Aidane through the underbrush. There was just enough moonlight for Aidane to see the path that had once led this way. They headed up the hill, and Aidane could barely make out the outlines of the foundation of a house on the hilltop. The upper structures were long gone, but the steps to the front door remained, as did portions of the lower walls. In its day, it must have been a large house, perhaps quite grand, Aidane mused.

Over there. Elsbet directed Aidane's attention toward the family burying ground. As was the custom in Dhasson, crypts were built to look like the manor house. They stood in front of a building that was a miniature version of an impressive home. The part of her consciousness that was still mortal became more and more uneasy as they neared the crypt. It was, Aidane guessed, a trick to turn bothersome mortals away from where the *vayash moru* took their shelter for the night. Elsbet was not deterred. Aidane scrambled to find her locked-away sanctuary in her mind as Elsbet opened the iron door to the crypt that had been her final home for over two hundred years.

The crypt smelled of dust and decay. A damp, loamy smell

spoke of disuse. It was obvious from the leaves that had piled inside the entranceway that the crypt was long unused. Judging by the pathway, it had been decades, perhaps longer, since anyone mortal had come this way. Elsbet moved surely, although once inside the crypt, there was no light. Even hidden away in the furthest corner of her mind, Aidane fought back panic as Elsbet began to descend the carved, stone steps into the deepest reaches of the crypt.

In the darkness, there was a rush of air. Strong hands seized Aidane's arms roughly. The darkness was complete, suffocating. "Why have you come?" It was a strange voice, rough and angry. But before Aidane could fight her way back to consciousness, Elsbet's assured voice answered their assailant.

"I'm here to see Kolin. Tell him that Elsbet has come."

The grip on Aidane's shoulders did not loosen. She was pushed more than led down the pitch-black corridor. In the distance, Aidane could hear stirrings, as if many beings moved in the darkness. The deeper they went, the colder it became. Suddenly, the man pinning Aidane's shoulders turned her sharply. She expected to slam into a wall, but instead she stepped through a doorway into a large, darkened room.

"Kolin. We have a visitor. A mortal. Says her name is Elsbet."

Aidane saw a spark strike, and a candle flared into light. Kolin held the candle, and the shadows made the angles of his face more severe. He was staring at her intently, with an angry gaze. "What kind of trick is this?" Kolin's voice was a cold growl.

Elsbet's spirit swelled within Aidane's consciousness. "I've waited over two hundred years, my love," Elsbet said, words pouring from Aidane's lips in fluent Dhassonian. Aidane had enough consciousness left to recognize that the voice, though it spoke from her mouth, was not her own. The gestures as her body took a tentative step toward Kolin were unfamiliar, though her body moved gracefully. "I've seen you come to the crypt, come to my body. I've seen the gifts you've brought to me. I wept, but you couldn't hear me. But tonight, we can be together again."

Kolin's eyes widened. His face was a mixture of curiosity and horror. "Leave us," he said to Zhan and the others. They hesitated, looking at Aidane, and then slipped into the dark corridor, leaving Kolin and Aidane alone. In the candlelight, Aidane could see that the room had been furnished like a comfortable parlor. A wide couch and upholstered chairs sat at either end of a Noorish carpet. There were other candles and lamps on a small table, but they were dusty with disuse. *Vayash moru* had little use for light and reason to fear the fire.

"How can I believe you?" Kolin's voice was uncertain, wavering between disbelief and anger.

Elsbet's spirit moved Aidane's body another step closer, and Kolin backed up a step, wary. "The night I died, I wore a blue velvet dress," Elsbet said, her Dhassonian accent growing thicker. "I wore the onyx necklace you bought for me. Father tore the necklace off my throat. It left a gash. He struck me with the candlestick from my room. The blow laid open my scalp, and when I fell, my forehead hit the hearth. I think I died then, but Father struck my body several more times before he seemed to come to his senses.

"You broke through the window. I'd never seen such a look in your eyes. You saw my body, and you struck Father with your open palm. It hurled him across the room. He was drunk, and sobbing, saying that he didn't mean to go so far, but you were a wild thing." Her voice became hushed, choked with tears. "You tore him apart. And when he was dead and you were covered in his blood, you found the necklace and you put it in your pocket. You carried me out of the room and up to the crypt, and you made a place for me to lie. You put the necklace back

291

on my throat, and you held my body, rocking me like a child." Tears were running down Aidane's face. Elsbet's voice was just a whisper. "No one was there but the two of us, my love. I was dead. If you didn't tell the tale to anyone, then who but you and I would know?"

Kolin had not moved. Aidane had meant to lock herself away in the place within her mind where she went to hide. *Don't go yet*, Elsbet pleaded. *If I know Kolin, he'll want to know that you've given me permission to use this body, that you haven't been forced to it. Please, don't go yet.* Now, Aidane saw the scene as if she were detached, as if the images she saw with her eyes weren't quite her own. Kolin stood completely still, and if it were possible for a *vayash moru* to be ashen, then Kolin was pale with shock. Denied tears by the Dark Gift, his expression was agonized. His grief looked as fresh as it had been on that night more than two hundred years ago. With a cry, Kolin fell to his knees and pressed Aidane's hand against his cool cheek.

"I should never have let you go home that night," Kolin whispered in a strangled voice. "Or I should have gone with you, to protect you. I knew your father hated me, but I never really thought he would hurt you. When you were delayed, I came to the window after I woke. And I saw you, lying there—" Kolin squeezed his eyes closed as if he were seeing the scene fresh in his memory. Elsbet moved Aidane's hand to stroke Kolin's hair.

"I know, my love. I know. Everything you said to me that night, everything you've said to me all the nights that you visited me in the crypt, I heard every word. My spirit was with you, reaching for you, but I could never touch you, never comfort you. Until now." Elsbet knelt, taking Kolin's face between her hands. "For tonight, we can be together once more. It's been too long. Let me warm you. Love me, and remember."

Kolin closed his eyes and shook his head. "I don't know how this is possible. I hear Elsbet, but I see Aidane. And yet, in every movement, every breath, you *are* Elsbet. How can that be?"

"She is a true *serroquette*. We made a deal, Aidane and I. I bargained with her for one last night with you, before I went to my rest in the Lady. She wished to show her gratitude. She gives herself willingly to this arrangement."

Kolin's eyes searched Aidane's face. "Is this true?" Aidane knew that the question was addressed to her, and not to Elsbet's spirit. "Aidane, if you can hear me, I must know. Is this done with your consent? I won't force this on you."

Aidane felt Elsbet's spirit pull back, and Aidane moved out of her hiding place. It was odd cohabitating her body with a spirit; Aidane couldn't remember ever doing so. It took thought and effort to make her own voice speak. "Elsbet and I have an agreement," Aidane said, in her own voice, speaking Common instead of Dhassonian, with a strong Nargi accent. "I consent. You and Elsbet have my blessing. Elsbet can inhabit my body for two candlemarks, but no longer. Don't waste the time you've been given."

Aidane pulled back, giving Elsbet the forefront of her consciousness. Aidane's shielding during her clients' encounters was always imperfect. This night, it seemed especially difficult for Aidane to completely block out how the spirit used her body. She tried not to hear the long-delayed endearments, tried to ignore the urgency of Kolin's touch. If there had been any doubt about whether the love Kolin and Elsbet shared had been genuine, the passion of their reunion left no room to question. Aidane could feel Elsbet's grief begin to ease as tentative touches gave way to long overdue passion.

Kolin was a gentle lover. The candle had gone out, and in the darkness, Aidane knew it would be easier for Kolin to imagine that the face and form of his lover was Elsbet's, and not Aidane's.

Elsbet returned his caresses joyously, without reservation. Aidane wondered whether in life, Elsbet had been just as uninhibited and whether she had a similar zest for living. Perhaps it had been the life that burned so brightly within Elsbet that had attracted Kolin. In Nargi, the idea that a *vayash moru* might take a human lover was unthinkable, let alone that they might be free to marry. But over the weeks she had traveled with Jolie and Kolin, Aidane had watched Jolie and Astir together. Their affection looked as genuine as any couple's, and more heartfelt than most.

Now, as Kolin and Elsbet made love, Aidane could not shut out the intensity of their emotions. Elsbet was overjoyed at the reunion and the unexpected possibility to reunite with her lover. Kolin's joy was bittersweet, tempered by the knowledge that this night would be one brief homecoming. Elsbet's spirit looked forward to a final rest. But for Kolin, Aidane knew, after this night, his grief would continue, made fresh and new by losing Elsbet all over again.

Why do the vayash moru *risk loving mortals, when we die so quickly?*

Aidane heard Elsbet's murmur in reply. *Because our life and our blood warms them. They remember what they've lost. Kolin meant to bring me across. We were to be together, always. Except things didn't go as we had planned.*

Aidane tried to draw back, giving the lovers as much privacy as she could. But always in these couplings, her consciousness was not as far removed as she gave her clients to believe. Aidane had sensed many motives from both the living and the dead lovers she had served. Few reunited with pure intentions. Some returned to cause guilt, and others came to complete old fights. Some came for revenge and others for emotional sadism. But there had been a few over the years who had lost themselves in the sheer joy of reunion. Because a *serroquette* was unlikely to ever win real love of her own, then Aidane accepted that these few reunions were as close as she would ever experience of anything akin to true love.

Too soon, Aidane could feel the possession waning. Elsbet felt it, too, and fear and sadness thrilled through Aidane as Elsbet knew her hold was slipping.

"So soon?" Kolin's voice was achingly plaintive.

Elsbet reached up in the darkness to run her fingers along his cheek, down his shoulder and arm, letting her palm slide along his chest. His skin was warm, letting Aidane know that earlier this evening, Kolin had fed well. "It was chance alone that let us have this evening." Elsbet smiled, and leaned up to kiss Kolin gently. "I've missed you."

Kolin wrapped his arms fiercely around her, burying his face in her hair. "Don't leave me again." But even as he spoke, Elsbet's consciousness was slipping away.

"Good-bye, my love. Let me go now, and go on. You've been faithful long enough."

Elsbet's voice grew soft, finishing in a whisper. This time, the ending of the possession was gentle. Aidane had an instant's image in her mind of a beautiful, amber-eyed woman in the Aspect of the Lover holding out her hand to Elsbet's spirit before the two of them walked off along the edge of a gray sea. Then Aidane was fully back in her own body, still wrapped in Kolin's arms.

It took a moment for Kolin to realize the shift, and he pulled away awkwardly. "Aidane?" he asked, his voice shaky.

Aidane took a deep breath. In any transaction, this was the most awkward moment. Beginning the tryst was fueled by anticipation, both the client's and the possessing spirit's. That eliminated any awkwardness about disrobing or intimacy. But ending the tryst was inevitably awkward, as Aidane usually found herself naked in a stranger's bed, and the living lover was forced to deal with the reality that their endearments, anger, or passion had all been aimed at the spirit of their loved one in the body of a whore.

"If you wouldn't mind lighting that candle again, I'll gather my clothes and go." Aidane had found that a detached professionalism got her and the client through this phase the easiest. She made it a practice to collect her money up front, which had served her well on the nights when the lovers' reunion was unhappy. Now, she just wanted to minimize her own discomfort and reduce Kolin's embarrassment.

"Aidane?" Kolin's voice was a little stronger. He released her from his embrace and moved back so that their bare skin no longer touched. "I don't know how to thank you." In his voice, Aidane heard loss and sorrow, but also a sense of wonder and completion.

"It was the only way I had to repay you," Aidane murmured. She felt around for her clothing. Behind her, Kolin moved and then lit a candle, casting its glow over the small room. Kolin was still naked, and only belatedly did it seem to occur to him that Aidane was no longer Elsbet, and then he moved quickly to turn away. Aidane blushed. No matter how long she had been a *serroquette* and how intimate she and her client had been while the spirit was upon her, the aftermath was always uncomfortable.

Aidane coped by keeping her eyes averted and turning her back, dressing quickly. Her working outfits were designed not only for their seductive appeal but for the practicality of being easy to take off and quick to put back on. The borrowed clothes from Cefra were more conventional, made of stiffer fabric and more elaborate fastenings. Aidane strained to reach a button and was surprised when Kolin stepped up behind her to fasten it.

She turned and looked up at him. His face still held a look of pain and confusion, as if he had not yet worked through the abrupt appearance and equally abrupt disappearance of his ong-lost lover. "Is it always like this for you?"

Aidane looked down, and she felt her cheeks flame. When the ghosts possessed her, no discussion or intimacy was off limits. But few clients ever inquired about the private life of their *serroquette*, and Aidane was sure it was because it made it easier for them to think of her merely as a vessel for the spirits to inhabit. "No, not always," she said, embarrassed. "Not everyone is happy to see each other again. It's nice when I can help people who really missed one another."

"How much are you aware of?" Kolin's eyes searched hers.

"Almost nothing," Aidane lied. "It's best that way, for everyone."

Something in Kolin's blue eyes flashed, giving Aidane to know that he understood the fabrication for what it was, and why she told it. He reached out to touch her arm. She looked up at him sharply. "I can't do this for you again. Elsbet's gone. I can't channel anyone once they've gone to the Lady."

Kolin still looked shaken. He always seemed so self-assured, so completely self-possessed, that it unnerved Aidane to see the naked grief in Kolin's eyes. *I always thought how wonderful it would be to be immortal. To watch the years go by like a play on a stage, to enjoy the best things forever. I never realized there was a cost. Maybe some* vayash moru *don't care. Maybe they didn't care when they were alive. But immortality means outliving everyone you love, over and over again. No wonder they say that the very old ones go mad.*

"I know," Kolin replied. "I wouldn't ask that of you. I just want you to know that there isn't a greater gift in the world than what you gave me, gave us, tonight. And when we get to Dark Haven, I'll make sure there's a safe place for you, with Jolie, or with Lady Riqua, or somewhere. I owe you that, at the very least."

Aidane managed a smile at his sincerity. She gathered the last of her things. "That's kind of you. But what I'd really appreciate right now is someone to escort me back to the camp. Elsbet knew the way here, but I don't think I'll find my way back in the dark."

Kolin shook off enough of his mood to manage a smile. "I believe I can arrange that, m'lady."

The camp was quiet when they arrived. Kolin nodded to Aidane in farewell before heading back towards the crypt. It was still long before dawn. Ed the peddler lay wrapped in his cloak, near his pushcart wagon piled high with a jumble of wares and tools. The four minstrels lay not far away, always their own small grouping. Astir and Jolie sat near the fire, talking in quiet tones. Astir's arm was around Jolie's waist, and Jolie leaned on his shoulder. They both looked up as Aidane joined them, and Jolie looked questioningly from Aidane back to Kolin, but said nothing. True to her word, Cefra had saved a spot on the pine branches for Aidane. Cefra mumbled in her sleep as Aidane picked her way carefully among the sleeping women and stretched out in exhaustion, wrapping her cloak around her. The nights had grown cold, and the farther north they went toward Dark Haven, the more Aidane was glad for her borrowed cloak.

Everything I have is borrowed, Aidane thought as she got as comfortable as possible. The pine branches smelled of balsam, as did the smoke from the fire. *My clothing, my cloak, even my place with Jolie and her girls, it's just borrowed. My lovers aren't my own, and the things they whisper aren't about me.* She remembered the passion Elsbet and Kolin had shared, and sighed. Among the whores she knew well, most doubted that such a thing as true love existed. But as a *serroquette*, Aidane knew better. Even in the trysts that went wrong, beneath the anger and even the hatred, there was some form of love, even if it was twisted and starved. And there had been enough of the trysts like the one tonight between Elsbet and Kolin to let Aidane know that some lucky few did, indeed, find the kind of love that the minstrels honored in their songs. She squeezed back tears. Usually, she was good at not crying. But tonight, alone among strangers, far from home and cold, Aidane wept silently until she fell asleep.

Aidane was so tired, she almost did not hear the ghost's call. *Please, please, wake up. Wake up.*

Aidane woke groggily and sat up, drawing her cloak around her. It was late enough that Astir had gone and Jolie had taken her place near the fire, asleep. The ghost of a woman sat just beyond where the pine branches made a bed. The woman had long, straight hair that was as black as the night around her. Her skin was dark, and Aidane guessed that the ghost was Eastmark-born. She had dark eyes and features that would have been considered exotic in Dhasson or Margolan, high, angular cheekbones, a faintly almond shape to her eyes, and a narrow, thin nose. She was dressed in an expensive but provocative gown. Its fabric was rich brocade, and it glistened with pearls and gemstones sewn into the bodice. The neckline was scandalously low, revealing the curve of ample breasts, barely hiding the darker ring surrounding the nipples. *Too daring for a noble woman. Too rich for a whore*, Aidane thought. Then she noticed one more thing. Even for a ghost, the woman was ashen. *Not just a spirit. The ghost of a* vayash moru.

I need your help.

Aidane shook her head. *I can't, not tonight. I've already had one...client. I don't know which of the* vayash moru *you've come for—*

None. Please, I have a message for Jolie, and a warning for Lord Vahanian. You're all in terrible danger.

Tired as she was, something about the urgency in the ghost's voice woke Aidane like a hot cup of *kerif. How do you know Jolie, and Lord Vahanian?*

The ghost held out a hand to Aidane, and grudgingly, Aidane left the warmth of her spot on the pine boughs to join the ghost near the banked fire. *My name is Thaine. I used to be a whore in Eastmark. It's a long story, but one night, I got into a lot of trouble and my handler sold me to a traveling merchant, who abused me and then sold me for a gallon of brandy to a Nargi general. That was ten years ago. The general bought me as a present for his fight slave. The fighter was winning a lot of money for the general, and since slaves have no need of coin, the general rewarded him with money and brandy. A lot of brandy.*

Did he kill you?

Thaine shook her head. *Oh, no, he didn't want me.*

He preferred men?

Again, Thaine shook her head. *No, he grieved for his dead wife, and he hated his life as a slave. But he was the best fighter anyone had seen, and although he stayed drunk until it was time to fight, he earned the general enough money and glory that the man would have done anything to make his slave happier. They had a big match coming up, and the general thought I might do the trick.*

Did it help?

No, the fight slave made it clear I wasn't welcome, and he would have sent me away like he did the others that the general tried to provide, but this time, the general said that if the slave refused me, I'd be given to the soldiers. I'd be killed. The fight slave let me stay, but he kept me from his bed. At least, until he won the match but nearly died from his injuries. I nursed him back to health. And I convinced him that while it wasn't love, there was something to be said for warmth, and someone to hold on to during the night. He took me to his bed then, but we

300

were never in love, not really. Allies, perhaps.

What happened?

One night, the fight slave won the biggest match in all of Nargi. He made the general a very rich man. The general told him that he could have any prize except his own freedom or the general's commission. He asked for my safe passage to Margolan.

Truly?

Thaine nodded once more. *The general even let him come along, in chains, to see that I was put across the Nu in a sound boat and reached the other side.*

And Jolie's Place was on the other side?

Yes. She took me in. I was mortal then. A year later, a man washed up on the riverbank, nearly drowned. It was the fight slave. He had escaped. Astir almost slit his throat because he wore a Nargi uniform, but I recognized him and begged Jolie for his life. Another patron, a soldier, also recognized him and offered to pay Jolie for his care.

What happened?

When he was well enough, Jolie let him mind the door. We didn't have any problems that season with drunks. He and I became lovers again. Later, Jolie had him tend bar, and then she put him in charge of provisioning the house and taught him to smuggle on the river. In time, he was gone so much that I took another lover, a wealthy vayash moru *who gave me jewelry and fine dresses and turned my head. I thought he loved me, and I left Jolie's and went with the* vayash moru, *let him bring me across. But it didn't last, and for a time, I was passed around as a mistress to wealthy card sharps and thieves, the* vayash moru *who aren't welcome in the honorable broods.*

That explains Jolie, but why would you warn Lord Vahanian? Why would he listen?

Thaine met her eyes. *Jonmarc Vahanian was the Nargi fight slave.*

Aidane gasped. *I'd heard rumors that he had been a brigand, but I never thought they were true.* She paused. *How is it that you're really and truly dead?*

Thaine's ghost sighed. *I was captured by Black Robes. Given to them, really, by a lover who'd grown tired of me and wanted rid of the inconvenience. They murdered me to do their magic, but I've heard their plans. Please, Aidane, you've got to help me. I know Jolie will go to Jonmarc in Dark Haven, and I know he'll give her sanctuary. He's like a son to her. But I have to warn him. It's more than just the Black Robes stealing from tombs. They're part of something bigger, something from outside the Winter Kingdoms. There's going to be war, Aidane, and right now, no one knows it. What's coming makes the Black Robes look like children. Please, please, help me.*

Aidane rubbed her eyes. *We're going to Dark Haven. But that's another two weeks' travel. I've never met a ghost that could go so far from where they're buried. And I can only hold a spirit in my body for two candlemarks at a time.*

Thaine gave a bitter chuckle. *I'm not buried. My bones lie in a heap of dust just over that mound, where the Black Robes left me. But I had a patron who dabbled in blood magic, and I learned a few things. As I lay dying, I bound my spirit to the necklace I was wearing. You can carry my spirit with you if you wear the necklace. And it probably wouldn't hurt if you took some of my dust.*

Dust?

Vayash moru *crumble. But you should gather the dust from my bones. Just three: my skull, my breastbone, and my right hand. That will help you hold my spirit long enough to travel to Dark Haven.*

Show me.

Aidane braced herself, and Thaine's spirit entered her. It was as gentle as possession ever was, but for Aidane, the wrenching shift of giving herself over to another entity was never completely without pain. Aidane adjusted to the presence that filled her. Thaine seemed determined but unsure as her spirit entered Aidane's body. And while Aidane could feel Thaine's willfulness, she did not detect any immediate threat. Thaine opened her memories to Aidane, showing her the truth of her tale. Aidane took all of it in, though only minutes passed.

Now do you see why it's so important for me to warn Jonmarc?

Yes, I'll do what I can to help.

Moving carefully to avoid waking the others, Aidane picked her way through the crowded space around the fire towards the large hill not far from their campsite. As they drew closer, Aidane realized that the hill was unusually shaped, too regular to be a natural part of the landscape. *It's a barrow*, Thaine's voice supplied in her mind. *A very old burying place. The Black Robes were trying to awaken whatever spirits live inside.*

Did they succeed?

I don't think so. For some reason, I don't think the barrow held what they expected. But they raised strong magic. I was terrified.

Thaine guided her surely across the uneven land. When they reached the other side of the barrow, Aidane caught her breath. A gibbet hung from a wooden framework. Inside hung a rotting corpse. The stench made Aidane cover her mouth. Runes had been painted onto the wood, and the corpse was festooned with amulets of clay and wood. At the foot of the gallows lay other bones, some animal, and some, Aidane realized as she forced herself to go closer, were human. Behind the gallows, a shallow hole had been dug into the side of the barrow, but even by moonlight, Aidane could see that it stopped before it went very deep.

There, Thaine's voice directed. *What's left of me lies over there.*

Fighting down her own fear, Aidane worked her way through

the tall grass, toward where Thaine indicated. A mound of dust, like a scattering of ash, lay in the grass. It had the vague outline of a human form. Where the neck had been lay a necklace of silver with teardrops of amber and emeralds. The stones were favored by the Lover Aspect of the Lady and were popular with whores for their reputed magic to increase the wearer's sexual attractiveness. It was a beautiful necklace, and would have cost the buyer a small fortune.

It's beautiful, isn't it? Thaine sighed. *My patrons may have passed me around like a bottle of river rum, but they were wealthy, and when I pleased them, they could be generous. Immortality is a great way to get rich, for some, at least. When I've carried my message, you can keep the necklace, as payment for the trouble I've caused you. I won't need it anymore.*

Aidane hesitated, and then knelt by Thaine's dust. Grimacing, Aidane reached down to take the necklace. She swallowed hard, and then fastened it around her own throat. Immediately, she could feel its magic, and Thaine's spirit became clearer in her mind. It became easier, less draining, to carry the spirit inside her body.

Now take my bones, Thaine instructed.

Aidane steeled herself and reached for the spot where the body's right hand would have been. She gathered a handful of the dust and put it into a pouch she made from the cloth of her apron. Thaine guided her to take a handful of dust from the center of the shape's chest and from where the skull had dissolved. Aidane added those to the heap of ash and tied the apron shut.

I'm sorry to make you do that, but the spirit is strongest in the skull, hand, and heart bone, and since we have to travel far away, it's the best chance that I'll be able to make the journey.

In her lifetime of fending for herself as a *serroquette*, Aidane had done many things to survive that she tried not to think about. She'd traded favors for sustenance, and she'd acquiesced to demands from clients that filled her with revulsion. But never before had she desecrated the dead.

What are you waiting for? I don't like being back here. Things didn't go well last time, if you know what I mean. Thaine's voice held a trace of fear. *If you hurry, maybe no one noticed we're gone.*

Aidane paused, staring down at the rest of the dust that lay amid the tall, dry grass. "It seems wrong to leave you like this," she said softly.

It's all right. It's hard to explain, but it's like leaving an old dress behind, one you won't ever wear again. But thank you.

Aidane felt the cold before she turned. It was like a frigid wind, but even here, early fall was never that cold.

Aidane! Behind you!

Aidane screamed. Ghosts surrounded her, drawn to her magic from the burying ground on the hill, and another lot long overgrown by trees and scrub. *Let us in. Give us your warmth. There's room for my spirit in your lovely, warm flesh. Please, please, let me feel a heartbeat again.* Aidane could see them clearly in her mind. They were old dead, and some had lost the ability to project their image as they had been in life. Aidane saw them as they were now, rotted corpses, and bones draped with the remnants of their filthy shrouds. The spirits came closer and closer, filling the night air around her. Aidane was exhausted from hosting Elsbet's spirit, drained from the working with Kolin, and now from Thaine's possession. She cursed her lack of caution. She knew better than to sleep outside. She'd heard tell of *serroquettes* being consumed by spirits that overtook them when they were too weak to defend themselves. When she returned from trysts in the city, Aidane had always taken care not to pass by crypts or family plots. She'd worn charms to protect herself. But the charms were gone, along with the rest of her possessions. And the spirits were cold and hungry, so hungry.

Let me fill you. I can protect you from them. Thaine sounded sure, but Aidane had doubts.

Her body stiffened as the spirits fell on her, passing through her form, stealing her warmth. She screamed again, but her voice sounded distant. She gasped as another spirit passed through her. Aidane's control was barely strong enough to keep the ghosts from seizing her mind, but she could not stop the revenants from drawing breath and heat from her with every spectral pass. They were cold, so cold. She was growing cold. But she held on, guarding that last corner of herself. If, or when, her control weakened, whichever spirit was strongest could fully possess her. She'd fought off clients who had wanted to keep her body, but never so many at once. Now, their voices were a jumble in her mind, male and female, a cacophony of accents, all begging for her life, her warmth.

If I've filled you, no one else can. Together, we can hold them off.

Terrified, Aidane did as Thaine urged, and felt Thaine's warmth flow through her, felt the odd shift of another soul fill her body. Immediately, the ghosts drew back. They were angry, robbed of their prize. Aidane was surrounded by a host of spirits, some misty shapes of fog, and others glowing a faint green.

What do we do now? They're waiting for me to tire. I don't know how long I can let you possess me. It's never been more than a few candlemarks. If we run back to the camp, they'll follow. Aidane felt her fear rise up in her throat. And in the back of her mind, she knew that Thaine was frightened, too.

"Aidane! Aidane, can you hear me?" It was Jolie's voice, from far away.

"Help me!" Aidane shouted loudly enough to hear herself

over the low murmur of the circle of waiting ghosts. She didn't know whether the spirits would be visible to Jolie or any of the others, but she and Thaine were trapped inside their circle.

"By the Whore!" It was Ed, the peddler, and he continued to curse, fluently switching from Margolense to Dhassonian and then to the river patois.

Jolie started to run toward Aidane, but Ed caught her arm. "Can't you see? She's spiritbound. There're haunts all around her. They want a ghost whore, but they'll fall on the living if they think they can take you."

The four minstrels crested the barrow just then, and stopped abruptly. Aidane didn't know whether or not they could see the spirits, but Astir was with them, and Aidane was certain the *vayash moru* could see the ghosts.

"I don't see any ghosts," Jolie argued.

"He's right," Astir shouted. "Stay back."

"We can't leave her there." Jolie did as Astir bid, but even from a distance, Aidane could see that she was angry.

"I've got an idea." Cautiously, Ed worked his way closer. He reached beneath his shirt and pulled out two silver talismans. They glowed in the moonlight against his skin. Mumbling to himself, Ed began to make a wide circle, with one hand in his jacket pocket. The other hand dug something out of a pouch at his belt, and as he made his circle, he sprinkled a powder with his right hand and seemed to flick something small from his left hand into the grass at intervals. Above on the hill, the musicians began to play. The tune was different from the lively tavern songs they had played earlier that night. This song was a dirge, and it sent a shiver down Aidane's back.

What are they doing?

Magic of some kind. I can feel it. If I weren't bound to you with the necklace and the bones, it might work on me, too. The music is a charm, and whatever the peddler is sprinkling around us is making some kind of safe area. It may not tear me from you, but it's making me damned uncomfortable!

The ghosts gave a sudden, startled hiss. Before Ed could complete the circle, the host of revenants vanished as if pulled by an unseen hand. The musicians played a few more measures, and then lowered their instruments. Aidane fell to her knees as Jolie and Astir ran up to her. A few steps behind the minstrels, Aidane could see the rest of Jolie's girls crowding forward. There was a rush of air, and Kolin and the other *vayash moru* suddenly appeared in the clearing.

"Dark Lady take my soul," Kolin murmured, taking in the gibbet and the shattered skeleton. "Black Robes were here not long ago."

"A fortnight," Aidane said. For now, Thaine was staying in the background, and Aidane's voice was her own.

"How do you know?" Astir's voice was sharp.

"Because one of the ghosts is inside me."

Ed started forward, holding out his amulets. In Aidane's mind, Thaine squealed with sudden pain. *Make him put those things away!*

"It's all right, Ed. This ghost I invited. Please, you're hurting her. Put the amulet away."

Ed looked at Aidane skeptically, but did as he was told. Kolin traced Ed's path around the circle and bent to touch something in the grass.

"You made a circle of salt and you've left a trail of iron coins. How is it that a peddler comes prepared to bespell the dead?" Kolin asked. Aidane heard a wary edge in his voice.

Ed looked chagrined. "I'm a bit of a hedge witch, on the side. One of my many talents. I can't call the dead or hear them, but I can banish them, at least for a while, if they're not too strong. It's just a little magic, but it earns me coin for dinner and drink when no one needs their tin mended."

Jolie had reached Aidane, and he knelt beside her. "What are you doing out here alone at night? Are you mad?"

Aidane leaned forward, holding herself up with her hands. She was exhausted, and fought the urge to collapse. "A ghost came to me. She said she had a message for you, and a warning for Lord Vahanian."

Jolie looked up sharply. "A ghost, with a message for me?"

Thaine pushed her way to the forefront. Aidane felt the change in her posture and her expression before words in a voice very different from her own spoke from her mouth. "Hello, Jolie. It's me, Thaine."

Jolie's eyes widened, and Astir turned, looking at Aidane with suspicion. "That's not possible. You're *vayash moru*."

Thaine gave a bitter laugh. "Oh, even *vayash moru* can die. You were right, Jolie, about Reev. He tired of me after a while, when he'd brought me across and I wasn't warm anymore. It didn't go well after that."

"How did you find me?"

"Sheer luck. I was kidnapped by the Black Robes, and they murdered me here. I didn't know what to do, so my ghost stayed here. Then I heard you make camp. I couldn't believe it was really you, but when I saw you, I was sure. And I knew I had to warn you, warn Jonmarc."

Jolie shook her head. "Jonmarc's moved on, Thaine. He's a lord now, happily married, with babies on the way. You've no claim on him. Not anymore."

"You're not listening. I don't want Jonmarc. I'm dead, remember? I'd heard that he'd become a lord, and if he found someone to love, I wish him well. It was never going to be me. I know that. I'd also heard that he was Lord of the Undead. That's why I need to warn him."

"Warn him about what?"

"Before the Black Robes killed me, I heard them talking. There's something big coming, bigger than just the Durim wanting to bring back Shanthadura. They've been told that there's a war coming, a War of Unmaking. It's supposed to destroy everything, so everything can start over."

"What's that got to do with Jonmarc?" Jolie looked skeptical. "Martris Drayke perhaps could fight such a thing. But Jonmarc?"

"It's not just about magic," Thaine said, pleading for them to understand. "There's a real war, and the Black Robes were talking about ships, ships landing in Principality, maybe even in Eastmark. Ships with blood mages and a dark summoner."

Astir laid a hand on Jolie's shoulder. "Jonmarc is liegeman to King Staden, and Princess Berwyn's champion. If there's war coming, he's sure to be in the thick of it."

Jolie made the sign of the Goddess to ward away evil. "Is this the message you want me to take to Jonmarc?"

"No. There's a plot, a conspiracy. It's supposed to happen soon, at the Feast of the Departed, in Principality City. I don't know exactly what they plan to do, but I got a good look at the Black Robes without their hoods. I can identify them. I've got to get Jonmarc to take me to Principality City."

"Lady Carina may not care for that idea." Jolie's voice had a warning edge.

"Don't you understand? This isn't about me, and it's not about trying to win back an old lover. But with Jonmarc's position, he might be able to stop this. Please, you've got to believe me."

Kolin was watching her, and the look on his face was uncertain. Aidane knew that Thaine's expressions and gestures were completely unlike Elsbet's, or her own. Thaine moved with a sure confidence that was stronger, more dominant, than either Elsbet or Aidane. He stared at her as if he were thinking about Thaine's warning. Finally, he nodded. "I believe her. And I think it's something Jonmarc needs to hear for himself. Let him decide."

While Aidane had been talking, Ed and the musicians had

begun gathering branches. Ed took a handful of rags from one of the bodies on the ground and wrapped it around a long, sturdy stick, and then soaked it with river rum. When he pushed it into the campfire, the torch burst into flame. Cal did the same. Bez, Nezra, and Thanal began dragging the bodies to a central pile. Aidane and Cefra went to help, and a few more of Jolie's girls did the same when they realized they meant to make a pyre.

"I figured your friends would just as soon we handled the fire," Cal said with a half smile, directing his comment to Kolin. "We're not long past the Moon Feast; no one will notice another bonfire."

Kolin nodded. His face was stony. "Yes. Burn them. Burn it all."

Ed and Cal readied two pyres to burn the bodies, while Jolie and the others followed Kolin's instructions to cleanse the area and dispel the spirits. It had taken more than a candlemark, and Aidane was exhausted. Just as they were about to return to camp, a wolf's howl sounded, followed by another.

Kolin frowned. "Those are the sentries. They've seen something they didn't like. Everyone, stay close."

There was a blur of movement and a rush of air, and one of the *vayash moru* who had been on night watch appeared next to Kolin. "Something's coming on the road, but I've never seen the like," the guard reported. "Men and broken wagons and lamed horses, like some caravan of the damned. Don't know what they are, but the *vyrkin* thought at least some of them were *ashtenerath*, and I agree. Thought you should know."

In the distance, a sound carried in the darkness. Faint, discordant music filled the night air. "Sweet Chenne. They're coming." Ed the peddler had gone completely ashen. "We've got to break camp and get out of here. Now! They can't hurt the *vayash moru*, but the rest of us have to get out of here." Ed pointed, and the group turned to follow his gesture. A long row of shadows was visible on the next rise, just before the road turned toward their camp. From the horses and wagons, it looked to be a caravan, but as Aidane stood, her eyes widened. Even from a distance, she could tell that something was very wrong.

The clouds drew back and in the moonlight, they could see the travelers. Their wagons were broken and shabby. The tarpaulins that roofed the largest of the wagons were tattered and full of holes. Lamed horses so thin that their bones bulged from their skin struggled to pull the ruined wagons. Shuffling along with the wagons were men, or what used to be men. They walked with uneven gait, lurching from step to step, and a stench more foul than the gibbet's odor reached the watchers, even from a distance.

"*Ashtenerath*," Astir murmured.

Kolin grabbed the peddler by his collar. "What more do you know of this?"

Ed's eyes were wide with fear. "They used to be a caravan from Eastmark, one of the most popular in Dhasson. But plague fell on them, only it didn't kill them. Not completely. What's left isn't quite living, but not really dead. They wander by night, and if you cross their path, the plague will take you, too. They wander like that until they die, or just fall apart, or maybe, they'll wander like that forever. But if you're not going to get out of here, let go of me! I'm not staying." Ed struggled and kicked.

"What are *ashtenerath*?" Aidane hadn't thought she had the energy left to be afraid, but watching the shadowed caravan move toward them, she felt fear stir anew.

"They're men—or they were men—who've been changed by magic or plague," Kolin replied, never taking his eyes from the lurching figures. "Their minds die but their bodies keep on moving. They're violent and unstable."

"The peddler's right." It was Cal, the portly dulcimer player, who spoke. "Whatever they were, they're good as dead now. We need to leave. Now."

"They're coming!" Bez pointed toward the ghastly caravan.

Kolin turned to Jolie. "Gather up everything you can carry from the camp and run. Take the crossroads north, so you're going a different road to the caravan. Wait for us outside the next town. We'll find you after sunset."

"What about you?" Jolie asked, looking from Kolin to Astir and to the other *vayash moru*.

Kolin drew his sword. "We can't catch plague. If they come after you, we'll hold them off. If they don't, we'll catch up. Now go!"

Jolie grabbed Aidane's hand and pulled her along as the *vayash moru* made a line to block the progress of the oncoming caravan. Jolie's girls were whimpering with fear and some were chanting charms against evil, but to their credit, they kept their heads and did not scream. Aidane fought down both her own fear and Thaine's apprehension. More quickly than Aidane thought possible, they had gathered what little they had left at the camp and made their way down the road, in the opposite direction from the caravan.

Aidane cast a glance over her shoulder. The *vyrkin* had joined the *vayash moru*, some in human form and others in their wolf shapes. As they ran, Aidane could hear the low, warning growls of the wolves.

Jolie's expression was resolute. "Come on. We've got to get you and Thaine somewhere safe. If you're right, then you've just become the most dangerous woman in Dhasson. Astir and Kolin can take care of themselves. But the Winter Kingdoms might not survive if we don't make sure you get to Dark Haven. Now, run!"

16

"I hope you know what you're doing." Soterius's voice attempted to be light, but Tris could see the worry in his friend's eyes.

"So do I."

Soterius and a handful of guards had come with Tris to the shrine of the Mother and Childe along with Sister Fallon. Tris had already made an offering of flowers and live doves to the Childe and water and wine to the Mother. Now, he was as ready as he would ever be to descend into the resting place of Margolan's kings to seek the counsel of his long-dead ancestors. Although he had meant to visit right after his trip to Vistimar, the obligations of the throne had delayed him more than a week. Or perhaps, Tris admitted to himself, his own reluctance had allowed him to become delayed.

"If you run into trouble, just give a shout. We'll be there."

Tris gave a wan smile. "The kind of trouble I'm likely to run into down there isn't anything your swords can fight."

Soterius glanced at the sword Tris carried. "That's not your usual sword. It's that ghost sword your grandmother gave you, isn't it?"

"Ghost sword" wasn't exactly the right term for Nexus. At Tris's coronation, one of the Sisterhood had presented him with a sword that had once belonged to the sorceress Bava K'aa,

Tris's grandmother. A sword that was said to still possess a whisper of her soul and power. Tris had first dared to use the sword at the Battle of Lochlanimar, when desperate measures compelled him to draw on the sword's magic without a complete understanding of its power. Now, he better understood both its power and its price, and he did not carry Nexus lightly.

"I'm hoping that I don't need it."

"Does it really steal a breath from your soul each time it's used?"

Tris shrugged. "It held a memory of Grandmother's spirit, and that's the warning she gave me. If so, I've used a couple already."

Soterius's gaze was worried. "How many breaths are there in a soul? What happens if you use them all up?"

Several possibilities occurred to Tris, none of them good. "Let's try not to find out, huh?" Tris drew a deep breath and squared his shoulders. While he called or dispelled ghosts from all walks of life nearly every day in his Court of Spirits, this was the first time Tris had gone to seek the counsel of his ancestors. He had no idea whether the family reunion would be pleasant.

"May the Lady watch over your soul," Soterius said, clapping Tris on the shoulder before he stood back, making room for him to descend the shadowed stone stairway.

Above ground, the Shrine of the Mother and Childe was one of the most peaceful places Tris knew. Sacred to two of the Lady's Aspects, the shrine was a place for offering and quiet reflection. Unlike Isencroft, Margolan did not have Oracles to speak for the Lady, nor did it have *Hojun* seers like Eastmark or Nargi's Crone priests. Margolan's tradition invited each individual to listen for the voice of the Lady. That ambiguity was often both comforting and disconcerting, since it offered few certainties. Right now, Tris thought he would give a lot for an Oracle to spell out the confusing omens.

The garden of the Childe was in its glory. Doves cooed and flowers bloomed in profusion, nurtured by magic even in the chill of autumn. Delicate, graceful archways decorated the garden and led down into the sacred ravine. A waterfall and channel of water, favored by the Mother, ran through all seasons of the year, warmed by magic in the coldest months. The water flowed down the waterfall, into a decorative sluiceway and then down the stone walls of a V-shaped cut through the hillside to a reflecting pool. Tris could hear the calming sound of running water and smell the fragrance of the garden as he started down the stairs. He refused the torch Soterius offered, opting instead for a ball of cold handfire raised by a flicker of his magic. Nexus was ready in his hand.

Even Fallon had been unsure about the protocol for entering the realm of the dead kings. Bricen, Tris's father, had never attempted it. Neither had Bricen's father. Royster, the Sisterhood's archivist, had found a fragmentary text that mentioned the offerings made by long-ago kings who sought advice from the dead, along with a warning that the kings of past ages should not be disturbed lightly. Tris had taken that warning to heart.

As he descended into the crypt, Tris could sense the presence of the old dead around him. He felt the flicker of their spirits, and he also knew that they were not yet ready to reveal themselves to him. He had gone down enough stairs that the sunlight above was lost in shadow and there was no sound except for the scuff of his boots on the stone steps. Tris swallowed hard. *I am king of Margolan, and the summoner-heir to Bava K'aa. I have every right to come here.* But despite that, he could not dispel his sense of uneasiness as he moved farther into the crypt and left the living far behind.

At the bottom of the steps, Tris let his handfire flare, revealing a large chamber. Torches in sconces awaited the brave—or foolhardy—visitor. Tris used a flicker of magic to light the torches, illuminating the large room.

Arched passageways led off in eight directions, one for each Aspect of the Sacred Lady. Runes and gems, sacred to each Aspect, adorned the archway, inlaid in silver. Four catafalques sat in the outer chamber. One of them held the body of Bricen's father, King Larimore. The few resources Tris had found differed on the occupants of the other catafalques. He knew for a certainty that his own father was not among the kings buried here. Although Tris had seen Jared murder their father, by the time Tris returned to reclaim the throne, no one could say just what had happened to Bricen's body. Since Jared had killed Bricen with a dagger spelled to destroy the soul, Tris could not summon his father's spirit to find out how to lay his remains to rest. Now, Tris realized that he had no emissary among the dead to guide him.

"Why have you come?"

The ghost stood pale and seemingly solid, blocking Tris from moving farther toward the passageways. He was an old man, wizened with years, gaunt but not frail. The ghost's eyes held a keen intelligence, and though his body was wasted with age and sickness, in his youth, Tris guessed that he had been a powerfully built man.

Tris gave a half-bow, deep enough to be reverent but not so deep that he ever took his eyes off the ghost blocking his way. "I'm Martris Drayke, son of Bricen, King of Margolan, and summoner-heir to Bava K'aa. I come to ask the advice of Marlan the Gold and Hadenrul the Great. Let me pass."

The ghost began to laugh. It was not a friendly sound. His arms were crossed over his chest, and he did not move aside. "The old dead do not wake without cause. Few have dared to disturb them. The concerns of the living mean little to us. Why would you wake the old ones?"

Tris drew deep breath. "I would ask Hadenrul how he ended the domination of the cult of Shanthadura. The Durim have risen again, and they may serve an invader from the north." He paused. "I would ask Marlan the Gold about the Dread. The Durim have desecrated the mounds of the Dread and are attempting to break the wardings that hold the Dread—and their prisoners—within the barrows."

The ghost stared at Tris with a piercing gaze. "How do I know that what you say is true?"

Before Tris could answer, the runes along Nexus's blade burst into cold fire. Tris held the sword up so that both he and the spirit guardian could watch as the fire runes rearranged themselves along the blade. *Blood of your blood* slowly spelled out against the steel.

"Even the dead feel the strength of your magic," the guardian said. "But do you have the power to raise the old ones? They will not speak to you unless your power can call them back from where their spirits have wandered."

"My magic will have to do," Tris replied. "Margolan's in danger. If a dark summoner is really planning to raise the Dread with the help of the Durim, I'll need all the help I can get to stand against them."

The ghost seemed to consider Tris carefully in silence. Around them, Tris could feel the dead gathering. Some were drawn to the power of his magic. Others watched with detached curiosity. A few debated the matter among themselves. Whether or not the guardian spirit listened to the debate, Tris was not sure. Finally, the spirit stepped aside.

"We are agreed that you are Margolan's rightful king and heir to Bricen's line and to Bava K'aa's power." The ghost's eyes narrowed. "Her power is not the only magic you inherited, is it? Lemuel's power also fills you. I feel it."

Tris didn't flinch. "Lemuel was my grandfather."

The ghost appraised him with a gaze weary with age. "If you mean to keep your crown, I hope that magic is sufficient." He stepped aside and gestured for Tris to move deeper into the crypt, motioning for Tris to follow the fourth passage.

Handfire lit Tris's way. This passage was old, older than the catafalques in the front chamber or the shrine above them. In the glow of the magic, Tris could make out the cuts of the tools that had chiseled into the rock. He could sense the spirits around him, and he knew that the passageways went on, deep into the ground. There were more than just the spirits of Margolan's long-dead kings and queens. The ghosts of stillborn heirs and royal children who had died before their time walked these passages, as well as favored seers and mage advisors. Layer upon layer of magic warded these chambers. Tris passed through the wardings without effect, but he did not want to know what reception might have met an unauthorized explorer. Old magic pulled at his blood, as if the wardings verified the consanguinity of the visitor. Tris felt the weight of a host of watchers that gathered around him, felt their ghostly eyes on him as he made his way through the chamber, felt their presence in the unnatural chill that made his breath fog.

Frescoes had been painted onto the walls of the passageway. In the glow of the handfire, Tris could make out the images. The farther he descended into the crypt, the older the drawings appeared, until the images were faint ghosts of their original glory. The murals told of great battles and opulent investitures, with paintings of the kings and queens of Margolan in all their royal splendor. Some of the panels depicted bloody battles, and others showed Margolan's people celebrating with abundant food and wealth. It looked as if chroniclers had added both pictures and narrative as each king's remains were brought to the crypt. Tris was cynical enough to be certain that the tales had been varnished by the tellers to glorify the memory of the deceased king, but as the murals grew more ancient, he was surprised to find that famines and plagues were depicted as often as scenes of abundance.

They were deep into the passages now, and the paintings were quite old. Tris stopped to study the images. A robed man with a circlet on his brow stood next to what looked to be a mass grave. Pale bodies, many of them naked and emaciated, were heaped in carts and laid head to foot in a deep trench. In one panel of the mural, the robed king raised his hands in blessing over the dead. Even in the faded drawing, Tris could see that the artist had shown tears on the face of the king.

Hungry for more information, Tris moved to the next panel. Here, the king was shown in armor, wielding a sword. But it was the artist's depiction of the king's foes that caught Tris's attention. Some were drawn in chalk tones, crudely, like corpses standing upright. *Ashtenerath*, Tris thought. Around the battle-field, the trees were hung with the dismembered bodies of men and animals. And behind the chalky fighters was a line of black-robed opponents. The next panel showed the victory, but Tris stared as the details became plain in the glow of the handfire. All of the black-robed foes lay vanquished on the ground, and the corpse fighters were fallen. The trees with their rotting fruit of dangling bodies, offerings to Shanthadura, were aflame. But it was the figure of the king that made Tris catch his breath. Hadenrul was on his knees, hands pressed against his chest, eyes turned skyward. And an unmistakable fountain of blood poured from the chest of the king.

The next panel showed a great funeral procession. It was drawn in haste and lacked the artistry of the earlier murals. The materials used for the drawing had not held up as well, and some parts were smudged beyond recognition. But it was clear that the body of the king was borne on a bier carried by a sea of mourners. Musicians with drums and cymbals followed, and the faces of the mourners were painted to show unbearable grief. The king's hands were clasped over a sword that he held on his chest. On the King's right hand, the artist had taken pains to draw a gold ring. Tris bent closer, because the ring stood out. Whoever had drawn the mural had left out many details, giving only suggestions of the attire and adornment of the mourners or the king's grief-stricken court. But the king's ring was drawn in exceptional detail. As Tris squinted for a better look, he could see a complicated knot pattern set with dots of color that he assumed were meant for gems. He straightened, pondering the meaning of the mural.

Nexus thrummed with power and a faint nimbus shone around it. Whether that was warning or warding, Tris had no way to know. As he had often complained to Soterius during their last campaign, no one had told him how its magic worked. Neither Royster nor Fallon could find any details about its forging or its origin in the annals of the Library at Westmarch, except that it was made for Bava K'aa on the eve of the Great War against the Obsidian King and it was said to hold a shadow of her magic. Wary of the sword and its price, Tris used it as infrequently as possible. For combat against a mortal foe, he had a beautiful and deadly long sword. But one of Nexus's abilities was to manifest on the Plains of Spirit as a weapon that could destroy even the dead. And so, for this journey among the restless dead, Nexus was his weapon of choice.

Tris had worried that he might not recognize Hadenrul's tomb. Whoever had carried Hadenrul's bones to the shrine had been a devoted servant of the king. A chamber opened off of the passage, and above the doorway, runes marked the name of Hadenrul. It was old script, long fallen into disuse and difficult to read. Tris paused at the door and extended his magic, careful to sense for traps and wardings. He sensed none.

He let the mage fire illuminate the interior of the room. Unlike the catafalques in the outer chamber, there was no box to hold the body of the king. Instead, there was an altar in the center of the room. Tris entered, ducking to avoid the low transom of the doorway. Inside was a room with a domed roof. Murals covered these walls, too, as well as the ceiling. Eight panels of murals led the visiting mourner around the room. With a start, Tris realized that each panel depicted Hadenrul with one of the Aspects of the Sacred Lady, the deity whose worship he established in Margolan with the defeat of the followers of Shanthadura.

As a summoner, Tris had glimpsed the Aspects. Whoever had drawn Hadenrul's journey had been given accurate descriptions of the Lady in all Her faces. In the first panel, Hadenrul received his crown from the Mother, who was a generously proportioned woman with a broad face and full breasts and hips, standing on the bank of a wide river. In the next panel, Hadenrul received a blessing from the Childe, slim and robed in white. Doves ascended all around Hadenrul, and the Childe presented him with an armload of flowers and an ornate baldric.

Next, the sultry Lover greeted Hadenrul with a kiss and laid her hand in blessing on his groin, in what Tris guessed meant that Hadenrul's lineage would prosper and multiply. From Chenne, the Warrior Aspect, Hadenrul received a sword. Tris peered closely. Either the paint had smudged over the century or the artist meant to suggest that the sword itself shone with light.

The Light Aspects had given Hadenrul their gifts, and in the next panels, the four Dark Aspects bestowed their thanks. Istra, the Dark Lady, patron of the *vayash moru* and the outcast, handed Hadenrul an ornate chalice full to the brim with what appeared to be blood. Sinha, the Crone, splayed a reading of bone and runes, holding up the Jalbet card of the Victorious King, all omens of fate. From the Whore, Hadenrul received mountains of gold. Women knelt beside him, reaching up, caressing his body. Many of the women already showed bellies swollen with child. Heaps of grain, apples, and potatoes stood as tall as a man, and fields heavy with produce for the harvest

322

surrounded the goddess. Finally, Hadenrul stood before the Formless One, the Aspect of the Wild Host, so feared that there was no name spoken for her. Nameless was drawn as Tris had glimpsed her, a shrouded figure without a face. Behind her were her ghostly Host, wraiths, and revenants riding the skeletons of steeds. Nameless did not bestow a gift. Instead, the Aspect of chaos and genesis held out her hand, demanding a gift of the king. Hadenrul's hand held out a human heart, torn from the gaping wound in his chest.

Tris felt a shiver run down his spine as he turned back to the altar in the center of the room. Four candles made a semicircle around the three golden boxes. Someone had replaced the candles far more recently than Hadenrul's death, Tris thought, and he wondered where the acolyte was hidden. Tris passed his hand over the candles and willed them into flame. Respectfully, Tris knelt in front of the altar and made the sign of the Lady in blessing. Then he stretched out his magic and carefully opened the first box. A man's skull, yellowed with age, lay on a bed of crumbling velvet. The second box held the king's sternum on silk that might once have been a brilliant red but now was the color of dried blood. In the third box lay the bones of a right hand, and on the index finger was the golden ring Tris had seen in the mural in the passageway.

Tris felt the temperature in the crypt plummet. He felt the ghost's presence behind him before he had time to rise. Nexus flared blindingly bright in his hand.

"What do you seek?" The voice was deep and resonant, weary with years. It held both command and sorrow in equal measure, and a power that seemed to vibrate through Tris's bones. Cautiously, Tris rose to his feet and turned, inclining his head in respect.

"Tell me how you defeated the Durim," Tris said. Hadenrul's appearance without Tris's need to summon him gave Tris to guess that the spirit of the dead king knew who he was and judged his lineage worthy.

"You mean the Black Robes. The followers of Shanthadura."

Tris nodded. "You vanquished them four hundred years ago. But they've returned. They may be working with a dark summoner from across the Northern Sea. I don't know how to fight them."

Hadenrul's ghost looked solemn. "The Durim had caused great turmoil in Margolan when I saw the vision of the Sacred Lady. She wanted to end the slaughter, and her ways won over many of the worshippers of Shanthadura. As the worship of Shanthadura declined, so did the power of the Black Robes. But they had enough power for a final stand. It took all of my army's strength and my mage's cunning to win the day."

"You died in that battle, didn't you?"

Hadenrul nodded.

"Were you a summoner?"

Hadenrul looked startled for a moment, and then he smiled sadly. "Is that what the chroniclers say? My, how the stories have grown! No. No, I had no magic, unless you count exceptional intuition."

"Some would call that a type of magic."

Hadenrul shrugged. "Perhaps. But to your question, I did not have power over the dead, or the spirits, or the undead. I sense that power in you. Your magic animates even those of us who have not stirred in centuries. I can...feel...your breath, feel the blood flowing in your veins, feel the beating of your heart. Things I have not felt in a very long time. Great magic courses through you, my son."

Hadenrul had been in his fourth decade when he died. He still had the features of a relatively young man, with dark hair cropped short for battle and a warrior's build. He stood a head shorter than Tris, with broad shoulders and solid arms. A dark beard was braided, common for men going into combat. Whether he was a warlord or a king, Tris knew that Hadenrul had been a supreme warrior.

"What turned the Durim? I need to know."

Hadenrul's eyes were solemn. "Blood called them, and blood turned them. Not the blood of their sacrifices, taken by force. The blood of my troops, given in loyalty, given freely. Many men bled that day. But from that blood, the mages turned back the Durim." His voice was a low whisper. "Not all magic that involves blood is to be feared, my son. In blood we're birthed, and with the shed blood of the deer and cattle we fill our bellies. Blood can damn, and blood can redeem. It is the first magic, and the strongest."

Hadenrul's image began to waver. "Stand firm, my son," his voice said, as if from a great distance. Hadenrul's spirit was gone. Shaken, Tris extinguished the candles and said a prayer to the Lady in blessing. Hadenrul's ghost had not required his power to appear, and had not asked his permission to leave. Tris might have been able to follow the ghost on the Plains of Spirit, but something warned him not to try.

Here in the gloom of the crypt, Tris had no idea how much time had passed. But before he could return to the world of the living, he had one more visit to make. Tris took a deep breath to steady himself. Nexus still had a faint glow, but if the sword sensed either danger or strong magic, it gave no sign. Making one last bow in respect, Tris left Hadenrul's crypt and returned to the outer corridor, calling handfire once more to light his way.

The murals ended with Hadenrul's crypt, and, for a while, Tris walked along a passage with bare stone walls. He wondered if he had missed a side corridor or a hidden room. The passageway rounded a bend and ended in a dark opening. Once again, Tris extended his magic. He sensed no threat, but there

325

was a presence in the darkness, something ancient that was waiting for him to enter.

Nexus glowed brightly, and Tris sent more magic to the handfire, illuminating the end of the corridor. At the doorway to the darkened room were two very old vases. They were finely shaped and painted with faded images, fit for the grave goods of a barbarian king.

Tris sent his magic into the room, and the handfire filled it with a cold, blue glow. Tris felt the echo of magic, a preservation spell. A man's form lay on a slab of stone. A coat of animal skins covered the body from shoulder to ankle. Gold vambraces glistened from wrist to elbow on both arms. Rings sparkled on the corpse's fingers, and an intricate talisman of hammered gold set with gems glittered on his chest. A thin, plain circlet was held between the corpse's hands. A crude iron sword lay beside the body. All around the king's resting place lay a wealth of items intended to secure his comfort in the Nether. Leather quivers, fine sets of bows, knives with carved bone handles, and beautifully made spears and pikes lay ready for their master's use. At the foot of the slab lay the skeletons of two large dogs. Wolfhounds, Tris guessed by the bone structure.

The walls of the crypt were covered with runes and symbols Tris did not recognize. Even after a thousand years, he could feel the vestiges of old magic in the room, magic that preserved Marlan the Gold's body and his grave goods. Tris took a deep breath and willed his magic to fill him. He felt his magic resonate with the wardings in the tomb. His intent had been to probe the wardings and not to disturb them, but at the first touch of his power, a blinding light flared, and a rush of magic forced Tris to his knees, knocking his breath from him.

The crypt grew cold, and a fine mist formed in the torchlight, swirling and coalescing into the shape of a man. The figure scowled, as if the interruption displeased him, but when he spoke, Tris did not recognize either his words or his accent.

It's been a thousand years. His language is as dead as he is.

The power that had forced Tris to his knees receded, allowing Tris to regain his feet. An image became clear in Tris's mind. A man with long, unruly golden hair and a thick, reddish beard wore clothing that matched that of the ancient corpse on the slab. Marlan looked to have been late in his third decade, at the height of his power as a warrior. His eyes glinted with intelligence and ruthlessness, and the set of his mouth was a grim, thin-lipped half smile, as if, even now, he was sizing up Tris. Marlan's gaze lingered on the signet ring on Tris's right hand, the crest of the kings of Margolan.

Tris held up his hands, palms outward in a placating gesture as he stood, watching the spirit warily. He pointed toward the runes and markings on the crypt walls. "Tell me about the war," Tris said carefully. The ghost frowned. "About the Dread."

Marlan's eyes widened as if he recognized that single word, "Dread," and images flooded Tris's mind. Memories that were not his own overwhelmed him with the sights and sounds of battle. Tris suddenly stood at the fore of a large force, facing the army of the Cartelasian Empire, whose numbers looked to be much greater than his own force. The battle raged all around him, and Tris knew he was seeing through Marlan's eyes. What Marlan's forces lacked in powerful weapons they made up for with courage and savagery. More of the empire's soldiers than Marlan's troops lay dead on the ground, and Tris watched as Marlan's soldiers drove off the Cartelasian soldiers, riding down the stragglers and beheading the captives.

On Marlan's side, there were score upon score of men wearing crude helmets and leather armor, wielding maces or swords. But among them, Tris glimpsed shadow warriors, opaque, black forms without faces. These shadow warriors carried no visible weapons, but the Cartelasian generals fled before them, stumbling over their own men to escape.

The shadow warriors moved like a cloud against the enemy. In front of the dark shapes, soldiers ran screaming, casting away their weapons as they ran for their lives. Behind the shadows, mangled corpses and skeletons lay on the battlefield.

Are they the Dread, or the beings that the Dread guard? Tris wondered.

Other strange shapes caught Tris's attention. *Dimonns?* Tris wondered, and immediately decided differently. The shapes were amorphous balls of light, dark blue or bright red, and the light shifted to take on different, glowing forms. Some became huge beasts with fangs as long as a man's forearm and claws that could eviscerate with a single swipe. Others became great winged reptiles that ripped their prey into pieces. Still others took on the form of men, but these fighters had six arms and carried vicious scythes, dismembering the enemy soldiers unlucky enough to get in their way.

Marlan's soldiers held the field, but few men remained on their feet, and most of those were badly wounded. Severed arms, legs, and heads were strewn across the ground, along with entrails and the torn carcasses of battle steeds. The flag of the Cartelasian Empire lay bloody in the muck, trampled underfoot as its soldiers fled.

The creatures turned on Marlan and his soldiers.

Trapped within Marlan's memories, Tris saw a yellow glow radiate from Marlan's body. Light streamed from his hands, and the corpses of his fallen soldiers staggered to their feet against the new enemy. Against this foe, the former victors were badly outclassed. The creatures of blue and red swept aside Marlan's soldiers, living and dead, and Tris realized that they wanted the magic that surrounded Marlan. Powerful magic. Summoner magic.

Just as the blue and red creatures reached Marlan, the shadow warriors rallied, raising their arms in a gesture of warding. Blinding light filled the sky. Tris felt the memories blur, and he guessed that Marlan was choosing which images to show him. When the memories once again took shape, Marlan stood beside a large mound, one of the barrows of the Dread. His hands were outstretched in warding, and a procession of shadow warriors filed into the mound. Behind Marlan stood what remained of his living soldiers.

The onslaught of images ended abruptly enough to make Tris stagger. Tris drew on his own power as he turned back to face the ghost, drawing them both onto the Plains of Spirit.

Why have you come? Whether Marlan's voice sounded in the tomb or just within his own skull, Tris could not tell. Here in Nether, their spirits could communicate without the barriers of speech and language.

Someone is trying to raise the Dread—or whatever it is the Dread guard. I need to know how to stop them.

What the Dread bind, they choose to bind. And if they choose, they can loose the First Spirits, the Nachale.

Were you a summoner?

The old king's spirit hesitated, as if it had to search to understand Tris's words. Finally, Marlan spoke. *We did not use that word, "summoner." My people called me a ghost caller, and my enemies called me Sja Kun. It meant Death-bringer.*

How can I persuade the Dread to ally with us? We think a dark summoner is trying to win the Dread to his side. It may become a War of Unmaking.

There were tales, even in my day, about Wars of Unmaking. For the dead, every war is a war of unmaking.

Tris remembered the warning Alyzza had given him. *What of a bridge? Is there a bridge between the Dread and the Nachale? A bridge that the Dread guard?*

I know nothing about a bridge. The Dread guard the passage to the world of the living. The Sworn are their guardians.

How can I persuade the Dread to side with Margolan to defend your kingdom again? How did you gain them as allies?

The Dread sought me. I did not seek them.

If they're as powerful as you say, what did you have that they wanted?

Marlan paused. *I was a channel for their power, and they were a channel for mine. They had not been alive in so long, I believe they had lost their connection to the power of breath and blood. Magic is born of both spirit and sinew. Whether they could have found another channel, I do not know. But together, we were enough to bind the Nachale, although they were too ancient to destroy. Whatever power now calls to them, it will be up to the Dread to decide whether to listen or whether to turn away.*

If a dark summoner has the power to call to the Dread and raise the Nachale, how can I protect my people?

Tris felt Marlan's full power crash over him. It lanced through him, as if weighing him to take his full measure. *You are a true heir of power. If you wish to protect your people and defend the kingdom, then when the time is right, surrender yourself to that power. Take the talisman from my body. When battle comes, wear it into combat. If your offering is sufficient, it will open the magic of your fathers.*

Abruptly, Marlan's presence was gone, thrusting Tris from the Plains of Spirit and leaving a silence so complete it made Tris's head pound. He fell to his hands and knees, waiting for the pain to subside. When his vision cleared, Tris got to his feet and moved cautiously toward Marlan's body. The wardings yielded to him, and he reached out to carefully remove the golden talisman from the preserved corpse. It thrummed against his skin with a strange, old magic. For an instant, Tris felt Marlan's magic sizzle through the channels of his power. It left him breathless and unsteady. When he could trust himself to move, Tris put the talisman into a pouch safe within his tunic and made his way back up the winding passageways of the crypt.

As he moved toward the world of the living, the magic seemed to part around him, receding like water. Once, when he had been a boy, he had gone swimming in the depths of a lake in the forest. He had accidentally gone almost to the bottom, not realizing how the press of the water would drive breath from him and that its cold would draw the warmth from his blood. Even now, he remembered how it had felt to kick his way towards the surface, for the grip of the depths to loosen as the water grew lighter and warmer, and how he had gasped for air when at last he broke through the surface into the light. It was magic, not water, that pressed him now from all sides, that stole his breath and leached the heat from his marrow. Tris quickened his step, and it felt as if the magic pulled at him, as if it would draw him back into the darkness where the ancients slept.

With a burst of both physical and magical power, Tris willed himself forward, and he felt the tendrils of magic snap, as if he had passed an invisible barrier. He stood, shaking, for a moment, feeling as if, freed of the encumbrance, his body was light enough to float. Tris sucked in deep lungfuls of air and realized that he was nearly to the outer chamber and the crypt entrance. Light reached into the doorway, though it was the golden glow of late afternoon, and not the bright light of morning. He quickened his footsteps, and something deep and primal within him urged him to run. With an effort, Tris kept himself from fleeing, more because he did not care to hear the laughter of the dead than because he cared what the soldiers at the door might think.

Relief swept over Tris as he stepped from the crypt into the late-afternoon sun. Soterius and Fallon ran to him, but Tris held up a hand to stave off questions.

"Yes, yes, I'm fine. Really." Tris could see the concern in Soterius's expression, and he knew that Fallon was using her magic to make her own assessment of his condition.

"You've been in there for nearly two days," Soterius said, touching Tris's shoulder as if to reassure himself that Tris was alive. "We tried to go in after you, but the magic wouldn't let us pass. Even Fallon couldn't get through the wardings."

"Two days?" Now that he stood in the sun and fresh air, Tris realized that he was weak from hunger and his throat was parched. Fallon guided him to sit on the ground and pressed a flask of brandy and a wedge of cheese into his hands. "Eat. Drink. You've spent a long time in the realm of the dead. Ground yourself and remind your soul that you belong among the living." She glared at Soterius as if to deter him from questioning Tris until he had finished eating.

"Did you talk with them?" There was a note of excitement in Soterius's voice.

Wearily, Tris nodded. "Yes, and I'll tell you all about it on the ride home. Just give me a chance to catch my breath."

By the time they reached Shekerishet, Tris was exhausted. He and Soterius and Fallon had debated and dissected from every angle the meaning of what the ghosts had said. In the end, Tris had no more certainty about a course to protect Margolan from its enemies than he had before he entered the tomb.

"We'll have to convene the war council," Soterius said as they approached Shekerishet.

Tiredly, Tris nodded. "I know. And we'll have to go over all this again and again. I don't know if they'll believe me. Margolan doesn't have the resources to waste mustering the army again to sit by the edge of the sea and wait for an invader who might not be real."

"You've got more than a hunch to base it on. You've had warnings from Staden, Jonmarc, even Eastmark. Fallon told you that even the mage Sentinels think there's a blood mage or a dark summoner headed our way."

"The council can argue that those are reasons for caution, but not war. We don't have proof that there's an invading fleet on the way—we just have Cam's guess for the reason Alvior dredged the harbor. We don't know for certain whether a fleet that invaded Isencroft would try to invade Margolan, let alone Principality and Eastmark. The council could argue to wait and see."

The set of Soterius's jaw told Tris his friend was already spoiling for a fight. "Wait and see? And if Cam's right, does the council think we can snap our fingers and have an army provisioned and at the shore? We've barely recovered after Lochlanimar—"

"And that's the point. They'll argue that we're stretching ourselves too thin. They'll say that we're risking revolt by calling up the army to play a game of wait-and-see."

"And if it is a War of Unmaking?"

"Then they might say that nothing we can do will matter." Fallon had spoken little since they had left the shrine of the Mother and Childe. Her comment made both men turn to look at her. Fallon shrugged. "Think about it. We have only legend to tell us about the Wars of Unmaking. After all, by definition, if it wipes the slate clean and begins time over again, even the legends are suspect. Who's left to tell the story?"

"Do you think such a war is possible? Is it just a myth?"

Fallon frowned as she took a deep breath. "Some people say myth and they mean fable, a made-up tale. But the real myths, like the legends that endure, have a truth inside them, although it might be hidden in disguise. Do I think a War of Unmaking will actually destroy the entire world?" She shrugged again, palms open and upward. "Who knows? I haven't seen the whole world. I take it on faith that there are lands and people outside the Winter Kingdoms, but I haven't seen them with my own eyes. But do I think there could be a war that would unmake *our* world as we know it? That's another question. And the answer to that is yes. We know that the Mage Wars happened. We know that the first battle against the Obsidian King nearly destroyed the Winter Kingdoms. We know that before the Mage Wars, the Blasted Lands were full of people and cities and farmland, and now they're barren. Maybe that's as much 'unmaking' as we need for the threat to be real. And by that measure, I'd say it's a very real threat."

A different kind of headache was starting at the back of Tris's neck. It was a headache born of stiff muscles and the tension of trying to figure out something that might not have an answer. Right now, Tris decided, he wanted nothing so much as a hot dinner and another glass of brandy.

"You're probably right," he said, and he knew that the others could hear exhaustion in his voice. "But let's tackle the rest of this tomorrow. There's nothing more to be done tonight."

At the entrance to the palace, Tris left Soterius and Fallon behind and headed for the private quarters he shared with Kiara. He was not surprised that she was waiting for him in the parlor. She looked tired and worried. Cwynn was not in the room, and Tris guessed that Kiara and the nurses had finally managed to get him to sleep.

"What's wrong?" Tris gathered Kiara into his arms and she leaned her head against his shoulder.

"Cwynn had another bad night. I don't know how to soothe him. We've already found that some parts of the castle bother him more than others, so we keep him clear of those areas."

"And when I went over those places with my magic, there was nothing," Tris said, smoothing his hand down her long, auburn hair. "No ghosts, no energies, nothing."

"I don't know why he screams. The last few days it's been like he's been touched by madness."

Tris felt a coldness settle through him. He pushed away from Kiara and met her eyes. "What did you say?"

"I said that it's like Cwynn's been touched by madness. He rocks back and forth in his crib, but nothing soothes him. We'll finally get him to sleep and he'll wake screaming. Sometimes, he won't let anyone near him except Ula and Seanna, but they're ghosts. They can't hold him or clean him. Why?"

"When I went to Vistimar, the Sister in charge said that the residents there seemed to be more restless than ever, and that the restlessness came and went, almost like the waves in the sea or the cycles of the moon. Sometimes worse, sometimes better, but never gone completely."

"You think Cwynn is mad?"

Tris shook his head. "No, of course not. On the other hand, I'm not convinced Alyzza is completely mad, either. There's enough of her magic still intact to tell me that she senses something, even if her mind can't explain it. Or even if it's too frightening for her mind to explain."

Kiara looked at him sharply. "And you think Cwynn...senses something like the crazy mages at Vistimar? You and Sister Fallon told me that he's far too young to have power, even if he is your mage heir, which isn't guaranteed."

Tris shrugged, and reluctantly let go of her. "I don't know. Forget I said anything. Even if he could sense something, it doesn't solve the problem. Until he stops screaming, you and I and the rest of the castle aren't going to get much sleep, and neither will he." He shook his head. "If all firstborn children are this difficult, it's a wonder there are ever siblings."

Kiara drew a breath and turned away from him. "In a way, that brings up something I've been meaning to talk with you about."

"Oh?"

"I've been thinking about the problems Isencroft is having, first with the Divisionists and now with Alvior. Father's enemies are playing on the fear that because you and I are married and the throne of Isencroft will pass to me when something happens to Father, Isencroft has somehow been colonized by Margolan."

"You know that's not true."

Kiara nodded, walking as she talked, as if she needed the motion to help her sort out her thoughts. "I know that, and you know it, and Father knows it, but it's the kind of thing that can be hard to explain to a plowman in the field. Now we have a son, and that child is heir to both crowns. From the Divisionists' standpoint, that's no better. But if there were a second child, an heir designated for the Isencroft throne—"

Tris met her eyes, suddenly guessing where the conversation was headed. "No, not yet. We've talked about this before. There's barely been time for you to heal since Cwynn was born. You're only just recovered enough for us to be together again. It's too early to have another child."

"It's not completely our decision," Kiara said, and Tris heard the sadness in her voice. "Like it or not, what you and I want personally comes second to the crown—to both crowns—and to our kingdoms."

Tris turned to her with a stricken expression. "This is why I never wanted the crown. We aren't just prize horses for stud."

Kiara took a long breath. "Maybe not. But more depends on our children than on the children of a tinker or a smith. It's not about passing down the family business. There's already a threat from Jared's bastard. We know he's hidden away in Trevath, waiting for the right moment to challenge you."

"Jared's son is only a year older than Cwynn. Any challenge will be awhile in coming."

Kiara shrugged. "Maybe. Then again, one hundred years ago, Mortimer the Bald raised a challenge for the Isencroft throne in the name of a toddler he claimed was the rightful elder son. It took a war to defeat him, and a panel of mages to determine the consanguinity."

"We both know that wars can start over almost anything. Bad whiskey. Taxes. Empty bellies. I can't rule looking over my shoulder."

Kiara stepped closer. "If war comes to Isencroft, like it or not, part of the fight will be over our child. And if it comes, I'll have to help Father stand against it."

"Kiara, that doesn't make sense."

"Maybe not to the Margolense, but in Isencroft, yes, it does. I'm Donelan's heir. And don't forget, I saw a vision of the Lady on the battlefield when I rode with Father to put down the border war. To the Crofters, that makes me 'goddess blessed.' If Isencroft had a civil war and I didn't go home to show where my allegiance lies, it would undermine Father and give more fuel to the conspiracies that people already think are brewing."

"Maybe I could help—"

Kiara shook her head. "If the king of Margolan and his troops set foot on Isencroft soil, I guarantee you that a civil war will become a war with Margolan in a heartbeat. Nothing unites us like the idea of a common threat, and you have to admit that more than once in its history, Margolan has tried to annex Isencroft. Trust me, my people haven't forgotten that."

Tris sighed. "Carroway wrote a play once about lovers from two feuding families. In the end, everyone died. I hated that play. Now, I feel like I'm living it."

"There's something else to think about." Kiara's voice fell nearly to a whisper. "If it's true that there's going to be another war, if there's an invasion coming from across the sea, then it's more important than ever to make sure there's a safe succession. I don't want to even think that it's possible for something to happen to you, but I've been to war. I know what can happen.

And if something did happen to you, and if Cwynn really can't take the throne—"

Kiara did not have to finish the sentence for Tris to understand. Without its king and with a crippled heir, Margolan would be defenseless. The challenge to the throne would come both from across the sea and from the supporters of Jared's bastard, while Isencroft dissolved into chaos. Both kingdoms would almost certainly fall to outsiders, and the resulting war could well draw in the rest of the Winter Kingdoms.

Which course leads to a War of Unmaking? Is it the threat of a dark summoner, or the risk of a weak succession? Or is war certain to come, no matter what we do?

As if she guessed his thoughts, Kiara took Tris's hand. "It's in our power to reduce the threat of war in one way. If I'm pregnant with a second heir, then if Cwynn turns out to be healthy, Isencroft has its new king. And if there's really something wrong with Cwynn—" She couldn't finish the sentence, but Tris knew what she was thinking.

If Cwynn isn't suitable to take the throne, then, Goddess help us, we have a spare. It wouldn't solve the Isencroft issue as neatly, but it would secure Margolan's throne and the joint throne with Isencroft, and it might keep outsiders at bay. Tris folded Kiara into his arms.

"I anchored your soul when you gave birth to Cwynn," Tris murmured, resting his cheek against Kiara's hair. "It took all my power not to lose both of you. So many times, it was close. Too close." His voice caught. "Crowns and kingdoms be damned, Kiara, I don't want to lose you. Maybe that makes me a bad king. So be it." His fingers trailed through her hair, tangling in the auburn strands.

Kiara leaned against him. "I have no intention of leaving you or Cwynn. This isn't the timing I'd choose under other circumstances. But we don't get to choose. Please, Tris."

Tris swallowed hard, and nodded. "All right. What do Esme and Cerise say? How soon would it even be possible?"

Kiara turned in his arms. A bittersweet smile touched her lips. "Neither of them likes the idea any more than you do, but when I laid out the options, they had to agree that it's less risky than all the other choices."

"Which isn't saying much."

Kiara ignored his comment. "It's been almost six weeks since Cwynn was born. Esme tells me that in the farmlands, many a wife is already pregnant with the next child well before the first is three moons old. You and Esme can use your magic to assure that we conceive quickly."

"Most days, I'd give anything to be one of those farmers, with nothing to worry about except getting the crop in," Tris said and sighed.

"And no control over soldiers riding across your fields or the taxes you pay or whether or not your lord conscripts your sons into the militia."

"Point taken. On the other hand, we've just discussed how little control a king really has—over much of anything."

Kiara gave him a mischievous look. "And is making a baby such an onerous duty to the king?"

Despite his gloomy mood and the exhaustion of the day's working, Kiara's smile quickened his pulse. Tris bent to kiss her hand with a flourish. "Absolutely not, m'lady. The crown is at your service."

Kiara grinned broadly. "It wasn't the crown I had in mind."

The next afternoon found Tris presiding over a war council. Soterius sat to his right, along with General Senne. To his left, Sister Fallon sat next to a newcomer, Nisim, one of the Sentinels. Lord Dravan represented the Council of Nobles. Mikhail was both seneschal and the official representative of the Blood

Council for the *vayash moru*, and with him was Kolja, from the Margolan *vyrkin*.

The council listened with growing concern as Tris and Fallon shared their news. The warning letters from Cam, Jonmarc, and Eastmark lay in the middle of the table. Tris's summary of the situation in Isencroft elicited worried outcry.

"We may have no control over it, but this couldn't be worse timing for the army," Senne said. Tris had learned to depend on Senne's experience and clear thinking during the siege of Lochlanimar. Senne was twenty years older than Tris, and his dark hair was gray at the temples. His eyes were a cold, dark blue, and there were fine lines at the corners of his eyes from time spent squinting against the sun. Bricen had always valued Senne's advice, and after having seen him in battle, Tris now shared his father's admiration. "With the soldiers home, we barely have enough men to bring in the crops. The plague's made it hard enough, but if we call back the soldiers, can we really expect the women and elders to bring in a full harvest by themselves? I don't fancy fighting a war when the townsfolk behind the lines are hungry. It'll make it the Crone's own to provision the troops, and hungry people have little patience. We could have a revolt on our hands, even without civil war in Isencroft."

"Lady knows, the Council of Nobles has no desire to see another pretender to the throne, whether it's from across the Northern Sea or it's Jared's bastard." Lord Dravan was a generation older than Tris's father and had been one of the nobles who remained loyal to Bricen throughout Jared's rule. Dravan's white hair showed his age, but his blue eyes were sharp and his angular features showed keen intelligence. "With the three new additions to the Council of Nobles, I trust Your Majesty will find the support you need if it comes to war, but I pray to the Lady such a course is not necessary."

Tris nodded. Political maneuvering among three of the former members of the Council of Nobles had nearly resulted in unfounded charges of treason against Kiara and a warrant of execution for Master Bard Carroway, one of Tris's dearest and most loyal friends. When Tris had returned from battle to set the matter straight, one of the Council had been hanged for treason and two were banished permanently from court. Their replacements had been chosen both for loyalty and the ability to think rationally on matters of policy. With any luck, the new Council reduced the threat of betrayal from among the most prominent nobility.

"We can't count on support from the Sisterhood." Fallon's voice made her disdain for the ruling body of mages clear. "I've tried to get Sister Landis to rethink her position of neutrality, but she's adamant that her mages will not get involved in 'temporal' concerns."

"By the Whore!" Senne roared. "Will she stand by and do nothing if we're invaded by a dark summoner?"

Fallon met the general's eyes. "She'll see to the safety of her mages. If they were attacked, she would use magic to defend them. But she won't provide battle mages for the army or bring the Sisterhood to the aid of the crown." She paused. "On the other hand, if war really does break out, I know of quite a few mages who might find their consciences tried by Landis's edict. I think we could count on many of those mages to go rogue and join us, as some of us did during the battle for the throne."

Dravan leaned over to Tris. "Refusing to aid the king—isn't there something on the books about that?"

Tris managed a wan smile. "With the rest of Margolan's problems, do you really want to skirmish with the Sisterhood?"

Dravan sat back in his chair with a muttered curse. "Of course not. It's the principle of the thing."

"Unfortunately, after the battle for the throne and the siege of Lochlanimar, the number of *vayash moru* who could join our forces is smaller than it used to be," Mikhail observed. "We've also had more than a few *vayash moru* flee to Dark Haven after some of the locals tried to burn them out, blaming them for the plague. On the other hand, we've got more *vayash moru* than usual as refugees at Huntwood and Glynnmoor. They might prefer taking an active role, especially against a threat like a dark summoner. I could see who I can personally recruit, but we won't have a very large contingent under the best of circumstances. There are never as many of us as the mortals believe, and now, there are fewer still."

"Your people fought bravely at Lochlanimar," Senne said. "Our losses would have been much heavier without them."

"I'm afraid that the *vyrkin* are in much the same situation as the *vayash moru*," Kolja said. "Our numbers were never very large, and Jared did his best to hunt us to extinction. He may have come closer to success than he knew. Many of my people have also fled for sanctuary in Dark Haven, but even there, I hear that mortals are hunting us for fear that we carry plague." He spread his hands. "Ironic, isn't it? Neither we nor the *vayash moru* can carry or die of plague, so they kill us for the crime of not dying." Kolja paused. "Like the *vayash moru*, many *vyrkin* have found sanctuary at Huntwood and Glynnmoor. I will see whose pledges I can secure."

"If the warnings are true, and Alvior's invasion includes a dark summoner of real power, then we're at a disadvantage without more mages and without significant numbers of *vayash moru* and *vyrkin*," Tris said. He knew they could hear the weariness in his voice, and a glance in the mirror that morning had told him that his tiredness was plain on his face. If he hadn't been born with white-blond hair, he was quite certain that the burden of the crown would have turned his hair gray within his first year as king.

"The *vayash moru* have strength and speed and they're just plain tougher to destroy. That's an advantage when we're fighting magic. And as we saw at Lochlanimar, fever and pox spring up quickly in army camps. It helps to have some of your troops who are immune," Senne said.

"It's not just immunity to disease," Fallon added. "Taking mortal troops up against a dark summoner means magic will be as much the weapon of choice as your catapults and trebuchets. *Vayash moru* and *vyrkin* are more immune to mind-meddling or magicked terrors than mortal troops, and they're better at seeing through whatever glamours a mage might cast to trick soldiers into a trap." She shrugged. "But if we don't have the numbers, we don't have them. There's not much we can do about it."

"What kind of a fleet can Margolan put to sea?" It was Nisim, the mage-Sentinel, who spoke, and Tris startled. Except for his report to the council of the warning signs observed by the Sentinels, Nisim had said nothing.

"There's been no serious threat from across the Northern Sea in generations," Tris said. "And while there are explorers who've gone into larger, open waters, the seas near Margolan are icebound for months out of the year. There are fishing boats and trading vessels that move from Isencroft to Margolan to Principality—some even to Eastmark, and the privateers who keep the pirates away from the villages. The fishermen from the Bay Islands are probably our best sailors. They go far out to sea for the best catch, but I'm not even certain they really consider themselves to be Margolense. Margolan's never had much in the way of a real navy. If we were ever to go to war with our neighbors, it would make more sense to march rather than sail!"

Nisim nodded as if he had expected Tris's answer. "That had been my observation, but I wanted to hear confirmation." He leaned forward. "To my thinking, and to my fellow Sentinels, the evidence is overwhelming that an invasion fleet from across the

Northern Sea is coming. We don't have time to build ships to counter that. But we might be able to rally the good shipping folk of the Bay Islands and the Borderlands to our cause if they knew that foreign troops and dark mages would be ravaging their lands and villages."

"Say on," Dravan said, stroking his chin as he listened.

Nisim looked uncomfortable being the center of attention. He was a thin man, perhaps ten years older than Tris, with long, straight, dark hair. His accent gave Tris to guess that Nisim came from the Borderlands he now protected. "Even mages have their limits when it comes to personally gathering information," he said, with a glance toward Fallon, who nodded encouragingly. "The other Sentinels and I have been making contacts among the shipping folk for a while now. They agree to be our eyes and ears, and in exchange, we help them fill their nets with fish and keep the rough seas to a minimum."

"Spies," Senne said. "You've built a network of spies."

Nisim nodded. "The shipping folk and the privateers were quick to spot evidence to confirm the dangers we observed in the currents of magic. There's a powerful bond between those folk and the sea. If it isn't magic, it's near enough as to be no different. They've practically got brine for blood, and they can scent the winds almost as well as any weather mage.

"My point is, no one's got more of a stake in this than they do. If invaders land their ships on the Margolan coast, it'll be the shipping folk's families who are first to die. And if it comes to a Mage War, then it'll be their fields and homes blasted into oblivion," Nisim continued.

"So you think they might help us?" Tris asked.

"The privateers have already offered their aid. And the fishermen are angry enough about anyone spoiling the catch that, with or without the king's flag, they'll fight any foreign ships that enter their waters."

"You don't need to convince me that Borderlanders are good fighters," Tris said. "After all, Jonmarc Vahanian hails from those parts."

"Could their flotilla hope to engage a navy?" Senne's skepticism was clear in his voice.

Nisim shrugged. "Do you have an alternative?"

"I don't like putting civilians in harm's way."

Nisim met Senne's eyes. "And isn't that exactly what happens when farmers become soldiers?"

With a growl, Senne sat back in his chair and crossed his arms. "I still don't like it."

"I don't think we have a choice." Tris knew he sounded more certain than he felt. "The truth is, we can barely field an army. Many of the people who fled Margolan because of Jared haven't come back yet. They might never return. Then there's the toll the plague's taken, and the food shortages last winter. We lost a lot of men at Lochlanimar, even if we did win the siege." He turned to Soterius and Senne. "How many troops do you really think we can muster and still have people left to harvest the crops?"

Soterius shrugged. "I've been working on the counts for a week, and no matter how I run the numbers, I don't like them. We took four thousand men to Lochlanimar, and lost more than a third to battle and disease. If we call up every able-bodied man from fifteen to fifty—and every woman inclined to wield a sword—we might muster up six thousand." He spread his hands. "It's the best estimate I can come up with."

"We might persuade fifty or so *vayash moru* and *vyrkin* to fight, but some of the *vyrkin* will need to stay with the pups, and some of the older *vayash moru* feel much like the Sisterhood, that the affairs of the living are no longer their concern," Mikhail added.

"I think I could bring in about twenty mages, but they won't all be true battle mages," Fallon said. "That's everything from hedge witches to healers, and no guarantee we won't be overly supplied with one type of magic versus another."

"So we could have ten land mages and only a few water mages?" Tris asked. "It would be good to have all four elements represented. Lady knows, we needed all the magic we could get at Lochlanimar."

"I think you'll find water magic, large and small, among the fishing folk," said Nisim. "And my fellow Sentinels will do all we can."

"Bricen's army was twenty thousand at its peak strength," Senne said. "How far we've fallen in so little time!"

"I'd guess that at least ten thousand of those soldiers lie in the shallow graves Jared's men dug for them," Soterius said bitterly. A thought crossed his face, and he turned to Tris. "Is there any chance—"

"If it comes to that, yes. I can call on the armies of the dead. But not without great cost, and only as a last resort. You saw what toll that kind of magic took at Lochlanimar. I'd rather not depend on it, if we have any other options."

Soterius met his eyes. "As you've heard, our options are sparse."

A knock at the doors to the council chamber startled them. Harrtuck, Captain of the Guard, leaned into the room. "Beggin' your pardon, but there're visitors here for you. I think you'll want to see them right away."

Tris rose and walked toward the door. "Who—"

The door opened farther. Framed in the doorway stood Jair Rothlandorn, and beside him a Sworn shaman.

17

"Please forgive our intrusion." Jair's formal language was for the benefit of the council, but his grin was directed at his cousin. Tris Drayke stepped forward and embraced Jair, then drew back, still holding him by the shoulders.

"Lady True! You're the last one I thought to see walk through those doors. You're supposed to be on the Ride, aren't you?"

Despite the urgency of the situation, Jair felt a rush of pleasure just being back with his cousin. It hadn't been quite a year since the last time Jair had seen Tris. Then, at Tris's wedding, it had struck Jair how the battle for the throne had changed his cousin, forced him into a maturity beyond his years. Now, after a year that would have tried even a seasoned monarch, Jair could see the tiredness in Tris's features. "Technically, I'm still on the Ride. I'm here with the Sworn, not on behalf of Dhasson."

Tris looked from Jair to Talwyn. "And this must be—"

Jair grinned more broadly. "May I present *Cheira* Talwyn, daughter of the Sworn chief, shaman of her people—and my wife."

Tris bowed. "Honored, m'lady. Jair's written me about you, and I see that his praise was not undeserved."

Although he was in Tris's palace in Margolan and not his father's war room in Dhasson, Jair knew quite well what he and

Talwyn had interrupted. Although most of the time, he much preferred the riding garb of the Sworn to the fancy dress of court, now that he had come to court on business, he felt uncomfortable not being dressed for the part. Harrtuck had permitted him his *stelian* and had not made any move to relieve him of the knives in his baldric. Jair saw the appraising looks of Tris's war council, and he could only imagine how he and Talwyn must look to them. *Enter the barbarians.*

Tris's smile had faded as he began to realize what Jair's appearance meant. "Your Ride doesn't bring you anywhere close to Shekerishet."

They were speaking Common, which Jair knew both the council and Talwyn could follow. "We weren't far from Ghorbal."

"That's a week's ride."

Jair managed a lopsided grin. "Four days if you ride hard and change horses. Who needs sleep?"

"Then this isn't a social call."

Jair's grin disappeared. "No, it's not. We've come with a warning, and a request."

"Say on."

Jair looked from Tris to the waiting council. "The Durim have been desecrating the barrows from Margolan into Dhasson. They're trying to raise the Dread—and the spirits that the Dread guard."

"Why?" Fallon's voice was sharp with alarm. Nisim sat up straight, and his eyes darted from Jair to Talwyn.

"The Durim are preparing for war. They've been making sacrifices—animal and human, and a few weeks ago, the ones we fought were preparing for a soul harvest."

Tris blanched. "They were Hollowing?"

Jair glanced sharply at his cousin. "You know of this?"

"It was done by blood mages. And the Obsidian King."

"We brought the Durim we captured before the Consort

Spirits," Talwyn continued. "The Durim want to usher in a War of Unmaking. From the currents of magic, they believe the war is coming, and they want to feed from the destruction."

"That's bad enough," Jair interrupted. "But when Talwyn walked among the spirits of the Dread, they said that they've felt the power of a dark mage, a spirit mage," he said, meeting Tris's eyes.

"Is that why you came here, to warn us?" Fallon had left her seat and now stood next to Tris. Nisim looked conflicted, as if he wanted to join them but was unsure his rank permitted it. He made do by straining to bend as close as he could to catch every word.

"In part," Jair replied. "But the night before we left, Talwyn walked the spirit paths again. This time, the Dread came to her."

"The Dread have asked that I bring Martris Drayke to them," Talwyn said. "They wish to determine on whose side, if any, they will fight when war comes."

"For the benefit of the rest of us poor folks without magic, could someone please explain what's going on?" Dravan's tart voice cut through the tension in the room.

Chagrined, Tris and Jair turned toward the others. Jair wondered if the rest of the council saw the family resemblance between them as clearly as he did. Bricen's sister was Jair's mother, and though Tris was as fair as Jair was dark, the similarities in features were stronger than the differences. "Sorry," Tris said, and gestured for Jair and Talwyn to join them at the table. "Bear with us; this may take a bit of explaining."

Tris and Jair took turns describing the full meaning of Jair's news to the council. Fallon and Nisim jumped in from time to time to clarify an unfamiliar phrase or a bit of magical lore. Talwyn did her best to explain the mystic connection between the Sworn and the spirits that they guarded. When they were finished, the expressions of the council made it clear that as ominous as the indicators had been before Jair's arrival, the likelihood of war was now almost certain.

"*Cheira* Talwyn," Senne said, and he seemed to be struggling to find just the right phrasing. "I have certainly learned to respect the validity of information gained through magical means, although I don't have a magic bone in my body. But... with all due respect... can there be any room for error? If what you say is true—"

Talwyn might be a stranger to court, Jair thought, but council meetings in the palace differed more in form than in substance from the tribal council over which Talwyn presided with her father. If she felt uncomfortable among the uniforms and brocades of the men around her, she did not show it. She was, Jair noted with pride, in every sense a warrior and the spirit-speaker for her people.

"I would not have come to you if any doubt remained." Talwyn spoke deliberately, enunciating carefully to make up for her strong accent. "I have tested the spirits. I've walked with the spirit guides and with the Consort Spirits. The Dread do not come lightly to the living. No one living can remember another time when they have requested that a mortal mage be brought to them for... evaluation."

"We're on the brink of war. There's no way Tris can leave for Ghorbal right now," Soterius protested.

"We don't need him to leave the palace," Talwyn replied. "The meeting is in the realm of spirit."

"You mean the plains of the dead?" Fallon asked.

"No. I'm not a summoner like your king. I can't walk the Plains of Spirit in the same way he can. The Durim are no more 'dead' than *vayash moru* are 'dead.' There are... places... between the extremes of living and dead. The Dread dwell in those places."

"And what of the 'things' the Dread guard? Whose side are

they on?" The challenge came from Nisim, and there was a hint of fear in his voice.

Talwyn turned to look at him. "If the Dread intervene, it will be for the first time in a thousand years. But even if they do, the spirits they guard, the Nachale, can remain bound—if the Durim don't release them."

"And the last time the Nachale and the Dread walked the world of the living, the legend says there was a War of Unmaking," Fallon said quietly.

"I spoke with the soul of Marlan the Gold. He ruled this land when that war was fought, and he was the last king to see the Durim before they went into the barrows," Tris said quietly. "He said that the Dread sought him, as a channel for their power. But I had the distinct impression that their reasons were their own."

"Is it a trap?" Senne's eyes had narrowed. "With all respect, *Cheira* Talwyn, might the Dread have an agenda of their own for asking our king to come to them? Maybe they've already allied with our enemies and intend to eliminate the threat King Drayke poses to their invasion."

Talwyn seemed to consider his argument for a moment, and then she shook her head. "I understand your caution, General. You do well to protect your king. But the Dread are ancient beings. Mortal politics don't concern them."

"Some say the same of the *vayash moru*, that because we live for centuries we care little for the maneuverings of mortals," Mikhail said quietly. "They're wrong."

"Can I go on record to say that I don't like this at all?" Soterius's jaw was set. "Tris went to seek counsel from the ghosts of his long-dead ancestors, and he barely had enough energy to stagger out of the crypt. I've seen how much this kind of magic costs him. How many times can he do these kinds of workings before our luck goes bad and something goes really,

really wrong? It's not like my soldiers and I can go in after him."

"I will walk with him." Talwyn's voice was firm but not defensive. "His mages can help to anchor him, if they wish." She gave a tired smile. "To tell you the truth, it would be nice to have backup, for once."

"We don't have a choice." Everyone turned to look at Tris. "Marlan's ghost told me that the Dread also sought him out. This isn't just the chance of a lifetime; it's the opportunity of a millennium. If the Dread want to size me up, then it's not a meeting I can afford to miss." He met Talwyn's gaze. "I'll do it."

Since it was agreed that Tris and Talwyn needed a day to rest and prepare for the working, it gave Tris an excuse to clear the remaining meetings from his afternoon and left the evening free. Jair and Talwyn were happy to join Tris in the parlor of the king's private chambers after servants saw to it that they both had cool baths and time to clean up from their long journey.

"That's a healthy-looking boy you've got there," Jair said, getting a glimpse of Cwynn as Kiara handed him to a nursemaid after his feeding was finished.

A shadow seemed to cross Tris's face for a moment. "He's got an appetite like a horse. And he's grown by the length of my thumb just since he was born." He took a deep breath. "How's Kenver?"

"He's every bit his father's son," Talwyn answered.

Jair chuckled. "Funny, I was going to say that it's clearer every day that he's got your blood."

"Aunt Jinelle and Uncle Harrol are well?" Tris stretched out in his chair, moving as if he were stiff from battle or the salle.

Jair nodded. "They were when I left Dhasson, and I pray to the Lady and Her Consorts that they remain so."

Tris shifted in his chair and leaned forward onto his knees.

Kiara returned to a seat near him and curled her legs under her. "How badly is the plague hitting Dhasson?"

Jair sighed. "Bad, especially on the southern border. And it's making its way north toward Valiquet. I think this is the first year Father's actually been relieved for me to leave on the Ride. He's worried what might happen if the plague really takes hold in the palace city. I know you had no choice in the war on the southern plains, and I know that the plague wasn't of your making, but it crossed the river quickly into Dhasson just a few months after the Margolan army decamped from Lochlanimar. Although, if it's any consolation, it appears to have hit Nargi just as hard."

"The last letter I received from my cousin, Carina, said that King Staden in Principality had sent his daughter, Berry, to Dark Haven for safety," Kiara said. "Plague's already gone upriver into Principality, and from what Carina says, it's going badly up there."

Jair looked to Kiara. "You know that King Kalcen has opened relations with Dhasson. There'd been diplomatic envoys before your wedding, but Kalcen and Father hit it off at the ceremony."

"As I recall, they were back to back wielding swords against that magicked beast the assassin turned loose," Kiara observed dryly.

Jair chuckled. "You should hear the way Father tells that tale to the court! It's been years since he's been allowed to be in harm's way, and he's relishing every moment. The beast gets bigger with every telling. But as I was saying, Kalcen and Father actually left Margolan with a draft of an alliance handwritten on some scraps of parchment. They made it official a few months ago. So we get news regularly from Eastmark and have full diplomatic exchange." He sighed. "Unfortunately, the news isn't good, even from there. They've had two outbreaks of plague, and once that happens, more's sure to come."

"And Trevath? Has anyone heard news of them?"

Jair shook his head. "Father and King Nicolaj have never been on entirely good terms, although obviously better than relations between Margolan and Trevath. Most of what the spies bring us is related to trade and smuggling, and nothing at all about Jared's bastard."

Tris grimaced. "I'm not surprised. Ah well. That particular problem will have to wait its turn." He arched backward, and his face twitched in momentary pain, as if he'd pulled on a sore muscle.

Jair looked at him worriedly. "You know, Tris, I might be one of the few people who can say this without landing myself in the dungeon, but... you look like hell."

Tris's chuckle was bitter. "Actually, I've heard almost those exact words from Fallon and Soterius, and Kiara keeps telling me I look 'tired.'" He glanced sideways at his wife. "I think that's code for the same thing."

"If I weren't already dreading the day I take the crown, you're certainly making it look less fun than anyone imagines."

Tris closed his eyes and slumped back against the chair. Kiara reached over to take his hand and tangled her fingers with his. "We've both read the old histories. Some kings were lucky enough to come to the throne during peace and prosperity. Some had to fight for their crowns, and some had to battle just to stay alive." He sighed. "I'm afraid it's our lot to live during 'interesting times.'"

Jair slipped his arm around Talwyn. "I always found the histories to be boring, pretentious, and, in all probability, lies. But it's alarming how few kings get to die of old age in bed."

"I went into the crypts to summon the spirits of King Hadenrul and Marlan the Gold. Both of them died in battle."

Jair's surprise was clear on his face. "You spoke with them? If it were anyone but you saying that, Tris, I'd be sure they were making it up."

Tris shook his head. "It was a hard working, and that's one of the reasons Soterius and Fallon were so adamant that we wait before we walk with the Dread. I was pretty spent afterward."

Talwyn leaned forward. "Our magics are very different, but I am intrigued by your summoning. I can spirit walk, but it's not the same as being present in soul both on the Plains of Spirit and in the realms of the living."

Tris frowned, thinking. "So you can walk in the Nether?"

Talwyn conversed for a moment with Jair in the Sworn's language, asking for a translation. Finally, she nodded. "We have other names for the Place Between, but perhaps it is the same." She smiled. "We'll see when we try to walk there together, no?"

"I don't know that your visit will allow it, but I would also like to learn more about your magic." Tris grimaced. "My education was rather rushed. I learned about warding and blasting, and I picked up on what not to do the hard way. Every time I do a working, I'm reminded that there is a lot I didn't have time to learn, and one of these days, that's going to catch up with me."

Talwyn turned to Kiara, who had been quiet. "And you, Kiara, you have some magic, too?"

Kiara smiled. "A little Regent Magic, although up till now, it's been mostly scrying and self-protection. Maybe I just don't have the talent."

Talwyn shook her head. "I don't believe that." She closed her eyes and was very still for a moment. When she opened her eyes, she met Kiara's gaze. "No, there is magic in you. Perhaps it isn't time yet. But power is in you."

Tris and Kiara exchanged glances. "Fallon and I have both tried to sense Kiara's magic, and something seems to block us," Tris said. A look passed between Tris and Kiara that Jair could not decipher. "How is it you can feel it and we can't?"

Talwyn shrugged. "Magics work in different ways. I call on the Consort Spirits instead of the Sacred Lady. That's one difference between us. My magic is grounded not just in the four elements, as yours is, but in the magic of each Consort. Perhaps I walk different passageways."

Again, a look passed between Tris and Kiara, and Jair knew that something in Talwyn's words had been very important to his cousin.

"Talwyn, I have a favor to ask," Tris said. Kiara gave him an encouraging look. "Could you use your power to sense whether Cwynn has magic? I know it's early but…"

Kiara leaned forward, laying a hand on Tris's arm. "The truth is, I was attacked by an assassin when I was pregnant with Cwynn. The blade used wormroot, and it was a massive dose. We both nearly died. The birth was very difficult, and although he seems healthy, Cwynn's had a rough time of it. 'Fussy' doesn't begin to cover it. Right now, he's the heir to two thrones, so if there's truly something wrong—"

Kiara's voice caught and she looked down. Tris wrapped his arm around her, but Tris's worry was plain on his face. "Even the runes and omens refuse to speak. In better times, we could wait and see. But now, with a war looming…"

Talwyn nodded. "Of course. We know something of succession problems ourselves."

Tris glanced at her. "But you have Kenver, and he's healthy, isn't he?"

Jair knew that his own distaste for the situation in Dhasson was clear on his face. "Health isn't the issue. It's parentage. The court has made it clear that they will never accept Talwyn as my wife, or Kenver as heir to the throne." He sighed. "And Talwyn wouldn't be able to leave her people any more than I could leave Dhasson."

"What will you do?"

Talwyn was first to speak. "We will make an 'accommodation.' Among the Sworn, Jair and I are ritually wed and Kenver is both Jair's heir and next in line, behind me, for the chieftainship when my father goes to the Consorts." She shrugged. "Jair will have to make a suitable arranged marriage, a business proposition, to produce an heir of acceptable lineage. So long as the other party knows what to expect, life moves on. It's hardly the first time such a thing has happened." Jair looked at his wife. Although her tone had been objective, he knew her well enough to see the pain that flickered in her eyes.

Kiara leaned forward to touch Talwyn's hand. "I'm sorry."

Jair glanced at Tris, and he knew that Tris could see that his own feelings were far from happy with the arrangement. "I've always envied you two the chance to make a love match. You know how rare that is among kings and queens."

Kiara gave a dry laugh. "We only had to break a betrothal contract that was put in place to stop a war, then fight for the crown. Even so, it's brought Isencroft to the brink of civil war." She shook her head. "It wasn't as romantic as the stories make it sound." She closed her eyes and rubbed a hand across her forehead as if it pained her. "That's why we really need to know about Cwynn. Two kingdoms hang in the balance."

Talwyn nodded. "Bring me your son."

Kiara slipped from the room and returned holding Cwynn. He was already beginning to fuss. "It's not like I woke him," she said apologetically. "He doesn't sleep much, or for long at a time. There are places in the castle that we can't take him at all, because he shrieks like a wild thing. He coos to himself, or we think it's to himself. He responds best to the two ghosts who have been nursemaids to the children here for hundreds of years, but we aren't certain whether he can see other ghosts." Gently, she folded back the light wrap that covered Cwynn's face.

Talwyn threw up a hand to cover her eyes.

"What's wrong?" Tris asked.

Talwyn shook her head and blinked several times, gradually

lowering her hand. "He glows so brightly it hurts." She looked to the others in astonishment. "Can't you see?"

The confused shakes of their heads made Talwyn's eyes widen. "I see him bathed in many-colored light, like I'm told the Spirit Lights of the far north shine. I'm certain he sees the light, too." She held out her arms. "May I hold him?"

Carefully, Kiara transferred Cwynn to Talwyn. "He's not good with strangers. In fact, he's not very good even with the people he knows."

Talwyn said nothing. Her lips began to move, and Cwynn's fussing grew quieter. Tris closed his eyes, and Jair guessed that Tris was opening his own magic, perhaps even stepping into the Plains of Spirit to see if he could see the glow. Slowly, Talwyn began to move around the room, speaking in a whisper. Jair could make out just enough of her words to know that she spoke in the Sworn's language, and that her words invoked the Consort Spirits.

"Careful! He tends to scream if you get too close to that wall," Kiara cautioned.

A faint, yellow light began to glow around both Talwyn and Cwynn as Talwyn moved closer to the north wall. Cwynn gave a sharp cry, and Talwyn took a sudden breath. The yellow light wavered, and then grew stronger, and Cwynn's terror subsided. Talwyn walked full circle around the room. When she returned to the center, she held Cwynn in one arm while her right hand pulled at the amulets around her throat, lifting them above the neckline of her tunic. She wore one amulet in honor of each of the Consort Spirits, and a talisman of the Lady's mark. Eyes closed, Talwyn handled each amulet one by one, waiting for several breaths as if she were expecting a reaction from Cwynn.

Whatever she found, Talwyn said nothing. Her eyes opened, and she walked toward a clustering of candles on the side table. She drew a pouch from her belt with her free hand, still holding

Cwynn against her side with her left arm. From the pouch, Talwyn poured a mixture of dried leaves onto the side table, and dropped a pinch into the candle flames. A dense, musky smoke rose, filling the air with its scent.

"Consort Spirits, I ask the honor of your attendance. Trouble the smoke for me, and help me see."

Cwynn had fallen completely silent, watching with round, open eyes but making no sound. His gaze seemed to follow the rising smoke. With her right hand, Talwyn made a series of gestures. The smoke began to move, rearranging itself. From where he stood, Jair caught glimpses of images in the smoke, ever-changing scenes that appeared and disappeared between breaths. He wondered what Tris's magic made of it, or whether anyone but Talwyn could read the messages in the smoke.

After a few moments, Talwyn bowed her head and made a gesture of thanks to the spirits. She seemed to come back to herself, and she turned toward the others. Cwynn gurgled happily in her arms, and she returned the baby gently to Kiara, who looked from Talwyn to Cwynn with astonishment.

"He's never this happy. What did you do?" Kiara asked, nestling Cwynn against her chest as she patted his back.

Talwyn lowered herself into a chair, and Jair could see fatigue in her face as he slipped an arm around her to steady her. Tris hurried to pour a goblet of sherry, which Talwyn accepted gratefully. "The Eagle Consort answered my petition. She's the wildest of the Lady's Consorts, an untamed spirit. I see a glow around Cwynn that augurs of power, but what kind of power, I can't tell. I sense no magic, and no lack of magic. I sense nothing at all. That's highly unusual. But whether he possesses magic or not, Cwynn can sense power. When we reached the north wall, I felt his terror. I didn't feel what caused his terror, but I felt his reaction. It changed the light around him, in color and intensity." She looked up at Tris and Kiara. "I sense no sickness or damage in the child. But at the same time, there is a difference. I don't know what that difference means, or how it would affect his ability to rule. But with or without a crown, he is a spirit of power." She frowned. "There was one other image. I don't understand it, but I should mention it. A bridge. I saw a bridge the moment I touched him, and that image never left me until I handed him back to you."

"What kind of bridge?" Kiara asked. "Did you recognize it?"

Talwyn shook her head. "It seemed to be made of light, so I don't think it was meant to be a real bridge, a place that we'd find. Maybe it's a symbol of something that connects two sides. I don't know."

Tris's face was pale. "Alyzza said 'protect the bridge.'"

"What?" Jair asked. Kiara had moved to the door to give Cwynn back to his nursemaid, but she rejoined them and laid a hand on Tris's arm, her expression troubled.

Briefly, Tris recounted his journey to see Alyzza and her manic pronouncements. "So much of what she said was almost in code, but there was one thing she said clearly, although I had no idea what she meant. She told me to 'protect the bridge.'"

"You think now that she might have meant Cwynn?" Jair asked.

Tris shrugged. "It's an odd coincidence, don't you think? But if he is *the* bridge, or *a* bridge, then the question is, a bridge to where? A bridge between what two things?"

"And from whom does he need protecting?" Jair murmured.

"I don't think there's any doubt about the last question." Talwyn's voice startled them. "We face a common enemy. Potent magic is calling the Durim and courting the Dread. Something terrifies Cwynn, even if he's too young to understand. It may be that our enemy has found something attractive about Cwynn, or perhaps Cwynn will come to his attention. You don't yet know what Cwynn's gifts are. Maybe right now, we don't need to know what Cwynn bridges. If the enemy wants him, then he is a prime asset in the war that's coming. Protecting him is more than a matter of succession. For all we know, Cwynn might be the point of the whole war."

At dusk the next evening, Tris and Talwyn met to answer the summons of the Dread. Kiara and Jair insisted on coming. Fallon and Nisim came to provide warding and a magical anchor, grounding Tris and Talwyn in the realm of the living. Ban Soterius also was adamant about being present, and he brought with him half a dozen handpicked guards to seal the area from intruders during the working.

The only ancient barrow near Shekerishet had been desecrated. After making a quick scout of the area, Talwyn had selected a suitable compromise. The spot she chose was near the mouth of a cave just at the forest's edge, not far from the banks of a stream. It was a place where many small shrines had been erected over the years by passersby. Stacked stones and guttered candles marked the offerings people had made in this place, sensing that the other realm was close here. Bits of colored cloth fluttered in the trees, tied to the lower branches as petitions to the Lady.

"Why here?" Soterius grumbled. "There are too damn many places someone could shoot from cover. Why can't you do magic out in the middle of a nice, flat field where I can see who's coming?"

Talwyn smiled. "I really don't pick the place for magic like this. The spirits pick it. There is power in this place." She swept a hand to indicate the small shrines. "I'm not the only one to feel it. And I'll bet that if you look closely at the rocks around that cave, you'll find runes scratched into them, maybe some more offerings. The deep places have their own power. Barrows or not, the Dread and the Nachale walk in the deep places. Those realms belong to them."

Tris nodded. "I feel it. You know, I spent my boyhood avoiding places like this, and I didn't know why. Grandmother didn't tell me about my magic to protect me from Jared. She thought he'd kill me if he suspected, and I think she was right. I just knew that the ghosts I wasn't supposed to be able to see were stronger in places like this. Ghosts—and other things that weren't friendly."

Talwyn shut her eyes. "I don't sense dark spirits here. This area feels neutral. That's another reason why I chose it." She opened her eyes and glanced up at the setting sun. "I'd like to work this before full dark, just to be on the safe side. Let's get started."

Fallon and Nisim raised wardings around the area. An outer warding protected a large area around the group. A second warding separated the four mages from the others. Soterius's guards were prominent and fully armed, creating a third, practical level of protection. While the others prepared the space, Talwyn readied the materials for the working. She built a small fire midway between the creek bank and the cave opening, just paces from the edge of the trees.

The shadows were stretching long as Talwyn called to the Consort Spirits while she set the fire. Herbs from her pouches raised thick smoke that smelled of juniper and sandalwood. Around the fire, she placed polished stones in recognition of the eight Aspects of the Lady. Chalcedony, aventurine, peridot, and citrine for each of the Light Aspects, and at the cross quarters she placed bloodstone, garnet, iron, and salt, tribute and wardings for the Dark Aspects. Talwyn took a talisman for each of the Consorts and placed them atop the stones on the four quarters: an eagle feather, a bear claw, the tooth of a stawar, and a wolf's tooth.

Through Talwyn, Tris could feel the light touch of Nisim's magic like a gossamer rope to secure her return. He knew that

Fallon was anchoring him in a similar manner. When Fallon and Nisim were satisfied, Talwyn looked to Tris. "Ready?"

"Ready," he said, and his voice was steady.

Talwyn took his hand. "Since we don't know for certain whether I spirit walk in the space you call Nether, watch me make the shift, and then see if you can follow." She managed a smile. "It wouldn't do for us to end up in different places."

Talwyn gathered her magic around her, drawing on the images of the Consorts and the Faces of the Lady. Tris was very aware of her magic, and he could sense it through their bond. Talwyn let the musky incense fill her lungs and Tris felt the loosening of the bonds that secured her spirit within her body. It wasn't the complete separation Tris could make with his summoner's magic. As Talwyn had explained it to him, it was her spirit, her consciousness, that walked, and not what some called a soul. Beneath his tunic, Tris wore Marlan the Gold's talisman on a strap around his neck, hoping that it might serve as a vouchsafe.

Once Tris joined her, Talwyn let her magic call to the Consort Spirits. In his mind's eye, Tris saw a figure with the head of a wolf and the body of a man step from the mists. The being wore the mantle of a Sworn shaman and a beaded belt hung with charms and amulets. The Consort Spirit wore the rough woven pants of a Sworn warrior but he was bare chested. His body was covered with thick, brown hair, although he was clearly in the form of a man. The guide beckoned for Talwyn and Tris to follow him, and then turned and began to walk down a path that appeared out of nowhere just a step in front of him.

Still clasping hands, Talwyn and Tris followed. Tris could feel their magics resonating through the skin of their palms. Their powers seemed to feed each other, and Tris almost expected to see an arc flash between them, although none did.

The Wolf Consort guided them through heavy mist. Tris could

see few features of the terrain, but there was enough to tell him that their spirits walked somewhere far different from the landscape they had left behind. Time ceased to have meaning. They might have walked for a candlemark or a day. Finally, the Wolf Consort stopped, and with a bow and a sweep of his hand, he indicated that they should pass in front of him.

"Thank you, Spirit Father," Talwyn said. "I ask that you await our return, to guide us back safely."

The Wolf Consort nodded in assent, and then vanished into the mist.

Before Talwyn could say anything, Tris felt the coming of the Dread. Cold, ancient power rolled over him, like a wave on a storm-ravaged sea. It was enough to make Talwyn stumble. Tris tightened his grip on her hand, but he did not move. The mist roiled, but it did not part to show a solid figure, although Tris thought he could make out an outline blurred by the fog. The Dread's shape was larger than most men, and taller. Its arms and hands seemed too long—not quite, and perhaps never, human. Its face was darkness, and as the mist shifted, Tris could not make out any clear features.

"Yes, you are indeed a true summoner." The voice might have sounded in their minds, or all around them.

"Why have you called me?" Tris's voice was firm, making it clear in his tone that the Dread had issued an invitation, and a king had chosen to respond.

"We would take your measure." Now, Tris heard the low murmur of multiple voices, and he sensed that more shadows moved beyond the veil of fog.

Tris withdrew Marlan the Gold's talisman from beneath his tunic. It glowed in his hand. "See for yourself. I'm Marlan the Gold's heir in blood and power. What more would you know?"

A rumble of voices sounded just below Tris's ability to catch their words. Or perhaps they spoke a language that he did not recognize, even on the Plains of Spirit.

"Your power is great. We have been touched by another power from beyond these borders. Others have tried to call us to their aid. Always, we have refused. We may still refuse this call, but we would know more of you, Marlan's heir. What would you offer us in exchange for our support?"

Tris took a deep breath. "Honored spirits, I didn't choose to call you from your slumber. I respect your choice to be apart from mortal concerns. But if you choose to walk among the living once more, then I would ask you to protect Margolan and the Winter Kingdoms from those who would cross our borders unbidden. Judge the measure of the magic by how it's worked. I have not called you with blood magic."

"And yet, it is your blood itself that calls to us," the voice replied. "Blood is the oldest magic, and the most powerful. Marlan knew this."

Tris nodded. "Yes, as did Hadenrul. But I don't shed human blood in sacrifice, or destroy the undead as offerings. And if it's possible, I would rather avert this war than pay its price in blood, although if it comes to that, I would pay in my own blood to protect my people."

"Interesting," the voice replied. "What spoils would you offer us to ally with you? What payment would you make for us to tip the balance?"

There was a note of anger in his voice when Tris spoke. "Once, long ago, you walked these lands. My ancestors trusted you as their protectors. Marlan trusted in your power to protect his people. I would call on those vows to ask that you protect Margolan once more, if war comes. I have nothing to offer you as payment, except honor's satisfaction. I won't barter my kingdom's freedom. I won't accept any power as master of Margolan, yours or the invader from across the sea. We will fight any hand that tries to dominate us. We may lose, but we will die free."

Tris's jaw was set. He felt the Dread's power like a low hum that reverberated in his bones, almost too low to hear but impossible to ignore.

"You are indeed Marlan's heir. He, too, was not afraid to challenge us." Tris thought he heard a note of amusement in the voice. "What of the Nachale? You're the Summoner King. You've called the recent dead to your aid in battle. We felt your power across the graves when you raised the spirits in your recent war. Would you seek the power of the Nachale to win your cause?"

"If Margolan faced defeat, I would ask for help from all allies, living, dead, and undead. I would use my power to gain their willing help. But I would not loose a greater bane upon my people to rid us from a mortal threat."

Again, the sound of low conversation just at the threshold of sound. "We must give this matter thought."

"Wait!" Tris moved a step closer, nearly pulling his hand out of Talwyn's grip. "Is this a War of Unmaking? Is there still a way to keep this war from coming?"

"Whether or not this becomes a War of Unmaking lies in the decisions made upon the battlefield. Great powers, mortal and magical, will align against each other, great enough to destroy everything you have known. And yet, the end is unclear. Only one thing is certain. War will come."

The Dread did not ask their leave. One instant, Tris could feel the oppressively heavy power of the dark shapes beyond the mist, and the next, the shapes were gone and with them, their power. Talwyn tugged on Tris's hand and nodded toward the Wolf Consort, who had emerged behind them, ready to guide them home. Neither Talwyn nor Tris spoke until they stood in the mist back in the clearing. The Wolf Consort stood between them and the fire, and beyond him, their bodies waited.

"Honored Consort," Talwyn said. "Thank you." She and Tris both made a low bow. The Wolf Consort inclined his head, and then his image dissipated like smoke on the breeze. Talwyn dropped Tris's hand, and Tris felt her energy return to her body. Tris shuddered as his spirit returned.

Fallon and Nisim withdrew their anchoring presence, and Tris felt the wardings fall. Jair and Kiara rushed forward, each of them bearing bread and wine so that Tris and Talwyn could ground themselves.

"Did the Dread come? What did you see?" Fallon's voice was uncharacteristically curious.

Tris nodded, finishing a mouthful of bread and taking the time to gulp down the wine before replying. "Yes, the Dread came. As for what I saw—it was a shadow more than a clear image. But the legends are right. They're powerful. Really powerful. We want them on our side, if they choose sides, but I think it would be better for everyone if they didn't play at all."

"What did they want from you? Do you think they'll side with Margolan?" Kiara reached out to touch Tris on the shoulder, as if to reassure herself that he was fully back among the living.

"He wanted to size me up. Whether that's as a potential ally, or as an enemy to defeat, I still don't know." Tris's voice showed the fatigue of the working.

Jair slipped his arm around Talwyn's shoulders to steady her, as if he could read how much the working had drained her. "Did they answer your questions?"

Tris exchanged glances with Talwyn before he replied. "After a fashion. They believe war is inevitable. Whether or not the war ends everything is apparently up to us."

18

"Here's what we think of your whore-spawned king!" The rebel's face was partially covered by a kerchief, but the dung that flew through the air to land with a wet thud against Cam's shield made the protester's meaning abundantly clear.

"Disperse to your homes! Disperse now!" Cam's voice was raw with shouting, and the crowd facing them seemed in no mood to hear. That he and the Veigonn were helping to put down rioters should have given anyone an idea of just how bad things had become.

The palace city of Aberponte was aflame.

What had begun as a tavern brawl between a soldier and a townsman with Divisionist sympathies had spilled out into the street. Whether the first fire had truly been from a lantern knocked over in the brawl or whether it had been set intentionally no longer mattered. From where Cam sat astride his battle steed, the smoke was thick and the fall night was unseasonably hot. The entire horizon glowed orange with flames. At least a third of the city was on fire, and though he could hear the cries of the bucket brigades behind him, it was anyone's guess as to whether they could stop the flames from leaping from roof to roof.

A hail of rocks answered the shouted warning. They slammed

against Cam's shield and helm, clattering off his horse's armor. Cam tugged on his reins to keep his warhorse still. As one, the line of mounted soldiers advanced, forcing the crowd back a pace.

"Disperse, by order of the king! Go home now, and no one gets hurt."

"Pox take you and your king! Go to the Crone!"

The rioters surged forward, fueled by rage and ale. Cam knew that their orders to put down the riots with as little violence as possible could only control the situation for so long. At some point, one side would push the other too far, and blood would flow. The soldiers were armored and mounted on massive horses with iron-shod hooves. The crowd had its fury and its sheer size, emboldened by alcohol and provoked by fear.

A row of men with homemade pikes rushed forward to hold the mounted soldiers at bay while the crowd pelted them with larger objects, fist-sized pieces of stone, broken bottles, and sharp shards of pottery. Though Cam's armor deflected the worst of the blows, one of the pottery pieces opened a gash on his cheek and a large stone hit his left forearm hard enough to momentarily numb his hand.

"Swords out!" Cam and the other soldiers drew their swords. Half a dozen men armed with sickles and barn rakes ran at them with a cry as the crowd roared. Before their makeshift weapons could do damage, the soldiers' swords whistled down, sending heads and limbs rolling.

Cam winced. It was one thing to fight invaders; it was another thing entirely to slaughter townsfolk. He had hoped it wouldn't come to this. A collective gasp rose from the crowd. *Run away*, Cam willed to the angry mob. *Do the smart thing and run away.*

Plague, famine, and fear fueled rage. The mob surged forward, hurling anything that wasn't nailed down and grabbing whatever they could carry as weapons. Two burly men wrenched a watering trough free from its moorings and ran at full speed toward the line of soldiers.

"Defend yourselves!" Wilym shouted. Cam's stallion reared up on his great hind legs and kicked at the attackers. The horse's massive hooves connected with a sick thud, taking the top off one man's skull and sending the other man flying back.

Enraged, the crowd kept coming. All around him, Cam could hear the snick of swords meeting flesh and the sound of bodies hitting the ground. Curses flew from both sides, and the rioters had begun to climb for higher ground, scaling the balconies and drainpipes for better advantage. The hail of muck and solid objects now rained down from above. Out of the corner of his eye, Cam saw a small boulder slam down on one of the soldiers. The crowd cheered wildly as the soldier toppled from his horse, and three men ran forward to slit the downed man's throat, scrambling out of the way before the soldier's comrades could ride to his defense. The cobblestones were red with blood and strewn with shattered glass, and the air smelled of burning thatch and open sewers.

We're damned, no matter what we do. Fall back, and the mob storms the palace gates. Cut them all down, and they become martyrs, while the soldiers become the enemy. Even if we win, we lose.

If the soldiers had held back before, the sight of one of their own lying dead on the road put an end to restraint. Cam heard battle cries tear from the throats of the men around him as they urged their war steeds forward, laying into the crowd with their swords with as much fury as if they were on a field of battle. Half of the mob held their ground, hurling broken bottles and rocks. Behind them, the others put up hastily made barricades of overturned wagons and upended barrels and crates. From behind the cover of the barricade, slings and slingshots replaced hand-thrown rocks, firing their missiles with better aim and deadly force.

If we've got to take back the city from our own people street by street, Goddess help us!

The alleyway was littered with severed arms and mangled bodies, but the sight seemed to drive the mob beyond fear. Across the barricades, down the alleys that fed into the street, Cam could hear running footsteps and see more fighters coming to join the rebels behind the barricades.

"Forward!" Wilym gave the order, and as one, the soldiers headed straight for the barricades at full gallop, their heavy hooves making a deafening roar as the sound echoed from the buildings. Even the most stalwart of the rabble fled their ramshackle fortification as the wall of battle steeds charged toward them. The iron hooves smashed through the wagons and barrels, sending a rain of wooden bits into the air. Cam grimaced as one of the rioters stumbled underneath the hooves, screaming.

Farther down the alley, Cam could see the mob rallying again. This time, they used the stone wall at the edge of the common grazing area as their redoubt, and the hail of insults and rocks resumed.

"This is going to take the whole bloody night," Cam heard Wilym curse.

Instead of scattering, more people were streaming toward the fight. Some of them might have intended to be onlookers, and others might have been fleeing the fires. But like it or not, they had become combatants.

"Bows drawn!"

Reluctantly, Cam sheathed his sword and drew the crossbow that was slung across his back. An ugly night was about to become even uglier.

The first salvo of quarrels sailed through the air, and a row of men at the front of the opposition crumpled and fell. Rocks and bits of wood studded with nails sailed through the air returning the fire. A chunk of wood the size of a man's fist barely missed Cam's shoulder. Another round of arrows flew, and more rioters fell.

Suddenly, three small barrels sailed through the air, slamming into the cobblestones just ahead of the soldiers and their horses. Cam had a heartbeat to recognize the smell of the liquid that burst from the kegs to realize what the rioters intended.

"Fall back!"

Torches landed in the pools of brandy, and a wall of flame flared, forcing the horsemen to back up. Too late, Cam could hear the pounding of footsteps behind them and he realized that more rioters had closed in on them from the rear.

"Ride for it!"

Cam wheeled his horse and rode hard as the alleyway behind them began to close, choked off by rioters who were screaming obscenities. Bodies scattered as the heavy war steeds forced their way through. Blows fell on the soldiers and horses as they passed, and Cam knew blood was running down his good leg where a dagger had been jammed into his thigh.

Suddenly, the night was as bright as day. A blinding white light illuminated the alleyway, forcing soldiers and rioters alike to turn their heads and shield their eyes. To Cam's utter astonishment, the rioters began to topple over, their expressions showing total confusion as their bodies, still frozen in place, wavered and fell over.

"By the Crone! What—"

Cam and the others turned to see two gray-robed battle mages behind them. Wilym grinned broadly and motioned for his soldiers to lower their weapons. "You're a welcome sight, my friends."

One of the battle mages, a tall man with graying temples, stepped forward. "Sorry it took us a bit to get to you. The king sent us out to do what we could to stop the fires, and when riots broke out, it got to be difficult to move from place to place."

Cam could see the concern on Wilym's face. "It's like this all over the city? By the Whore! What about the fires?"

Even as Wilym spoke, the second battle mage, a woman with a long, dark braid, raised her hands and put out the sputtering fire that still guttered in the pools of spilled brandy. The alley reeked of blood and scorched alcohol.

"We've put the worst out," the man replied. "Some of the rest will have to burn themselves out, but we've managed to contain them."

"And the rioters?" Wilym asked with a jerk of his head toward the jumble of bodies that lay still behind their barricade.

The battle mage's face was streaked with soot, but he managed a tired smile. "They're not dead, though they'll wake up with headaches that might make them wish they were. I dare say that a bout of diarrhea will keep them from taking to the streets again for a few days, at least."

Wilym looked at the mage skeptically. "Glad you're on our side."

The mage turned his attention to Cam and seemed to note the crest on his breastplate and shield that marked him as King's Champion. "Cam of Cairnrach?"

"Aye."

"We were told to tell you and the leader of the Veigonn that the king wants you in the palace as soon as you can be spared from the fight."

Cam and Wilym exchanged glances. "Any idea why?" Wilym asked.

The battle mage shook his head. "I didn't think it wise to ask. We were all told to keep an eye out for you, and to tell you to come straightaway, without taking time to clean up."

Cam spread his arms and looked down at himself in dismay. "I'm covered with filth!"

The mage shrugged. "Those were the orders. I'm guessing that the king could guess what you look like and doesn't care."

They paused only long enough for Cam to pull the dagger from his leg and bind up the wound. Wilym shouted terse orders to his second in command, and with a nod of thanks to the mages, he and Cam headed uphill toward Aberponte. As they made their way to the palace, the night's toll became more apparent. Injured townsfolk stood aside to let them pass, following them with baleful gazes. Whole blocks of buildings were charred wrecks, with smoke still rising from fallen timbers. Many of the stores and pubs had broken windows, and more than one woman leaned out of an upper window to shout curses at them as they galloped by.

"Why do I have the feeling that the night isn't going to get any better once we reach to the palace?" Cam asked.

Wilym's expression told Cam that the other had shared the same thought. "I hope Donelan meant what he said about coming straight to the palace. We both look like we've been to war, and we smell like a sewer!"

The portcullis had been dropped, blocking their entry into the palace. Soldiers behind the gate motioned for them to leave their horses outside and come through a door in the thick bailey wall that allowed only single-file entry. Cam and Wilym motioned for the servants to help them hurriedly unbuckle their armor, hoping to leave the worst of the blood and muck behind. Heeding Donelan's orders, they did not take time to clean the grime from their faces and hands, although Cam cast a longing look at a trough of fresh water as they ran for the palace door.

Inside, Allestyr was waiting for them. "Thank the Goddess you're safe. The king asked me to send you to the Council Chamber as soon as you arrived."

"What's going on?" Wilym asked.

Allestyr looked from Cam to Wilym. "The king's in chambers

with The Council. He's arguing to muster the army to defend the coastline."

The men took the stairs two at a time, with Wilym leading the way. At the entrance to the Council Chamber, they slowed. The guards at the door gave a sharp rap, and Tice, one of the king's advisors, leaned out. "Good. You're here. Come in."

Cam drew a deep breath and followed Wilym into the chamber.

"Perhaps that's not a bad idea," Lord Mannon spoke. His arms were crossed and he sat back sullenly in his chair. Cam had the thought that perhaps he and Wilym were not the only ones facing a long battle this night.

"Are you completely mad? Do you have any idea what you're saying?" Count Renate was purple in the face with rage.

"A kingdom can't exist in anarchy. If it takes a dark summoner to put things in order, then perhaps it's a gift from the Lady," Mannon retorted.

"A curse from the Formless One, you mean!" Renate looked as if he were about to launch himself across the table. Cam glanced at the other faces. Donelan sat, stony faced, at the head of the table. Next to him was Kellen, head of the palace guard and a trusted protector. On Donelan's other side was Tice, whose thin face clearly showed his displeasure with the way the debate was going. Lady Marja sat beside Tice. Her eyes were bright with emotion, but Cam could not guess whose side she was on. Beside her, Baron Tahvo's fists were balled.

"Isencroft does not have the manpower or the will to wage a war. Our own people are burning the city as we argue!" Duke Yrje's voice cut through the debate.

"Yrje, you're an ass," snapped Tahvo. "We have no choice. Isencroft has never stood by and let invaders take our land."

"Unless they marry into the family." Mannon's face was flushed and it was clear his blood was high for a fight.

"Silence!" Donelan's roar quieted the room. "Wilym, report!"

Wilym squared his shoulders and stepped forward. "With the help of the battle mages, the rebels were stopped. The worst of the fires have been put out, and my men remain with the other soldiers and the mages to mop up."

"How do you expect to fight a foreign invader when we can't stop the damn Divisionists?" Mannon's tone was acerbic. "Where are your conscripts going to come from, and how will you keep them from knifing you in the back?"

Donelan's barely contained rage made his eyes glint. "Cam, give The Council the full report you gave me from Brunnfen. Hold back nothing."

Cam swallowed hard and moved to stand beside Wilym. He repeated the account he had provided to Donelan, leaving out no detail, even though his cheeks flamed with the shame of Alvior's treachery. Although he did his best not to look at the Council while he spoke, he had the sinking feeling that even if the Formless One and her Wild Host were at the gates of Aberponte, Mannon and Yrje would remain resolute. When he finished, the chamber was quiet for a moment, and then Yrje leaned forward.

"I would ask Your Majesty exactly what we would be protecting if we raise the army for this supposed 'threat.'"

Donelan glowered. "Isencroft." Though the king did not say it, Cam was certain that Donelan had mentally added, *You idiot.*

"But we've already given Isencroft as a wedding gift to Margolan. What is a joint throne if not a peaceful coup? Our heir has been brokered off to marry the king of our hereditary enemy, the kingdom that has attempted to invade Isencroft more times in our history than any other. Sire, the invasion has already been accomplished, and we are but a Margolan territory."

Renate rose to his feet and in one, swift moment hurled his wine at Yrje, dousing the man. "What kind of treason are you spouting, Yrje? We've been at peace with Margolan for a generation."

Yrje shook himself off and gave a killing look at Renate. "Perhaps that's because the Margs took with a betrothal contract what they always wanted to seize with an army."

"We've been over this before—"

"Been over what? Been over how we delivered our heir like a purchased whore right to the Margolan doorstep?" Yrje spat.

"Look around yourself, Yrje." Tahvo's voice was like ice. "Neither the Margs nor the king caused three poor harvests in a row. Naught but the Crone brought plague on us. The alliance with Margolan makes sense, and if we're about to be invaded by Temnotta, then we can be damn glad that Margolan is an ally instead of a worry."

"You think Margolan would risk a hair on its king's head to save Isencroft?" Yrje was standing now, shaking with rage. "For all we know, they're in league with Temnotta. Margolan's army doesn't have the manpower to invade us, but they could let Temnotta do their dirty work and then share the spoils."

"Enough!" Once again, Donelan's growl brought the room to silence. He got to his feet and sent a sheaf of papers and his goblet flying from the table with a sweep of his arm. "Isencroft is endangered from within by the Divisionists and from outside by Temnotta. We must fight."

"Fighting is not an option." Mannon's face was set. "Perhaps we can win an accommodation from Temnotta. We have no issue with them."

"Are you deaf?" Renate's voice was loud enough to make himself heard even if Mannon were hard of hearing. "We already know Alvior has a deal with Temnotta. And we know Alvior used his gold to support the Divisionists. The die is cast, Mannon. Temnotta comes to our shores as an invader, with a puppet king already in hand. We must fight, or die."

"Our city is on fire, burned by our own people. There's your 'no confidence' vote if ever there was one," Mannon shot back.

"And you hope to do what with your *accommodation*?" Contempt was thick in Renate's voice. "Keep the Temnottans from pillaging your lands while they loot the rest of the country? Hand over our women so long as they keep their hands off *your* daughters?"

"Ask Donelan. He knows all about handing over a daughter to invaders."

Renate's answer was a punch that caught Mannon square in the jaw and bowled him over the back of his heavy chair. Lady Marja screamed. Kellen rose to his feet, protecting Donelan, and both Cam and Wilym closed ranks around the king.

Mannon rose to his feet slowly and waved off assistance from Yrje. Tahvo had gone to stand beside Renate, and from the look of him, he was ready to finish the fight if Mannon came at him.

"It's clear the crown seeks capitulation and not counsel," Mannon said, rubbing his jaw. "I am through with this charade." With that, Mannon turned and stalked from the chamber, with Yrje close at his heels. Lady Marja looked as if she meant to call after them, and then sank back into her seat miserably. Renate and Tahvo still looked ready to fight, and neither one of them made a move to stand down until Donelan cleared his throat.

"That went about as well as I expected," Donelan said and sighed. He motioned for the others to sit, and waved Cam and Wilym forward to take the seats vacated by Mannon and Yrje. "Let them carry that tale back with them."

Lady Marja glanced sharply at the king. "You suspect their loyalty?"

Donelan shrugged. "I suspect the loyalty of any man with more spleen than spine." He leaned forward. Cam thought that Donelan suddenly looked older and very tired. "Let me make myself completely clear. There will be war, and it will be hard fought. I don't know whether or not we can win, but I'm damn

378

sure not going to make an *accommodation* with a traitor." He sighed and passed a hand over his forehead as if a headache pounded in his temples.

"Tonight won't be the last of the riots. People are scared and hungry. The plague advances farther into Isencroft every day. By the Whore! I don't even know if we can field an army, or how long we can hold the line. But I will not give up the crown or give an inch of land without a fight." Donelan's eyes narrowed. He looked in turn to each one seated around the table. "Where do you stand?"

Kellen and Tice pushed their chairs back and knelt. Cam and Wilym stepped up and knelt beside them. One by one, Marja, Renate, and Tahvo joined them.

"We will support you with our lives, lands, and honor, my king," said Renate, his voice catching.

Cam could see the emotion in Donelan's eyes. "Thank you," Donelan said wearily. "Ready your people. Those who can fight should muster. Have the rest put back supplies for your households." He looked to Tice. "Work with Allestyr to provision the castle for a siege, and then work with the generals to supply them for war."

Donelan's gaze fell to Cam and Wilym. "I know your men are tired. I've asked a lot of them, and I'm going to have to ask more."

"They're ready, my liege," said Wilym. "Ready and willing to serve."

Donelan nodded. "Good. Let them know what we're up against. The Veigonn will be the last line of defense if Alvior's goal is the crown."

"Alvior's mine." They all turned to look at Cam. He barely recognized his own voice, thick with anger. "I want to be the one who kills him, for the troubles he's brought down on Margolan and for betraying his kingdom." Cam held up his maimed hand. "And I owe him for this."

"May Chenne grant your vow," Donelan murmured. He motioned for them to rise, looking genuinely touched. "Realize that your loyalty may place each of you in danger. It's clear the Divisionists are hardly vanquished. Go nowhere without a trusted armed guard. Our numbers are few enough. We can't afford to give those bastards any more of an advantage than they already have."

Renate, Marja, and Tahvo each bowed low and kissed Donelan's ring in fealty, reaffirming their loyalty before they left. With a nod and a glance that seemed to speak volumes, Tice went to find Allestyr to begin preparations, and Kellen went to stand guard inside the door. Cam and Wilym lingered, and Donelan waved at them to sit back down.

Donelan went to the decanter of brandy that sat on a table near the fireplace, and he poured three generous measures, returning with nearly full goblets for each of them. Donelan sank heavily into his chair, nearly sloshing his brandy.

"By the Crone's tits! I hope you appreciate the restraint it took not to put my sword through Mannon's tongue!"

Wilym and Cam chuckled, accustomed to Donelan's dark humor. "I was actually wondering how put out you'd be with me if I had slipped a blade between Yrje's ribs." Wilym's tone was dry, and Cam wasn't quite sure how much Wilym was joking.

Donelan chuckled. "Now there's a pleasant fantasy. Perhaps I'll fall asleep tonight picturing it." He shook his head. "Dark Lady take my soul! This is not the legacy I'd hoped to leave Isencroft." The smile faded from his face, and his eyes grew dark.

"Have you heard from the other kingdoms? Will they give aid?" Wilym sipped at his drink, and from his expression, Cam knew Wilym was already formulating battle plans.

Donelan nodded. "I'm trying not to take it as a bad omen that all of them sent replies by *vayash moru* to shave time off the trip. Kalcen is readying his army, and he says we can count on him to hold their coast. Of all the allied kingdoms, Eastmark is probably in the best position to defend itself. Plague hasn't taken hold there, and their last harvest was good. Word came from Principality that their mercs would rise to the cause, but Staden's seneschal added a note that the king is very ill."

"Jonmarc Vahanian is Princess Berwyn's liegeman," Cam said quietly. "If war comes, he'll be at the forefront. I know Dark Haven will rally."

"Tris Drayke pledged his support, of course, but that's a thorny problem." Donelan took a long drink of his brandy and sighed as it burned down his throat. "We don't dare let the Margolan army onto Isencroft soil, and it's anyone's guess whether Tris can put much of a force together after all they've been through over there."

"What of their navies?" Wilym asked.

Donelan shrugged ill-humoredly. "I'm not entirely sure what Eastmark has in ships. Principality runs its navy the same way it runs its army. It provides sanctuary to mercenaries and privateers who pledge never to sell sword against them. The letter from Principality said they had the gold to assure the privateers' loyalty. Margolan never has had much of a navy, but I believe Tris when he says he'll bring everything they have against the invaders. Damn it all to the Abyss!"

"Do you believe what the Oracle said? That this could be a War of Unmaking?" Cam asked quietly.

"You know what I usually think of those shrouded biddies," Donelan grumbled. "Skulking around without showing their faces, always talking in blasted riddles. It'll be a War of Unmaking for the poor bastards who die on the field, that's for certain. As for the rest of us," he said and paused, then upended the rest of his brandy. "I'll worry about chaos after we make it through the battle."

Donelan stood abruptly and stretched. "Damn, I wish Viata were here." He looked up at the painting of his late wife that graced the wall above the mantel. Viata stood tall and proud, forever young, with the darkly beautiful features that made her royal Eastmark heritage clear. She wore the signet of the queen of Isencroft clearly on her right hand, and at her throat was a necklace with the crest of Eastmark, although Cam knew that her father, King Radomar, never forgave her for marrying Donelan.

"She was a fine woman, very brave, and shrewd about things like war. She was Radomar's heir in backbone, that's for certain," Donelan said wistfully. He set his glass aside and closed his eyes, shaking his head. "Ah well, perhaps it's best she didn't see these dark days."

Donelan turned back to them, and it was as if he willed his mood to lift. "Well then, if we're headed to war, I want to hunt tomorrow. The stag are plentiful, and if we go to war I'm likely to miss another shot at them. I'd prefer a winter hunt, but there's no telling where we'll be by the time the snow flies." He nodded toward Wilym and Cam. "You'll come with me. A good hunt clears the head. It'll take time for the army to be ready to march. No one will miss us tomorrow."

"Are you sure it's safe, Your Majesty?" Wilym asked.

Donelan snorted. "I doubt Alvior managed to win over the king's deer to his treason. Bring along a guard or two if you must, but mind that you don't plan to march a squadron into the woods. You'll scare off all the game!"

Wilym chuckled. "Yes, m'lord. As you wish."

Donelan looked at Cam. "You'd best get that silversmith of yours outfitted. You'll need a battle squire."

"Rhistiart? I hardly think—"

Donelan's gaze was shrewd. "He's loyal and he's proven that he can keep a clear head under pressure. That's more than

I can say for most men. These are hard times, m'lad. He'll have to do."

Cam was sure Donelan could read his uncertainty in his expression, but he nodded. "He wanted an adventure. I think he's already gotten more than he bargained for, but I'll tell him."

Donelan clapped him on the shoulder. "Good. Good. Now both of you, make sure you're ready for the hunt tomorrow. It may be quite a long time before we have the chance to do this again, and I want to enjoy every minute of it."

The next day dawned clear and crisp. The Feast of the Departed at the equinox was still more than a week away, but the air had already turned cold in Isencroft. Cam felt his spirits come close to lifting for the first time since he had left Brunnfen. A glance at Wilym told Cam that the head of the Veigonn was almost enjoying the day as well. They'd left their horses tethered at the edge of the forest. Now, Donelan, Cam, Wilym, and two guards walked silently through the forest armed with bows in search of a prize stag.

It was the kind of sacrifice Donelan would only have made for war. Cam knew that Donelan much preferred to hunt when snow lay on the ground. Donelan was an expert tracker, and a good bit of his enjoyment came from the skill of finding his quarry. Cam also knew that the king was quite partial to venison. Although the king had helped to cull the herd earlier in the year when starvation threatened to weaken the deer, those had not been trophy hunts. Today's hunt might give Donelan a rack of antlers and bragging rights for the season.

Donelan moved slightly ahead, watching for deer. The two guardsmen were unwillingly forced to spread out, flanking the group to drive game into the king's path. Cam and Wilym watched the forest, but their interest was in protecting the king, and not in the wildlife.

The brush to his right shuddered and something streaked from cover. Cam had his bow leveled before his mind recognized that a rabbit had been flushed from cover. He held his shot and gave Wilym a grin.

"Must be my stomach aiming. I'm as fond of rabbit stew as I am of venison!"

Wilym returned the smile, but it did not reach his eyes. Instead, he continued to scan the brush for trouble. But as the morning wore on without incident, even he began to relax, just a little.

A pheasant burst from its cover, scared into flight by their approach. This time, Cam's arrow flew, catching the bird through the breast. It fell with a soft thump, and Cam tied off its legs and slung it over his shoulder.

Suddenly, Donelan stopped. He gestured silently for Cam and Wilym to freeze, and motioned ahead. Through the brush, Cam could just see a large rack of antlers. Donelan moved forward in a crouch, putting more room between himself and the others, drawing his bow for the shot.

Two arrows sang through the air. Donelan's arrow found its mark, lodging in the stag's shoulder, but in the same breath, a quarrel flew from the branches of a tree behind them, catching the king through the back.

"Up there!" Wilym shouted, running to cover the king, his own bow drawn and ready.

Cam gave a shout and launched himself at the tree where the bowman had hidden. He could hear the other soldiers crashing through the brush to get to them, but his full attention was on the tree.

Another quarrel tore through the air, barely missing Cam. Cam dove and lunged, coming up on the far side of the tree. Despite his bulk, Cam moved with surprising speed, something his opponents seldom realized until it was too late. And while Cam's bad leg shaved some time off his run, his upper body, muscular from a decade of wielding heavy swords, was easily up to the task of hauling himself into the branches and helping him scramble toward where the attacker hid.

"Guard the king!" Cam shouted to the soldiers. Yet another quarrel flew past him, but it went wide and sank into a branch over his head. Cam had dropped his bow, and he carried a knife between his teeth. He peered around the trunk, and another quarrel shot past him, flying wild as leaves and branches sent it off course. It was enough for Cam to get an idea of where the shooter was. In one fluid movement, Cam stood and released his knife. Heavier than the quarrel, the blade cut through the small branches without losing its course. Cam heard the blade strike flesh. A man cried out, and as Cam stepped around the trunk for a better view, he saw a man falling, spread-eagled, to the ground below.

By the time Cam shinnied down the tree, the two soldiers stood over the downed man. They, too, had slung their bows over their shoulders, and they held the prisoner at sword's point. In the field, Wilym knelt beside the king. Donelan wasn't moving, and Cam felt his heart in his throat as he ran to Wilym.

"Is he—"

Wilym shook his head and Donelan groaned. "He's alive. Thanks to the chain mail he's got on under his shirt, it's not as bad as it could have been, although since the bowman was above us, the angle made it penetrate more than a straight shot should have."

"Do we move him or have someone ride for Trygve?" Trygve, the king's personal battle healer, was back at Aberponte. It would be a candlemark's ride one way, a long time to lie bleeding in a field.

Wilym shook his head. "I certainly haven't got Trygve's gift, but there's a bit of hedge witch in my blood, enough to do some basic field healing. Cover us." With that, Wilym closed his eyes and let his hands hover just above where the thick shaft of the quarrel protruded from the king's shoulder. After a moment, Wilym frowned, and then let out his breath and opened his eyes.

"It's torn up some muscle and sinew, but it missed the artery, thank the Lady. He'll need Trygve to patch him up good as new if he means to fight soon, but, with the king's permission, I can get the arrowhead out safely. As far as I can tell, it wasn't poisoned. That's something else to be thankful for."

"Just pull the damned thing out!" Donelan's voice was muffled as he lay face down in the grass, but there was no mistaking his imperative.

"This is going to hurt," Wilym warned.

"Get on with it!"

Cam stood guard over them while Wilym braced himself and then kept up steady traction on the arrow to remove it from where it was lodged. Donelan grunted but did not cry out, although once the arrow was free, he showed a bent for creative cursing that made Cam shake his head in approval.

"Stay still, Your Majesty," Wilym warned. "I've got to stop the bleeding and do what I can to set the healing on the right path until we can get you to Trygve."

"Blast that! What about my stag?"

Cam walked toward the brush where they had spotted the antlers. A fresh deer carcass was held upright by a wooden rack, with the body mostly obscured behind brush. The antlers that had tantalized Donelan and lured him into range appeared to have been cobbled together from several pairs, upon closer inspection.

Cam returned to where Donelan sat, impatiently allowing Wilym to bind up his shoulder with strips torn from his shirt. "Well?"

"The deer was a trick. Someone knew you were planning to hunt and had a fondness for prize stag. The antlers aren't even real."

"By the Whore! Bring me the man who shot at me. I want answers!" Donelan was as angry as Cam had ever seen him, and Cam had the distinct impression that the king was as enraged about losing his deer as he was about the attempt on his life.

Cam motioned for the two soldiers to bring their prisoner forward. They had bound the man's wrists, but they left Cam's knife where it was, buried deep in the man's back. From the way the prisoner was struggling to breathe, Cam's aim had been truer than the assassin's, and their attacker had obviously not thought to wear armor.

"Who sent you?" Donelan's voice was firm, although what remained of his shirt was soaked with blood.

The prisoner raised his head, and it was the first good look Cam had gotten at the man's face. He had the look of the Isencroft hills, and when he spoke, his accent confirmed Cam's guess. "Death to traitors!" He spat in Donelan's direction.

"I'd be careful what you wish for, boy. From where I sit, 'tis treason to fire on your king," Wilym warned. "Tell us how you knew where we'd hunt, and who helped you, and perhaps one of the Light Faces will take pity on your soul."

"You thought you broke us, but we're stronger than you know," the would-be assassin boasted, and choked on blood. "We're everywhere, hidden in plain sight. And we won't rest until Isencroft becomes independent!"

"Funny way to show your loyalty, trying to kill the king," Wilym said, prodding the man with the point of his sword.

Donelan's eyes narrowed. "You can tell me now, or we can wait until you're dead. My daughter's husband is a very powerful summoner. I bet he could get your ghost to tell me what we want to know."

"You can try."

Donelan and Wilym exchanged a glance that spoke volumes.

"Bind him and haul him back to the palace. We'll let the battle mages have a turn at him, see what they can get from him."

"The hunt was a last-minute idea," Cam said thoughtfully. "How many people knew?"

The soldiers trussed the prisoner to drag him back to the horses. Wilym and Cam offered their hands to Donelan as the king got to his feet, but Donelan waved them off. "No one but Kellen was with us when the king proposed it last night," Wilym said thoughtfully.

"And I'd trust Kellen with my life," Cam said.

Wilym nodded. "So would I. After we left the king last night, I spoke to our escorts personally," he said, with a glance to the soldiers. "We were also alone, and they were quartered for the night."

"We saw no one and spoke to no one, sir," said the guard closest to Wilym.

Wilym frowned, thinking. "After that, I went down to the stables to see that the horses would be ready, and I spoke to the king's groom directly."

"Were there others about?" Cam asked.

Wilym shrugged. "It was late. I don't remember seeing anyone, but someone might have been within earshot. It wasn't intended to be a secret mission." He shook his head. "But I didn't say anything about where we meant to hunt. This fellow didn't follow us, hoping for a lucky shot. It took some time to set up that deer and make it look convincing, and then to get into position in that tree. Even the guards didn't know where the king wanted to hunt."

Donelan grunted. "I've had my eye on this spot for a while. Haven't told anyone, but I had a feeling that I'd find a good stag here. Wasn't about to talk about it and have someone beat me to it!"

"So that means that no one heard it from the king and stored

388

it away for future use," Wilym said. "That cuts down the suspects."

"Did you talk with anyone else?"

Wilym thought for a moment. "Come to think of it, I went to the armory after that to get the king's bow. Derry wasn't there, but his assistant was very helpful." His eyes widened. "Chatty, in fact. We were talking about where the deer have been plentiful this year, and he told me his favorite spots." Wilym sighed. "I can't believe how stupid I was. I told him enough about where we were headed that someone might have figured it out from that. I never thought—"

"Not your fault, lad, though in the future, I'll thank you to treat my favorite hunting spots like the state secret they deserve to be," Donelan said. "I'd trust Derry with my soul, but I don't know his assistant. Hasn't been with us much over a year."

Cam and Wilym exchanged glances. "We still don't know if it's the assistant who betrayed you, or whether he told someone else, who used the information," Cam said.

"It makes a short trail to follow. When we get back, I'll bring him in for questioning. Could be, like you say, that he mentioned it in passing. We'll find out." From the look on Wilym's face, Cam knew the other was blaming himself for the breach.

Cam nudged their prisoner with the toe of his boot. "Hear that? Whoever your man is inside the palace, we'll get him."

The assassin's face was pale. From the bluish cast to his skin, Cam wondered whether the man would make it back to the palace. But the glint in his eyes was defiant. "Cut one down, and another will spring up. Isencroft must be free!"

"Gag him," Wilym said to the guards, with a nod toward the prisoner. He walked over, knelt next to the man, and let his hands hover over the wound as he had done for Donelan. This time, Cam noticed, Wilym kept his eyes open. Wilym jerked the knife clear and the prisoner groaned. For a few minutes,

Wilym worked over the wound. "That should keep him from dying before we reach Aberponte. We'll see if he changes his mind about being helpful. If not, well—"

"If he isn't helpful, hang him," Donelan said. "That's getting off easy for trying to kill the king. It would serve him right to be drawn and quartered for losing me my stag!"

Now that the prisoner realized that death would not spare him imprisonment and interrogation, fear replaced defiance in his eyes. "He's not kidding about the stag," Wilym said in a cold voice. "The king takes his hunt very personally. If you want a quick death, and a painless one, you might want to cooperate." Wilym gave the man a cold smile that was ominous.

For the first time, the assassin looked uncertain. Though he said nothing as the guards manhandled him toward the horses, Cam would have bet money that Wilym and the mages would get what they needed from the man if it came down to a choice between the gallows or worse.

"Whoever's working with him probably isn't the only traitor inside the palace," Wilym said to Cam as they moved ahead, out of earshot of the prisoner. They stayed a pace behind the king, with their swords drawn.

"It's not necessarily the servants who are disloyal," Cam said. "It could be anyone they speak to outside the palace, from the woodcutters to their families."

Wilym nodded. "Give me a foreign enemy any day. This disloyalty from within is like leprosy. A kingdom can't stand when no one can trust his fellow countrymen."

Even if we can defeat Alvior and his dark summoner, what will the war do to Isencroft? Cam worried. *I can see what it's done to Margolan to unseat Jared. It could take a generation to repair the damage the Divisionists have done. Lady Bright! We haven't mustered the army yet, but the war's already begun.*

19

"That's Dark Haven?" Aidane stared at the dark, forbidding outline of the manor house. In the moonlight, the large building looked ominous. Aidane wasn't sure what she had expected, but not this gray, sullen fortress.

"Dark Haven isn't like the villas you've seen in Nargi," Kolin said over his shoulder. "It's a stronghold, not a place to lounge. You'll be glad enough for the walls once you're on the inside."

Now that they were at the gates, Aidane was nervous. Not all of the apprehension was her own. Thaine's spirit was positively jumpy. Thaine had been a reasonably pleasant traveling companion on the long trek from Dhasson, and in the nearly two weeks it had taken them to cross into Principality and reach Dark Haven, Aidane and Thaine had gotten to know each other through the silent conversation between their thoughts as Aidane bore Thane's spirit in her body.

But if Aidane had gained a friend in Thaine's ghost, it seemed to come at the expense of her welcome among most of the rest of the party. Cefra, once so outgoing, now regarded Aidane warily. Zhan's attitude made it clear that he tolerated her because of Kolin's forbearance. The peddler and the musicians kept to themselves. Only Jolie and Kolin made an effort to seek out

Aidane, but even they seemed to be guarded. Aidane turned as Jolie rode up next to her.

"I'm still not sure it's wise to bring you here." Jolie kept her eyes on the road, but her words were intended for Thaine. "Jonmarc has a good thing going for him, finally. I won't let you interfere."

Aidane felt the shift in her posture that indicated that Thaine was coming to the forefront. "I didn't come to bed him; I came to warn him. And if you recall, I'm the one who left him."

Jolie gave Aidane an appraising glance. "I recall. You thought you'd bettered your prospects with your *vayash moru* patron."

"It's not like I broke his heart. We were never in love."

"I just want to make sure that you don't suddenly change your mind now that Jonmarc's 'prospects' have improved."

Aidane could feel Thaine's impatience. "I haven't changed my mind. This is about preventing a war. It's the Durim I'm after. I want them to pay for what they did to me."

Jolie's gaze was skeptical. "I'll be watching."

Thaine's disappointment was genuine. "You used to trust me."

Jolie's expression softened. "You might not have hurt Jonmarc with the way you left, but I wasn't happy about it. You left a note and disappeared. Not much of a good-bye after you'd made your home with us for so long."

Thaine's regret was real. "I'm sorry. I was a fool. If it's any consolation, I died for my foolishness, and I continued to pay for it, long afterward."

The anger was gone from Jolie's face. Aidane was surprised to see genuine caring, something she hadn't expected. "You were free to go any time you wished," Jolie said quietly. "No one is ever forced to stay with me against their will."

"I know. You took good care of me. Of all of us." Thaine swept her arm to indicate the other whores who rode behind them just far enough to be out of earshot. "I've seen enough other houses in the business and enough other managers to know that you're one of a kind, Jolie."

"Damn right about that."

"Do you think Jonmarc will believe me?"

Jolie shrugged. "It's not him believing you that worries me. I'm fond of Carina, his wife. She's been good for him. Carina's a healer, Thaine. Not just the best damn healer in the Winter Kingdoms, but a mind healer, too. For the first time since I've known him, Jonmarc's actually happy. I don't want anything to go wrong with that."

Thaine looked away. "I understand. I'm dead, remember? Dead and without a body of my own. Let Aidane carry my warning. When I've done all I can, I'll leave and go to my rest."

Jolie's eyes held a sadness Aidane hadn't seen there before. "Principality's not a bad place for our kind to die. After all, they worship the Lover and the Whore. Perhaps the Lady will grant you favor."

"We're here." Kolin's voice interrupted whatever reply Thaine might have made. Thaine's spirit drew back into the recesses of Aidane's mind, leaving Aidane master of both her mind and her body. Jolie fell back, taking a position with her girls. Kolin looked at Aidane and shook his head. "I can't wait to see what Jonmarc makes of you."

Aidane watched nervously as guards opened the huge manor-house gates. The guards outside the gate were dressed in the livery of King Staden's soldiers, making it obvious that the king had a stake in protecting Dark Haven and its inhabitants. Aidane wondered if the guards inside the gates were *vayash moru*. They hailed Kolin and waved the group inside. A tall, flaxen-haired man was waiting for them in the courtyard. He was clearly of noble birth, Aidane thought.

"You're late," he said to Kolin, but Aidane heard worry more than censure in his tone.

"Had some unexpected complications," Kolin replied, handing off the reins to his horse.

The blond man looked at the newcomers, and his eyes widened in recognition. He went to where Jolie stood with her girls and gave a bow in greeting, kissing the back of Jolie's hand.

"Jolie? What an unexpected surprise."

Jolie grinned and held her head up as if she wore her usual finery instead of the plain traveling dress. "Good to see you, Gabriel. Even with the king's blessing, Margolan got a little too dangerous for my taste. Thought we'd throw ourselves on Jonmarc's mercy and sit this out somewhere safe."

Kolin had already begun to hand off his newest charges to Zhan, who took the rescued *vayash moru* and *vyrkin* toward one of the other buildings that ringed the courtyard. Kolin spoke in low tones to other servants, who motioned for Ed and the musicians to go with them. Soon, only Jolie's party and Aidane remained in the courtyard with Kolin and Gabriel.

"Where's Jonmarc?" Kolin had moved so quickly that Aidane hadn't seen him until he spoke from beside her.

"Inside. He'll be anxious to see you, and happy to see Jolie. I'll have the servants find a place for you and your girls."

"Any place that's dry and warm is fine with me. I thought perhaps we might set up shop in the village. We can earn our keep."

Gabriel frowned. "You might want to rethink that, at least for a while, Jolie. I know you've come for sanctuary, but Dark Haven's not as safe as it used to be."

"Jolie! What brings you here?"

Aidane looked up to see a man standing on the landing of the entranceway. His dark hair was loose around his shoulders, and he moved with the muscular grace of a swordsman. As he drew closer, Aidane could see intelligence and surprising humor in his dark eyes, and she glimpsed a nasty scar that ran from his left ear down into his collar. *That's him*, Thaine whispered in her mind.

Jonmarc embraced Jolie, and the two began to talk rapidly in the thick river patois that was a favorite of smugglers and thieves. Jonmarc's affection for Jolie was clear, and Jolie fussed over Jonmarc like a son she hadn't seen in years. As if he suddenly became aware of the others around them, Jonmarc switched back to Common.

"Of course you're welcome, all of you. Gabriel's probably told you that it's not the best time to try to relocate your house, but until things settle down, you're welcome here. I'll warn you; it's tight. We've been overrun with refugees, and it's kept Carina busier than she should be."

Something made Jonmarc turn and he looked Aidane up and down. "What do we have here?" To Aidane's surprise, he addressed her in fluent Nargi.

"That's one of our 'complications,'" Kolin said.

"Hello, Jonmarc. Been a long time." It was Thaine's voice that spoke, and her spirit surged forward, filling Aidane so that Aidane took on her stance, her mannerisms, all in the span of a single breath. And while Aidane knew that Thaine had told the truth about her intentions, Aidane could also feel Thaine's perverse pleasure in the stunned look on Jonmarc's face.

"That's not possible," Jonmarc whispered, his eyes widening.

"Aidane is a *serroquette*," Jolie said quietly. "We met up with Thaine's ghost by accident. Thaine says she has a warning for you."

"Perhaps we should have this conversation inside," Gabriel said, with an unhappy glance at Kolin. Gabriel gestured, and two servants came running to see to Jolie's contingent and their sparse luggage, although Jolie did not follow them.

Gabriel led them inside, and although Thaine was at the forefront of her consciousness, Aidane looked around as they entered the manor house. She had called on many highborn clients and was accustomed to the great homes of Nargi. While Dark Haven was easily their equal in size and construction, it was austere by comparison. There were no paintings of esteemed ancestors, real or purchased, no grand tapestries regaling tales of family history. What Aidane could see of Dark Haven and its rooms showed its furniture to be practical but not opulent, and its decoration to be minimal. The manor seemed as unpretentious as its lord, and Aidane was even more curious to learn more about Jonmarc Vahanian.

Kolin, Gabriel, Jolie, and Aidane followed Jonmarc to a small parlor. He closed the door behind them and lit the lanterns. Then he turned to face Aidane, hands on hips.

"What the hell is going on?"

Under Thaine's control, Aidane squared her shoulders, taking a defiant stance. "I thought you might be happy to know that I'm dead."

Something flickered in Jonmarc's dark eyes. "I'm sorry. How long?"

Thaine shrugged. "My patron brought me across as a *vayash moru* a few weeks after I left Jolie's Place. I guess it's been about five years now. It went badly after that." Thaine tried to sound nonchalant, but Aidane felt the pain behind the words. It was true what Thaine had told Jolie, that she had no designs on Jonmarc. But at the same time, Thaine felt keenly humiliated at having to admit just how badly her choices had turned out. "My last 'patron' tired of me and sold me for my blood to the Black Robes. They murdered me as an offering to Shanthadura."

Jonmarc paled at that, and Aidane saw pain in his expression. "Thaine, I—"

"I didn't come here for pity." Thaine's voice was sharp, and Aidane could feel embarrassment turning into anger. "I'd heard about the new Lord of Dark Haven. My patrons debated the uprising last year, and I heard all about how you put down the *vayash moru* who broke the Truce." She glanced at Kolin and Gabriel, and her smile was more of a smirk. "My patrons feared you, and they hated fearing a mortal. Congratulations, you have the same reputation as a fighter among the undead as you had among the Nargi."

"I'd have rather not had to earn either one."

Jonmarc's gaze seemed to see through her bravado. Thaine looked away. "The Black Robes talked in front of me, because I was expendable. They're planning something big in Principality City during the Feast of the Departed. They want to disrupt the festival and cause panic. But there's more to it. They want to slaughter as many people as they can as a blood offering to Shanthadura. They think that if they murder the priestesses, the Black Robes can take their place and bring the worship of Shanthadura back to Principality."

Jonmarc exchanged glances with Gabriel. "Staden and Berry don't need something like that, on top of the plague and everything else that's going on. Everyone's jumpy enough that a big disruption like that could do a lot of damage."

Gabriel nodded. "I'll alert my people in the city."

"There's more," Thaine said. "The Black Robes think something big is going to happen. They were excited about it. They called it a War of Unmaking. The Black Robes said that there's a new power, a dark summoner, who will help something they called an 'ancient darkness' rise again."

"A dark summoner," Jonmarc repeated. "Dark Lady help us." He looked at Thaine. "Where is this dark summoner? Where will he come from?"

"Across the Northern Sea."

Jonmarc swore and turned away. "It just keeps getting better." He glanced at Gabriel. "Well, at least we know now why the Black Robes seemed so intent on getting into the barrows.

They're hoping to wake up whatever lives in there, bring it back in time for the war."

Thaine met Jonmarc's eyes. "So you'll take the message to the king?"

"There's just one problem with that," Jonmarc said, grimacing. "Staden's very ill. I've got a direct order from the king commanding me to guard Berry and to keep both of us here until he sends for us, or until he dies. Short of those two options, I'm not to set foot in Principality City until the crisis is over."

"But you have to warn him!"

Aidane could feel Thaine's panic. It rose as she realized that Jonmarc seemed to be reconsidering the message.

"How do we know it's not a trap?" Jonmarc said, looking from Gabriel to Kolin. "The *serroquette* could have met Thaine anywhere. Maybe Thaine told the ghost whore her story. It doesn't mean that she's actually channeling Thaine's ghost. How do we know it's not a trick to get close to Staden or Berry?"

"Ask me anything," Thaine said, and Aidane felt the spirit growing more desperate. "Anything. I *am* Thaine. And what I'm telling you is true."

"Aidane's gift with the spirits is real." They all turned to look at Kolin. "She used it when we were escaping from the Nargi. And we saw her beset by spirits outside the camp where we found Thaine's body."

"Maybe she's a gifted actress," Jonmarc said, and a hard glint had come into his eyes.

He doesn't want to believe. He doesn't want to deal with me. Things are bad enough, without this. Thaine was upset enough she was making Aidane breathe too fast. Aidane struggled not to become light-headed. Then she met Kolin's eyes.

He knows my power is real. Aidane wondered if Kolin read the challenge in her eyes, and whether he would take it.

"She's not acting." Kolin hadn't fed recently enough to blush, but he looked uncomfortable, nonetheless. "Earlier on the night that we found Thaine's body, Aidane came to me in the crypt. She was possessed by the spirit of my long-dead betrothed, Elsbet. I, too, was skeptical. I've known too many *vayash moru* who were promised reunions by ghost whores who were nothing but frauds. But Elsbet has been dead for over two hundred years. There was no marker, no conversation to give Aidane any clues. No one in our party knew."

Kolin met Aidane's eyes. "No one knew the circumstances of Elsbet's death except the two of us. Aidane recounted it exactly. She had Elsbet's voice, Elsbet's ways. She was Elsbet." His voice caught, and he looked away. "Her power is genuine."

Gabriel moved closer. "Taru and Carina are mind healers. They aren't telepaths, but they can sense power and read memories. They could validate whether or not her power and her message is real."

Jonmarc passed a hand over his eyes. "Carina. How am I going to explain this?"

Jolie gave Aidane a hostile glare. "I have Thaine's word that she didn't come to make trouble."

"Somehow, that's not much comfort."

The door behind them opened. Carina stood in the doorway. "Neirin said Kolin was here with Jolie. I wondered where you'd gone."

Aidane felt Thaine's surprise as she took a first look at Lady Vahanian. Carina was dressed in healer's robes. She had dark hair, cut chin length, and intelligent, green eyes. But there was no sign of rank or wealth, no jewels, nothing other than the green healer's belt to indicate her status or position. She wore no cosmetics, nothing to enhance her appearance. And yet, when Aidane watched Jonmarc move toward Carina, it was apparent that he was completely smitten, and that the two cared deeply for each other. It was also very clear that Carina was nearly to term with her pregnancy. Thaine startled, and Aidane followed Thaine's gaze to a thin, twisted scar on the palm of Jonmarc's left hand. *Jolie said they were married. I thought a handfasting. But he's made a ritual bond. That's something I didn't think he'd ever do.* And although Thaine was sincere in disavowing any interest in the lord of the manor, Aidane felt a twinge of pain.

"There's someone I'd like you to meet," Jonmarc said, taking Carina's hand and leading her into the room. He stopped in front of Aidane.

Carina's eyes widened. "You're a—"

"*Serroquette*," Aidane finished for her, in her own voice. Thaine had stepped back in her consciousness. "The spirit I'm carrying has an urgent message for King Staden. Lord Vahanian is right to be cautious, but we need to prove that the spirit is genuine, that the message is real. Please, Lady Healer, if you can use your power to verify that, I beg you, do whatever you must."

Carina glanced at the necklace Aidane wore, the necklace Thaine had given her. She seemed to take in everything: the borrowed clothing, Aidane's heavy Nargi accent, even the way Kolin and Jolie watched Aidane. If Carina sensed that Jonmarc was ill at ease, she did not let on.

"Will you open your mind to me?" Carina met Aidane's gaze with green eyes that seemed to see into her soul. For the first time, Aidane was afraid.

"Yes. Not just my mind, but the spirit I'm carrying."

"Give me your hand."

Aidane stretched out her hand, and as Carina took it, Aidane saw the match of the scar on Jonmarc's palm that made a fine white line on Carina's hand, the mark of a ritual wedding. Such a vow bound the lovers' souls as well as making a formal commitment. Aidane had never known anyone sure enough of their choice to make a ritual bond.

Aidane felt a warm presence brush against her mind. It was different from the ghosts that possessed her, different from the way Thaine inhabited her. This warmth posed no threat. Aidane knew that Carina's power had no desire to harm her or to take control, and Aidane relaxed. It was as if a balm soothed her mind, easing the memories of the beating, her capture by the Black Robes, and the near-possession at the camp. The memories remained, but their ability to hurt had been dulled. Carina's touch was light, gentle, but Aidane knew its power. And while no words passed between them, Aidane was certain Carina could feel her own magic as a *serroquette*.

There was a shift, and Thaine's spirit came to the fore. Aidane was content to withdraw, uncertain of Thaine's reception. Thaine, too, was unsure, and Aidane could clearly feel the ghost's fear. After a moment, Carina's power drew back, and Aidane stood looking at the healer in a silence that seemed to last forever.

"Both Aidane and Thaine are what they seem to be," Carina said finally. It was impossible for Aidane to read any emotion in Carina's voice. What she thought of Aidane as a *serroquette* or what she made of Thaine's presence in her household, Carina gave no clue.

"Is Thaine telling the truth?" It was Jonmarc who spoke.

Carina seemed to consider her impressions from the mental touch, and then nodded. "Yes. At least, she believes it's the truth. Thaine is afraid."

"Damn." Jonmarc began to pace. "Now what do we do?"

"Perhaps if you contacted Captain Gellyr, he could give her safe passage to Principality City, make sure her word reaches the king," Carina suggested.

Kolin shook his head. "If the Black Robes get any inkling that Aidane is carrying Thaine's spirit, they'll try to kill her. Will Gellyr take the message seriously enough to protect her?"

Aidane knew that Kolin's real question was different, and she shared his fear. *Will Gellyr bother protecting a whore?*

"If the king is barely conscious, then he's not going to be able to stop this threat personally," Gabriel said. "I would not expect General Gregor to give Aidane a worthy hearing."

"The Feast of the Departed is barely a week away. That's not much time to find the traitors and stop the plot." Kolin chewed on his lip as he thought, and despite the gravity of the conversation, Aidane smiled at how mortal the gesture was.

Jonmarc sighed. "I don't see an option. I have no choice about staying here to protect Berry. Gellyr is our best shot, and perhaps he knows someone other than Gregor who would hear Thaine out. But we can't send her alone." He looked at Kolin. "You're not due to make another Nargi run for a while. Would you go with her?"

To Aidane's surprise, Kolin nodded. "I'd just worked through the options and come to that same conclusion myself. Yes, I'll go."

Before the conversation could go further, there was a sharp knock at the door, and a man Aidane did not recognize peered from around the door.

"What is it, Neirin?" Jonmarc asked, distracted.

"Sorry to bother you, m'lord. But Captain Gellyr is here. He says it's urgent."

Jonmarc exchanged glances with Gabriel and Carina. "Is he alone?"

"Yes, m'lord."

"Send him in."

A man in the uniform of the king's army stepped into the room. He held his helm under his arm. From his expression, Aidane knew something bad had happened. Even Thaine drew back, afraid.

"You're always welcome in Dark Haven, but it's rather late

for dinner," Jonmarc said, extending a hand to the officer, who clasped both hand and arm as if greeting an old friend.

Gellyr's eyes held a deep sadness. "Once again, I'm afraid it's not a social call. I came as soon as I received news." He swallowed hard, and although he kept his composure, Aidane could see the struggle in his face. "King Staden is dead."

20

Carina gasped, and made the sign of the Lady in blessing. Jonmarc was silent, as he worked through the implications of Gellyr's announcement.

"We'll need to tell Berry," Jonmarc said quietly.

Gellyr nodded. "I thought it might be best coming from you."

"Can we take her back to the palace without risking her life?" Jonmarc asked. "If the plague is that bad—"

"It seems to have subsided from its peak," Gellyr said. "That's what I've heard. Staden survived the initial bout of it. He was a very strong man. But it went to his lungs, and that's what killed him." He met Jonmarc's eyes. "Without a crowned monarch, Principality is vulnerable."

Jonmarc drew a deep breath. "You have no idea." He turned to Aidane and motioned for her to come forward. Gellyr's eyes widened, just a bit.

"Aidane is a *serroquette*," Jonmarc said matter-of-factly. "The spirit she's harboring has a warning you need to hear. Carina has verified that the spirit is who she claims to be, and that she believes the message to be true. I know this is...irregular...but please, you have to hear her out."

Gellyr nodded. "I fear that in the next few weeks many things will be 'irregular.' Let the lady speak."

Thaine came to the fore of Aidane's consciousness, and once again gave her warning. Jonmarc watched Gellyr's face as he listened. Doubt, concern, and mistrust all showed in his expression, but to the captain's credit, he listened without interruption. When Thaine finished and Aidane stepped back, Gellyr shook his head.

"That's quite a tale."

Jonmarc nodded. "We've only just heard it ourselves, before you came. Kolin's brought back another group from Nargi, and Aidane was one of the Black Robes' prisoners." He met Gellyr's eyes. "You know the trouble we've had right here in Dark Haven with the Durim. I've been afraid they were after something big. A disruption on the scale Thaine's describing would be bad under any circumstances—"

"But with the death of the king, it could throw Principality into chaos, right as a foreign invader comes to the northern shore," Gellyr finished. "Damn."

"You know Gregor won't believe this," Jonmarc said. His voice was level, but there was an undercurrent that made his dislike for Gregor plain.

Gellyr nodded. "Gregor is my superior officer, but my rank doesn't close my eyes. He has many strengths as a military man, and many weaknesses."

"Is there someone else who could help us? When I was in Principality last year, I was part of the war council that helped Tris put his strategy together. Staden gave us General Darrath, and a man named Hant, who Staden called his 'chief rat catcher.' Hant's the guy we need."

"Would he remember you?"

Jonmarc shrugged. "Maybe. Would he believe a ghost whore? Don't know. Berry and I are going to be on thin ice—her, newly crowned, and me, a Champion people don't know or trust. I'd rather not make Berry force her generals into something. But we don't have time to cut through a lot of bureaucracy. Haunts is less than a week away."

Gellyr thought. "I'll have to arrange it outside of the normal chain of command. My wife's uncle is a general. He's fond enough of me to see me if I use her name. I can get you an audience, but I can't guarantee how he'll receive the information, or that he'll do anything." He paused for a moment. "If he buys in, he can get Hant to listen. I'm almost positive."

Jonmarc nodded. "Even if he won't act, we've got a backup plan. We'll know the Durim are up to something. I'll be there, escorting Berry. I'll take Kolin with me, and Laisren. If you could accidentally have more men stationed where there's likely to be trouble..."

Gellyr smiled. "I'd heard it said that before you earned your reputation as an outlaw, you were a fine military officer. I see the rumors were correct."

A shadow seemed to cross Jonmarc's face. "That was before I was court-martialed and left to die."

Gellyr sobered. "Even here, we've heard about Chauvrenne. When orders conflict with true service to the king, orders must be disobeyed."

"Not everyone sees it that way."

"Before we leave for Principality City, I've been instructed that there has to be a field coronation." Gellyr looked to Jonmarc.

Jonmarc looked at him quizzically. "A field coronation? How?"

"In extreme circumstances, a titled noble can convey the crown," Gellyr replied. "You're Staden's liegeman, and the princess's sworn protector."

The irony that Dark Haven's brigand lord would crown the next monarch was not lost on Jonmarc, but a new possibility crossed his mind, and he looked to Gabriel. "I'd like to invite the Blood Council and the *vyrkin*," Jonmarc said, and Gabriel nodded, as if the same thought had occurred to him as well. "If Thaine's prediction is true, then it's going to take a real alliance of the living, undead, and shapeshifters to defend the kingdom. This is a good place to start."

"Tonight's far spent. It will take most of tomorrow to prepare for your trip back to Principality City. By tomorrow night, I can have the Blood Council here—those who will come—and I am sure Sior can bring the *vyrkin*." Gabriel looked at Gellyr, as if expecting an objection, but the captain shrugged.

"We're going to need all the allies we can get, if what your lady here says is true," Gellyr said. "The more the merrier."

Carina touched Jonmarc's arm. "Perhaps we should both go to see Berry."

Jonmarc nodded. He looked to Kolin. "Find Neirin. Tell him what's going on. It's not an occasion for a feast, but he'll need to make a room ready for the ceremony. Then see what Taru knows about these things. I don't want to do it wrong and find out we've left a door open for someone to challenge the succession."

"Done." Kolin disappeared at *vayash moru* speed.

Jonmarc looked to Jolie. "Who'd have thought, huh?"

Jolie smiled sadly. "I knew there was more for you than smuggling the river, *cheche*. You take care of the princess. My girls and I will take good care of Aidane. We've got some work to do to get her ready if she's palace-bound." And with that, Jolie took charge, slipping her arm through Aidane's and leading her out of the room.

"I've brought a small contingent to escort you and your party to the palace," Gellyr said.

Jonmarc nodded. "Thank you, Captain. I'll have Neirin see to it that you're well fed and given a place to sleep." He spread his hands wide to indicate the manor house. "If you hadn't noticed, it's gotten crowded here with the refugees, but we'll do the best we can."

Gellyr managed a half smile. "Even the barn will do, m'lord. My men and I have slept in worse places."

Too many thoughts were tumbling around in Jonmarc's mind as he and Carina headed for Berry's room. The enormity of the news still left him feeling shock. Staden had been the first king to back Tris Drayke's quest to reclaim the Margolan throne, and Jonmarc, Carina, Carroway, Harrtuck, Kiara, and Soterius had been Staden's guests for much of that year as Tris had trained with the Sisterhood and prepared to retake his kingdom. And while nothing in Jonmarc's background had prepared him to be the guest of a king, he'd grown to genuinely like and respect Staden, and to see him through Berry's eyes. It made the loss much more personal than he had ever imagined.

But aside from the human loss, Staden's death put Principality in a dangerous position. *Margolan's reeling from plague, famine, and Jared's aftermath, plus the battle at Lochlanimar. Isencroft's on the brink of civil war. If Principality falls into chaos, it endangers Eastmark and Dhasson. And if Trevath and Nargi are backing the Durim and this new dark summoner, the Winter Kingdoms are doomed. Dark Haven can't hold them all off alone. I made a vow to protect Berry. I promised to keep Carina and the twins safe. I swore I'd defend Dark Haven. And I have no idea how the hell to do that.*

"Jonmarc?" From Carina's tone, it was clear she had been calling him without response.

He grimaced. "Sorry. My head's still spinning."

Carina nodded toward a closed door. "We're here." She stepped forward and knocked. "Berry? It's me, Carina. I've got Jonmarc with me. Can we come in?"

They heard footsteps, and the door opened. Berry was wrapped in a dressing gown, although from the lamp that was lit on a table and the open book, Jonmarc guessed she had been reading rather than napping. "What's going on?" But before her voice faded, Berry's expression froze. She looked from Carina and Jonmarc and her eyes widened as she found in their faces confirmation of her worst fear.

"He's dead, isn't he?"

Carina nodded, and Berry collapsed against her, sobbing. Jonmarc closed the door behind them and Carina guided Berry to a chair, while Jonmarc went to pour a small amount of tea from a kettle near the fire, and brought a cup to Berry.

"I didn't get to say good-bye," Berry whispered, as sobs racked her body and she clung to Carina. Tomorrow, she would become a queen. Tonight, Berry was a grieving young girl. At a total loss for what to say, Jonmarc stood behind Berry's chair and laid a hand on her shoulder.

"I'm sorry, Berry," he said in a strangled voice. "I'm sorry."

After a while, Berry's sobs subsided. Carina handed her a kerchief, and Berry blew her nose, wiping the tears from her face with the back of her hand. She took a deep breath and sat up straight. In that moment, she seemed to be several years older, and the regal bearing Jonmarc had glimpsed in the confrontation with Gregor reasserted itself. Whatever turmoil Berry was feeling inside, she knew her duty to Principality. "What now?"

Carina smoothed back the hair from Berry's face and sat back. "Neirin is pulling together what we need to have a ceremony here tomorrow night, before you head for Principality City. We'll do a version of the coronation here, and then once you reach the palace, they'll make the public display."

Berry reached up to clasp Jonmarc's hand on her shoulder, and she drew him around to where she could see him. "You're coming with me." It was both a statement and a plea.

Jonmarc nodded. "Of course. I'm bringing Laisren and Kolin, and we'll have someone else with us. Aidane."

Berry looked puzzled. As quickly as possible, Jonmarc filled her in on Aidane's role and Thaine's warning. Berry seemed to push the grief aside and she frowned as she thought. "If all that's true, it's a really bad time to lose Father and put a young, untested girl on the throne."

Jonmarc had to smile at her perceptiveness. "Thanks for saving us all a week's worth of polite attempts to explain that. Yes, it makes it dangerous for you, and dangerous for Principality."

Berry's eyes looked haunted. "There's going to be war, isn't there?"

Jonmarc and Carina exchanged glances. "It looks that way," Jonmarc said. "Although I wish there were another path."

Berry looked up, and Jonmarc could see in her expression that she'd reasoned it out for herself. "But there isn't. The Durim aren't just trying to revive the Shanthadura cult, which would be bad enough. They're set to betray us from within to whoever the invaders are from across the sea, whoever's backing this dark summoner. This war is going to pull in all of the Winter Kingdoms."

Jonmarc sighed. "I'm afraid so."

Berry rose and walked over to one of the trunks she'd brought with her from the palace. She worked the complicated lock, and dug down below a mound of gowns that she'd refused to wear at Dark Haven to withdraw a wooden box. It was beautifully made, covered with Noorish inlay, and Jonmarc guessed that it was spelled to open only for Berry. At her touch, the clasp snapped open. With an expression both resigned and sorrowful, she withdrew a sheaf of papers. Berry held out the papers to Jonmarc.

"Here, you'll need these for the ceremony. Father forced me to take them with me when he sent me away from the palace. I tried to tell him they weren't necessary. Maybe he'd had a premonition. They're the instructions for a field investiture and the legal papers attesting that I'm really the heir to the crown."

Jonmarc accepted them, handling them gingerly. "I'm sorry, Berry. It would be a bad situation even for someone as seasoned as Staden. I thought Tris came to the throne under rough circumstances. I'm afraid it's not going to be any easier for you."

Berry managed a half smile that did not reach her eyes. "Then it's a good thing I've got friends."

Jonmarc and Carina walked back to their rooms in silence. When they were inside, Jonmarc placed the papers in a leather pouch for safekeeping and poured himself a glass of brandy. Carina walked to the window and opened it. She leaned against the frame, staring out into the night.

Jonmarc's stomach clenched. "Carina—" When Carina did not answer, he walked toward her slowly, feeling at a total loss. "About Thaine..."

Carina sighed. "You'd told me about her, about what it was like with the Nargi. And when I did the mind healing, I saw your memories from those times."

"That's not the same as having her ghost show up on our doorstep."

Carina shook her head. "No, or having you go off to war, taking her with you." Her hand fell to her belly. "I can't go along to help this time. And if war comes, you might be on the battlefield when the twins are born."

"We don't know that for certain. There might still be a way to avoid war."

"You don't really believe that."

Jonmarc looked down. "No, not really."

Carina looked up at him, and he could see that her eyes were bright with unshed tears. "I'm afraid for you, Jonmarc. If there's a dark summoner involved, this won't be a normal war. And if the Durim are able to raise the things that live in those barrows, it really might be a War of Unmaking."

Jonmarc stepped up behind Carina, wrapping his arms around her shoulders. She leaned back against him, and he let one hand splay over her belly. "If I hadn't promised Staden I'd be Berry's protector, I wouldn't go. You know that. I want to stay here and protect Dark Haven, the twins, and you. I've had my fill of war."

Carina swallowed back tears. "I know. But you *are* the best fighter in the Winter Kingdoms. And you're the Dark Lady's chosen warrior. When you saw your vision of Her, She said that without you, the future would change for the Winter Kingdoms. Perhaps this is what She saw, or part of it."

"Right now, I'm more worried about you." Jonmarc kissed the top of Carina's head. "That's why I'm going to ask Laisren to go with us to Principality City, instead of Gabriel. I want Gabriel here to protect you. As it is, if war comes, most of the mages will have to leave Dark Haven for the front lines. I want to make sure that you—and Dark Haven—are protected."

They stood in silence for a few moments. "Did you miss her?" Carina's voice was quiet.

Jonmarc sighed. "Miss her? Not really. I've thought of her from time to time. On the other hand, I try hard not to think about those years."

He turned Carina's hand so that the scar on the palm showed, and he put the scar on his own palm against hers. "If you've seen my memories, then you know that after the time in Nargi, I wasn't really very...human...anymore. I wanted to die. And since I couldn't fight the things that took my life away from me, I fought everyone else. It was always worst at night. Thaine and I held on to each other, and it was bearable. Thaine knew I didn't love her. She didn't love me. I don't think either of us had it in us at the time. We looked out for each other. It was enough to get us through."

"Do I have to tell you that I'm not thrilled about my husband leaving for Principality City with the ghost of an old lover in the body of a beautiful *serroquette*?" Her tone was sad, not angry, and Jonmarc could hear an edge of hurt beneath the worry.

He clasped their hands together so that the scars touched. "Touch my mind, Carina. I know you can. I've made my choice. I don't want anyone but you." He felt the warmth of Carina's magic brush against his mind, and he met her eyes. "No secrets. No lies. I won't betray your trust. And I'll do everything in my power to be home in time to be with you, when the twins are born."

Carina laid her cheek against their clasped hands. "Then I'll make an extra offering to the Dark Lady, and to all the Aspects for good measure."

The next night, a small group gathered behind closed doors in Dark Haven's great room. Jonmarc and Carina were dressed for court. Carroway and Macaria came at Berry's personal invitation, both as her guests and to play a favorite song in tribute to Staden. Kolin and Jolie were present, as was Captain Gellyr, whose soldiers guarded the door. Raen, one of Dark Haven's resident ghosts, glowed a faint blue in the corner. Berry wore one of the gowns she had disdained all season, a fitted dress of Mussa silk in a deep emerald color that set off her auburn hair. Carina had plaited Berry's hair and covered it with a mesh of gold. Dressed for court, with a new somberness in her manner, Berry looked older than her fourteen years.

"Where's Gabriel? Did the Blood Council refuse the invitation?" Berry's voice had a nervous edge to it that told Jonmarc that she would have found something to fret about even if the full Blood Council was already in attendance.

"I'm sure they'll be here," Jonmarc said, although he was not as confident as he sounded.

Just then, the doors opened and Laisren ushered in their guests. Riqua went straight to Berry.

"I'm so sorry about your father," Riqua said, giving Berry a hug. During the months Berry had been at Dark Haven, she and Riqua had often helped Carina tend to the refugees. Now, Jonmarc saw genuine sorrow beneath Riqua's usually unreadable expression. "I've seen many kings rise and fall over the last several hundred years. Staden was among the best to rule these lands. He will be missed."

"Thank you," Berry murmured.

Jonmarc had his eye on who was entering behind Gabriel. Rafe slipped in quietly, murmuring condolences. Uri followed, but he remained at a distance. Behind him were Vigulf and Sior from the *vyrkin*, followed by Sister Taru and Lisette, who brought with her the chalice that the investiture ritual required.

"Astasia didn't come," Gabriel murmured from behind Jonmarc. "In fact, she and her brood appear to have gone missing. Her manor house at Airenngeir is empty."

Jonmarc turned to meet Gabriel's gaze. "Do you think she's sided with the Durim?"

Anger glinted in Gabriel's eyes. "We must assume so. Rafe agrees. Given the circumstances, we've voted her outlaw to the Council, which means her lands are forfeit and she's lost any protection as a member of the Council until she explains herself. If she really has sided with the Durim or the invaders, we'll be bloodsworn against her and her brood. That's not a step we take lightly."

When the guests had taken their places, Carroway and Macaria played the song Berry had requested. To Jonmarc's surprise, it was a bawdy tavern song, not one of the pieces of chamber music often favored at court. Despite the solemnity of the moment, the song brought a smile to many faces in the small crowd, even Berry, who managed a smile although a tear was on her cheek. Jonmarc wondered how much Macaria's music magic had to do with the feeling of calm that seemed to settle over the room. When the music ended, Carroway came forward and knelt in front of Berry.

"Let me be the first with a coronation gift," he said, and while his manner was solemn, a glint of mischief sparkled in his eyes. From inside his vest, he withdrew a velvet-wrapped bundle. Berry undid it to find a beautifully made set of throwing knives with inlaid handles. Despite the occasion, Berry giggled.

"You've used the first set so much, I figure they're scratched by now. I was going to give them to you at Haunts, but since you'll be in Principality City, I thought I'd do it now. I hope you never have to use them."

Berry threw her arms around Carroway's neck and gave him a kiss on the cheek. "Thank you. You never know when they'll come in handy. I've kept in practice. I'm afraid Carina will find new holes in the beams in my room."

Taru cleared her throat, and the room fell silent. Lisette handed the chalice to Taru, who held it up. "We are here to crown a new queen. Tonight, Berwyn, daughter of Staden, will accept the throne of Principality for all subjects, living, dead and undead, mortal and immortal."

Berwyn rose and walked slowly to where Taru stood beside Jonmarc. Lisette took the circlet crown Gellyr had brought with him from its velvet pouch and handed it to Jonmarc.

Berry knelt in front of Jonmarc. He swallowed hard. Berry had been a courageous tomboy when he and the others had rescued her from slavers. He'd watched with the pride of a godfather as she returned to court and grew into her responsibilities. Now, he felt both pride and apprehension, and he knew that it was just a shadow of what he would someday feel for his own girls. He took a deep breath and was pleased to see that, as he accepted the circlet from Lisette, his hands were almost steady.

"Berwyn, daughter of Staden, heir to the throne of Principality and to the crown of your ancestors. Staden, King of Principality, bestowed on me the title of Lord of Dark Haven. By that power, whose source is the king's authority, I give to you the crown of Principality and name you Queen Berwyn." Jonmarc felt relief sweep over him that the long-memorized piece was at an end. Berry rose, and everyone in the room knelt. Jonmarc met Berry's eyes as he sank to one knee, and she held out her hand. Jonmarc took her hand, kissing the signet ring.

"As I was to your father, so also to you," he murmured.

One by one, the others in the room made their oaths. Finally, when everyone had vowed their fealty, Carroway and Macaria struck up a festive tune, one that heralded the arrival of the king at festivals. Neirin leaned into the room.

"I've taken the liberty to prepare a repast suitable for our new queen," he said. "May we all toast the good health and long life of Queen Berwyn."

At that, servants entered, bearing platters of roasted venison, ramekins of baked onions and leeks, and a large pudding, along with pitchers of wine. Jonmarc nodded his approval, knowing how little time the staff had had to prepare for the occasion.

The evening passed in subdued gaiety. Staden's death cast a pall over the celebration, and Jonmarc, seated at Berry's right hand, often caught a glimpse of Berry sniffing back tears or struggling to maintain her composure. Still, she did her best to rise to the occasion, and Carroway and Macaria kept the music festive. Jonmarc noticed that Carroway was playing better than ever with his injured hand, and he wondered when, given the plague in Margolan and the possibility of war throughout the kingdoms, the two bards would attempt to return home. After hearing about Carroway's valiant efforts to protect Kiara while Tris was besieging Lochlanimar, Jonmarc found himself hoping that Carroway and Macaria might stay in Dark Haven until he returned from Principality City.

As was the custom, the guests departed just after midnight, having kept watch with the new queen into her first full day as monarch. When the last of the guests had gone, Berry leaned against the wall and closed her eyes.

"Well, that's done," she murmured, massaging her temples. She opened her eyes and gave a wan smile to Carina and Jonmarc. "I appreciate everything you and Carroway and Neirin did on such short notice. It was wonderful, all of it. But everything's happening too fast." She sighed. "By the time we get back home, they'll have burned Father's body. I won't get to say good-bye."

Berry glanced from Carina to Jonmarc. "I thought I'd spend a few candlemarks down in the chapel, making an offering to Istra for Father's soul. With the way Principality celebrates Haunts, I know I'll have plenty of opportunity to make offerings to the Lover and the Whore." She paused, thinking. "Do you think Aidane will decide to stay in Principality? After all, Athira the Whore is our patron Aspect of the Sacred Lady. What Aidane does isn't that different from the way the Sacred Vessels prophesy. They claim to be possessed by the Lady, or the spirits. And the Temple Consorts believe it's their divine duty to couple with as many pilgrims as possible." She giggled. "Principality has its own ways of celebrating a holiday, that's for sure!"

Jonmarc had to chuckle. "I was an eighteen-year-old merc in Principality once upon a time, or had you forgotten? Harrtuck and I served with the War Dogs, and you won't find a merc company with a more sullied reputation for drinking, wenching, and dice. Our commander, Captain Valjan, told us that our lives were going to be short and our deaths painful, so we had the Lady's blessing to enjoy every moment until then as if it were our last." He shook his head. "I've often wondered what became of Valjan, and whether he stayed true to his own words. He was the Crone's own in battle."

Carina fixed both of them with a playful glare. "And did you both forget that Cam and I joined up with a Principality merc group as well, when we were just Berry's age? It was my duty to patch up the sorry lot of them after they staggered back to the barracks. At least the Temple Consorts are divinely immune to the clap. Can't say the same for the rest of the whores in Principality." She shook her head, and her eyes seemed to see something far away. "Gregor was just a merc commander then, with Ric as his captain. Goddess! How were we brave enough to fight, not even twenty seasons old?"

"I suspect most of us were running from something, or some-where," Jonmarc said, slipping his arm around Carina. "I was. And for many of the men in the War Dogs, Valjan's prediction was true." He took a deep breath, trying to shake off the gloomy mood. "We leave early tomorrow, Berry, so don't stay too long in the chapel. We'll have Gellyr's soldiers to ride with us by day, and Laisren and the *vayash moru* will join us each night. Sior said he'd give us a *vyrkin* escort until we were close to the city, but only a couple of the *vyrkin*—in their human form—will stay with us once we get to Principality City. They're not as comfortable there, and it's harder for them to hunt."

"Thank you," Berry said, giving both Jonmarc and Carina hugs. "I'm going to miss Dark Haven." The look in her eye gave Jonmarc to suspect that it wasn't just the people Berry would miss. Gone forever was her chance to move among a crowd anonymously, to be free of the strictures of court and the burdens of the crown. Once they entered Principality City, "Berry" would be replaced forever by "Queen Berwyn."

"We'll miss you, too, Berry."

The next morning was crisp and clear. Neirin, Carina, and Jolie saw them off. Although he and Carina had made their good-byes in private, Jonmarc could not resist a backward glance as the group rode out. Although the odds were against it, he fervently hoped that he would be home for the birth of his daughters, and that the war that seemed inevitable could somehow be averted. Neither possibility seemed likely.

The main roads were crowded with pilgrims headed to the festival in Principality City. While the proper name of the holiday was Feast of the Departed, most people knew it as Haunts. It was a time when the ghosts of the Winter Kingdoms became visible to everyone, without the aid of a summoner. During the rest of the year, only those spirits who had enough power to manifest themselves were visible. The other ghosts were present year-long, but invisible to all who did not have the magic to see them.

It had been at Haunts two years previously that Jared the Usurper had murdered King Bricen of Margolan, sending Tris Drayke, Soterius, Harrtuck, and Carroway running for their lives, and beginning the adventure that had changed Jonmarc's future. Last year, Jonmarc had celebrated Haunts in Dark Haven, which tended to keep its holidays differently from the rest of the Winter Kingdoms, due to the centuries-long existence of many of its *vayash moru* residents. Now, heading to Principality City, Jonmarc tried to recall Principality's customs beyond wenching, games of chance, and drinking to excess, and remembered little else. He glanced at Berry. Returning to the city during its most excessive and licentious festival as the guardian of a young queen suddenly made the city's high spirits and wanton revelry seem more dangerous than exciting.

Jonmarc and Gellyr rode point. By day, Anton and Serg, the two *vyrkin* representatives in human form, rode at the back, with Berry and Aidane in the middle. At night, Kolin and Laisren rode behind the group, while Anton and Serg went hunting.

They stopped for a cold lunch of sausage, bread, and cheese in a clearing along the road.

Jonmarc sat down next to Berry. "How are you?"

Berry took a deep breath before she replied. "Struggling. It's just—I never really thought he'd die while I was gone." She squeezed her eyes shut, but a tear slid down her cheek. After a few moments, she looked up, but from her reddened eyes, Jonmarc knew she had probably been crying for much of the ride.

"I hope Jencin knows what's been going on while I've been gone," Berry said, taking an all-business tone. "When I left, Father was deep into the negotiations with Eastmark."

"Do you know what that involved?"

Berry shook her head. "They'd had a few meetings face-to-face, and there were lots of messengers back and forth. I had the feeling it was still coming together. I asked him, but he said he'd tell me more when I got home, that he still needed to check into some things." She sighed. "That's why I hope Jencin knows where he left off. The last letter I had from him said that he was expecting a delegation from Eastmark for Haunts to finish the negotiations."

Jonmarc took a swig of wine from his wineskin. "So we could get to the palace and find a bunch of Eastmark diplomats waiting on the doorstep?"

Berry giggled. "I think Jencin might let them in the door. But, yes. They could show up on our heels, or beat us there. If they were already on their way, there'd have been no way to tell them not to come, to tell them about Father's . . ." Her voice trailed off, as if she couldn't bring herself to say "death." Jonmarc took her hand and squeezed it, and she turned her face for a moment until she collected herself.

"I have to do better than this," she said, swallowing hard. "This won't do at all for a queen."

Jonmarc smiled and took a kerchief from his pocket to wipe her face. "Maybe not. But until we get to the palace and have the second coronation, it's not totally official. So you've got a little longer to just be Berry, and no one here will tell anyone if you need to grieve."

Berry stretched up to kiss him lightly on the cheek. "Thank you."

They headed back onto the road. The next candlemark passed without incident. Jonmarc was still thinking about what Berry had said when he saw Gellyr riding up alongside him.

"*Skrivven* for your thoughts," Gellyr said.

Jonmarc shrugged. "Just wondering how in the hell we're going to keep Berry safe in the crowds at Haunts. She told me that after the coronation, it's her duty to go to the Temple of the Sacred Vessels to make an offering, and that it's considered a good sign if the spirit of the Lady falls on the monarch to make a prophecy."

"Please tell me that the monarch gets to keep his or her clothes on," Gellyr said. "I've seen the Sacred Vessels prophesy. For some reason, shedding their clothing seems to help them, um, make the connection to the afterlife."

"I already asked. Yes, she gets to keep her clothing."

"Thank the Goddess for something."

"We're going to have thousands of drunken revelers in the costumes of the Aspects, and wagons pulling huge effigies of the Aspects, and one big street party throughout the entire city with enough ale to give the whole place a monster-sized hangover." Jonmarc shook his head. "How are we going to find the Durim in all that and stop them from whatever they mean to do?"

Gellyr grimaced. "I've been wondering that myself. Isn't there a Citadel of the Sisterhood in Principality City? Can they help?"

Jonmarc shrugged. "Taru sent letters of introduction with me to the mages she thought would help us. Some of them are as powerful as she is, and others are more on the hedge-witch side of things. On the other hand, I've seen what a hedge witch can do when she decides to kick up a fuss, and it's not something to dismiss. Unfortunately, none of them are summoners. But Rigel is an air mage, and if he agrees to help, Taru said that a good air mage has some power to attract and repel spirits and *dimonns*, though nothing like a full summoner can do. The problem is, we don't know what the Durim plan to bring against us."

Gellyr looked at him thoughtfully. "You know Martris Drayke in Margolan well, don't you?"

Jonmarc chuckled. "Carina and Queen Kiara are cousins. So Tris and I are kin. Donelan certainly sees it that way."

"If war comes, is Martris Drayke as powerful as the rumors say?"

Jonmarc raised his eyebrows. "Truth be told, I'd say Tris is much more powerful than I've heard the rumors give him credit for. I was there when he called the ghosts of the Ruune Vidaya forest and set them on the slavers who'd captured us. It was sheer, raw power that let him do that. He barely had any training. I've seen the worst war has to offer, but I'd never seen anything like that, and I hope never to see anything like it again." He shook his head. "I've seen Tris go up against magicked beasts, and I was in the room when he fought Foor Arontala and the Obsidian King. If there's a war, he's definitely the guy you want on your side. What worries me is the idea that there might be someone just as powerful going up against us."

They were quiet for a few moments. "How connected is Gregor? How much trouble can he make?"

Gellyr gave him a sideways glance. "You mean, how much of a pain in the ass can he be for you?"

"Uh-huh."

Gellyr shrugged. "You're the Queen's Champion. Even he wouldn't dare move against you. Within the ranks, he can spread the usual rumors. Gregor's a good soldier. He's tough, he treats his men decently, and he gets the job done. I've never known him to play politics, and I've served under him for years now."

"When did he come across from being a merc into the service of the crown?"

Gellyr thought for a moment. "Not long before I was assigned to him. The merc group he led disbanded after his brother died, or so I heard. Principality doesn't have much of a formal army. We rely on the merc groups for defense, in exchange for a safe haven for them. But there are a few hundred troops that owe allegiance only to the king—or queen. Maybe Gregor just got tired of the merc business. It's a young man's game."

"That it is." *Young and suicidal.*

"Truth be told, I've never seen Gregor get in a brawl—before I took him to Dark Haven." There was a pregnant pause, and Jonmarc guessed that Gellyr was hoping for the story.

"You could say that there's some history," Jonmarc said. If Gellyr was going to stick his neck out to help him, he needed to understand what he was getting into. Jonmarc gave him the short version of the story: Ric's death, Carina's failure to save him and her own near-death, and Gregor's capture of them the year before.

"Is that all?" Gellyr asked with wry amusement. "Goddess true! That's a tale for the bards. Well, that explains a lot."

"Here's the big question, and I know I'm putting you on the spot, but with what's coming our way, I need to know. Gregor's an ex-merc. So am I. So's my friend Harrtuck, who's now Captain of the Guards for Martris Drayke in Margolan. Some mercs find something bigger than themselves to believe in. Somewhere to pledge their loyalty. Some mercs are only ever loyal to themselves. Which kind is Gregor?"

Jonmarc could see the conflict in Gellyr's face and guessed he was weighing his words carefully. "I've seen General Gregor perform his duties admirably," Gellyr said finally. "He received a commendation from King Staden for his performance handling some border raiders a few years ago. Personally, I have no quarrel with the man. He's been a good commander." He met Jonmarc's eyes. "But I know what you're asking, and I don't know the answer. I've never seen him with his back against the wall. The kind of war your *serroquette* is predicting—that's going to put the allegiance of most men to the test. Fighting men is one thing. Fighting magic and monsters, well, some men aren't cut out for that."

Jonmarc met his eyes. "Are you?"

He saw old pain flash in Gellyr's eyes. Jonmarc guessed from the other man's scars that he was a seasoned veteran, someone who had seen real battle and lived to tell about it. "I keep my vows," Gellyr said, and there was steel beneath his voice. "I'll do everything in my power to protect Principality and the queen. And if necessary, I'll die for her."

Jonmarc nodded. "Then we have an understanding."

21

"Is it always like this?" Aidane swiveled from side to side in her saddle as they rode into Principality City. Although it was night, the view was still impressive. Colorful flags, banners, and streamers waved from every building and post. Music filled the air, along with the sound of raucous laughter. The night air smelled of incense, perfume, and roasting meat. Crowds jostled the riders. Many of the festival-goers wore elaborate costumes to the Eight Faces of the Sacred Lady. The vast majority celebrated the Lover or the Whore. Some wore barely any costume at all. More than a few men staggered down the sidewalk gripping a tankard or bottle, while others walked arm in arm with one or more female companions, all, by the look of them, equally inebriated. The alleys they passed smelled of vomit and urine, the byproducts of a successful feast. Sounds from the doorways indicated that strumpets were busy seeing to the needs of the festival crowd.

Jonmarc gave a protective glance toward Berry, who seemed preoccupied. She noticed his attention, and forced a smile. "I grew up here, remember? You look as though you'd like to put a bag over my head, but believe me, I know what goes on at Haunts."

Jonmarc shrugged. "Just doing my job."

Berry sighed. "It's really all the same to them, isn't it?"

Jonmarc followed her gaze to the merrymakers. "What do you mean?"

"One king's as good as the next, so long as the taxes don't rise," she said softly.

Jonmarc could see the sadness in her eyes. "I told Kiara once that until I traveled with the lot of you, it never occurred to me that a king was a real person, someone's father or husband. Kings were like statues, up on high, not quite real. You paid your taxes to them and vowed loyalty and if it came down to it, you died for them. But loving them? I didn't understand that until I saw how things affected you and Carina and Kiara and Tris. Don't be too hard on them. They mean no offense."

Berry nodded. "And until I was captured by the slavers and spent time on the road with you and Tris, and then at Dark Haven, I don't think I realized just how far away the palace seems to most people. Like something out of a storybook. Not real at all." She swallowed hard. "Father loved Haunts. When he was a prince, he used to slip out into the crowd unannounced and have a grand time until the guards found him and dragged him home, usually drunk and singing." She chuckled, despite herself. "I wish I could have seen that."

"Look at that!" Aidane was pointing, her voice amazed. A huge stage had been erected in the center of the city for the appearance of the Sacred Vessels, the Lady's oracles. It was an elaborate dais with eight pillars and eight statues, one for each of the Lady's faces. Diaphanous cloth wafted between the pillars in shades of red and yellow. Behind the dais, a small city of white tents marked the area where the Temple Consorts welcomed those who sought to make a more personal, intimate connection with the goddess.

Above the sound of the crowd came the ringing of the chimes that marked the brothels. Legend had it that wenching was especially encouraged at Haunts to replace the lives of the departed. Jonmarc had always suspected that the prodigious consumption of alcohol had more to do with it than any religious significance.

All around the city's center, giant straw effigies of the Lady in all of her eight Aspects towered over the crowd. Bonfires flared into the sky in front of the empty stage, and musicians were playing a lively dance song. Many of the revelers wore the beads that signified their devotion to the Lady. At least for this night, everyone appeared to be quite devout, festooned with dozens of strings of the many-colored beads. Some of the women wore little else.

"Nice beads," Jonmarc commented.

Berry chuckled. "Good thing for some of the women out here that it's not any colder. They aren't wearing enough beads to stay warm. Do you remember what the colors mean?"

"It's been awhile. Red for the Whore, right?"

Berry nodded.

"Yellow for the Lover. Istra's beads are dark red like blood. I remember that from Dark Haven. Black is the Crone. Picked up on that in Nargi."

"Orange for Chenne and Green for the Childe," Berry prompted.

"Blue for the Mother," Jonmarc added, searching his memory. "I know I'm forgetting one."

"Clear for Nameless," Aidane supplied. "The Formless One." She shrugged as they turned to her. "I saw clear beads on one of the Black Robes. It stuck in my mind because, in Nargi, wearing anything except the black beads could get you flogged."

Costumed dancers twirled and shook tambourines or dried gourds filled with seeds. Puppets large and small entertained the crowd. Some were doll sized, telling stories from a movable stage on a cart. Others were child sized, suspended by strings.

Still others towered above their handlers, worked by a clever series of pulleys and wands. Food vendors offered every type of repast imaginable from stalls and carts along the street, while ale, wine, and stronger spirits sold at a brisk pace from taverns as well as from barrels on the backs of wagons.

"How are we ever going to spot the Durim in this mess?" Jonmarc murmured to Gellyr.

"If they're clever enough to leave their black robes behind, they could be anywhere," Gellyr replied. "We'll see what my wife's uncle, the general, has to say. Maybe he'll have a good idea."

They made their way slowly through the press of the crowd. Berry and Aidane were in the middle, with their traveling cloaks drawn up around them to avoid attention. Jonmarc, Gellyr, and the soldiers formed a knot around them, but even so, Jonmarc's hand never strayed far from the pommel of his sword. As they followed the road uphill, toward the palace, the crowds thinned out. They rounded a bend, and Lienholt Palace came into view, lit by torches and a bonfire in the bailey.

Berry caught her breath. A gray flag of mourning flew from the palace's highest tower. In stark contrast to the colorful banners in the city below, gray banners flew from every window and post. As they neared the gates, Jonmarc could see that a large wreath made of dry vines had been placed above the archway, signifying that there had been a death. Principality City might be going about its festival as usual, but it was clear that the palace was in mourning.

Jonmarc and Gellyr flanked Berry as she rode forward, dropping her hood. The gate guards bowed low, and the captain of the guards came out to greet them.

"Your Majesty," he said, making a deep bow. "We were expecting you. You must be tired from your journey. Everything is ready for you."

The large wooden outer gates creaked open. Jonmarc stole a glance at Berry as they entered. Her face was stoic, but her eyes were filled with grief. As the massive gate shut behind them, Jonmarc and Gellyr looked around, scanning for danger. Jonmarc had been a guest of Staden's for nearly six months when Tris was preparing for his return to Margolan. He'd gotten to know the palace well. Now, he planned to use that familiarity to protect Berry.

Servants ran to take their horses. Jonmarc and Gellyr stayed beside Berry, while Kolin, Laisren, and Aidane came behind them with Anton and Serg, and Gellyr's soldiers walked ahead and behind. A man in his middle years was striding down the palace steps toward them, and Jonmarc recognized him as Jencin, Staden's seneschal. He looked exhausted, and his face was drawn.

"Your Majesty," he said and greeted Berry with a hurried bow, as if he was reminding himself about her recent change from princess to queen. "It's so good to have you home again, although I wish it were under other circumstances."

Berry's gaze strayed past Jencin, to a scorched mark on the cobblestones of the bailey courtyard where Staden's pyre would have been. "Me, too, Jencin. Me, too." She collected herself, and her features slipped into regal neutrality. Jonmarc began to wonder if it was something royals practiced from birth. "You remember Jonmarc Vahanian, my Champion, and Captain Gellyr?"

Jencin smiled. "Of course. I'm glad your ride was a safe one."

Jonmarc nodded. "So far." Jencin looked at him as if he suspected there was a story behind the comment, but he said nothing as Berry continued with the introductions.

"Kolin and Laisren are emissaries of the Blood Council," Berry said with a nod. Both men inclined their heads in greeting. "And Anton and Serg represent the *vyrkin* packs. Aidane is the liaison for the dead," Berry said with a totally straight face. Aidane swallowed wrong and began to cough; Jonmarc suspected she was utterly unprepared to be introduced as a visiting diplomat.

"M'lady, do you think it wise—"

"I do, or I wouldn't have brought them." Berry's voice was sharp. She might have left Principality City as a girl, but she was returning as a queen, and as fond as Jonmarc knew she was of Jencin, old roles had to change. "I am queen of Principality, the living, dead, and undead. These are difficult times. If we expect the allegiance of all our subjects, then we must recognize and reward their fealty."

"Of course, Your Majesty."

Jencin led them into the palace. The servants they passed made low bows, welcoming Berry. Jonmarc watched as she swept by them, acknowledging them and thanking them. He wondered how many of them could see the strain in her face, the effort it was taking for Berry to return home, knowing that Staden was gone forever.

Jonmarc had had a chance to brief Berry before they arrived on the plan he and Gellyr had concocted, and she had agreed with him. Best not to start off her reign by forcing the military into something, even if she turned out to be right. They'd see if Gellyr's uncle would act as a go-between with Hant. If not, Berry would take the issue to Hant herself. "The festival was well attended when we rode through," Berry commented.

"Yes, m'lady. We didn't think it wise to cancel festivities, even with your father's passing. Such energy needs a release." Jencin looked nervous, and Jonmarc wondered if the seneschal was fully prepared for Berry's sudden return.

Berry gave a sad smile. "Father would never have stood for the festival being changed. It was one of his favorites. Better to remember how well he loved a feast."

"That he did, m'lady, better than anyone."

"Still," Berry said, pausing as if the idea was only just occurring to her, "it might do to have more guards about, to keep the peace."

"M'lady?"

"I'm not yet formally crowned. As the *vyrkin* say, the most dangerous time is between what was and what will be. It might tempt some revelers to get out of hand, knowing that Father is gone."

Jencin gave her a look that said he suspected there was more to it, but he did not question. "A wise observation, m'lady. I'll notify the guards and ask for additional men. I'll request that they remain vigilant but not heavy-handed."

Berry nodded. "Thank you."

They had moved out of the public areas of the palace and into the private rooms. As they walked, Jencin assigned the visitors to their rooms with Aidane's quarters on one side of Berry's rooms and Jonmarc's on the other. "As for the *vayash moru*, I can open the crypts in the cellars. You won't be disturbed." Jencin glanced from Kolin to Laisren. "And for meals, am I correct that deer or goat blood is acceptable?"

"Yes, thank you."

Jencin looked relieved, and Jonmarc suppressed a smile. "The *vyrkin* will be quite happy with meat, so the deer and goat will be appreciated," Jonmarc said, with a nod in the direction of Anton and Serg. "Tell the kitchen not to bother cooking it."

Jencin glanced at the *vyrkin*. His hand fluttered a bit at his side, but he controlled his nervousness. "Absolutely. I'll see to it right away."

"Jencin, what are the coronation plans?" It was Berry who spoke, and Jonmarc could see in her eyes the strain of maintaining her composure.

Jencin's voice softened as he turned to her. "We're all agreed that soonest is best. Your father left some unfinished business that can't wait. Now that you're here, I'll convene the nobles at the tenth bells. You'll find the robes of office in your room. I've taken the liberty of choosing a coronation gown. I hope it's to your liking."

Berry nodded, as if the selection of a dress was the furthest thing from her mind. "We'll have the ceremony here at the palace," Jencin continued, "to make it official with the nobles and the heads of the merchant guilds. Then tomorrow night, the custom is for the new monarch to journey to the Lover's Temple to receive the crown from the Sacred Vessels and perhaps receive a blessing from the Lady. In this case, falling on the Feast of the Departed, we'll go to the dais in the city for you to make your offering and hear the prophecy."

Having the Black Robes disrupt the festival is bad enough. Having them endanger the new queen makes this a whole new game. Jonmarc looked at Gellyr, and from the look on the captain's face, Jonmarc guessed Gellyr was thinking the same thing.

"Is it really necessary? I mean, the part about going out to the dais in the middle of the festival?" Berry's voice suddenly sounded fatigued, and while Jonmarc was sure that some of it was real, he was aware of just how good an actress Berry could be when necessary. He was betting she'd realized the danger as well.

"Without it, you haven't fulfilled the requirements of coronation, Your Majesty," Jencin said apologetically. "I can only guess how much strain you're under, especially after your ride. But we must do everything correctly, to avoid a challenge."

Berry nodded. "I'm just not in a festival mood this year. You understand, I'm sure."

"Of course, m'lady."

"With the queen's permission," Gellyr said, clearing his

throat, "I have some duties to attend to and some things to arrange."

"Yes, please," Berry replied. Jonmarc knew Gellyr went to send a message to his uncle to arrange a meeting after the coronation.

"I've had servants draw baths for you, to refresh you after your ride," Jencin said with a glance to Jonmarc and the others. "You'll also find food and drink in your rooms." He looked to Jonmarc. "As Queen's Champion, you'll have a role in the ceremony. I remember that you had a fondness for wearing your sword even in the presence of the king," he said with the barest trace of a smile. "That won't be a problem."

"Good, because I'm wearing it anyhow."

The candlemarks passed quickly, and tenth bells found a group of twenty people convened for the coronation. Some of the nobles looked vaguely familiar from his stay in the Principality court, but Jonmarc could not put names with the faces. He fervently hoped that the nobles would defer to Berry and that he would have no reason to get to know any of the nobility better. In his experience, the only reason for one of the Council of Nobles to come to his attention would be if they caused a problem. They had enough problems with the Black Robes.

Jencin led the procession into the room. All the waiting guests stood. Berry followed Jencin, looking regal in her elegant gown of Mussa silk. Her elaborate royal robes were covered with Noorish embroidery that seemed to move and shift. Berry wore the gold circlet that she had received in Dark Haven. Jonmarc followed in the procession, wearing all black, as he preferred when forced to be at court. Gellyr and three other guards followed, and while they were in their dress uniforms, Jonmarc noticed that they were all well armed. His hand rested on the pommel of his sword, making him feel ever-so-slightly more at ease. The doors shut behind them.

Berry had given Jonmarc some insight into the audience. Eight of the guests were seated in the front row. Jonmarc was sure that meant they were the Council of Nobles. Aside from the fact that each one was dressed in enough lace, velvet, and brocade to cost a master craftsman a full year's wage, Jonmarc saw nothing remarkable or memorable. They were unarmed, and they looked slightly bored. Behind them were five more finely dressed men and women, Staden's favorites among the lesser nobility, lords and ladies whose loyalty and allegiance were as certain as their friendship with the late king. These guests appeared to be more interested in the proceedings, although once again, aside from their obvious affluence, nothing marked them as a threat or worthy of notice in Jonmarc's mind.

Six prosperous-looking merchants sat behind them, and Jonmarc noticed with a smile that one of the merchants was quite probably the head of the Whores Guild. She was a blonde woman with a figure to rival Jolie's and, like Jolie, was in her middle years, although a casual glance might have said otherwise. Her dress was expensive and revealing, and her jewelry attested to a wealthy clientele. Beside her sat a man with a scarred face who was dressed in leather armor but lacking his weapons; obviously, the Master of the Mercenary Guild. The portly man next to him wore rings set with large gemstones, stones also glittered from a pendant at his chest. Gem mining was the main industry in Principality, and the reason it had been carved out as its own territory centuries ago by agreement of the other six kingdoms, to stop the endless battling over its precious resources. The Gem Master looked wary and uncomfortable.

The head of the Brewers Guild was a thin man who looked more like an exchequer than an ale master. To his right was the Merchant Guild master, a man Jonmarc knew was in the pay of Maynard Linton. It didn't guarantee his friendship, but it would keep him from siding against them in a dispute. The head of the Smiths Guild was a strongly built man. Although Jonmarc did not doubt that he had cleaned up before the event, telltale soot still lingered beneath his nails.

To Jonmarc's surprise, Sister Landis, head of the Citadel of the Sisterhood in Principality City, sat apart from the others. He'd glimpsed her at court, and Carina and Tris had told him quite a bit about her after Tris had trained for months at the Citadel. Taru had added her own comments. Jonmarc remembered that Landis had been cool to the idea of training Tris even though the crown of Margolan was at stake. Landis was in her seventh decade, with short gray hair and a determined expression. *Would the witch biddies really stand by and let the Black Robes bring about a War of Unmaking?* He met Landis's cool blue eyes, and decided that he didn't want to bet money on the answer.

Kolin and Laisren sat behind the guild masters, along with Anton and Serg. They were dressed in somber finery and looked to be the noble equals of the Council. Aidane sat beside Kolin. To Jonmarc's surprise, Jolie had acquired a traditional *serroquette*'s gown for Aidane. Dressed in the colors of flame, Aidane's dark complexion was set off to its exotic best. Her black hair was loose, with golden combs. A river of fine gold strands seemed to nearly fill the deep-cut bodice of the gown, and gold bracelets on each arm attested to a position of status and wealth. *Jolie never misses a trick, does she?* Jonmarc thought and smiled to himself. The head of the Whores Guild had definitely noticed Aidane, and the look was both intrigued and hostile. *I'm going to guess there aren't a lot of serroquettes in Principality City. She's probably worried Aidane will be a competitor.*

Jencin cleared his throat. "We're gathered here to crown Berwyn, daughter of Staden, as the new Queen of Principality," he said in his most formal manner. He made a gesture that indicated that the guests should take their seats. "Since she has already received a field coronation upon the news of the king's death, she wears the circlet. Today, she receives Staden's crown, forged for King Vanderon, father of Aesille, father of the late king."

Jencin removed a velvet cloth that covered a carved wooden box that stood on a pedestal in the center of the room. Next to the pedestal was a cushioned kneeling rail. The cushion was a deep red velvet, and the crest of the House of Principality was worked into the finely wrought support for the gold railing.

"If you please, Your Majesty," Jencin said, with a fluid gesture motioning for Berry to kneel.

Berry took a deep breath and made the sign of the Lady, and then knelt. She removed the circlet and gave it to Jencin, who put it into the box.

"With this crown, I accept the throne of Principality. I will be the guardian of all its residents, living, dead, and undead. I will keep the covenants my fathers have made with the guilds, especially the Mercenary Guild, that protect our lands. I will honor the treaties with our allies, and so far as it is in my power, I will strive to live at peace with those countries with whom we are not allied." Berry's voice was clear and strong as she recited the vows, but Jonmarc could see tears glistening, unshed, in her eyes. "I will preserve the sovereignty of Principality and defend it with my life. Before the Sacred Lady in all her Aspects, I make these vows."

Berry accepted the ornate crown from Jencin and turned it, feeling for a hidden clasp. A small, sharp point sprang from behind a gemstone, and Berry took another deep breath and then pressed the palm of her right hand against the point. She winced, and when she withdrew her hand, a few drops of blood ran down her palm. Berry turned the crown so that the large gemstone on the front faced her, and she covered the stone with her bloody palm. The crown seemed to glow in her hands, and the elaborate symbols on her cloak swirled, making it clear that their movement was not a trick of the imagination.

The temperature in the room plummeted. Jonmarc saw Aidane grip Kolin's arm, her eyes wide. A glowing mist began to form between the kneeling rail and the audience, and Jonmarc's hand gripped the pommel of his sword, although he doubted it would be of use against a spectral foe. As they watched, forms took shape in the mist, growing more solid and identifiable.

The figures of three men stood in front of Berry, and behind them, more shapes were obscured by the mist. Two of the men Jonmarc did not recognize, but the third he knew well. Staden.

"I am King Vanderon, your great-grandfather, and in my time, ruler of all Principality," the first ghost said, his voice clear and strong. Vanderon laid his ghostly hand on Berry's shoulder, and Jonmarc could see her repress a shiver.

"I am Aesille, your grandfather, also King of Principality, like my father and forefathers." He laid a hand on Berry's other shoulder.

Berry's eyes were fixed on only one of the ghosts. Staden's spirit came to stand before her, and his eyes were sad, although he managed to smile. "My daughter," he said, taking the hand Berry held out to him. She did not try to hide the tears streaming down her face. "How I wish that I did not have to leave you in such troubled times. This burden should not have fallen to you for many years." He shrugged. "But our days are in the Lady's hand. I will miss you, my dear."

"I'll miss you, too," Berry managed to whisper.

Staden's ghost placed a hand on Berry's head. Jonmarc guessed it was the touch of blood that activated the crown's magic, enabling the spirits to be seen and heard, and he wondered if it worked as well at coronations that were not on the eve of the Feast of the Departed.

"The blood of the monarchs of Principality runs in your veins," Staden said. "You're our flesh, our bone, our breath. Let there be no doubt that you are the rightful ruler of Principality. You are Berwyn, Queen of Principality. May the Sacred Lady smile upon your rule and give you long life, good health, and a peaceful and prosperous reign."

As Berry looked up at Staden's ghost with tear-filled eyes, the three specters began to dissipate. A moment later, the mist and the ghosts were gone. Jonmarc glanced at Jencin, trying to decide whether the seneschal had expected the ghostly visitors. Jencin did not seem to be as amazed as their audience, and Jonmarc wondered whether Jencin had actually seen something similar at Staden's coronation, or merely read about the possibility. From the nervous way Jencin handled the wooden box, Jonmarc guessed it was the latter.

"All hail Berwyn of Principality. Long live the queen!"

Berry stood, and once again, the onlookers lined up to make their vows of loyalty. Jonmarc was first, and he gave Berry's hand a reassuring squeeze as he took it to press her signet ring to his lips. She returned the squeeze, and the look in her eyes told him silently that she appreciated his presence even more than he might have suspected. Jencin followed, then Gellyr, and then the rest of the guests.

Aidane was the last to pledge her fealty. Jonmarc heard a low buzz of conversation as the nobles and merchants remarked on the newcomer. He could tell that Aidane was nervous, but she walked forward with assurance and knelt gracefully in front of Berry. She looked up at Berry and took her hand.

"What gifts I have, I offer you, for the protection of your kingdom," Aidane whispered. A flash of understanding seemed to pass between Aidane and Berry, although what the others made of Aidane's pledge, Jonmarc could only guess.

"I accept your pledge," Berry said, and clasped Aidane's hand with both of her own for a moment. A murmur spread through the nobles and guild masters, but Berry did not look up.

Let them think what they want to, Jonmarc thought. *Right now, Aidane just might be the key to saving Berry's life, and the Winter Kingdoms.*

It was after midnight when Jonmarc, Gellyr, and Aidane slipped through the palace gates without fanfare. Aidane wore a traveling cloak that covered both her dress and her head, sparing them the glances of curious passersby. Gellyr led the way as they left the palace walls behind them and wound through the cobblestone streets to the grand homes and villas of the wealthy and powerful.

"Are you sure he's still awake? The coronation took longer than I expected." Jonmarc looked around the alleyway cautiously.

Gellyr nodded, and pointed to the lit downstairs windows of the home in front of them. "He's awake."

As was the fashion, the house had its own outer wall around a small courtyard and an iron gate with a guard. Gellyr spoke to the guard, who opened the gate for them. Jonmarc looked around at the garden with its fountain and benches. If this was a general's home, then he had been successful by any standards.

The polished wooden door to the home opened, and the shadow of a broad-shouldered man stood in the entranceway. Jonmarc turned to look at their host, and froze.

"By the Crone's tits! Is that you, Jonmarc?"

Gellyr turned to look at Jonmarc. It took Jonmarc a moment to find his voice, but then he smiled broadly.

"Valjan! So this is what becomes of an old War Dog!"

Gellyr and Jonmarc were welcomed into the house with backslaps and embraces. "Dark Lady take my soul! I'd heard that you'd been at the palace with Martris Drayke last year, but I was leading a patrol out on the western border, and I didn't get back until after you'd gone. They told me Staden made a lord of you, and gave you the biters' refuge in Dark Haven."

Valjan was half a hand taller than Jonmarc and twenty years older. He wore a patch over one eye, and Jonmarc knew Valjan had lost that eye to a raider long before Jonmarc had joined his merc group. Although he was dressed informally in trews and tunic, the cut of his clothing and its cloth further attested to his success. He was tanned from years out of doors, and his arms and face carried the scars that marked him as a military man every bit as much as his stance marked him as a fighter.

"Lady Bright! It's true then? You're the Queen's Champion?"

Jonmarc chuckled. "It's true, all of it, although I doubt Staden expected it to come to this when he made me his liegeman."

Valjan brought a hand down on his shoulder, and he was still strong enough to have knocked Jonmarc off balance if he hadn't braced for it. "Gellyr told me you had information, a source who says we're in for trouble." He looked toward Aidane, who had still not removed her hood. "This is your source?"

Jonmarc nodded.

Valjan drew them into a sitting room. To Jonmarc's surprise, Hant was already seated there, along with one man Jonmarc had seen at the coronation, the head of the Mercenary Guild. "I took the liberty of asking them to join us, as they may have a stake in what's afoot."

"Hello again, Jonmarc." It was Hant who spoke, and a half smile crossed his thin features. His small, intense eyes seemed to look through the visitors as if he could see their bones. Staden might have considered his head of security as his "chief rat catcher," but Jonmarc knew that for a spymaster to live to be Hant's age, he must be very, very good at his job.

"Hello, Hant."

"This is Exeter, head of the Mercenary Guild," Valjan introduced the man who sat next to Hant.

"You don't remember me, I wager, but I knew of you when you were a merc," Exeter said, with a glance that seemed to appraise Jonmarc head to toe. "I heard about Chauvrenne and Nargi. Your friend, Harrtuck, rode with us to the Margolan border when Martris Drayke took back his throne." A dangerous smile crossed Exeter's face. "If you recall, we were insurance, in case something went wrong."

"I remember."

"My nephew says that your source might not get a fair hearing from some at the palace," Valjan said with a shrewd look toward Gellyr. "Let's see what you've got."

At Jonmarc's nod, Aidane lowered her hood and set her cloak aside. She was still dressed from the coronation, and it was clear from the reaction of the three men that they knew immediately what she was.

"*Serroquette*," Exeter murmured, but Jonmarc could not tell whether it was recognition or a curse.

"Aidane is a true *serroquette*," Jonmarc said. "We've proven her ability to channel spirits, and we've tested her messages. Her power is real. She's harboring the spirit of a *vayash moru* named Thaine, who was murdered by the Black Robes. While Thaine was a prisoner of the Durim, she overheard their plans. I'd like Thaine to tell you for herself."

At Jonmarc's nod, Aidane closed her eyes. She took a deep breath and let her head fall back. Her whole body trembled, and she startled, eyes wide, with a sharp inhale. As they watched, everything about Aidane's manner changed, until Jonmarc knew before she spoke that it was Thaine, and not Aidane, who stood before them.

Jonmarc and Gellyr watched the men's reaction as Thaine told her story. Hant leaned forward, tenting his fingers, his lips pursed. Exeter's arms were crossed and his face had a hard set to it. The eye patch made his expression difficult to read. Valjan's frown grew deeper as he listened, and his face colored with anger. When Thaine finished her tale, Valjan rose to his feet.

"On Chenne's sword! If they mean to move on Haunts, it's tomorrow night."

Exeter had not unfolded his arms. He had not moved at all. "How do we know she's telling the truth?"

Jonmarc and Gellyr exchanged knowing glances. Aidane moved forward, and her expression and bearing shifted, letting Jonmarc know she was herself again. She concentrated for a moment, as if listening to voices they could not hear. Then she met Exeter's eyes unflinchingly.

"You lost a lover when you were eighteen, before you ever thought to become a merc. She died in a house just beyond the city walls, trying to bear your child. She died cursing your name. Her parents cast her out because of the baby, and your parents withdrew your birthright. You were alone with her when she miscarried, when she bled to death on the floor. Would you have me bring her to you now? Do you remember Bellajera?"

Exeter had gone pale. "No. No, I believe you." He took a shaky breath and pulled himself together. "I believe." He was quiet for a moment, and then he looked up at the others. "Gentlemen, we have a very large problem."

It was third bells before Jonmarc and the others returned to the palace. Come morning, Hant and Valjan would take the news to the other generals, hiding Aidane's identity as the source. Exeter also vowed to have his mercs among the feast day crowds, watching for signs of danger amid the throng. Gellyr had delivered the letters of introduction Sister Taru sent with them, and Jonmarc fervently hoped that there would be some word awaiting him back at the palace. They were too tired to sleep, and too exhausted to function, but they headed back to the palace knowing that they had done everything possible to guard against the Durim's attack.

"That went reasonably well," Gellyr remarked.

Jonmarc sighed. "Considering that they didn't throw us out, laugh in our faces, or pack us off to the madhouse, yeah, I'd say so."

"Tomorrow, once I've rested, I'll see what the spirits can tell me," Aidane said quietly.

Jonmarc gave her a sideways glance. "Can you do that? I mean, with Thaine already in there?"

"Being possessed by more than one spirit at a time isn't comfortable, but I've done it before." A shadow crossed her face, giving Jonmarc the idea that "not comfortable" was an understatement. "What choice do we have? If the Black Robes are in the city, then they may have done some killing. Their victims might want revenge." Her eyes became distant. "So many ghosts, calling. Oh, yes. Fresh kills." She began to shake her head. "Buka. Buka."

Gellyr came to a dead stop, with a look of horror on his face. "Buka," he whispered.

Jonmarc looked at him warily. "What did you say?"

Gellyr shook his head as if to clear it. "Sweet Chenne, I don't know why I didn't see it before. What Aidane just said about the Durim killing here in the city. She's right."

They were nearly at the palace walls. Gellyr indicated for them to get inside the palace before he finished. "I'd had some word of it before we came back to Principality City, from the couriers who came to Jannistorp, and the letters my men got from home. There's a murderer loose in Principality City. He's a slippery one. I'm ashamed to say it, but since he tends to prey on cutpurses, drunks, and the absinthe strumpets, it hasn't gotten an all-out manhunt. They call him Buka. It's a lowlands term for 'slayer.'" Gellyr shook his head. "He's a butcher, that's what he is. Make a career in the ranks, and you see a few of that type. I thought he was just a madman. But now—"

"Either it's an amazing coincidence, or he's working with the Black Robes," Jonmarc finished. "Maybe even part of the Durim themselves."

Aidane's eyes were haunted. "We knew that kind in Nargi. Not long before I was captured, there was a killer loose there as well. I lived among those cutpurses, drunks, and absinthe trollops," she said, quietly reproachful. "Sometimes the whole bodies would show up; other times, only pieces." She shivered and wrapped her arms around herself. "No one looks too hard when they think the killer is only hunting vermin." Her voice was soft, but there was a note of hurt in it, and the last word stung.

Gellyr swallowed hard. "Apologies, m'lady. 'Tis too easy, sometimes, to forget that the victims were people." He took a deep breath. "I knew about the problems in Dark Haven, but I never put the two together." He shook his head. "I know we're running out of time, but we all need to get some sleep if we're to fight tomorrow. If Aidane can manage it, I'd like to find out anything we can from Buka's victims. It may give us a clue about the Durim's plans for the festival, or at least we might get a break in trying to catch the bastard."

"I'll help if I can," Aidane said. Jonmarc could hear the strain in her voice. He knew from the time he'd spent with Tris Drayke how much of a toll magic took, and while Aidane's gift might be slightly different, he bet it came with a cost.

"We're no good to anyone if we're too tired to move," Jonmarc said. "Let's get some sleep."

The next morning, Jencin knocked on Jonmarc's door. "You've got visitors."

Jonmarc dressed quickly and stepped into the hallway, where Gellyr was just closing the door to his room. He looked at Gellyr, who shrugged. "I'm not expecting anyone," Gellyr said. "Are you?"

"Who are they?" Jonmarc asked as Jencin walked with them down the corridor.

"Mages, by the look of them. Said you'd called for them." His tone clearly gave Jonmarc to know that a warning would have been appreciated.

"Sorry for not mentioning it, but I had no idea they'd show up this quickly," Jonmarc said. He glanced at Gellyr. "Looks like your messages got through."

Jonmarc followed Jencin into a parlor off the main corridor. He was surprised to see a dozen people waiting for him. Some of them dozed in chairs or on the floor, while others looked up from where they had been talking in low tones. All wore mage robes. One of the men rose and started toward the door to greet them. He looked to be in his third decade, with reddish-blond hair that fell to his shoulders. His eyebrows were almost white, and he was clean-shaven.

"Lord Vahanian?" The mage looked from Jonmarc to Gellyr. "Are you Rigel?"

The mage smiled. "I see Taru mentioned me. She's well, I hope?"

Jonmarc nodded. "Very well. I'll give her your greeting. You've brought friends?"

Rigel swept his arm in a gesture to include the others in the room. "Landis wouldn't approve of our being here. Some of us have already left the Sisterhood; others were planning to do so sooner rather than later. We don't agree with Landis's notion that mages should lock themselves in a tower and refuse to use their magic to help."

"I never thought I'd be so happy to see a room full of mages, but you're a welcome sight," Jonmarc said. Two servants entered the room, bearing trays of bread, cheese, and sausage and a large kettle of *kerif.* One of the servants brought Jonmarc a cup of *kerif*, and Gellyr also accepted one. They sat down as the mages grouped themselves into a circle. Rigel made introductions, but Jonmarc was tired enough that the names didn't stick in his mind. He paid attention to the color of their robes. Rigel's robes were light blue, and he remembered that Taru said that Rigel was an air mage. Not quite the powers of a summoner, but magic that was closer than any other type. He spotted a couple of green robes, indicating healers. Nice to have in a fight. Light brown robes usually meant a land mage. There were three of them. Tired as he was, Jonmarc began to smile when he saw six mages with dark blue robes. Water mages would come in handy if they faced an enemy from across the Northern Sea. The twelfth man wore red robes, and Jonmarc frowned. Fire mages were trouble.

Rigel seemed to follow his gaze, and guessed his thinking. "That's Tevin. He's a fire mage."

Jonmarc's eyes narrowed. "The last fire mage I met was Foor Arontala. It wasn't a good experience."

Tevin seemed to wince at the name. He was very pale, with lank, straw-blond hair. He might have been anywhere from seventeen to just under thirty. Jonmarc bet he was older than he looked. Tevin didn't look up, and he spoke just above a whisper. "We're not all like that. We choose what we are." His voice was quiet, but when he looked up to meet Jonmarc's gaze, Tevin's eyes were determined. Jonmarc guessed that he wasn't the first to question Tevin's integrity, or the first to suspect a fire mage's motives.

"We've got trouble at the festival," Jonmarc said. "If you've got the stomach for a fight, it looks like there's more bad news coming from across the Northern Sea. Help us, and I'll ask the queen to find patrons who'll take you out of Landis's reach."

Rigel was silent, looking from face to face, and Jonmarc wondered if he had the ability to mind speak with the other mages. Finally, he met Jonmarc's eyes and nodded. "You have yourself some mages. There're more coming. They couldn't be here this morning, but they should arrive before the festival begins." He smiled then, a look that seemed to anticipate the danger and accepted the risks. There was a glint in his eyes that told Jonmarc that Rigel knew what they were signing on for, knew before they set foot in Lienholt Palace.

"All right then," Jonmarc said, setting his empty cup aside. "Let's get started."

22

Later that day, just before tenth bells in the evening, Berry's procession left the palace to head for the festival. Despite all their preparations, Jonmarc still didn't feel confident that the ceremony would finish without incident. Thanks to Hant and Valjan, Jonmarc knew that the number of soldiers who were visible in their uniforms was only a fraction of the number of their men who were dressed as festival-goers throughout the crowd. Rigel and Tevin rode with the queen's entourage. The others had dispersed into the crowd, without the robes that marked them as mages, indistinguishable from the celebrants. They, too, would watch for trouble, using their magic. Kolin and Laisren had agreed to meet them near the dais. Anton and Serg were already in position. Jonmarc hoped that the heightened senses of the *vayash moru* and *vyrkin* would pick up some clue before the Black Robes made their move.

Aidane also rode with the queen's party. Unlike their entry into Principality City, when she hid her *serroquette*'s outfit with a traveling cloak, Aidane seemed to flaunt her status. Whether it was bravado or she knew that here at Haunts a *serroquette* would be welcome and not reviled, Jonmarc couldn't say. She had a determined look, and if he watched, her expression changed so that he guessed that she was alternating with Thaine to scan the crowd as they passed.

"Smile," Berry whispered as Jonmarc rode next to her. "This is supposed to be a celebration."

"I don't feel like smiling."

Berry chuckled, but the humor didn't reach her eyes. She patted the folds of her skirt. "I have both sets of knives Carroway gave me. Spent a candlemark last night practicing. It's good for the nerves."

"I wish we'd had more time. For all we know, the Durim have been planning whatever they're going to do for months." As he spoke, Jonmarc scanned the crowd, but all he saw were drunken revelers. He'd told the others to watch for people who didn't seem intoxicated, who weren't doing their best to get laid or score a free drink. If anything, this year's Haunts seemed to be more out of control than Jonmarc remembered it to be, as if the news of plague and the rumors of war had convinced people to live it up while they still had time.

"You know, I've had more complaints from the constables this year than ever before," Gellyr murmured, echoing Jonmarc's thoughts. "It's been like a weeklong drunken binge, and even by Haunts standards, 'orgy' seems too mild a word."

"Back when we were mercs, Valjan's motto was 'Drink it, eat it, win it, and bed it, because tomorrow you die.' In a business where most people didn't live to see thirty seasons, I'd say it was taken to heart."

"Indeed. Although I don't think everyone here is a merc."

Jonmarc shrugged. "If there were a year that would convince people to make the most of it while they're still breathing, I'd say it's the year we've just lived through. Or at least, it's an excuse to get their minds off it."

They reached the dais without incident. Soldiers in palace livery stood shoulder to shoulder along the pathway through the crowd and lined the edge of the raised platform. Behind the dais and creating a semicircle around the center of the crowd were the eight straw effigies of the Aspects of the Sacred Lady. Each effigy stood as broad as a tall man and four times as high, made of straw over a frame of wood.

At midnight on Haunts, the effigies would be lit and the revelry would reach its frenzied peak. A child conceived near midnight on Haunts was considered to be especially fortunate and said to be fated for wealth and happiness. Jonmarc noticed that more women in the crowd than usual appeared to be very near term, and he fought down a stab of loneliness, missing Carina. Beyond the dais, the white tents of the Temple Companions had long lines of both men and women, waiting to seal their good fortune for the next year by coupling with the Companions. They were going to have a busy night. Throughout the crowd, bead-draped revelers sang, hooted, and danced, and the smell of ale, wine, and stronger drink hung as heavy in the air as the incense of the Sacred Vessels. Local legend said that anyone too drunk to remember midnight on Haunts would be blessed by having their troubles erased like their memories of the evening. By the look of it, most of the crowd had a lot they wanted to forget.

Jonmarc turned his attention to the dais. Eight white pillars were draped with swags of fabric. In front of each pillar was a statue to one of the faces of the Lady, and at the foot of each statue, a brazier glowing with incense. Smaller braziers ringed the large common area, and the wood for a huge bonfire was stacked, ready to be lit at midnight. Prayers, requests, and thank-yous to the Lady could be written on scraps of wood or cloth and tossed into the braziers or into the central bonfire, and it was said that the sparks would carry the messages to the Lady Herself.

Eight women were already standing on the dais, and Jonmarc

knew they were the Sacred Vessels, seers, oracles, and rune scryers who had dedicated themselves to the worship of the Lady, especially the favored Aspects of Principality: the Lover and Whore. At the moment, they wore loose white robes. Before the night was through, they would shed the robes to make their predictions sky-clad. Tonight, with the unusual circumstances of a feast night coronation, Berry would join them on the dais. Their predictions were expected to be focused more than usual on the fortunes of the new queen, and Jencin had told him that it was not unheard of for the spirit of the Lady to fall upon the newly crowned monarch with visions and prophecies. Such an occurrence was considered to be a very good omen. Jonmarc found the prospect unsettling.

Even with the guards, the crowd seemed too close, now that they knew the Durim were among them. Jonmarc scanned the crowd, but nothing seemed amiss. Still, his gut feeling warned him that something was very wrong.

When they reached the dais, Jonmarc helped Berry down from her horse, while Gellyr assisted Aidane. Jonmarc knew for a fact that Berry could have swung down on her own, but an unaided dismount would not convey the proper queenly reserve. As they had hurriedly arranged ahead of time, Berry held out her hand to Aidane, asking Aidane to accompany her to make the sacrifices that protocol demanded. Soldiers weren't allowed on the dais, so having Jonmarc attend her wasn't an option, and they had all agreed that Thaine would be in the best position to search for enemies, seeing through Aidane's eyes if Aidane were on the dais with Berry.

The crowd murmured when they realized that Berry had chosen a *serroquette* as her attendant. Although there were plenty of whores, concubines, consorts, and plain old strumpets in Principality, real *serroquette*s were rare, and even more rarely seen in the company of a monarch. If the attention bothered

Aidane, she didn't show it, and then Jonmarc realized from her walk that it was Thaine in charge. He smiled despite himself. Thaine would have loved the show.

"I don't like them up there by themselves," Gellyr murmured just loud enough for Jonmarc to hear.

"Agreed. Let's hope it's worth the risk."

Jonmarc thought he had caught a glimpse of Kolin in the crowd, but the press of people was too heavy for him to be certain. It was nearly too crowded for him to be able to draw his sword without injuring a bystander. He flexed his fingers just above the pommel of his sword. *I'd much rather start a fight than stand around waiting to get hit.*

Berry moved with a gracefulness she rarely showed as her tomboy self. If Jencin could see her, Jonmarc knew the seneschal would be both proud of her bearing and astounded that the lessons that had seemed to go unheeded had actually sunk in. Beside her, Aidane was doing her best to scan the crowd, even as she carried the basket with the gifts Berry brought to present to each of the Aspects.

The Sacred Vessels greeted Berry, but did not bow. "Your Majesty," said one of the robed figures. With their cowls raised, all of the Sacred Vessels looked alike. "Have you come to make your coronation gifts to the Lady?"

"I have."

"She awaits. May the Sacred Lady, in all of Her faces, look on you and your reign with favor, and may your life and reign be prosperous."

Berry inclined her head, slightly, in acceptance of the blessing. The Sacred Vessels stepped aside for Berry to approach the statues and their glowing braziers. Aidane followed her, carrying the ornate basket of offerings.

Berry bowed to the statue of the Lover first, and took a flagon of wine from the basket. "My Lady, Lover of your children, grant us peace and prosperity." She poured out the wine onto the feet of the statue and she dropped a handful of rose petals into the brazier.

Then she moved to the statue of Athira, the Whore. "Athira, most generous in your favors, give increase to our crops and herds, and to our people. Make our children fat and our women fertile." She withdrew a bunch of plump, ripe grapes and laid them at the statue's feet and she sprinkled a handful of cardamom on the brazier. The sweet, spicy smell spread on the smoke, mingling with the rose scent.

Berry moved from statue to statue in turn, making her gifts and asking for blessing. Finally, she stood in front of the statue of Istra, the Dark Lady, patron of Dark Haven's *vayash moru* and of outcasts everywhere. Against his will, Jonmarc felt himself drawn to look up at the face of the statue, and he shuddered. Amber eyed and wild, Istra was more beautiful than any of her statues. Once, when he lay close to death, he had seen that raven-haired beauty on the shores of the Gray Sea, the sea all souls must cross at the end of their days. He had bargained with Her, and She had claimed him as Her champion.

"Istra, patron of outcast souls and Those Who Walk the Night, protector of my champion, look on us with favor. You know the dangers we face. M'lady, I beg of you, make us wise to know the vipers among us."

Jonmarc felt a shiver go down his spine. He realized he was holding his breath. There was power in the air, and even though he had no magic of his own, he could feel *something*. The energy made the skin on the back of his neck prickle in warning.

When Berry had made her offerings to each of the figures, she turned and moved to the center of the dais. Aidane stepped back, her eyes scanning the crowd. The eight Sacred Vessels clustered around Berry, and the queen knelt. Each of the Sacred Vessels moved closer to lay a hand on Berry's head. They murmured together in a language Jonmarc did not recognize, and he dimly remembered hearing once that the acolytes of the Lady spoke in a tongue all their own.

Near the stage, drummers began a complicated rhythm, and flutes picked up a descant. It started slow, but increased in tempo, and the Sacred Vessels began to sway with the music, even as the crowd felt its rhythm.

The Sacred Vessels fell silent, and one of them moved away from Berry. The white-robed woman let her cowl fall back, and she shrugged out of her robe, letting it pool around her feet. She was a beautiful woman, with chestnut hair that covered her shoulders and spilled down to partly cover her breasts. Strands of red beads draped across her chest, all lengths, falling to her navel. She lifted up her arms and let her head fall back as she let the music take her.

"A prophecy for the queen. Plague will depart from Principality, but War will take its place. Blood will feed the crops of the next harvest. Blood and flesh will fatten the birds. Death and birth begin in blood."

Still possessed of the spirit of prophecy, the Sacred Vessel began to dance, caught up completely in the music that was moving faster and faster and in the pounding drumbeats. A second of the oracles stepped forward, and when her robes fell, blue beads, sacred to the Mother, covered her body in a cascade like sea water, with the torchlight glinting off the facets of hundreds of beads. "A prophecy for the queen. Alliances will be forged, and new life will replace the fallen. Night and day will become one." She joined her sister oracle in the dance as yet another of the Sacred Vessels stepped to the front.

Bright green beads and feathers festooned the oracle's nude body, like a short, fringed dress. She threw open her arms as if she would embrace the crowd, but her eyes were distant, possessed. "Hear the prophecy of the Childe. Water births and

454

water kills. From the waters comes darkness. To the waters return the souls of warriors. The future is born of water and fire."

As she joined the dance, the fourth oracle left her place by Berry. She wore a more revealing cascade of yellow beads around her neck, but bracelets of beads covered her from wrists to shoulders and belled anklets chimed as she moved. "A prophecy for the queen. Hear the vision of the Lover. Hearts break. Hearts bleed. Bury love and fear together. Reap a harvest of souls, and a hollowing of spirits. Weep for the lost ones, never to wake again. Kings will fall and crowns will rise, and the old ways will be forever changed."

The crowd, drunken as it was, had stilled despite the music that played faster and faster. Some of them were sober enough to hear the warnings in the words of the Sacred Vessels, and as much of a hush as was possible for several thousand people fell over the throng as the fifth oracle moved to the front.

Orange beads, for Chenne the Warrior, covered the prophetess. She was of mixed blood, and Jonmarc guessed she had Eastmark heritage. "Soon my horses will ride your lands, and your blood will whet my steel. Hear me, Berwyn of Principality. In the rising and the setting of the sun lies your salvation. From across the sea comes death. Look to the course of the sun."

The sixth oracle let her robes fall. She had short, chopped brown hair and white, sightless eyes. She was thin, too thin, like an animated corpse. *Vayash moru* looked far more healthy than she. Clear beads, the color of Nameless, the Formless One, did little to hide her nakedness or the bluish pallor of her skin. "I ride across your land with my Host, harvesting what belongs to me. Beware the Hollowing. My servants have heard another voice, someone who would be their master. The Night Ones wake. Dread their coming. Dread and blood come and what will remain when they have passed?"

The crowd was now nervously quiet. While the oracles danced across the stage, whirling in a frenetic motion that drove out reason and opened them to the passions of the divine, two more seers had yet to speak. Jonmarc felt a coldness in the pit of his stomach as the seventh seer revealed herself.

Beads black as night covered her, making her pale skin glow in the torchlight by comparison. Or perhaps, Jonmarc thought, the seer was *vayash moru*. The beads made the sound of rattling bones as she moved, and unlike those that adorned the other seers, these strands seemed to move on their own, followed by a blur of shadows that almost formed a misty covering for their wearer. "Hear the words of the Sinha, the Crone. My cauldron fills with blood and spirits. Shadows awaken from long slumber. Days grow short, and night remains. The battle is coming, between day and night. Dawn and sunset war with each other. In darkness lie both defeat and victory."

Jonmarc's throat tightened as the eighth seer moved forward. Berry knelt alone in the middle of the dais, surrounded by a circle of sky-clad dancers. Sweat formed a sheen on their bodies and their beads flew as they danced, making brilliant swirls of color in the torchlight. Tambourines had joined the drums and flutes, along with pipers, and it seemed as if the heartbeat of everyone in the crowd had synchronized with the music of the dance.

When the eighth oracle's white robe fell, a gasp went up from the crowd. A dark-haired woman stood at the front of the stage, covered in a cascade of blood. Jonmarc blinked, and realized that it was a trick of the light, that the wash of dark red that covered the woman was made of beads, and not blood. He felt a tingle of familiar power and knew that the Dark Lady's presence was very near. He remembered the voice he'd heard in his vision, and the amber eyes that had fixed on his as he argued for death. Perhaps others in the crowd had as clear a vision of one of the other Aspects, but for Jonmarc, it was the Dark Lady who was frighteningly real.

"Istra, protector of Those Who Walk the Night and those for whom the night holds no comfort, speaks to you, Berwyn of Principality. I give to you both blessing and curse. Your crown will be remembered forever, and until the end of the world, men will speak of the days of your rule. You do well to favor my Chosen, and my children of darkness. Remember that my strength is in the night. I am with you." Her head turned as she spoke the last words, and although he was surrounded by a mob, Jonmarc swore that the seer stared right into his eyes.

There was a hush, and Berry rose slowly to her feet. Her face was turned skyward, and her arms were open, palms up. Her eyes were closed, and while the crowd murmured at the queen's obvious possession, all Jonmarc could think was that she made a wide-open target. When she spoke, her voice was deep and raspy, like the voice of a much older woman.

"When the north sky drips with blood, soldiers rise and fight," Berry prophesied. "Only the oldest magic will prevail. When the last days come and the War of Unmaking is upon you, look to the darkness. Born of curses, raised in fire, anointed with blood, the Son of Darkness may yet prevail. Before the end, you will hone your swords with tears and temper your spears with blood."

Out of the corner of his eye, Jonmarc glimpsed movement and saw a man brandishing a knife. "Get down!" Jonmarc shouted to Berry, as he barreled onto the dais to cut off the assailant as the man vaulted onto the stage. Jonmarc collided with the man before the attacker could reach Berry, and the knife sank into his left shoulder as both he and the assassin fell to the ground. Laisren seemed to come out of nowhere, adding his strength to pull Jonmarc free and subdue the wild-eyed man whose hand and shirt were slick with Jonmarc's blood.

"Not again," Jonmarc muttered, looking at the wound.

Before they could do anything, a scream came from the back of the dais, and all eyes went to Aidane, who was standing, stiff and staring, as if some other power suspended her on strings. She was quivering, and her eyes were wide like someone taken in a fit.

The music stopped, the drumming ceased, and the Sacred Vessels turned to stare at Aidane.

"Who has your body, *serroquette*?" It was the seer for the Dark Lady who spoke.

"I am Helja, the rune speaker."

Even Jonmarc recognized the name of one of the legendary oracles of Principality, a rune speaker who had counseled the kings of Principality a century ago. Helja's wisdom was still sought with gifts and incantations by the battle mages of every merc outfit in the kingdom. Berry rose slowly to her feet, advancing a step toward Aidane with Jonmarc right behind her. "Honored spirit, thank you for your presence. What message do you bring to us?"

Helja was pleased by Berry's deference. Aidane could feel the spirit's pleasure. "I have a message for you, Berwyn of Principality."

Berry nodded soberly. "Speak. I will hear you."

"Look to the Son of Darkness, when all is lost."

"Who is the Son of Darkness?"

"Ask my children who hear the music. They will know. They can hear the Blood Stalker rising, and they know the Hollowing is near. Mad eyes watch the horizon, and they flee the call only they can hear. But they know. They know. Look to the Son of Darkness, when all is lost."

As quickly as Helja's spirit came, it departed, and Aidane staggered as the ghost left her. Thaine's spirit rushed in to fill the void with a new and urgent excitement. "Black Robes are among us," Thaine cried. She stared at a man with close-cropped brown hair who was standing in the crowd. "You're one of them." Thaine's voice was loud and certain.

One of the huge straw figures of the Aspects burst into flames. The man Thaine accused let out a shout and hurled a knife at Aidane's chest. Aidane barely dodged out of its way, crying out as the knife slashed her shoulder. As the crowd screamed and tried to flee, Aidane saw Berry's hand flick once, twice, and Aidane's attacker fell, with one of the queen's knives in his throat. Kolin dove for Aidane, taking her down to the stage. Jonmarc, still bleeding, shielded Berry from the crowd.

Aidane felt Thaine's death memories pour over her as Thaine pointed out the Black Robes disguised as revelers in the crowd. Laisren and the *vyrkin* reacted first, tackling the men Thaine identified. The crowd began to stampede toward the rear.

Amid the chaos, the Sacred Vessels had somehow gathered their robes, but they did not run. Instead, they formed a ring around where Jonmarc lay covering Berry, facing outward, peering into the crowd. Aidane felt their power, their spirits, as if they were seeking out Thaine's ghost. Thaine spotted another of the Durim in the crowd.

"Black Robe. Murderer. I see what you are." It was the voice of the seer for the Crone.

Guards barreled through the crowd to apprehend the man. Another of the straw effigies burst into flame.

The seer for the Formless One turned her blind eyes toward the flames. "There is death in the straw. Death in the straw."

Flames roared to life along the straw outline of the third effigy, and then the fourth, although it was not yet the appointed time.

The first effigy began to crumble with the ferocity of the flames that enveloped it. Mats of straw and thatching fell away, exposing the burning wooden structure underneath it. Aidane had just an instant to glimpse some kind of apparatus inside the effigy, something that intuition told her should not be there, before there came a sound like swords singing through the air on a field of battle.

A hail of solid, silver objects sailed over her head, glittering in the light of the festival torches. Screams rose from the crowd. *Blades. Someone rigged the effigies with blades.*

She dared a glance up, to see if any of the Sacred Vessels had been hurt, and to assure herself that Jonmarc and Berry were safe. She saw a ring of coruscating light, translucent, like the film of oil on water, surrounding the seers and their royal charge. In the crowd, people were screaming and crying. Aidane strained to see. Many of the people close to the first effigy lay on the ground covered with blood. Others were shrieking in shock and terror, holding motionless bodies.

"Take down those damn effigies!" The voice sounded with authority from the crowd, and Aidane recognized it as belonging to the general with the eye patch. Her vision was limited from where she lay, but she saw a red-haired man come to a standstill facing the second effigy and raise his hands in a gesture of warding just as the straw giant began to tumble.

This time, she saw it happen. The belly of the effigy burst open and a hail of objects was propelled at high speed through the air toward the crowd. The red-haired mage moved his hands slightly, and his lips formed words she did not hear. The blades dropped from the sky as if the air itself had been drawn out from beneath them, and they clattered harmlessly to the ground.

The third effigy began to sway. A woman with short dark hair ran at the toppling figure and thrust out both of her hands, palms forward, and then brought them down sharply. Water flowed out of the nearby well and a watering trough for horses and it slammed into the burning effigy, extinguishing the flames. It groaned and wobbled, and then collapsed to the ground as the crowd fled as best they could in the press, but the deadly payload inside did not discharge.

It was impossible for Aidane to tell from the crowd who was trying to flee for their lives and who was running toward the effigies to stop the carnage. With the mages and many of the soldiers out of their normal dress, she had no idea who was who. A dozen men ran at the legs of the effigy to the Crone and brought it to the ground. It crashed with a solid thud, far too heavy for a straw shell, but none of its weapons discharged.

Two more of the effigies were burning. A dark-haired man with a determined look planted himself in front of the third effigy, the figure of the Mother. He brought his open palms up from his sides in a swift gesture. A wall of dirt rose into the air high enough to reach the effigy's head, and then the full weight of the airborne ground struck the effigy, cracking its supports and toppling it as the crowd surged to outrun its falling weight.

Men Aidane assumed were soldiers were trying to keep the panicked crowd from stampeding, with only partial success, but they had cleared a swathe around the last burning effigy, the figure of Istra, the Dark Lady. A thin young man with lank, straw-blond hair stood alone in that no-man's area. He brought his hands together with a clap that sounded like thunder, and then pushed out with both palms at once, sending a stream of red fire to match the flames of the burning figure. For a moment, flame seemed to fight flame, and then the red fire won, consuming the figure in a blaze of lethal heat that singed Aidane's hair although she was a distance away. The fire mage held his ground, although his clothing began to smoke. Whatever weapons the effigy might have held inside never had the chance to discharge. One moment, the figure was intact, identifiable; the next, it crumbled to the ground in a mound of cinders and ash.

The soldiers had pushed down the rest of the effigies that were not on fire, aided by some of the clear-headed men in the crowd.

A thick blanket of smoke hung over the festival area, which was much emptier of people than it had been not long before. Over the din of voices, Aidane could hear soldiers shouting for order. She blinked against the smoke, amazed to still be alive.

Aidane became aware of chanting, and she looked up to see the Sacred Vessels standing in a protective circle around Berry, who was still shielded by Jonmarc. As if they had suddenly agreed that the danger was passed, the chanting stopped and the curtain of light winked out. Kolin helped Aidane stand. To Aidane's astonishment, the seer who wore the yellow beads of the Lover's oracle walked toward her.

"We heard your spirit, Thaine of Nargi. Know that you have the thanks of the Sacred Lady."

Aidane's heart pounded, and she did not know whether her own fear or Thaine's was greater. She stammered for words, still in shock over her role in the turmoil. "Thank you, m'lady," she managed to say.

The oracle looked at her and her eyes grew sad. "You would leave us, Thaine of Nargi?"

Thaine's spirit came to the fore. "I've given you all the information I had. The men in the crowd were the men I saw in Nargi. I have nothing else to offer. I would go to my rest."

The oracle nodded. "You did not die in vain, Thaine of Nargi. I cannot make your passage to the Lady, but I give you my blessing. May you cross the Gray Sea in safety."

Thank you. For everything. Thaine's voice brushed along Aidane's mind. Aidane felt the spirit flow through her, taking one last, full breath. As she exhaled, the spirit seemed to follow the breath, gradually leaving her body, until nothing of Thaine remained. Aidane shook herself, as if awakening, and she found Jonmarc staring at her with an expression on his face that she could not read. Surprise, concern, and sadness mingled in his dark eyes.

A moment later, Jonmarc helped Berry to her feet. His shirt and coat were bloody, and he had grown pale. Berry looked at him with concern, but Jonmarc shook his head as he jerked the blade from his shoulder and threw it aside.

"Guess this one wasn't poisoned. I've had worse."

Berry turned to the Sacred Vessels. "Thank you," she said, making a low bow.

The speaker for the Childe inclined her head, just a bit, in recognition. "This is our gift from the Sacred Lady in all Her Aspects," the oracle said. Her eyes seemed to darken, as if she saw shadows they could not. "Darkness is coming. You must be wary but bold in your attack."

"Your Majesty." It was Gellyr. He looked uncomfortable trying to extricate Berry from the circle of seers. "While the crowds are clear, we need to get you to safety."

"Yes, of course," Berry said. Although Aidane hadn't seen him draw his weapons, Jonmarc stood slightly in front of Berry with a sword in each hand. Gellyr led them toward the edge of the stage, and for a moment, Jonmarc looked behind them at the soldiers who had taken command of the wreckage and the aftermath as if he wanted to join them. Then he looked down at Berry and managed a lopsided grin.

"You know how to make an entrance."

Aidane stepped over the body of the first attacker, the man who had jumped on stage. Only then did she see the hilts of two throwing knives embedded in his chest. Berry moved past her, defying the guards, and bent over the man, removing her knives and cleaning them on the dead man's shirt before returning them to the folds in her skirt. She straightened.

"Hant will find out who he was. If I know Hant, he'll have the mechanism that was inside those figures analyzed by daybreak." The queen looked up at Jonmarc, and the look in her eyes was much older than her years. "Let's patch you up, and then I want you there when Hant questions any prisoners. I want to know who they are and what they know." There was an undercurrent of cold, hard rage in the young queen's voice. "I will not lose this kingdom to the Durim, or to invaders from the north. If the Lady wants a vow from me on my coronation day, then there it is. We're going to fight this, Jonmarc, with everything we've got."

Aidane shifted her attention to Jonmarc. She saw resolve in his face, and anger, but there was something more, something she might have noticed because of Thaine's memories, something Berry did not see. *He knows, even though Berry may not, that the Lady hears vows like that. And he knows just how costly that vow will be to uphold.*

Jonmarc drew a deep breath and looked away. "Let's get back to the palace. We've got a mess to clean up, and a war to plan."

Early the next morning, a commotion in the courtyard roused Jonmarc from sleep. He looked out his window. Three fine carriages fit for royalty were in the courtyard. Each carriage was pulled by a team of sleek black Eastmark stallions, horses Jonmarc knew to be worth a small fortune each. With the carriages were wagons for servants and a dozen men at arms mounted on war steeds. Though the guards wore no livery, Jonmarc knew their origin from the fit of their armor and the style of their saddles. He swore profusely under his breath as he dressed quickly, belting on his sword as he left his room.

He caught up to Jencin in the castle's grand entranceway. "Were you expecting company?"

Jencin sighed. "The delegation from Eastmark was due, but I was hoping they wouldn't arrive until after Haunts."

"Actually, they're right on time." Berry's voice came from behind them, and Jonmarc turned to see the queen approaching, looking regal in a dress of forest-green Mussa silk. "Father and

King Kalcen made several treaties and agreements after the wedding in Margolan last year. We were told that they would send an ambassador, and a gift to seal the alliance. I doubt there was time for word to reach them about Father's death."

Jonmarc shrugged. "Let's just hope everyone remembers that Kalcen repealed the death warrant his father issued on me. Otherwise, there might be a 'diplomatic incident.'" He looked at Jencin. "How many of them are there?"

"An ambassador, two military strategists, two of their *Hojun* priests, a dozen servants, a contingent of bodyguards—and Prince Gethin."

"Prince Gethin?" Berry repeated in astonishment.

"Any idea why he came along?" Jonmarc asked.

Jencin shook his head. He seemed more nervous than usual. "No. No. The king didn't include me in his negotiations with Eastmark. He said he still had some details to work out. The Eastmark delegation has been very polite, but they've made it clear their business is with the queen."

Berry and Jonmarc looked at each other. "Well," Jonmarc said, "let's see what brought them all this way."

Berry composed her face and drew herself up to her full height. Jonmarc saw her expression take on a blankness that made it difficult to guess what she was thinking. Something else he imagined that royals practiced, a necessary survival skill.

"All rise to greet Queen Berwyn of Principality."

Jencin announced their entrance as he swung open the doors to the great room. Nearly twenty Eastmark visitors rose as the queen entered. Their dark skin made them stand out, even in Principality, which had more than its share of mercs and merchants from throughout the Winter Kingdoms. Eastmark was a proud kingdom, and under the previous king, King Radomar, it had maintained an aloofness from the other kingdoms.

Jonmarc noticed a dignified older man and a sullen but

handsome young man at the forefront of the group. Behind them, two Eastmark *Hojuns* wore the elaborate robes that marked them as shaman-priests. The *Hojuns*' heads were shaved bald, and intricate runes covered their scalps, designs that had been cut into the flesh and left to scar. Complex patterns of tattoos wound down their arms onto their hands. The *Hojuns* wore carved amulets and bracelets of wood, bone, and gemstones, and disks of copper around the hems of their robes made bell-like sounds as they moved. The rest of the group looked to be functionaries and bureaucrats. Whatever servants or valets the group brought were likely to already be housed with the rest of the palace staff.

The older gentleman, a poised man with close-cut, white hair, stepped forward first. He gave a polite bow that stopped short of real deference. "Your Majesty. We offer condolences on the untimely death of King Staden and our sincere best wishes for a long and prosperous reign, even in these difficult times."

Berry gave a polite half smile that did not reach her eyes. "Thank you."

"I am Avencen, and I have been sent by King Kalcen as ambassador to Principality." He smiled, and it made his finely featured face more open, although his black eyes did not soften. "It's been long overdue. Before we departed, I welcomed my counterpart to Eastmark. You may rest assured that he is comfortable."

"Again, our thanks."

Avencen paused, and Jonmarc thought he looked nervous. "King Staden's sudden death left important negotiations with Eastmark unfinished. Those negotiations must now be between you and King Kalcen." He seemed to steel himself and took a deep breath. "It leaves us in an awkward situation."

Berry frowned. "How so?"

Avencen stepped to the side. "May I present Prince Gethin, son of King Kalcen, third in line for the throne of Eastmark."

Gethin stepped forward and made a stiff bow. To Jonmarc's eye, he looked to be about nineteen years old. Jonmarc saw Berry's attention move to the prince. Gethin was a good-looking young man, and Jonmarc guessed that that was not lost on the new queen.

Gethin stood a bit taller than Jonmarc, with a trim, lithe build. His coal-black hair was shoulder length, and straight. Ebony skin indicated that he was from the highest ranks of Eastmark society, and his eyes glinted like obsidian. A medallion in the shape of a silver stawar joined the symbol of the Lady on a leather strap at his throat. A complicated tattoo on the left side of his face curled from brow to chin, and Jonmarc knew it indicated his rank in the succession. He had seen such a mark before when he had served as a soldier in Eastmark, at Chauvrenne.

Gethin was dressed in traveling leathers that were only slightly lighter than his skin. Where Avencen and the others favored the bright orange and yellow colors popular in Eastmark and loose, flowing pants and billow-sleeved shirts, Gethin's close-fitting leather outfit seemed stark, almost military. Jonmarc noticed that he wore a scabbard and a baldric, though both were empty. From Gethin's stance and manner, Jonmarc guessed the young man was an accomplished fighter.

Avencen cleared his throat. "King Staden and King Kalcen had agreed to all but one provision of the accord. Staden insisted that Prince Gethin travel here so that he could meet the prince and take the measure of his character."

The same possibility seemed to dawn on both Jonmarc and Berry simultaneously, as they exchanged wary glances. Berry drew a short breath. "For what purpose?"

"To seal the alliance, King Kalcen has offered something unprecedented: the hand of his son in marriage." Avencen swallowed. "As Your Majesty surely knows from Eastmark's history, when the king's sister, Princess Viata, eloped with Prince Donelan of Isencroft, the Winter Kingdoms nearly came to war. Such an alliance was forbidden until King Kalcen changed the law in his sister's memory."

"Yeah, and the betrothal contract that Bricen of Margolan brokered between Donelan's daughter and his own firstborn son to stop that war almost caused another," Jonmarc replied. That contract, which bound Kiara of Isencroft to Bricen's eldest son, Jared, created scandal and complications as Tris Drayke fought to take the throne from his hated half-brother and found himself in love with Kiara.

Avencen shifted uncomfortably. "I believe that history was not lost on King Staden. He had no desire to see his daughter paired to a...to someone like Jared the Usurper. That's why he insisted that the prince visit. King Kalcen had already had the good fortune of meeting Princess...Queen...Berwyn at Martris Drayke's wedding. All that was left was winning Staden's approval to the match."

Gethin's face was impassive, but his eyes flashed fire. *He doesn't really want to be here*, Jonmarc thought.

"Your deal just became more complicated," Berry said tersely. "No one asked me what I thought of an arranged marriage." She looked Gethin over and met his eyes defiantly. "I don't think anyone asked your prince, either. While I appreciate this historic first and am honored by the gift you offer, I'm queen now, not a princess to be bargained off. You began your negotiations with my father. Now, you're dealing with me." Her expression suddenly softened, just enough to give Avencen hope, and Jonmarc knew Berry was using all of her acting skills to navigate the situation.

"On the other hand, it would be unwise to reject such a historic offer out of hand. No doubt Father and King Kalcen had the best interests of both kingdoms at heart and, I would hope, the best interests of their children as well." She paused. "Your delegation and the prince are welcome to stay at the palace while I give this matter further consideration.

"There is another complication," Berry continued. "Our intelligence sources lead us to believe that war is imminent between the Winter Kingdoms and an invader from across the Northern Sea. Once war breaks out, you'll be unable to return to Eastmark for the duration."

Avencen and Gethin exchanged a glance. "We knew when we left Eastmark about the danger from the north," Avencen said. "The kings of all the lands have been communicating with each other for some time now about the threat. King Kalcen has already committed our army to the coast." Avencen paused. "Even knowing the danger, we came. The alliance between our kingdoms is that important."

Berry looked to Gethin. "Does he always do your talking?"

Gethin glowered at her. "No. While I agree with what he has said, I can speak for myself." He looked from Avencen to Berry. "The alliance between our kingdoms makes sense. It would protect both our peoples. We're also the best available marriage partners for each other. Neither of us would consider an agreement with Nargi or Trevath, even if they had partners of suitable age. Isencroft and Margolan have only one heir, an infant. There is honor in this pairing. I am not opposed."

But you're not exactly jumping for joy, either, Jonmarc thought.

Berry nodded. "Your reasoning's sound. The burden of the crown often removes choices others take for granted. On the other hand," she said, her eyes narrowing, "I would rather rule as a spinster queen than be tied forever to a man I loathe. An unhappy consort has opened many a kingdom to disaster."

"You dare to impugn the prince's honor?" Avencen's eyes widened and his cheeks darkened.

"I believe the queen has merely stated the case for getting to know one another before rushing into things, given the danger of our times," Jencin said in a placating tone.

Berry inclined her head slightly to indicate agreement. "The coming war must take precedence over everything else, for now," Berry said, and Jonmarc saw a glint in her eyes that told him Berry was certain that she had won this round. "You'll be our guests indefinitely. Let's use that time to get to know each other without the pressure of a deadline. Surely by the time the war is over, we'll both have made up our minds."

"That sounds fair," Gethin said before Avencen could speak. "And it permits both sides to save face, should the alliance not go as our fathers planned." He gave an unexpected bow, and in one graceful movement, he took Berry's hand and kissed it. "It means I'll have to court you and win your favor." He flashed a rebellious grin. "I prefer to stand or fall on my own merits."

The corners of Berry's lips twitched as she concealed a smile. "So do I."

23

For the second time in his brief reign, King Martris Drayke led his army to war.

Tris muffled a sigh as he reined in his restless horse. Moving an army was a monumental task, as was keeping it provisioned in the field. And while the Margolan coast was only a week's ride north, the fact that food would be scarce again this year would make a difficult task that much harder.

"Final count is five thousand two hundred and forty-six," Soterius said as he rode up beside Tris.

Tris nodded. "I'm afraid to ask, but how did we manage that? We barely pulled together four thousand men to fight Curane last year without leaving the palace undefended."

Soterius shrugged. "Rumor has it that the plague hasn't taken hold as much near the coast. I think some people signed up to outrun the fever. Most of the *vayash moru* and *vyrkin* refugees at Huntwood and Glynnmoor and Lady Eadoin's manor also signed on. Trefor earned a field promotion; he'll be leading them. As for the others, frankly, we weren't as choosy on age if the recruits would swear they were between fourteen and fifty." He grimaced. "And if they lied convincingly, we took them anyhow."

Soterius paused, looking out over the group. "We've also

taken more women as soldiers this time. Maybe it's the queen's influence, or maybe it's the lack of better options that made so many come forward, but if they could wield a sword and provision themselves with equipment, we took them."

"Do you think they realize what a fight this might be?"

"On one level or another, yeah, I think they do. Curane was a family feud, an internal problem. It's a whole different game when there's an invader headed for your coastline. That hasn't been something Margolan's worried about in a long time."

Tris scanned the ranks. Most of the soldiers were on foot. Those with a horse were promoted into cavalry. Wivvers, their genius inventor, had brought along several of his killing machines, covered with tarpaulins and hauled by oxen. Wivvers's machines had helped to turn the tide in the war against Curane at Lochlanimar, and Tris was glad to have him with them against a new enemy.

"The good news is that we've recruited more mages than before. Fallon's been busy. We're taking them all, from hedge witches to healers," Soterius said. "Maybe it's not surprising, but most of them already know that there's dark magic afoot. They can feel it, even if they don't know where it's coming from."

"We lost two generals last time out," Tris said, watching the organized chaos of an army on the move. Supply wagons followed the infantry and mounted soldiers, and the wagons held everything from extra weapons to tents and bedding and food. Four blacksmiths' wagons trudged along with them, as well as armorers and farriers. To move an army of soldiers, it took an army of civilians who would work behind the lines but often in no less danger to keep the army fed, sheltered, armed, and repaired. Tris glanced to one side and spotted the mages and healers. Most of them had horses, but they also took turns driving a wagon with their own supplies, both magical and medical. Even all of this, Tris knew, might not be enough to keep the army in true fighting shape, especially if the war dragged on.

"You've got Senne, Rallan, and me for starters. Trefor's a colonel now. We were going to need to include him in our planning sessions; it's good for him to have the rank to back it up. Senne and I put our heads together to promote talent within the ranks. We promoted Kiril and Taras to general based on how bravely they performed at Lochlanimar." His eyes took on a haunted look. "Kiril assumed command when Palinn was killed. His men were the first through the wall, and they took heavy casualties, but they cleared the path. Taras handled the mop-up of sifting through the wreckage after the fighting stopped and he took charge of getting the army home. They're both good men, and loyal." Soterius paused. "We needed more generals. We don't want you exposed the way you were the last time, against Curane."

Tris grimaced. "That's going to be hard to manage. If we really are coming up against a dark summoner, I can't hide behind the ranks. I need to see what I'm fighting."

Soterius gave him a sideways glance. "You're still the king. Keeping you alive and as far out of harm's way as we can is still our top priority."

Against his will, Tris's thoughts strayed back to Shekerishet, and to Kiara. Soterius picked up on the shift. "You're not completely with us, Tris. Tell me what's got you worried, and if I can fix it, that's one thing off your mind."

Tris gave a bitter chuckle. "I'm afraid it's nothing you can fix. Kiara's pregnant again. She was only a few days along when the army left; it's only by magic that we knew so soon." He let his voice trail off, not putting his real worry into words.

Soterius finished the thought for him. "And you're worried, because Cwynn's birth was so hard on her."

Tris nodded. "That, and we don't know what's going to happen with Isencroft. She's still heir to the throne there, and although the Divisionists are angry about our marriage, many Crofters see her as a hero."

"You're afraid something is going to happen that forces her to go back there, aren't you?"

Tris gave him a grim smile. "Am I that easy to read?"

"Only for someone who's been doing it since we were twelve years old."

"Yes, I'm worried. I'm worried about Cwynn, worried about Kiara with the new pregnancy and me gone, worried about the Isencroft problem. Fallon tells me it's the king's business to worry. But she says that doesn't mean I have to be better at it than anyone else," he added with a self-deprecating chuckle.

"Your Majesty!" Tris and Soterius turned to see Coalan riding toward them. The young man stood half a head taller than he had been just the year before, when he had accompanied Tris on campaign as his valet and squire. "General Senne sent me to tell you that he plans to camp for the night in another candle-mark, with your approval."

Tris nodded. "Tell him that's fine with me. We're nearly at the meeting point we arranged with the Sworn. Jair will have scouts watching for us."

Coalan grinned. "Thank the Lady that we're calling it a night. I'm about to die from hunger." Coalan was Soterius's nephew, and attaching his duties to the king had kept the young man out of the direct line of fire. But even behind the line, his loyalty had been valuable. At Lochlanimar, Coalan's bravery and quick thinking had foiled an assassination attempt, and in this battle, he was officially one of the king's personal bodyguards.

"Tell the truth; you were starving before we even broke camp this morning," Soterius grumbled good-naturedly.

Coalan's grin widened. "An army moves on its stomach. Don't you know that?" He patted his belly. "I've got to keep my strength up to take care of our king."

Soterius eyed the new baldric and sword that Coalan wore, as well as his cuirass. "You're rather well armed for a squire, aren't you?"

Coalan's grin slipped, and Tris jumped into the conversation. "Those are my gifts," Tris said, hurrying to avert a disagreement between Soterius and Coalan. "Just because he's behind the lines doesn't mean he's safe. If he hadn't known how to use a sword at Lochlanimar, I'd be dead now."

The tight-lipped expression on Soterius's face told Tris that his friend couldn't argue with the logic, although Tris knew that Soterius desperately wanted to keep Coalan safe. "For defense of the king only, you hear me? I don't want to have to explain to your father that you've gotten yourself cut up or worse, no matter how much of a hero it makes you." Soterius gave Coalan a stern look.

Coalan barely contained his glee at winning this round of the argument. "Absolutely, Uncle Ban." He grinned again. "If you'd like, you can put me in charge of guarding the cook wagon whenever Tris is in the field."

Soterius rolled his eyes. "Like having the fox guard the hen house, isn't it?"

Tris listened to them banter and he smiled with the first genuine glimmer of happiness he'd felt since leaving Shekerishet. Ban Soterius and Coalan were among a precious handful of old friends who had been close to him before Jared's coup, before the fight for the throne, before the burdens of the crown. For just a moment, Tris remembered what it had felt like, only a little over two years ago, before his world had upended and everything he knew had been plunged into chaos. Such glimpses were fleeting, and increasingly rare, and Tris treasured them for every second that they lasted, knowing that they came too seldom.

Soterius's voice brought him back to the business of war. "So

Jair and the Sworn will meet us tonight? Does that mean the Dread will support us?"

It was late in the afternoon and the low, rolling hills cast long shadows. There were barrows not far from their chosen camp site, and the long shadows made Tris suppress a shiver. "All we've gotten from the Dread is a warning that they're being courted by both sides. No promises that they'll back one or the other, or that they'll do anything at all. Probably best for everyone if they just stay out of it, but if the other side is trying to raise the spirits the Dread guard, then it may force a choice. The Sworn decided this was their business once someone started meddling with the Dread. So they'll fight to keep the Nachale bound in the barrows, but they're not signing on for more than that, at least, not yet," Tris said.

It was the seventh day since the army had left Shekerishet, and although the Northern Sea was not yet in sight, there was a change in the winds and a faint tang of sea water in the air. This part of Margolan was known as the Borderlands, a rocky area with hard-scrabble farms and small fishing villages. It was an area Tris had seldom visited, and what little he knew came from Jonmarc Vahanian, who was born in one of the villages that traded with the fishermen, sailors, and itinerant tinkers who sometimes passed through these parts.

Tris could swear that his sore muscles felt every league of the journey. Although it had been less than a year since he had returned from the siege of Lochlanimar, the duties of kingship made it difficult to spend as much time in the salle or in the saddle as he would have preferred. In times of peace, kings had the luxury of enjoying a ride into the countryside for the hunt, or even extended visits in the homes of the nobility. When, or if, such opportunities might come his way depended on surviving long enough for peace to come again. Tris felt a weariness that had nothing to do with sleep or the fatigue of travel. Very soon, Margolan would be fighting for its existence. Many of the soldiers around him, and no small number of the mages and *vyrkin* and *vayash moru* as well, would die in that effort. Tris remembered his conversations with both Marlan the Gold and Hadenrul the Great. This new invader would push an already strapped kingdom to its limits. Tris could only hope that the resistance they could muster, however valiant, would be enough.

The army camped far enough back from the coast to create a defensive line. At sunset, Tris climbed one of the low hills. In the distance, the setting sun cast an orange glow across the ocean. If all the signs were true, then before long, those rocky beaches would be red with blood. Tris sighed as the dying light shifted to a crimson hue as if it anticipated his thoughts. Along the horizon, Tris thought he could make out the faint shapes of ships, and he fervently hoped they were the make-shift navy Nisim had worked to assemble. A large ship that had the look of a privateer's vessel was anchored out from shore, and two smaller boats were beached near camp.

"Ban told me you were up here."

Tris turned as he recognized Jair's voice. He wasn't surprised to see Talwyn with him, and Tris welcomed both of them with an embrace. "I'm glad you could make it."

Jair and Talwyn stood beside Tris, and Jair frowned as he looked out toward the sea. "Your ships?"

"I hope so. We'll hear more about that tonight. Nisim is due with a report, and Fallon's mages should have some new intelligence for us by then, also."

"The attacks on the barrows have suddenly stopped," Talwyn said. "While I'd love to think it was because of us, we really don't know why they've ended, or whether they'll start up again." She nodded toward the ships on the horizon. "There's no way to tell whether whoever was in league with the Black Robes got what they wanted, or gave up because they didn't."

"And the Dread?"

Talwyn shrugged. "They haven't sought me out, and I don't go looking for them unless it's an emergency. For now, silence is probably good news." She paused and looked at Tris as if studying his expression. "What magic do you feel?"

Tris gave a wan smile. "I was about to ask you the same thing. I've been jumpy since this afternoon, and the closer we got to the ocean, the worse it's become. I'm tired from the ride, but I feel like I've had an entire pot of *kerif*. It's a prickly kind of feeling, like when a storm's coming."

Talwyn nodded. "I feel the same way. I've tried to read the omens, without any clear results. Last night, I went to the spirit guides, but they had nothing to offer me. And yet, there's something out there. It's as you said back at the palace. There's a hum, a vibration, just beyond what I can identify. I've tried to ignore it, but it's still there."

"And it's growing stronger," Tris agreed. "I keep thinking about Alyzza and the mages at Vistimar, wondering if it's affecting them more or whether whatever they've been hearing is just now breaking through to the rest of us."

"That's a pleasant thought."

Coalan's head and shoulders came into view as he hiked up the path from where he stood guard below. "They're calling for you, Tris," he said, with a nod to Jair and Talwyn. "The meeting's ready, and more to the point, so is supper."

With a chuckle, Tris, Jair, and Talwyn followed Coalan down the pathway and back to camp. The sun had just set, and scores of campfires dotted the flat plain, and thousands of campaign tents, large and small, fluttered in the breeze. Beyond the tents, a newly built corral sheltered the horses and oxen. In the distance, Tris could hear the sound of axes, and he knew that Wivvers was busy directing work crews to fell the trees he needed for the catapults and trebuchets that could launch boulders and more deadly missiles into the harbor should the enemy's fleet break past the defending ships. Tris sincerely hoped Wivvers's machines would not be needed.

They returned to camp to find that Tris's campaign tent had been assembled. Coalan had ransacked the officers' tents to gather enough portable campaign chairs to offer everyone a seat. A small brazier warded off the autumn chill.

"We couldn't manage a table just yet, but at least no one has to sit on the ground," Coalan noted cheerily as the others filed in. Coalan handed them each a bowl of hot stew and some hard biscuits as they entered. "Cook tells me that he'll bake some bread tomorrow, and I have his word we won't have stew every night, like last time."

General Senne chuckled. "Most soldiers don't join up for the food, lad. I thought your uncle would have told you that."

Coalan grinned. "He did. But I can still live in hope."

Tris looked around at the group that filled the tent. Senne, Rallan, and Soterius from the generals. Trefor for the *vayash moru* and *vyrkin*. Sister Fallon and Sister Beyral. Jair and Talwyn from the Sworn. And Nisim, who wore a grim look. Two other men sat with Nisim. The first man was in his middle years and looked like he knew hard work and time spent out of doors in bad weather. His hands were calloused and broadened and his clothes were plain. He wore a heavy sweater with an elaborate knot design, and Tris guessed that he was one of the Bay Islands men Nisim had been recruiting. He'd heard that the fishermen wore sweaters knitted with patterns distinct for each family, so that when a drowned man was reclaimed from the sea, the remains could be identified. A sextant and spyglass hung from leather straps on the man's belt, and a wicked-looking fish knife was sheathed beside them. *Not just Bay Islands, but a ship's captain*, Tris guessed.

The second man had the look of a mercenary. He was better dressed than the other stranger, with a coat and breeches that looked like they had once been expensive, although they had seen wear. His clothing and jewelry were a mixture that spanned the Winter Kingdoms and beyond: a vest of Mussa silk, leatherwork on his cuirass and baldric that looked to be some of the finest Isencroft had to offer, and a jacket with Noorish weave. His rings and the pendant at his throat were gold, set with Principality gems, and the charms that hung beside them were the carved stone and amber that were famous in Eastmark. The stranger wore a selection of knives on his belt and in his baldric that would have made Jonmarc envious, Tris thought. The man seemed to notice that Tris was looking at him, and he leaned forward before Nisim could speak.

"I'm Tolya, captain of the ship *Istra's Vengeance*, and leader of the Northern Fleet." Tolya watched Tris as if he were daring him to respond.

Tris met his eyes. "Happy to have you here, Captain. Nisim's told you what we're up against?"

Tolya snorted. "More like we told Nisim. Been scoutin' for his Sentinels for a while now. The ships of the Northern Fleet are all run by their owners, profit-minded traders, we are, with a charter since the time of King Larimore to board and raid hostile ships in the name of the king of Margolan."

Who gets to determine "hostile"? Tris wondered, but he kept his expression neutral. "What have you seen, Captain?"

Tolya smiled, a predator's expression. "We've seen more ships, large ships, coming and going to Temnotta than ever in my memory. Big ships, carracks, and caravels." His unpleasant smile did not reach his eyes. "We know they're not trading. We'd have seen them in the ports and the trade routes. Can only be one reason why they've got ships like that. They mean to carry men, not cargo."

Tris nodded. "And your ships? Are they fast?"

Tolya guffawed. "They're rigged for maneuvering. Aye, they're fast. Fast as anything in port in Temnotta, I'd wager. Our ships are built for pursuit and boarding. They're outfitted to ram, if need be, and we have fire throwers to set the other ships ablaze." His eyes tightened. "If we need to, we can fight in a line abreast. We've got crossbows and archers, and slings that can put heavy iron through a deck or a sail, or put a nice hole at the waterline." He chuckled. "Got more than a few water mages, too, who know how to churn the sea and call the weather. Oh, yes, m'lord, we're fast and we're armed."

"Good. We're in your debt."

Tolya smiled. "Yes, m'lord, that you are. And when the fightin's over, I have some business propositions to discuss with Your Majesty in light of our brave service to the crown."

Senne cleared his throat, and Tris could see the general's obvious distrust of the privateer. Rallan looked as if he were calculating profit and loss. Tris met Soterius's eyes, and he knew his friend well enough to read grudging approval. "I'd like to see Margolan's trade increase, Captain Tolya. If you and your ships can do that, I am open to waiving certain port fees and tariffs."

"Aye, then, we have a bargain and you have a fleet."

Nisim looked as if he had been holding his breath. Conversation lapsed as the group turned its attention to the food, and for a few moments, it was quiet. They ate quickly, and Tris knew that as pressing as the business at hand was, they were all equally spent from the long ride. When Coalan had taken away the remains of dinner and poured brandy for all who wanted it, he moved to his post outside the door, and Tris looked at the others who had gathered.

"I'd like to hear from you and your other guest," Tris said, looking to Nisim. "You've been closest to the sources."

Nisim nodded. "We sent out spies in small boats to see if we could spot the enemy. Two weeks ago, we had reports that a large fleet was on the move coming from the direction of Temnotta, on the other side of the Northern Sea. They were still a distance away, but the spies spotted them in their scrying glasses and made visual contact.

"Last week, our spies were due to report. They didn't. We found a couple of their boats drifting empty, but of the spies themselves, nothing." Nisim met Tris's eyes. "They were mages. They should have been able to leave some kind of trace, send some sort of signal. Our far speakers have listened for them, and our dream speakers have waited for them, but there's been nothing at all."

"You think they were captured?"

Nisim nodded. "Captured, maybe killed."

"It's not the first time." They all turned to look at the man beside Nisim.

"This is Pashka. He's the leader of the Fisher Guild out in the Bay Islands."

Pashka looked at Tris with sea-gray eyes. His expression held no particular deference, and Tris recalled Nisim's comment that the Bay Islands barely considered themselves to be part of Margolan. Tris wondered how long it had been, if ever, since the islanders had heard from their king, and whether or not Pashka believed himself subject to any monarch.

"Our boats started to disappear last year," Pashka said in a weather-roughened growl. He had an odd accent, more guttural than the hill country, flatter than the Borderlands. With a start, Tris knew where he had heard such an accent before. It reminded him of the Margolense spoken by ancient vampires, and by the ghost of King Hadenrul. It would seem that the Bay Islands had kept to themselves for a very long time. "First just one or two." He shrugged. "Such things happen. Fishing is a dangerous business. But it was odd, because there were no storms, and the men who went missing had fished those seas all their lives. They weren't reckless.

"Then a few more went missing, and our wives took to painting runes and sigils on our boats to protect us. Our hedge witches told us about dark omens, and our seers had dreams about the bodies of long-dead men rising from the ocean." A pained expression crossed Pashka's face. "My brother was one of the men who disappeared. Two of my nephews went missing along with him. I don't believe they drowned."

"Why not?"

"Because our rune scryers found a warning carved into one of the empty boats." Pasha's eyes narrowed. "It wasn't carved by our folk. It was in old runes, she said, hard to read."

"What did it say?"

For the first time, Tris saw a glint of fear in Pashka's eyes. "It said to beware the cold north wind that raises the dead and buries the living."

"Pleasant," Soterius muttered.

Pashka sighed. "That's not all, m'lord. Been bad omens all summer. You've heard of the Spirit Lights, I wager, the curtain of light in the sky far to the north?"

Tris and Soterius nodded.

"Well, there've been strange lights to the north, like nothing even the old men have ever seen. The Spirit Lights are cold colors, green and blue and white. These lights look like blood in the clouds. Puts a chill to your bones, it does, to see it. Fearsome as Nameless and the Wild Host. Got so that people stayed indoors after dark, wouldn't look up, for fear of it." Pashka paused, as if uncertain whether to go on, and then plowed ahead.

"Then two of our hedge witches went mad, not long after the strange lights began. One of them ran off a cliff, screaming, and drowned herself in the sea. The other set herself on fire." He shook his head. "Our seers say that they hear voices in their heads, evil voices. They draw runes around their beds to keep the spirits out of their dreams, but they say they can hear the voices singing, screaming, all the time." His eyes were haunted. "Our healer had to drug one of our seers to make her sleep, it got so bad. Every time she wakes up, she starts screaming again."

Tris exchanged glances with Soterius and Fallon. "We've had similar problems as far inland as Vistimar."

"Truly?" Pashka said in surprise. "Then you know I didn't invent this tale."

"Our mages have felt it, too," Fallon replied. "Something dark and hungry, just at the edge of the light. Most of them won't sleep without a lantern lit, and some have gone to sleeping in shifts, so that someone is always awake and watching."

Pashka leaned forward. "For generations, we Islanders have been happy to be left alone. We don't bother no one, and no one bothers us. But we know how to fight. Whoever is taking our men, our ships, as far as we're concerned, they've struck the first blow. Nisim says you mean to fight them. If that's true, we'll fight beside you." He sat back and crossed his arms over his broad chest.

"Thanks to Pashka and the Bay Islanders, we have more than a hundred small boats patrolling in shifts," Nisim added. "Their boats will be perfect for harassing the enemy fleet, since they're small and fast. They've also agreed to mount a lookout on the highest hill on the island, and if they see foreign ships, they'll light the bonfire. We'll be able to see it from here." Nisim took a deep breath. "We've been recruiting from all the coastal towns as well, from the Isencroft border to the Principality border. In addition to Tolya's privateers and Pashka's fishermen, there are plenty of small boats that would be perfect for hit-and-run skirmishes, and some larger ships, cargo ships, that should be able to help hold off warships, depending on the size of the Temnotta fleet."

"Thank you, Nisim," Tris said. He looked to General Senne and the men next to him. Trefor, leader of the contingent of *vayash moru* and *vyrkin*, sat beside Senne, next to General Rallan. "What about the troops?"

Senne nodded. "We have men out on the beach digging trenches and laying snares. If the Temnottans get past the fleet, they won't just stroll up the beach." He gave a cold smile. "Wivvers has been doing what he's best at: inventing things to cause mayhem and panic. We have a few surprises in store." He glanced at Trefor and Rallan. "Trefor's working with his troops. A fair number of the *vayash moru* served with one army or another, depending on when they lived, and for some of them, since they've been undead. Fewer of the *vyrkin* have any soldiering, but he's getting them organized. We should have his scouts out by nightfall tomorrow, and surveillance from the *vayash moru* who can fly."

Tris turned to Fallon and Beyral. "Are the mages ready?"

Fallon and Beyral nodded in agreement. "They've been on alert since we left Shekerishet, scanning the road ahead of us and the land around us. We've needed to rely more on charms and warding than ever before, because of that hum Talwyn was talking about, but so far, no one's been damaged by it."

"And has your magic picked up anything?"

Fallon grimaced. "Yes and no. We've got a good variety of mages with us: healers, seers, scryers, and dream seekers, as well as air, land, water, and fire mages. Anyone with any kind of far sight is taking shifts on watch, and Beyral has been reading the omens in a variety of ways. There's nothing conclusive yet from any of that, but we should be in position to pick up some-thing when it happens." She paused. "It may be that whoever is behind this knows we've raised an army. Maybe they've backed off from using magic—as Talwyn said, the Black Robes have stopped their attacks—because they're getting ready for something."

"Like a big strike?"

Fallon nodded. "That's what I think." She sighed. "We knew it was going to come. I have a mage from each element on watch in shifts. This time, we have enough mages to do that, thank the Lady. It should help us respond faster and to get a warning sooner."

Fallon met Tris's eyes. "What of the dead?"

Everyone looked to Tris. "I called to them when we first made camp. I know you chose this spot for the army because it's been a battleground before."

Senne nodded. "More than once, and that's just in Margolan's history. Given that it's wide and flat and near the coast, I wouldn't be surprised if there've been battles fought here no one remembers."

"You're correct," Talwyn said. "My magic works differently from Tris's, but I, too, sense the Ancient Dead here. Not just the Dread and the Nachale in their barrows, but mortal dead, just as ancient, beneath us."

"I called them and they came," Tris said. "They called this land home, even before Marlan the Gold claimed it, before it was Margolan. Some of them were Marlan's troops. Some served Hadenrul, and some fought here before the bards and the scribes began their histories."

"Will they fight for you? Will they join us?" Senne leaned forward, his eyes alight. Senne had no magic of his own, Tris knew, but after seeing what Tris's summoning magic was capable of doing at Lochlanimar, Senne had become passionately interested in the military advantage a true summoner could pose.

Tris took a deep breath. "I've asked them to join us."

The air became suddenly cold enough that those in the campaign tent could see their breath. Three glowing forms took shape in the open area circled by the chairs. The first ghost wore the armor common more than a hundred years before. His breastplate was shattered, and his death wound left a gaping hole in his chest. Next to him stood a man clad in leather and skins, with a crude, two-handed sword in a back scabbard and a necklace of bone and shells.

The third ghost carried a shield and sword of old design, and Tris knew the ghost to be one of Hadenrul's men. All of them had the look of leaders, and Tris knew that, in their lives, they had commanded legions of men.

"Welcome, honored dead."

The third ghost looked at the talisman that Tris wore at his throat, the amulet he had taken from Marlan the Gold's tomb, and then to Nexus, the spelled sword Tris wore in his scabbard. The three ghosts bowed.

Tris motioned for them to rise. "Have you taken my word to the spirits of your men?"

The ghost with the shattered breastplate nodded. "We have."

"And what is their decision?"

The man who had served Hadenrul stepped forward. "We are agreed. In life, and in death, we serve the land that bore us." He inclined his head. "We've felt the call of another power, one from beyond our land, a voice we don't know. It would command us, conscript us, force us to serve against our will, to fight those descended from our blood. We have agreed, Your Majesty, that we would rather be destroyed than fight against our countrymen. We are yours to command."

The ghost knelt then, joined by the other two spirits. The soldier who had served Hadenrul pressed his lips against the signet ring on Tris's hand that bore the crest of the House of

Margolan, and the others followed suit. Tris gestured for them to rise.

"This is Vitya, one of the most feared of Marlan the Gold's warlords," Tris said, introducing the leather-clad warrior. "Estan fought in the service of King Hadenrul the Great and was rewarded by his king for being crafty and ruthless in battle." The second ghost inclined his head in recognition. "And this is Dagen, who served my grandfather, King Larimore, with great valor."

Tris turned his attention back to the ghosts. "When this is over, I'll make the passage to the Lady for those who want to go to their rest. Those who want to remain, to guard your land, we welcome."

"Will you protect us from the Hollowing?" It was Estan who asked, and his dead eyes were fearful. "Whatever calls to us wants more than our defeat. It would consume us. You're a summoner. Can you protect us? We're past fearing death. We don't fear the passage to the Lady, whichever Aspect calls for us. But to be consumed, to be hollowed out, that has the power to frighten even the dead."

Tris met Estan's eyes. "On my crown and on my soul, I will use all my power, in life and in the Plains of Spirit, to protect you from the Hollowing. I swear it."

Whatever else the ghost meant to say was interrupted when a runner burst into the tent.

"Your Majesty! The island beacon is lit. There are ships on the far horizon, lots of them, and the sky is red with blood."

Tris led the way out of the crowded tent to where the entire camp stood staring at a sky gone crimson, as if a glistening curtain of blood shimmered across the dome of the night, blotting out the stars and darkening the moon.

Around him, Tris could hear commanders barking orders. Senne, Rallan, Soterius, and Trefor ran for their troops. Soldiers rushed to mobilize, and Tris caught a glimpse of *vayash moru* taking to the sky.

Only the ghosts remained with Tris. Estan raised his face to stare at the glittering, blood-red light. Then he turned to meet Tris's eyes. "It begins."

Acknowledgments

Thank you to everyone who helped make this book a reality, especially my husband, Larry, and my kids, Kyrie, Chandler, and Cody, who have to live with a writer and manage to do just fine anyhow. Thanks to my agent, Ethan Ellenberg, to my editor, DongWon Song, and to all of the team at Orbit for bringing this book into being. It truly takes a village!

extras

www.orbitbooks.net

about the author

Gail Z. Martin discovered her passion for science fiction, fantasy, and ghost stories in elementary school. The first story she wrote—at age five—was about a vampire. Her favorite TV show as a preschooler was *Dark Shadows*. At age fourteen she decided to become a writer. She enjoys attending science fiction/fantasy conventions, Renaissance fairs, and living-history sites. She is married and has three children, a Himalayan cat, and a golden retriever. Find out more about the author at www.chroniclesofthenecromancer.com

Find out more about Gail Z. Martin and other Orbit authors by registering for the free monthly newsletter at www.orbitbooks.net

interview

The Sworn **is your first book with Orbit, but it's not your first fantasy epic, isn't that right?**
Yes. *The Sworn* is my debut with Orbit, but since 2007, I've written The Chronicles of the Necromancer for Solaris Books (*The Summoner, The Blood King, Dark Haven, Dark Lady's Chosen*). With The Fallen Kings Cycle books, the world of the Winter Kingdoms jumps to Orbit.

So *The Sworn* marks a new beginning for you?
For me and for the Winter Kingdoms.

Is *The Sworn* related to your other books? Can someone pick up this book and start here?
I intentionally wrote *The Sworn* (and its sequel, *The Dread*, coming in 2012), to be a starting point for new readers, people who hadn't read any of my previous books. It's the beginning of a new adventure, and the threat faced by the characters has nothing to do with the villains in the previous four books. Having said that, I like to read a book where it feels as if the characters have their own pasts, so that it doesn't seem like they have been sitting at home doing nothing until their "big adventure." So the characters in *The Sworn* have personal histories and

relationships, with the same kind of complexity you'd expect in real life. You don't have to have read my prior books to enjoy *The Sworn* and *The Dread*—but of course, I always like it when people do!

What should your long-time readers expect?
For people who have read all of my prior books, *The Sworn* picks up about six months after the end of *Dark Lady's Chosen*. Tris Drayke, Jonmarc Vahanian, and the other main characters (and some new ones) head into a brand-new adventure that's unlike anything they've faced before. For long-time readers, this book should feel like a comfortable homecoming. And, of course, they'll know the landscape and the characters very well.

What do you enjoy most about writing epic fantasy?
I was a history major in college, so I enjoy getting to build my own histories, cultures, and religions into a believable world. And, of course, I enjoy creating characters in that world who have problems and triumphs that make for an exciting and enjoyable adventure. My goal is to create a really fun theme park with a killer roller coaster of an adventure and then open the gate and let everyone enjoy it.

if you enjoyed
THE SWORN

look out for

THE DREAD

Book Two of The Fallen Kings Cycle

by

Gail Z. Martin

"I had hoped that I wouldn't see war again in my lifetime."
King Donelan of Isencroft took a deep breath and swirled the
brandy in his goblet. "I had my fill of it in my younger days.
It was a bad bargain then, and it hasn't gotten any better."

"It's not by your choosing, m'lord." Wilym, the head of the
elite Veigonn guards, set aside his drink. "Temnotta's made the
first move."

Donelan sighed. "Spare me any words about a 'good war.'
There is no good war. The only thing worse than war is slavery.
I know we have no choice, dammit. I know Temnotta cast the
die. But it's a funny thing about war. Even when you win, you
lose. There are several thousand men having a good night's sleep

tonight who won't be breathing by war's end. There are villages that won't exist when the fighting's through. I never thought a king's reputation was earned on the battlefield. I always thought it was earned by making sure fields never saw battle. War is easy. But keeping peace for any length of time; well, that's the tricky part."

Donelan downed the last of his brandy in one gulp, and for a moment, Cam thought the king might pour himself another draught. Instead, Donelan let his head rest against the chair and closed his eyes. And although Cam had been the King's Champion for years, never had he thought Donelan looked so worn and tired. "There are no thoughts in my head fit to fall asleep with," Donelan said, his voice gravelly with fatigue. "Tell me just one good thing before I turn in for the night. I'd rather not dream of war."

Cam exchanged glances with Wilym and saw that his friend shared his worry for the king. "Think on the packet you received this morning from Kiara," Wilym said. "You told me her letter says that she and Cwynn are doing well, and that the baby has a fine appetite. The portrait she sent showed a healthy, strong boy. And they're safe from this madness, far from the coast, in Margolan." He chuckled. "I've heard it said that no one except Martris Drayke himself ever breached the walls of the palace Shekerishet. Count that as your good thing to sleep on, Your Majesty. Kiara and Cwynn are safe."

Donelan seemed to relax, as if the brandy was doing its work. The king was known both for his appetite for strong drink and for his ability to seem utterly untouched by it, even when he put his drinking companions under the table. Just for tonight, Cam wished that the brandy might do its work and give Donelan a few candlemarks of untroubled sleep.

"Aye, that's a fine thing," Donelan agreed, his voice a deep rumble. "A fine thing to sleep on. Thank you."

"The firesetter's been to your room a candlemark ago," Wilym replied. "The chill will be off and the fire should be banked for the night. We have a few more days before the army heads for the coast. Perhaps you should enjoy your bed while you have the chance." He chuckled. "Even the finest cot gives a poor night's rest once we're in the field."

Donelan stretched and twisted in his chair, as if to loosen his shoulders. "I think I will," he said, and he smiled, but Cam saw that it didn't reach his eyes. "Thanks to you both for sitting with me awhile. I'd best let you get some rest as well." Donelan rose and walked across the sitting room to where a guard stood by the door to his bedchamber. He glanced over his shoulder. "Mind that you're careful going about your business. I'll need both of you beside me when we ride for the coast."

The door closed behind Donelan, and the guard resumed his place. Wilym gave his brandy one last swirl and then tipped his head back and finished the drink, even as Cam did the same. "I'm worried about him," Cam remarked quietly.

Wilym was silent for a moment. "Donelan drew his first blood on the battlefield when we were still sucking on our mothers' teats. Does it surprise you that it gets tiresome after twenty-some years? By the Whore! I'm wholly sick of every campaign by the end of the first battle, and I haven't seen as much of it as he has."

Cam nodded. "I've never met a sane man yet who enjoys battle, even if he loves soldiering. I'm just not used to seeing Donelan look so haggard. Now it seems his dreams are dark. Makes me worried—"

A man's scream cut off the rest of Cam's words. Cam and Wilym jumped to their feet as the guard threw open the door to Donelan's chamber.

"Sweet Chenne," the guard whispered, blanching. Cam and Wilym shouldered past him at a dead run and stopped at the foot of the king's bed.

Six stout pikes thrust up through the bed, spanning from one side to the other. Donelan lay impaled, with one of the spikes protruding from his chest. Blood spread down the king's nightshirt, soaking the bedding, enough blood that Cam was sure the spike had taken Donelan through the heart.

"Get Trygve!" Wilym shouted. He grabbed the guard by the shoulders and spun him around, shoving him out the door. "Run, dammit!" He turned back to the king. "Hang on, Donelan. Trygve will be here in a moment."

Donelan's whole frame shook. His hands opened and closed convulsively, grasping at the covers. The king's eyes were wide with pain and shock, and his mouth opened and closed, as if gasping for breath. Wilym took the king's hand. "Hold on, please. Just hold on."

Cam drew his sword and made a thorough inspection of the room. The king's private quarters were large, but by design, they offered no easy hiding place. Cam flung open the wardrobe doors, but found nothing except dress robes. The garderobe alcove was empty, with an opening too small for even a slender boy to navigate. But when Cam knelt to look under the bed, he caught his breath.

"By the Crone!"

"What?"

Cam got to his feet. "Someone's rigged a bow contraption beneath the bed. Must have gone off once there was weight on the mattress."

Trygve barreled through the doorway, followed by the guard, who seemed close to panic.

"Mother and Childe!" Trygve swore under his breath, never breaking stride until he reached Donelan's side. Cam and Wilym melted back along the wall, giving the healer room to work. Trygve was one of the finest battle healers in all of Isencroft, but by the set of his mouth, Cam could tell that Trygve was worried.

"We've got to remove the stake, and the moment we do, he'll start bleeding." Trygve's voice was clipped.

"Tell us what to do," Wilym said, as he and Cam stepped forward.

"Can you retract the weapon from below? I'd rather not try to lift him."

Cam dropped to his knees. "I think so. It's been bound to the frame with rope."

"Then on my mark, with one of you on each side, slice the ropes while I try to stanch the bleeding." Trygve climbed up on the bed and straddled the king's body so that his hands were best positioned above the wound. "On three: one . . . two . . . *three*."

The two swords swished through the air simultaneously, slicing the ropes and hitting the bed frame with a thunk. The stakes dropped, but did not completely retract.

Trygve cursed. "Get on your knees. On my mark again, grab each side of that cursed thing and pull straight down."

This time, the apparatus gave way. Cam and Wilym rose back to their feet. Donelan gave a sharp cry, and Trygve murmured healing incantations while his hands cupped the hole in Donelan's chest. Blue healing light glowed beneath Trygve's hands. But from where Cam stood, Donelan's skin looked ashen, and his body had gone still. Trygve's tension gave Cam no reassurance.

Blood spattered Trygve's healer's uniform and his hands were slick. Donelan's breathing was slow and labored. Trygve leaned closer, and the blue light flared. Donelan murmured something Cam could not hear, and then, with one heavy breath, the king lay still.

"Donelan!" Cam said, starting forward.

"No!" Wilym cried.

Trygve bowed his head and his shoulders sagged. "I'm sorry. It was too much damage. Perhaps if we'd had a summoner to bind his soul we might have bought more time for healing. The stake...it tore through most of the heart..." His voice faded. Slowly, he climbed down from the bed and drew up a sheet to cover Donelan's body.

Cam turned to the guard at the door. The young man stared wide-eyed at the king's body. "Who beside the firesetter entered the king's rooms tonight?"

It took two tries for the guard to find his voice. "No one, m'lord. There's been a guard at the door to the king's bedchamber all day. The chambermaids set out his night clothes, but they come on the watch before mine, just before supper."

"We'll find the firesetter and the maids and the previous guard." Wilym's voice was tight and emotionless, and only his eyes revealed his sorrow. "I handpicked the king's guards myself, and I'd swear to their loyalty on my own life. As for the servants, we'll get to the bottom of it."

Cam looked at Wilym and Trygve. "The army's about to head to war, and the king's dead."

Wilym took a deep breath. "How fast can a *vayash moru* travel from here to Shekerishet?"

Cam met his gaze. "You're not proposing—"

"Yes, I am." Wilym's expression was resolute. "Kiara may be Queen of Margolan, but she is also the rightful heir to the Isencroft throne. We have no choice except to call her home to lead her people. Alvior's behind this. He'll count on chaos slowing our response. Maybe he's betting that without Donelan, we'll fall into a full civil war and he can sweep up the pieces. The army can move without the king. But the people need someone who can rally them, someone to remind them why they fight."

Footsteps in the doorway made them turn. Both Cam and Wilym drew their swords. Kellen stepped into the room, followed by Tice and Allestyr. "By the Whore!" Kellen swore softly. Tice froze, a look of shock on his face. Allestyr swallowed back a sob.

"It's true, then." Allestyr was the first to speak. Tears ran down his cheeks. "The servants found us when the guard came for Trygve. Is he—"

Wilym nodded. "Donelan is dead. And if Isencroft is to survive, the six of us must make it happen."